The Strivers' Row Spy

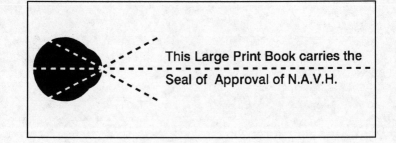

This Large Print Book carries the
Seal of Approval of N.A.V.H.

THE STRIVERS' ROW SPY

JASON OVERSTREET

THORNDIKE PRESS
A part of Gale, Cengage Learning

Farmington Hills, Mich • San Francisco • New York • Waterville, Maine
Meriden, Conn • Mason, Ohio • Chicago

LIBRARY OF CONGRESS CATALOGING-IN-PUBLICATION DATA

Names: Overstreet, Jason, author.
Title: The Strivers' row spy / by Jason Overstreet.
Description: Large print edition. | Waterville, Maine : Thorndike Press Large Print,
2016. | Series: Thorndike Press large print African-American
Identifiers: LCCN 2016032144 | ISBN 9781410493194 (hardback) | ISBN 1410493199
(hardcover)
Subjects: LCSH: African Americans—Fiction. | Harlem Renaissance—Fiction. |
Nineteen twenties—Fiction. | Harlem (New York, N.Y.)—Fiction. | Historical
fiction. | Suspense fiction. | Large type books. | BISAC: FICTION / Mystery &
Detective / Historical.
Classification: LCC PS3615.V4738 S77 2016 | DDC 813/.6—dc23
LC record available at https://lccn.loc.gov/2016032144

Published in 2016 by arrangement with Dafina Books, an imprint of
Kensington Publishing Corp.

Printed in Mexico
1 2 3 4 5 6 7 20 19 18 17 16

*This book is dedicated to
the memory of my father,
Eddie Leon Overstreet, Sr.*

"Providence has its appointed hour for everything. We cannot command results, we can only strive."

— Mahatma Gandhi

ACKNOWLEDGMENTS

I am indebted to the following people for their help and support:

To my brothers, Eddie and Joshua, thanks for always believing in me and for keeping me grounded.

To Frank Weimann, thanks for making sure the book found a perfect home. You're the man!

To Selena James, thank you for pushing me and for making sure the novel reached its full potential.

To Cathy, thank you for being my soul mate, and for spending countless hours listening to me read and reread page after rewritten page.

To my mother, Yuma, thank you for being the writer who showed me the way. You're my hero and the one who inspired me.

1

Middlebury College, Vermont
Spring, 1919

It was graduation day, and the strange man standing at the top of the cobblestone stairwell gave me an uneasy feeling. It was like he was waiting on me. With each step I climbed, the feeling turned into a gnawing in my stomach, gripped me a bit more, pulling at my good mood.

I glanced at my watch, then down at my shiny, black patent leather shoes. First time I'd worn them. Hadn't ever felt anything so snug on my feet, so light. Momma had saved up for Lord knows how long and had given them to me as a graduation gift.

Again I looked up at him. He was a tall, thin man, dressed in the finest black suit I'd ever laid eyes on, too young, it appeared to me, to have such silver hair, an inch of which was left uncovered by his charcoal fedora. Even from a distance he looked like a heavy smoker, with skin the texture and color of tough, sun-baked leather. I had never seen any man exhibit such confidence — one who stood like he was in charge of the world.

I finally reached the top step and realized just how imposing he was, standing about six-five, a good three inches taller than I. His pensive eyes locked in on me and he extended a hand.

"Sidney Temple?" he asked, with a whispery-dry voice.

"Yes."

"James Gladforth of the Bureau of Investigation."

We shook hands as I tried to digest what I'd just heard. What kind of trouble was I in? Was there anything I might have done in the past to warrant my being investigated? I thought of Jimmy King, Vida Cole, Junior Smith — all childhood friends who, God knows, had broken their share of laws. But I had never been involved in any of it. The resolute certainty of my clean ways gave me calm as I adjusted my tassel and responded.

"Good to meet you, sir."

"Congratulations on your big day," he said.

"Thank you."

"You all are fortunate the ceremony is this

morning. Looks to be gettin' hotter by the minute." He looked up, squinting and surveying the clear sky.

I just stood there nodding my head in agreement.

He took off his hat, pulled a handkerchief from his jacket pocket, and wiped the sweat from his forehead. "You can relax," he said. "You're not in any trouble." He put the handkerchief back in his pocket and replaced his hat. He stared at me, studying my face, perhaps trying to decide if my appearance matched that of the person he'd imagined.

He took out a tin from his jacket, opened it, and removed a cigarette. Patting his suit, searching for something, he finally removed a box of matches from his left pants pocket. He struck one of the sticks, lit the cigarette, and smoked quietly for a few seconds.

Proud parents and possibly siblings walked past en route to the ceremony. One young man, dressed in his pristine Army uniform, sat in a wheelchair pushed by a woman in a navy blue dress. He had very pale skin, red hair, and was missing his right leg. Mr. Gladforth looked directly at them as they approached.

"Ma'am," he said, tipping his hat, "will you allow me a moment?"

"Certainly," she said, coming to a stop. She had her grayish-blond hair in a bun, and her eyes were some of the saddest I'd ever seen.

"Where did you fight, young man?" asked Gladforth.

"Saw my last action in Champagne, France, sir. Part of the Fifteenth Field Artillery Regiment. Been back stateside for about two months, sir."

"Your country will forever be indebted to you, son. That was a hell of a war effort by you men. On behalf of the United States government and President Wilson, I want to thank you for your service."

"Thank you, sir."

"Ma'am," said Gladforth, tipping his hat again as the woman gave him a slight smile.

She resumed pushing the young man along, and Gladforth began smoking again — refocusing his attention on me.

"I don't want to take away too much of your time, Sidney," he went on, turning and exhaling the smoke away from us. "I just wanted to introduce myself and tell you personally that the Bureau has been going over the college records of soon-to-be graduates throughout the country.

"You should be pleased to know that you're one of a handful of men that our new

14

head of the General Intelligence Division, J. Edgar Hoover, would like to interview for a possible entry-level position. Your portfolio is outstanding."

"Thank you," I said, somewhat taken aback.

"I know it's quite a bit to try to decide on at the moment, but this is a unique opportunity to say the least."

"Indeed it is, sir."

He handed me a card. "Listen, here's my information. We'd like to set up an interview with you as soon as possible, hopefully within the month."

He began smoking again as I read the card.

"Think about the interview, and when you make your mind up, telephone the number there. We'll have a train ticket to Washington available for you within hours of your decision. Based on the sensitivity of the assignment you may potentially be asked to fulfill, you can tell no one about this interview.

"And, if you were to be hired, your status in any capacity would have to remain confidential. That includes your wife, family, and any friends or acquaintances. If you are uncomfortable with this request, please decline the interview because the conditions are nonnegotiable. Are you clear about what

I'm telling you?"

"Yes, I think so."

"It's imperative that you understand these terms," he stressed, throwing what was left of his cigarette on the ground and stepping on it, the sole of his dress shoe gritting against the concrete.

"I understand."

"Then I look forward to your decision."

"I'll be in touch very soon, Mr. Gladforth. And thank you again, sir."

We shook hands and he walked away. Wondering what I'd just agreed to, I headed on to the graduation ceremony.

I picked up my pace along the cobblestone walkway, thinking about all the literature and history I'd pored over for the past six years, seldom reading any of it without wishing I were there in some place long ago, doing something important and history-shaping. I may have been an engineer by training, but at heart, at very private heart, I was a political man.

I wondered, specifically, what the BOI wanted with a colored agent all of a sudden. I was certainly aware that during its short life, it had never hired one. Could I possibly be the first? I thought it intriguing but far-fetched.

"Don't be late, Sidney," said Mrs. Carlton, one of my mathematics professors, interrupting my reverie as she walked by. "You've been waiting a long time for this."

"Yes, ma'am." I smiled at her and began to walk a bit faster. I reminded myself that Gladforth hadn't actually mentioned my becoming an agent. He'd only spoken of an interview and a possible low-level position.

"It's just you and me, Sidney," said Clifford Mayfield, running up and putting his hand on my shoulder, his grin bigger than ever.

"Yep," I said, "just you and me," referring to the fact that Clifford and I would be the only coloreds graduating that day.

"The way I see it," he said, "this is just the beginning. Tomorrow I'm off to Boston for an interview with Thurman Insurance."

Clifford continued talking about his plans for the future as we walked, but my mind was still on the Bureau. Working as an engineer was my goal, but maybe it could wait. Perhaps this Bureau position was a calling. Maybe if I could land a good government job and rise up through the ranks, I could bring about the social change I'd always dreamed of. I needed a few days to think it through.

Moments later I was sitting among my fellow classmates, each lost in his own

17

thoughts inspired by President Tannenbaum. He stood at the podium in his fancy blue and gold academic gown, the hot sun beaming down on his white rim of hair and bald, sunburned top of his head.

"You are all now equipped to take full advantage of the many opportunities the world has to offer," he asserted. "You have chosen to push beyond the four-year diploma and will soon be able to boast of possessing the coveted master's degree. . . ."

Momma had told me from the time I was five, "You're going to college someday, Sugar." But throughout my early teens I'd noticed that no one around me was doing so. Still, I studied hard and got a scholarship to Middlebury College. My high school English teacher, Mrs. Bright, had gone to school here.

"It seems," Tannenbaum continued, "like only yesterday that I was sitting there where all of you sit today, and I can tell you from my own experiences in the greater world that a Middlebury education is second to none. . . ."

I'd left Milwaukee, the Bronzeville section, in the fall of 1913 and headed here to Vermont. I had taken a major in mechanical engineering with the goal of obtaining a bachelor's and then a master's degree in civil engineering. I would be qualified both to assemble engines and construct buildings. Reading physics became all consuming, and I'd spent most of my time in the library, often slipping in some pleasure reading. Having access to a plethora of rich literature was new to me.

"I want you to hear me loud and clear," President Tannenbaum went on. "This is your time to shine."

As I looked across the crowd of graduate students and up into the stands, I saw Momma in her purple dress, brimming with joy. She was so proud, and rightfully so, having raised me all on her own. For eighteen years it had been just the two of us, Momma having happily spent those years scrubbing other families' homes, cooking for and raising their children. But now that I had turned twenty-five, I would see to it that she wouldn't have to do that anymore.

It was time for my row to stand. As we progressed slowly toward the stage, I became more and more painfully aware of my wife's absence. I'd first laid eyes on Loretta in the library four years earlier when she'd arrived at Middlebury, making her the third female colored student here.

I'd approached her while she was studying, introducing myself and awkwardly asking her if she'd like to study together sometime. She'd just given me an odd look before I'd quickly changed my question, asking instead if she'd like to have an ice cream with me sometime in the cafeteria. She said yes and it was easy between us from that day on.

"Sidney Temple!" called out President Tannenbaum, the audience politely clapping for me as they had for the others. I walked onto the stage, took my diploma from his hand, and paused briefly for the customary photograph. I looked at Momma as she wiped the tears from her eyes.

I longed for Loretta to be sitting there too, witnessing my little moment in the spotlight. Before coming to Middlebury she'd spent one year at the Pennsylvania Academy of the Fine Arts and another at Oberlin College. But she'd finally found her collegiate home here and earned a degree in art history.

Her graduation, which had come three weeks prior to mine, had been a magical affair. Unfortunately, that celebratory atmosphere had come to an abrupt halt. Today she was grieving the loss of her father and was back home in Philadelphia arranging for his funeral. His illness had progressed during the last year, and he'd rarely been conscious the last time we'd visited him together. I figured that would be the last time I'd see him and had said my good-byes back then. Still, it was comforting to know that Loretta had insisted I stay here and allow Momma to see me graduate.

With the ceremony over and degree in hand, I headed to the reception the engineering department was having for a few of us. My mind raced to come up with a good reason for visiting Washington, D.C. — one that I could legitimately tell Momma about. As I arrived at the auditorium, she was waiting outside. We embraced.

"I'm so proud of you, Sugar."

"I couldn't have done it without you. I love you, Momma."

The pending trip to Washington crept into my mind even during that long motherly hug.

A week later I was standing in the train station lobby in downtown Chicago on my way to the nation's capital. I'd said my good-byes to Momma back in Milwaukee earlier that morning. My "good reason"? I'd told her I'd been asked to interview for a position on the Public Buildings Commission, a government committee established in 1916 to make suggestions regarding future development of federal agencies and offices. It was the first time I'd lied to her, and the guilt was heavy on me.

The Bureau had sent an automobile to pick me up at Momma's place in Milwaukee and drive me to Chicago. It was a wondrous black vehicle — a 1919 Ford Model T.

When my train was announced, I headed to the car where all the colored passengers were sitting. Unlike the South, here in Chicago there were no Jim Crow cars I was required to sit in, but I guess most of us just felt comfortable sitting apart from the whites, and vice versa. Was the way things were in public. But it was a feeling I never wanted my future children to have.

All the folks on the train were immaculately dressed, and I felt comfortable in my cream-colored three-piece suit and brown newsboy cap. We gazed at one another with curiosity, each probably wondering, as I was, what special event was affording us the opportunity to travel such a distance in style. The car was paneled in walnut and furnished with large, upholstered chairs. It was the height of luxury.

I began studying the brand-new Broadway Limited railroad map I'd purchased. Ever since my first year of college, I'd been collecting every map I could get my hands on.

It had become a hobby of sorts, running my finger along the various lines that connected one town to another, always discovering a new place various rails had begun servicing.

The train passed by West Virginian fields of pink rhododendron, then chugged through the state of Virginia as I reflected on its history and absorbed the landscape with virgin eyes. This was the land of Washington and Jefferson I was entering.

2

Washington, D.C., struck me as a fantasyland. An agent picked me up from the station, and we made our way down Pennsylvania Avenue. Men in finely tailored suits with briefcases lined the streets.

As we drove by the Capitol Building, my heart began to race. It was everything I had imagined from an architectural standpoint. It symbolized power. For a brief moment, I imagined myself, the fresh engineer, building such a structure.

The closer we got to BOI headquarters, the more nervous I became. For the first time since meeting Gladforth, I began to have second thoughts about my interview. Why me? The magnitude of my being recruited by the Bureau hit me. Here I was, twenty-five years old and about to enter one of the most powerful buildings in the world.

The dull ache below my ribcage became a very uncomfortable twinge. The college nurse had chalked it up as stress. Clenching my jaw, I tried to shrug it off, fixing my eyes on the back of the agent's blond head.

I waited in the lobby to be called into Mr. Hoover's office. After what seemed a very long time, his secretary finally said he was ready. I entered the office and he stood from behind a desk, extending his hand without taking a step.

"J. Edgar Hoover," he said, shaking my hand and sitting again.

"It's a pleasure to meet you, Mr. Hoover. Sidney Temple."

"Please, have a seat."

Surprisingly, the man before me looked no older than twenty. He was about five-feet-ten with a boxer's nose, thick, bushy eyebrows, and a squatty neck. He looked very much like a bulldog, but he was an exceptionally neat, well-groomed, and organized bulldog; I gave him that much.

I took a seat in an uninviting metal folding chair in front of his desk. As I scooted forward, the chair legs screeched against the marble floor. The entire office had an empty, cold feeling to it, with unpacked boxes and gray file cabinets lining the ivory walls, recently painted judging by the smell. He was obviously just moving in.

A framed diploma from George Washing-

25

ton University hung behind his desk, and various photographs covered the wall to his right. There was only one window in the office, designed, it seemed, to hinder rather than let in the sunlight.

"We've been doing a bit of shuffling between office buildings around here, Sidney," he said, reading something. "I haven't even been officially named head of the General Intelligence Division. That will happen on August first. But official titles aside, I've been given my orders.

"The attorney general's office and those of us here at the Department of Justice have been told that these arbitrary locations are temporary — that we'll be getting a permanent home base soon. I'm told they've been saying that for nine years. We shall see."

I nodded while he stayed fixed on his report of some sort, flipping to another page.

"The BOI wants to make it a habit of tracking college students of all racial backgrounds who perform at the academic level at which you performed. We're fond of those students, especially those" — his finger scanned the page — "with a knack for physics, mathematics, psychology, and law."

He looked up from the file, seeing me for the first time it seemed, aside from the brief

26

look he'd given before brusquely shaking my hand. "We're even more enamored of those who remain apolitical," he said, tapping the file. "In going over your history here, I find it remarkable, even a tad hard to believe, that you've never been a part of any fraternities, social groups, or committees — even during high school — not even on the student council. Correct?"

"That is true."

"It's one of the reasons you're sitting in that chair. Your autonomy is appealing — that and the fact that you have the physique of a sportsman and not some bookwormy engineer. Have you ever been inclined to join any political party or national movement?"

"My focus from the time I left Bronzeville was on earning an engineering degree — nothing else."

He looked back at the file. "I also see that two years ago you attempted to enlist for the war but were turned down due to a letter that was sent to the Army by your college president regarding your" — again his finger scanned — "unique acumen for physics, your overall distinguished scholarship."

I was puzzled by that bit of information and responded, "I did attempt to enlist and was turned down. But I am unaware of any letter being written on my behalf."

"That's fine," he said. "I know you weren't aware of said letter. Your honest response is commendable." He looked directly at me again. "Ever fired a pistol?"

To this question I wanted to lie and say yes and that I had done some training in hopes of preparing myself to be a soldier someday. I wanted to impress the young man but figured he was the type to suggest a visit to a shooting range to gauge my comfort level with a gun. He would have been sadly disappointed.

I also knew that he was probably suspicious, like most, of any colored who'd ever fired a gun. As far as I knew, there wasn't a shooting range in America that allowed men like me onto their grounds. Therefore, any answer other than no would lead Mr. Hoover to believe that I had fired a pistol illegally. So I told the truth.

"Never," I answered.

"Doesn't mean you're not a good aim." Again, he looked at the file. "Your high school coach, a Mr. Sanders, says here your vision and hand-eye coordination is 'unmatched on the basketball court.' Based on the high marks and comments your coach gave you, I believe even Dr. James Naismith himself would be impressed."

He looked back at me. "Anyway, the Bureau hasn't been given the authority by Congress to allow its agents to even carry handguns. I'm hoping that will soon change, and when it does, I'm sure you'll take kindly to a sidearm."

"I believe I would."

"I need to sign a few papers here, Sidney. Bear with me. But I'll ask you while I'm signing. I want you to try to be as specific as possible with your answer. What do you know about the Negro scholar W. E. B. Du Bois — assuming you're familiar with his philosophy? Are you aware of his communist leanings and dangerous agenda?"

I froze, trying to make sure I'd heard him correctly. "Well, I am . . ."

"Hold that thought," he interrupted, as his focus was on signing the papers. "One minute."

I was bothered by what he'd said about Du Bois and felt foolish all of a sudden. I had allowed excitement to get in the way of common sense. Gladforth hadn't approached me to do the same type of work their other agents do. Of course not. They needed a Negro to spy on another Negro — one W. E. B. Du Bois.

"Just one more minute here, Sidney."

I watched Mr. Hoover turn page after

page, penning his signature on each. Little did he know he'd mentioned my idol. I'd read everything Du Bois had ever written. But I was certain that Hoover knew nothing about my views because I'd never written nor spoken publicly about the man.

I considered Du Bois the preeminent scholar of his time — the leader of colored America. And now, for that, the Bureau wanted to pry into his life. But they had the wrong man for this job. Besides, there would be nothing to find: He was completely honorable.

"All right, Sidney," he said, returning to my interview, which seemed to be becoming almost a distraction from his real job. "Go ahead."

"Well . . . I . . . I think that Du Bois's precise objective is unknown."

"Do you subscribe to the *Crisis*?"

"No."

"Why not?"

Just then there was a knock and his secretary opened the door.

"Mr. Hoover," she said, "Agent Lively needs you in the meeting next door for a brief moment."

"I'll be right there. Listen, Sidney, I want to apologize in advance for this, but I may be running in and out of here during our visit. I was to take part in another meeting next door but didn't see why I couldn't fit you in. Told them to call me in only when my opinion is needed. We all have to keep several balls in the air at the same time around here."

"I understand."

"Good." He stood. "I'll be back before you know it."

Once he exited, leaving the door open behind him, I stood and walked over to the window, looked out, and tried to gather my thoughts. I actually read the *Crisis* religiously but hadn't ever subscribed to it. Something Hoover *didn't* know was how voracious a reader I was of many subjects, not just physics.

One of my more political teachers, Professor Gold, provided me with several colored newspapers, all of which were, of course, controversial. But he knew it was critical for me never to appear to be part of any movement if I was going to get hired at any institution as an engineer or professor. Whenever I took one of these newspapers home with me, he told me to "burn after reading," and I always did.

"Mr. Temple," said his secretary, walking just inside the doorway, "Mr. Hoover will be back in just a second. Can I get you

31

anything?"

"No, ma'am. I'm fine. Thank you."

She half smiled, walked out, and I turned back to the window, my thoughts still on Professor Gold. He and I were very close. He was a white man with socialist leanings. He had changed his name from Jackson, a name his father had adopted on entering the country, back to Gold upon his graduation from Harvard in 1872 — likely out of pure embarrassment for bearing the seventh president's last name.

Simply put, Professor Gold was like a modern-day abolitionist. He hated inequality and had taken a strong interest in me my freshman year. He told me I was brilliant, took me under his wing, mentored me, damn near treated me like a son. I think he believed that helping me was like helping an entire people.

When I married Loretta, we moved from our dorm rooms into a tiny guesthouse on his ten-acre property, situated in the woods about five miles from the college. The grounds were nestled in between acres and acres of sugar maple trees. We would walk over to his chalet on most weekends, as our guesthouse was on the opposite end of the property.

It was at his place that I read and discussed politics with him for hours on end, while Mary, his wife, would work on her essays and Loretta would paint in the little bedroom they had converted into a studio just for her.

I knew Professor Gold would never tell a soul about me, including any Bureau agent who may have come around. Gold was concerned about hiding his own political activity, so he never would have said a word. Luckily for him, the Bureau had no interest in him or his activities — just mine.

"Okay," Mr. Hoover said on his return, closing the door behind him. "Where were we?"

"You wanted to know why I hadn't subscribed to the *Crisis*."

"That's right." He sat down. "Why not?"

I moved from the window back to my chair. "Well, I've never subscribed to it because . . . probably . . . or . . . let me rephrase that . . . precisely because during my twenty-five-year lifetime, I've never been given a reason to believe I wasn't the equal of any man, regardless of race.

"Perhaps my mother left Chicago with me when I was five because she wanted to, in some way, shelter me from reality. The Bronzeville streets, though they contain some rough elements, are not as brutal as those in Chicago. Truthfully, I have accomplished every goal I've ever set. My life has not been a crisis — no pun intended, Mr. Hoover."

"Does your own success desensitize you to the struggles of the greater Negro race, assuming you believe that there is a struggle?"

"No."

"In twenty words or less, define what America means to you."

"It means unparalleled courage, sacrificed blood, broken chains, and the relentless hope of a united people."

Hoover sat there for a moment and stared at me. I couldn't tell if his glare represented a newfound hate for me, a respect for my opinion, or a surprised reaction to the quickness with which I'd responded to his question.

His poker face was impressive. My bold answer about racial equality was likely a death sentence for this potential career, as I had no idea what theories on race Mr. Hoover might have, but at this point I didn't really care.

As he continued his stare, the desk phone began to ring. "That's likely the attorney general," he said. "There isn't enough time in the day. One minute, Sidney."

He picked up and it occurred to me just how ignorant I was being. If they wanted to spy on Du Bois, there was no stopping them. And if I turned the assignment down, if indeed that was what my role was to be, there would be some other colored graduate willing to infiltrate Du Bois's world — someone lacking my loyalty and respect for the scholar — someone willing to destroy him for the right amount of money.

"No, Mr. Palmer," he said into the phone, "that entire outfit has been turned over to Kirkland. But I can put it back in the hands of Fennison if you feel that Kirkland could be better utilized in Santa Fe."

Having heard Hoover call Du Bois "dangerous" felt like a call to arms. I could, especially as a covert agent, protect him and his integration agenda from his enemies, including the government. Du Bois surviving would ensure a better America for my unborn children. And if protecting him meant I needed to get inside the beast — the impenetrable beast that had played a role throughout American history in influencing the destiny of our nation — I needed to do it. This relatively new Bureau was part of the innards of that beast.

"You have my word on it, sir," continued Hoover.

I began to envision the potential spy mission as a sacrifice for Du Bois that only someone with my unique pedigree, intelligence, and beliefs would be able to make. I was also confident that I could outsmart this Mr. Hoover, especially considering we were roughly the same age. Perhaps my biggest flaw was that I'd always believed I could outsmart everyone around me.

He hung up the telephone. "Sidney, the Bureau has never hired a colored agent. Earlier today I interviewed a man by the name of James Wormley Jones, a soldier. Was stationed in France. I may hire him. Do you have any clue as to why I would even consider hiring him as the first-ever colored agent since the inception of our Bureau?"

"No."

"Loyalty."

"I see."

"The Bureau of Investigation wants men who care about what's in the best interest of America first. Jones obviously understands this — he was willing to die in a war. And I am quite certain that you, in your eagerness to enlist back in 1917, were willing to die as well. I can only imagine the pride these men must feel today as each returns to a hero's welcome across the country. I didn't fight in the war. I was already employed at the Justice Department at a very young age and was exempt from the draft. I regret that.

"Fighting in a war," he continued, "and surviving it, allows a man to brush aside the kinds of regrets a typical man becomes entangled in throughout life — regrets about trivial failures and whatnot. A willingness to die for this nation is the ultimate badge of honor. And I've examined the details of your life enough to believe that you possess such a badge."

"Thank you, Mr. Hoover."

He began jotting something down. The man had mentioned my willingness to die, and he was right. I'd do so for Du Bois. And had I gone off to war, I certainly would have made a good soldier. I would have tried to show the same bravery that American soldiers from past wars had. Men like General George Washington.

The image of him leading America into battle on horseback was imprinted in my mind, had been ever since I was six years old and Momma had read a story to me about Washington at Valley Forge, then about his exploits throughout the rest of the Revolutionary War. The image resonated with me. I had been fascinated by him ever since.

"You love America, don't you?" he asked, looking up from his writing.

"Very much."

Hoover cleared his throat and suddenly took on an even more serious demeanor.

"Two months ago you were quoted in, of all things, an issue of your college newspaper, saying that you believed Marcus Garvey was, quote, 'undermining the American Negro agenda.' I actually have a copy of the paper right here."

He picked it up from his desk, leaned forward, and handed it to me. "Go ahead and skim through it. Take your time and make sure it rings a bell."

I began thumbing through it, looking for the article. It took me a moment to digest his comment. *Wow,* I thought, *one remark about this Garvey individual had been the impetus behind their bringing me to Washington. This had nothing to do with Du Bois after all.*

"Take your time, Sidney."

I found the article and began pretending to read, trying to collect my thoughts. I'd read this article many times. Loretta had brought it to me, excited beyond words to see my name in print. I did know some things about Garvey. I'd been reading about him off and on since he'd arrived from Jamaica in 1916.

He was a powerful orator and operated out of Harlem. I'd read some of his remarks and took exception to his seeming disrespect for Du Bois, who'd been fighting the fight here in the United States, literally, before Garvey was even born. Based on what I'd read, I had myself convinced that Garvey was committed to destroying Du Bois, the NAACP, and everything it stood for.

Garvey's arrogance and seemingly quick dismissal of too many American colored leaders was upsetting. I didn't know if he appreciated the unique nature of the Negro American struggle compared with the struggles of coloreds in other countries, including his own.

My dislike for Garvey wasn't just about his politics but also about his approach to leadership. He was flirting with becoming a demagogue.

Based on what I'd read and heard from others, Garvey detested and was jealous of Du Bois because of his New England background, Harvard education, and close relationships with whites. The last thing our people needed was a conflict between two of its own leaders.

And Garvey would definitely have success if his aim was to rile up angry colored folk. Spying on him for the Bureau would actually mean spying on him for Du Bois as far as I was concerned.

"Yes, I remember making a statement to my college newspaper," I finally said, returning the paper to him.

"Just how familiar are you with Mr. Garvey?"

"I know nothing about him. I made that remark because a Middlebury newspaper reporter showed me a quote Garvey had made before coming to America regarding light-skinned folks in the West Indies.

"The quote seemed insensitive. I had never heard of Garvey so I flippantly made the remark, knowing that I was two months away from graduation. What I actually said was 'If Garvey truly has a problem with light-skinned coloreds, that attitude has the potential to undermine the American Negro agenda, especially considering how many people are light-skinned.' They took my quote out of context."

Hoover retrieved a file from his desk drawer and stood. "One minute," he said, heading for the door and exiting.

One minute turned to five so I stood and began pacing back and forth, trying to get the circulation going in my legs. I also took some deep breaths. Maybe he'd been simply leaving the room to share info about me with colleagues — to get second and third opinions about my answers.

Lying to Mr. Hoover about not knowing anything regarding Garvey was easy and important — especially if I intended to continue playing the apolitical character he seemed to like. But all the reading material Professor Gold had provided me with was enough to keep me well informed about the up-and-coming leader and soapbox orator. Nevertheless, I was actually telling Mr. Hoover the truth about the quote I'd made to the paper: They *had* taken my quote out of context.

"Here you are, Mr. Temple," said Irene, walking in and handing me a glass of water. "Was told you might be thirsty."

"Thank you."

She scurried off and I sipped. I walked over and took a closer look at the photographs hanging on the wall to the right of Mr. Hoover's desk. Some were group pictures, others of individuals — perhaps government officials or college professors who had influenced him. All of these men, some dressed in military uniforms, likely had leadership roles of some sort. And leadership was something Garvey was craving.

Glass still in hand, I downed the rest and began pacing again. I understood Garvey's desire to unify and strengthen coloreds throughout the world, but I was convinced his approach was dangerous.

Catching me in mid pace, Hoover reentered and took a seat. I eased my way back to my chair, setting the glass on his desk.

"We're just about finished here, Sidney. Just a few more items." He put the file away, made a note on a large desk calendar, then looked back at my file, which he'd left open on his desk.

"Apparently this Garvey, who until recently was an unknown figure, is quickly becoming known to the greater public. How do you think this classmate — college reporter — knew about the quote Garvey'd made?"

"I have no idea."

But I did know. The past November of 1918, the *New York Times* had reported on a meeting Garvey had led with five thousand people in attendance. That report had introduced Garvey to America.

A student reporter began investigating him, looking into his Jamaican past, his rise to a position of leadership in America. I guess since I was one of the only colored students at the school, the reporter came to me with all this information and asked for a response to the quote.

"Are you familiar with Max Eastman?" asked Hoover.

"No."

"He heads up the *Liberator.* It's a socialist-leaning magazine in Greenwich Village. He previously ran the *Masses,* in which he repeatedly railed against the United States's involvement in the war. He stood trial under provisions of the Sedition Act.

"We also have every reason to believe he's a Marxist. Although, I must say, to his credit, he's been able to sniff out any agents we've ever sent to infiltrate his businesses. But perhaps a colored agent wouldn't draw his suspicion."

Now I was truly confused. Was it Garvey or Eastman he wanted me to follow? Maybe it was someone else altogether. I was through trying to predict this young fellow's intentions for me.

"I'm due over on the Hill here shortly, Sidney." He paused and cleared his throat. "The Bureau does not provide formal training for its agents, and again, our agents have no congressional authority to carry a side-arm, though most of them carry a weapon for their own protection.

"Besides, I intend to change all this authority, no authority nonsense. We will eventually have a training academy for physical work and classroom study. In the meantime, I'd like you to follow a few of our experienced agents out in the field for some on-the-job training. You could say I'm going to throw you to the wolves for three weeks, Sidney. You'll also have to pass the official security clearance.

"James Wormley Jones and two other candidates will also be in the field with you. You'll be under the direct supervision of an Agent Lexington Speed — a decorated war man. He prides himself on doing rigorous physical training, even when he's out on assignment for weeks at a time. God knows I'd like for his work ethic and discipline to become the norm around here — to rub off on some of our less fit individuals.

"Anyhow, Agent Speed will be putting you four through his physical routine each morning. It won't be easy. He'll also be observing how you handle yourselves in the field. You'll likely be in some rather tense situations, ones that will test your mental mettle.

"Based upon Speed's evaluation, I will render my decision on whether you have the makings of a covert agent — assuming you even want to work for us at that point. You may have shown a willingness to die, an apolitical nature, and demonstrated high scholastic achievement, but those characteristics alone do not make an effective undercover agent.

"Besides that, many of the agents we hire have extensive military or police backgrounds. They've been schooled in weaponry, evidence gathering, etcetera. So, if hired, you'll be a unique case. But let's be clear, I say none of this to discourage you."

So I was in, or almost in. Into what, however, I knew little more about than I had when I'd stepped on the train for my first trip to Washington, D.C.

3

I took a train to Philadelphia the next day to meet Loretta at her childhood home, a nice three-bedroom in West Philadelphia. Her father had been a renowned Baptist preacher for some forty-plus years. Now that he'd passed, Loretta was without either parent; her mother had died of cancer ten years earlier. Her parents owned their home, and now, with no siblings, Loretta had inherited it.

Her intentions were to sell immediately and reinvest in a home of our choosing. She wanted to get out of West Philadelphia and start a new life in a place where I could find work and she could focus on her painting. The resources from selling the house would certainly allow her the time and freedom to do just that.

Before heading to Loretta's, I hailed a taxi to Leonard's Gun Exchange — a place owned by a man the cab driver had recommended. I needed a pistol. I had no intentions of being a sitting duck during my assignment and knew I'd eventually want a gun in the privacy of my own home. The exchange went quickly, and I purchased a Colt M1911. I liked the fact that it was small, easy to conceal. When and where I would learn to use it was the great unknown, but I felt safe just having it.

As the taxi eased down Locust Street, the red brick three-story Queen Anne house with a wraparound porch came into view. Loretta's father's prized possession — a beautiful, gray 1915 Chevrolet Baby Grand Touring — was parked out front. I thought about having to lie to Loretta about my activities in Washington but felt justified in doing so, forced to compartmentalize between home and work. Now I needed to come up with a believable story about why I'd be returning to D.C. in two weeks.

The driver stopped and I retrieved my belongings from behind the seat. Making my way up the sidewalk lined with gorgeous mountain laurels, I entered the house, sat my suitcase down, and climbed the stairs to the second floor. As I walked the hallway, I stopped for a moment, noticing a childhood photo of Loretta standing next to her mother.

They were the spitting image of each other, both a shade darker than my caramel-colored skin. I leaned in closer to get a better look at how her mother so lovingly had her pulled in close, snug against her leg. Loretta appeared overjoyed, her big grin showing a few missing teeth.

I reached the back room and stopped at the doorway. She was standing there like a statue; shoulders drooped, arms just dangling. With paintbrush in hand, she stared at a blank canvas.

"Hello, lovely lady," I said.

She looked up, half smiled, then approached me. We embraced for several seconds without saying a word. Felt like I was absorbing some of her hurt.

"It has seemed like forever," she said into my chest.

"God, you feel so good." I rubbed her back and touched my nose to the top of her head. "Smell so good too."

"My other half is home."

"Yes."

"Now maybe I can finally sleep. I'm exhausted, Sid."

"That makes two of us." I took her hand. "You have every right to feel tired. We don't have to talk right now. Let's just go lie down. I'll rub your wrist the way you like."

We lay down and slept soundly for the next fifteen hours, thus avoiding a conversation about D.C. for the time being.

Waking before Loretta the following morning, I made eggs, toast, grapefruit, and coffee for the two of us. I sat down to read the *Philadelphia Inquirer,* moving aside the dozens of art books she'd been reading. I buttered a slice of toast and took a big bite. Just as I opened the paper, into the kitchen she walked.

"Good morning, Love," she said.

"I hope you slept well," I replied, giving her a kiss.

A good feeling always ran through me when she called me "Love." It never got old. The morning brought about a renewed spirit in both of us. She was sad about her father's death, but he had been suffering ill health for about five years, so the blow was perhaps less shocking to her.

"Look at you already reminding me why I'm so lucky," she said, a bit of morning rasp in her voice. "Tucked me in last night, making me breakfast this morning. What's next?"

I lifted my eyebrows suggestively and bit down on the edge of my toast, freeing my hands to pull out her chair.

"Here, sit, sit, sit," I mumbled, the toast hanging from my mouth.

She took a seat and began scooping her grapefruit with a spoon. I noticed that the tired around her eyes was gone. She looked radiant, her long, wavy black hair resting against her milky-looking nightgown with an elegance that added to her alluring presence. I loved her angular chin, her long, thin limbs and narrow shoulders.

"How was Washington?" she asked.

"It was awe inspiring." I poured her some coffee. "The Public Buildings Commission is indeed going to hire several engineers and architects over the next few months. They would like several of us to come back in two weeks and attend twenty-one days of training seminars, Commission meetings, and lectures.

"We will be visiting several future building locations and participating in what they call group feedback sessions with civil engineers from all over the country. The Commission is trying to find a way to come up with only the best and brightest ideas."

"Wait," she said, chewing, "this sounds like a bigger deal than you originally made it out to be."

"It does, doesn't it?"

For some reason, I felt like I needed to

continue convincing her. That's what happens when you're telling a bald-faced lie.

"It's a unique situation," I continued, sitting. "They want to begin building several neoclassical government office buildings in what they are calling the 'Pennsylvania Avenue Triangle.' " I paused to gauge her reaction but she was simply listening. "You don't want any sugar on that grapefruit?" I asked.

She shook her head no, sipping her coffee. "I spent a lot of time thinkin' of D.C. while you were gone," she said.

"Good. And?"

"Well . . . ya know . . . I think I can see myself living there." She paused. "Or can I?" She playfully contorted her mouth and raised one eyebrow. "Yeah . . . I think I can. Sorry, Love. Continue."

"Okay." I forked and fiddled with my eggs. "Well, they are paying for my trip back to Washington and all accommodations. Any potential hire is predicated on how the training goes. But it sounds encouraging."

"It sounds important, too, Sid . . . like an opportunity to be on the cutting edge of something." She sipped. "Sounds very exciting."

"Well, we should hold back our excitement. They haven't offered me a job. Again, the training will determine everything."

"I will have plenty to do while you're gone. At least you'll be here for the next two weeks. We can spend that time getting the house ready to sell. Oh . . . what about all of the loose ends back at Middlebury?"

"Well, I left the guesthouse spotless and packed all of our things. Professor Gold said he'd arrange to have our items sent once we get settled. Mary was really missing you. They want to come see us as soon as we get situated."

"You know what I'm going to miss the most about them?" she asked.

"What?"

"Those snowy winters when the four of us would hunker down inside by the fireplace. I will never forget how they took us in as family, Sid."

"Me neither."

"I truly believe Middlebury is the most beautiful place on earth."

"It is," I said.

"And . . . I figure . . . at least . . . Daddy got to see it before . . . you know . . ."

"Right."

I watched her fiddle with her grapefruit and could tell she no longer had any interest in it. She set her spoon down, and we both sipped our coffee and were quiet for a while. Figured I'd wait for her to continue the conversation.

"Just a special place," she finally said. "Middlebury. Inspired so much of my work. Those autumn colors are magic."

"No . . . *you're* magic."

"Thank you," she said, placing both hands on her lap. She looked at me but it was more like she was looking through me, her dark brown eyes transfixed, obviously on the past.

"Sweetie," I said, bringing her back to attention. "How are you doing with the funeral now over . . . with all the extended family gone?"

"Ya know . . . I feel empty and full at the same time — empty in my head and heart, full in my artistic soul. I guess Daddy's death leaves me wanting to paint images that have no clear identity. I find myself moving in that direction."

"Well, you can certainly be proud of your figurative pieces."

She turned and looked at the painting of her father on the wall behind her.

"That one in particular," I said. "It captures him . . . his strength. And it captures the Vermont scenery just as well as any Charles Heyde piece. You're amazing."

"Thank you, Love."

She stayed fixed on the painting for a moment. Then she turned back around and there were tears in her eyes. I got up and approached her, taking her hand as she stood. I wrapped her in my arms, and she began to cry softly.

I could never take her father's place, but I could certainly be the rock she would need. And I knew that, in time, she could find joy again. In the meantime, all I wanted to do was protect her. Of course I had now convinced myself that being an agent wouldn't get in the way of that. Hell, I had convinced myself that it would *better* enable me to protect her. After all, I was now an armed man.

4

Back in June, Galleanists, followers of Luigi Galleani, an Italian-born anarchist who had been in the United States since 1901, had detonated several bombs across the country. They'd even managed to damage the home of Attorney General A. Mitchell Palmer. That act made them prime targets of the Justice Department and, perhaps not coincidentally, of my training program. Hoover had reason to believe a tiny group was operating out of Baltimore, site of my three-week training assignment.

It had been raining for seven straight days, and now my face was pressed down against a muddy quagmire in Patterson Park. Lexington Speed stood over me, demanding that I complete the twenty push-ups I had left.

"Get your ass in the air, Temple!" Speed yelled.

Speed had been around the Bureau long

before Hoover. He was a huge man, about six-foot-six. His head was shiny-bald and pinkish in color, the veins protruding from his temple like purple hookworms, his physique godlike. He was downright scary-looking. I couldn't decide whether his goal was to kill me or train me.

"Jones is wiping his ass with you, Temple."

This insult hurled at me was in reference to James Wormley Jones. He and the two other trainees had already finished doing one hundred push-ups. But, for some reason, I was being asked to do one hundred fifty today. Maybe because earlier we'd completed a one-mile run and I'd whipped Jones. In his defense, I was ten years younger.

Paul Mann was one of the trainees. He was an arrogant young man. The other, Bobby Ellington, seemed to be rather enlightened. He was from Hudson, Ohio, and fresh out of Ohio Wesleyan University. His obsession with Greek mythology was evident. I had enjoyed conversing with him the previous six nights and knew instinctively that he was a decent man.

My body was so sore that I couldn't wait to get back to my hotel room and lie down. I finally pained my way through the last push-up.

"All right, Temple," Speed yelled, "session complete. We've got a half-mile run back to the hotel. Ellington, you and Temple are assigned to relieve Knox and Long in one hour. You'll take night watch from sundown to sunup. Any movement whatsoever out of that alley house and you immediately notify the team."

So much for going back to the hotel and resting. Our tiny hotel was located four blocks from the Galleanists' hideout, which was close to the Phoenix Shot Tower. For the past seven days, two rotating agents had been parked across the street and down about twenty yards from the Galleanists' ground-level room in a red brick alley house.

So far, there had been no movement. There were only four rooms in the building, the two rear ones — one upstairs, one down — each occupied by single old men. We had seen both of them come and go and had sneaked around back at night and watched them through their windows. The front upstairs room was unoccupied, as the sign in the window read FOR RENT.

Based on a solid tip, we had reason to believe four male Galleanists occupied the downstairs front room. We were operating on the assumption the four were simply lying low inside, perhaps planning their next move and building bombs. Or maybe they were out of town and would soon return.

Either way, the week had left plenty of downtime for Speed to work us like dogs. He fancied himself a brilliant marksman and, evidently, expected us to follow in his footsteps. As this Baltimore job was considered a special assignment, the Justice Department had given our team the authority to arm ourselves. We had even visited a firing range earlier in the week, immediately after completing a rigorous exercise routine.

Agent Speed wanted us completely fatigued when we visited the range. Tired, wobbly legs and aching, shaky arms didn't make for accurate shooting. I accepted the challenge and wasn't going to let Speed break me. He hadn't called me a nigger yet, but it was right on the tip of his tongue.

It was getting dark and the rain was still pouring down. Ellington and I, holding our umbrellas, approached the black Lincoln. In it sat Knox and Long. They had been parked there for eight hours. From the look of things, there'd still been no activity in the hideout.

I wondered, privately, if the Galleanists had simply spotted us. But the street was lined with automobiles and had plenty of folks walking up and down throughout the day, so the Lincoln didn't stand out.

Taylor Knox and Sam Long were veteran agents like Speed. But they were not as physically imposing, though they seemed to enjoy physical training and, like Speed, had military backgrounds.

Ellington knocked on the passenger-side window and Knox opened his door. He threw a cigarette on the ground and spoke to Ellington.

"You workin' by yourself tonight?"

"No, I'm with Temple."

"Who?" asked Knox.

Ellington pointed at me, and Knox just sat there squinting his eyes and acting as if he couldn't see me.

"I don't see anyone," he said. "It's dark out here. Smile, boy. Let me see those teeth."

Knox and Long laughed as Ellington gave me a sympathetic look. It would take great discipline for me to ignore his antics for the next fourteen days. Ellington stood there as if waiting for me to react. I studied Knox, sizing up his pinkish, oily face.

He was a heavy drinker and smoker from Georgia who didn't see the value of men like me. Long, a Louisianan, was the quiet type who tended to follow Knox's every move. I never knew what he was thinking. People like him left me uneasy. At least in the case of Knox, he made it known that he despised my type. The two of them looked like twins — salt-and-pepper hair, average builds, white T-shirts, black slacks, and soulless-looking eyes.

"We're here to relieve you two," I said. "Agent Speed wants you to join him for supper at the spot next to the hotel. He's waiting on you."

Knox got out of the Lincoln, slowly stepped toward me, and we were briefly face-to-face. He spit tobacco on the ground and smiled.

"Well all right, then," he said with a twang. "Don't want to leave anybody waitin' on little ol' me."

Agent Long exited the driver side, circled around front, and approached us. He put his right hand on Knox's left shoulder, encouraging him to move on.

"Night-night, boys," said Knox as the two walked away.

Ellington got into the passenger side. As I sat behind the wheel, I briefly contemplated starting the engine, turning the Lincoln around, and running over the two Southern sons of bitches. The thought quickly passed. It was becoming abundantly clear that even though Hoover wanted me around for selfish reasons, the greater Bureau wasn't on board with his little experiment.

"I wonder how many bombs are in there?" Ellington asked, staring ahead and to his left at the pitch-black window of the hideout.

"Are they even in there?" I asked.

"Probably. Speed told me the tip came from an Italian bomb maker who some agents apprehended in Buffalo last month."

"Why aren't the local police involved then?" I asked.

"Because ever since April, when all of those mail bombs were delivered to prominent government officials, not to mention the one that exploded at Palmer's house last month, Palmer himself has made it clear that this is a federal matter, not a local one. We're probably one team of twenty staking out houses around the country. The local police don't even know about this particular location. And if they did know, they'd probably make the mistake of walking up and knocking on the door — aggressively seeking to catch them making the damn things."

"Good point."

"Also," said Ellington, wiping the rain from his forehead, "if they happen to have the bombs hidden somewhere else, such a visit from Baltimore's finest would only make them postpone or cancel their mission. We're hoping to follow the four and catch them planting the devices. I'm quickly learning that such patience is what makes the Bureau unique. It is slowly creating a new way of catching criminals. Why do you think they've chosen us? This is a thinking man's business."

"I'm tempted," I said, "to sneak over and see if they have something covering the inside of that window — a black cloth of some sort."

"Lose the temptation." He began rubbing the dashboard with his hand, clearing away the moisture.

"Hope you have some stories to tell," I said. "We're gonna be sitting here all night and nothing's gonna happen."

"You do know that Hoover is meticulous about everything, right? A friend of mine attended night school with him at George Washington. He said that when Hoover worked at the Library of Congress, he was such a perfectionist that he mastered the entire Dewey decimal system."

"He dresses sharp — I know that," I said.

Ellington and I were certainly following the dress code. Agent Speed had already informed us that Hoover expected all of the agents to wear black suits, white shirts, keep their hair very short, and have pristinely shiny shoes. Agents were also ordered to wear fedora hats.

Speed himself didn't follow Hoover's orders about hair and wasn't likely to change his bald look. He was the exception. I found it ironic that Hoover was so picky about the agents' appearance, considering that his own look was rather odd. And he was awfully young to be so in command — only twenty-four.

"Agent Speed told me something interesting," said Ellington. "Hoover is looking for young agents he can groom to head up various field offices. Agents who get those jobs have a great chance to rise high within the Bureau. Speed seemed to suggest that I had excellent prospects of securing one of those positions."

"Good for you," I said.

"Speed said Hoover is intrigued by my background."

I just nodded. I really liked Ellington. The twenty-one-year-old kid had good energy. His striking good looks suggested he should be pursuing a career as a film actor rather than an agent.

"What in God's name were you dreaming about the other night?" I asked.

"What do you mean?"

"Your stirring and mumbling woke me up several times."

"What was I saying?" he asked.

"You kept going on and on about Cronus, Dodona, and Aphrodite. You were tossing and turning like you were engaged in a fight with someone."

"Hmm," he said. "I don't know."

"Come on."

"I was probably just dreaming about my childhood."

"I don't understand."

"Look," he said, "it's a bit embarrassing. But when I was a kid, I used to pretend I was Zeus — the king of the gods. You know?"

"Yeah, the ruler of Mount Olympus and the god of the sky."

"Right," he said, growing restless. "I actually thought I was him."

"But you don't *still* think you're him?"

"I guess last night I did." We both snickered before he went on. "Actually, I still pretend I'm Zeus from time to time, especially when Agent Speed is busting my ass. I feel like wiping him out the way Zeus struck Salmoneus dead with a thunderbolt. But knowing Agent Speed, he'd probably laugh at the thunderbolt and crush me. The man is scary."

"Yes," I said, "he's a very scary man."

"Anyhow, I'll try to cut out the tossing and turning so you can sleep. Let you do the dreaming from now on. Did you dream a lot as a youngster?"

"Shoot," I said. "I wished. More like nightmares. Simple dreams would have been great."

"I know. Nightmares stink when you're a kid because you can't predict when they might visit you. And when they do, you can't understand what they mean."

"Oh . . . I knew what mine meant."

"No shit?"

"Yeah," I said. "When I was sixteen, I witnessed something horrific."

I paused for a spell.

"Look, Temple, if you don't want to go into it I understand."

"Nah. It's just . . . I've always avoided talking about it."

I thought back and contemplated whether I wanted to share this story with him. I closed my eyes. I started to see myself as that innocent sixteen-year-old, happy to be spending time with my cousin in the summer of 1910. We had been like brothers, so close, even though we only saw each other in the summers.

I glanced over at Ellington. For some reason I trusted the kid. Oddly, I hadn't been able to completely share this story with anyone for nine years, and now, unbelievably, I felt ready to get it out — to share the details with someone I barely knew. I turned my attention back to the hideout and the words began to flow.

"It really is still as clear as yesterday," I said. "It was a hot day in Chicago. I watched my cousin TJ engage in a fistfight with a white man. My cousin was eighteen and the man was probably thirty-five.

"TJ and I were riding our bicycles, approaching an intersection. TJ didn't see an automobile idling there at the intersection, preparing to turn. When it turned, TJ ran into the side of it and scratched the door a bit. No real damage."

"Right," said Ellington.

"The man jumped out and began shoving my cousin. He wouldn't stop. Finally TJ pushed back, and the two began fighting. All of a sudden the man pulled a knife and my cousin kept engaging him.

"Anyway, the man stabbed him in the stomach. Then he walked toward me and pointed it within an inch of my face. I lost all of my senses, just stood there, staring down the point of the blade for what seemed like a lifetime.

"But he then thought better of it, got back into his car, and drove away. I was shaking like crazy, but I fell to my knees beside TJ. I held him as he bled all over me and died right in my arms."

"Shit," said Ellington. "My God. Sorry, Temple. Sounds like there wasn't anything you could have done to stop it, though."

"Nah. I was never a fighter. I didn't have a fighter's mentality. If I had known how to use my hands, I would have intervened. And what adds to the anger I still feel is the fact that we were riding our bicycles in our part of the city.

"So, you see, this man had crossed the tracks and had entered 'Colored Town.' He was the foreigner. He was also a coward because my cousin never had a weapon to brandish. He was using his bare hands. That man was a cold-blooded murderer."

"Damn right, Temple."

"Whole thing has always made me want to change the way things work . . . the race thing and all. Know what I mean?"

Ellington nodded. But what I hadn't told him was how the police never even looked for the man. Two white officers arrived on the scene, questioned me, took the body away, and that was it. There had been two colored women who witnessed the event, and they told the policemen the story, but nothing came of it. I had to accept the horrific fact that a man murdering a Negro and getting away with it was routine in America. But accepting that reality had killed a part of me.

"To answer your original question," I said, "about dreaming — after he died, I began searching for some kind of skill I could learn to help me feel like I could defend myself. I told one of my teachers — my mentor — Mrs. Bright — about what I was seeking and why. She could sense that I needed something to help me focus because I had lost that ability.

"She had one of her colleagues in the white district go to the Central Library in Milwaukee. She checked out a book entitled *Scientific Boxing* by James Corbett. I was able to learn the basics of the sport and how to stay fit by sparring with an imaginary opponent in the mirror, but I was always seeking something more. Years later at college I found the answer in a book called *Judo Kyohan* by Yokoyama and Oshima. I read it and learned about a man named Jigoro Kano. He had created this form of Japanese fighting known as Kodokan Judo in 1882."

"I've heard of it," said Ellington.

"I began working on his techniques every night. The book was filled with pictures that showed the Leg Wheel, Advancing Foot Sweep, Shoulder Wheel, and lots of others. I actually made a dummy out of pillows, a broomstick, and some rope. I tried to master the moves, visualizing the dummy being real. Kano stressed the idea of 'maximum efficient use of energy.' Anyway, somehow it all helped me finally cope with my cousin's death."

"Sounds like some very intense shit."

"It is. I told myself that I would spend one hour a day for the rest of my life working on this form of hand-to-hand combat, and I would do it in my cousin's honor."

"Speed has no idea you know all this shit."

"Don't make it sound like too much," I said. "I'm no master, that's for sure. Kodokan Judo just gave me a starting point, a foundation. It gave me discipline in every facet of my life."

Ellington began flexing his arms and jokingly asked, "But do you think you could handle Zeus?"

I smiled. "No."

We both stared at the still-quiet hideout, wondering what those so-called Galleanists were doing in there.

■ ■ ■ ■

It had been seventeen days, and finally the rain stopped. With only four days left in Baltimore, I sat alone with Jones at dinner — basic fare — red meat, mashed potatoes, turnip greens, and corn. It was the first time the two of us had engaged in any substantive conversation.

Ellington and Mann were still sleeping, while Speed, Knox, and Long were on night watch. This was a first, as they had always reserved the day shift for themselves.

"This is something, isn't it?" I asked. "The two of us being in this position."

"Indeed," said Jones. "I knew it would happen eventually — just didn't know if it would be in my lifetime. Actually, let me slow way down. It still may not happen in my lifetime. They haven't hired either of us yet. And I learned in the police department, waiting for a brother to rise within the ranks is akin to watching paint dry. But I'm optimistic."

"You were a policeman, huh?"

"That's right." He sipped his lemonade. "After college I took a job as a policeman in Washington — as a footman. You a college man, Temple?"

"Middlebury College," I said. "Vermont."

"I'm a Virginia Union graduate."

"You're also a veteran of the war, correct?"

"Yes," he said. "But that doesn't seem to mean much to ol' Speed. To tell you the truth, the fact that we're training, eating, and sleeping alongside these men is something to behold in itself. When I was sent to Des Moines, Iowa, for training, the facility was segregated. And, of course, when we actually went off to fight in France, we were confined to colored units. My men and I battled the enemy in the Vosges Mountains. It was ugly."

"I can only imagine."

I watched him pick at his turnip greens, trying to think of a question worth asking. This was a man who'd seen hell.

"What unit were you in?" I finally asked.

"I wasn't just *in*. I was in command of a Company F. It was part of the 368th Infantry. Like I said, an all-Negro outfit. We fought like hell. And when the war ended, unlike the colored troops of Britain and France, who were very well represented in the grand victory parade down Paris's Champs-Élysées, we American coloreds were kept out of sight."

I could sense his uneasiness about think-

71

ing back. And as we finished our meal in silence, I believe he respected my decision not to press on. We understood each other. And when it came to being Bureau agents, we certainly understood the unique position we were in.

The next day Ellington and I arose before the others and walked to our training site at Patterson Park where we sat on damp grass waiting for the hard day to begin. I could smell the recently poured fertilizer and noticed the shoddiness of the fence around the field. Beyond, I could see the top of the Phoenix Shot Tower. As if out of nowhere, Agent Speed approached with Jones and Mann. He began yelling.

"All right, get your asses off the ground and get in position. This is going to be a sprint, not a goddamn jog. Understand?"

The four of us lined up and, on Speed's cue, ran the first of ten sprints. I felt like vomiting up my oatmeal from the morning's breakfast. Kodokan Judo hadn't worked my lungs the same way.

Later that night, Ellington and I walked from the hotel toward the hideout.

"Where do you think they'll send you?" he asked.

"My hunch is New York."

"I love New York. I spent spring break there once with some buddies. Down in the Tenderloin, at a place called the Kessler, I drank 'til I passed out. Worst hangover ever."

As we approached the Lincoln from behind, I wondered what smartass remark Knox would have for me this night. Instead, he leaned his head out and put his right index finger to his lips, signaling for us to keep quiet. He then pointed toward the hideout.

There was light shining through the window. Ellington and I froze for a moment and then eased our way up to opposite sides of the car, I to the passenger side. The realization that there'd actually been people in the house for fourteen days had all of us rattled. It was eerie.

Knox turned to me and whispered, "Head back to the hotel and fetch Speed."

Just then, a loud explosion came from the hideout. The blast lit up the entire front of the alley house. Glass and debris flew everywhere. It took me a minute to digest the fact that the Galleanists had accidentally killed themselves. And just like that, our Baltimore assignment had come to an end.

A few days later I was back in Washington, ready to meet again with this important man of my age, Mr. Hoover. He sat me down in his office while I waited with bated breath to find out if I'd been hired and, if so, where I'd be working.

"Sidney, I'd like to familiarize you with three individuals: Max Eastman, James Weldon Johnson, and Marcus Garvey."

I sat and listened to him rattle off the details about the three men's lives. One word he kept repeating was *Bolshevism.* He believed all three had ties to the Russian movement. And after going on and on about it, he finally finished and took out a file.

"Sidney, you're to be commended for the swiftness with which you've mastered the variety of skills generally reserved for a military man. We've decided to hire you as a special agent. And as such, that makes you — officially — only the second colored agent the Bureau has ever hired, Agent Jones being the first, as he signed a contract while on assignment in Baltimore. So, Agent Temple, welcome aboard."

5

Time stood still for a moment. I felt an excitement in my belly, a nervousness. I wanted to share the news with the world but knew I could share it with no one.

"I must say," said Hoover, still holding a file, "sounds nice and official, doesn't it? This new title of yours: Agent Temple."

"Indeed."

Hoover stood and walked over to a file cabinet in the corner behind him. He removed several documents and returned.

"Let's get down to business," he said, dropping the pages on the desk and taking his seat again. "With the growing threats toward a variety of government officials, the general increase of antiwar socialists and organized communists, Americans are starting to think we're on the verge of Armageddon. The Bureau and the country need you now more than ever."

"Thank you, Mr. Hoover. I'm committed

to upholding the law of the United States of America."

"Things are really heating up. We've had our New York office forward all information on Johnson, Garvey, and Eastman to headquarters here in Washington. These are three very smart men. We have to present something new to them — something foreign. We need colored agents for this assignment.

"Your mission is to move to Harlem. Get comfortable. As you've already been told, you are to tell no one of your status with the Bureau, including your wife. That is critical in assuring her safety and yours — and in not compromising the mission. Many of our agents' wives know what their husbands do, but your case is different. You're not just an agent; you're being hired specifically to go undercover, to act as a spy."

"A spy. Of course. I see."

"Once you're in Harlem, find a home, get situated, and make sure your wife's comfortable. It's vital that you both just blend in. Attend church, go to functions, make friends. You will need to set up a front company in the heart of Harlem as soon as possible — some kind of engineering consulting firm with your degrees on the wall would suffice."

Hoover was looking at me like a hungry

dog, chomping at the bit to get his jaws around one of these targets.

"You will work out of that office during the duration of your assignment in Harlem, which could be five weeks or five years. Pick a small office and give it an authenticity that will serve as a great cover for you. Be creative — we're paying the bill. It needs to be credible enough for you to feel at ease if Eastman, Johnson, or Garvey themselves eventually set foot in there. No other agent will work out of that office. Understand?"

"Yes."

"Get to know people connected to these targets. Be friendly, and become known as an independent businessman who's willing to donate bits of his money to their causes. Of course, it's actually our money. As far as you're to be concerned, not one of these men has priority over the other in terms of whom you target first."

This part I didn't believe. He seemed more fixated on Garvey. Every time he uttered his name the disgust on his face was all the more obvious, the clenched jaw, the frown lines. Still, time would tell.

"Take it as it comes," he continued. "Walk through the doors that open first. We have no reason to believe these three are connected in any way, but we have every reason to believe they are all independent threats to American democracy as we know it. You're to become our eyes and ears on the street. We know very little about these people. We know little of their intentions. We want you to be a floater. Make sense so far?"

"Perfect. Be your eyes and ears."

"Good. We may not be able to nail the big fish, but we want to at least take down the little ones. Who's giving money to the NAACP — to Eastman and the *Liberator*? Eastman may be a white man, but he has a history of opening his publication's door to Negroes. When he opens it for you, carefully walk through. James Weldon Johnson is a bit of an enigma, but he's becoming powerful; find out why. And Garvey isn't the only West Indian immigrant that's making noise. Give us details on the others. Are we clear?"

"Crystal."

"Once you've gained access to the inner worlds of these targets, we want to know as much as you can dig up on them — where they go, who they see, what they're thinking, what they're writing, the list of high-ranking individuals they correspond with, and who their stated enemies are. Eventually, once you're able to establish solid connections with these targets, if they so much as fart, we want to know what it smells like. Can you juggle all this?"

"Performing multiple jobs simultaneously has never been a problem for me."

"You're to keep records of everything. You are to report to me once a week, if not more, on the details surrounding at least one of these men's actions — even if the report simply says that there is no news that week. And any correspondence you send via courier or telephone will be under the code name Q3Z. Got it?"

"Yes. Q3Z."

"As of this moment, the name Sidney Temple is never to be written on any documents used for corresponding with the Bureau. That's critical. On the other hand, Sidney Temple will remain your street name. Most of our covert agents inevitably run into someone they know from the past, so it's important for you to remain who you are to the general public. And the targets will know that you are Sidney Temple, graduate of Middlebury College.

"From this point forward, unless otherwise notified, your sole duty is to demonstrate loyalty to the United States government. You have signed an oath to uphold the law, and the Bureau expects your complete honesty. Lying to the Bureau would be a death sentence for your career, and you would be terminated immediately.

"Lying to the Bureau would make it virtually impossible for you to ever find work in the United States of America again. Never compromise the integrity of this Bureau. Having said all of this, the question I pose to you — the real question — is can you even convince Eastman, Johnson, or Garvey to let you in — convince them to allow you to get close to them?"

"I can."

He stared at me as if deciding one last time whether he indeed felt I was up to the task. Then he continued. "Our agents, in general, may not have the authority from Congress to carry firearms, but by the authority of the Justice Department, I will permit you to obtain a sidearm for your personal protection . . . for this unique assignment."

I marveled at the way this Hoover had worked all of these details out in his mind. It was as if he were reading from a script. But he was doing no reading. In fact, he never even looked at the files in front of him. It was all from memory. Information just poured out of him.

"Harlem is hell, Temple."

"I see."

"Harlem is a new kind of code. It is . . . how should I say this? Let's just say you'd be the first to crack it."

Again I nodded. I intended to work for the Bureau only long enough to get the inside details on Garvey — and to assure that Du Bois's agenda would flourish. The NAACP's cause and survival were worth dying for. This was going to be my contribution to American history — my George Washington moment.

"I know you won't disappoint us, Temple." He stood and I did the same. "Good luck."

With that I shook his hand and headed for the door. I felt an overwhelming need to speak with Professor Gold. In fact, I was desperate to pay him a personal visit. I had every intention of telling him about my new covert mission. Maybe I wanted him to talk me out of it. Still, I knew he was the one person I could tell.

"Have a nice day, Mr. Temple," said Irene, the secretary, as I walked by her desk.

"Good day, ma'am."

An agent was waiting for me in a car out front. I had him stop at a nearby café and I grabbed a ham sandwich to go.

Once at the train station, I exited the car and headed for the nearest payphone. I called Loretta and told her that I'd be home three days late because of some extra training and examinations I needed to complete. I planned to board my scheduled train to Philadelphia. Once there, I would catch a series of connecting trains to Middlebury. I intended to sleep the entire way.

I arrived at Gold's early in the morning before the sun had risen. I'd called him from the Philadelphia station to inform him of my unplanned visit. He greeted me with a warm hug and a piping hot cup of coffee. I intended to spend the day with him and immediately head back to Philadelphia the next morning.

"Well, well, well," said the silver-haired Gold, still dressed in his burgundy bathrobe and slippers, "isn't this is a pleasant surprise."

"Yes, and I have good reason."

"Please, come inside and let's talk."

We entered the chalet and went into his office. He offered me some warm scones, and we made ourselves comfortable, he behind his maple-wood desk, and I on his warm, cozy, cowhide sofa. Professor Gold, unlike Mary, had always been an early riser. His energy was amazing, and a healthy diet had kept him a youthful-looking seventy-year-old.

"Talk to me," he said, scooting his chair back and crossing his bony, long legs.

"Has any agent from the Bureau of Investigation ever been to see you?" I asked.

"From the BOI? No. Why?"

I started from square one, explaining the details of what had taken place in my life over the last six weeks. He didn't seem surprised that the Bureau had contacted me. He knew the significance of the hire and was much more familiar with the Bureau's past activities than I. But I explained how the Bureau mistakenly believed that I was this neophyte who had spent his entire life with his head in a physics book, oblivious to the politics of the day.

I finished the story and dipped a scone into my coffee. I didn't know what to expect from Gold. If he had been readying himself to suggest that I get out, I wasn't sure if I'd oblige.

"You know the first rule of becoming a covert agent?" he asked.

"What?"

"Write a will," he jokingly said, flashing a wry smile.

I smiled back and we just sipped for a moment. Then I brushed aside some of the scattered, clipped newspaper articles that were decorating the sofa. His brown Chesapeake Bay retriever, Muddy, came into the office and began licking my hand. I noticed Professor Gold ruminating, squeezing the skin on his chin with his fingers. He could barely contain his excitement about what I'd just told him.

He had spent his entire forty-year career as a history professor attempting to unearth the hidden details about the government. He didn't teach the history that everyone knew, but rather the history that he was newly discovering. All of the books he had written were groundbreaking in terms of their specific subject matter.

He had been obsessed with researching the specificities surrounding Abraham Lincoln's supposed Civil War spies. Now he was sitting across from his pupil who was being hired by the government to do just that.

"Max Eastman is white," he said.

"Yes, I know."

"I just find it interesting that they'd hire a colored agent to shadow him."

"The element of surprise," I said. "Eastman is known for being good to us folks."

"I can tell you," he said, "the government is worried about Max Eastman for one reason. When he was running his first magazine — the *Masses* — just after the U.S. decided to go to war, he published several cartoons and articles that vehemently opposed the war. Government officials claimed that Eastman had violated the Espionage Act."

"What's your take on their targeting James Weldon Johnson?" I asked.

"Mr. Johnson is an interesting case. I know he was U.S. Consul to Venezuela in 1906. He's the man who wrote the song 'Lift Ev'ry Voice and Sing.'"

"I had no idea he wrote that," I said.

"I am mainly familiar with him as a poet. I'm fascinated that the government has him on their watch list. I certainly know why they're going after Garvey."

"Yeah," I said, "so do I. He has the loudest voice. And, of the three, I am only interested in shadowing him. Although I have to get information on all of them if I'm to satisfy Hoover's hunger for details."

"You know, Sidney, as a student of the abolitionist movement, I must confess a bit of forgiveness for Garvey's way of thinking. Because on one hand you've got this God-loving movement rooted in purity, and created to free slaves from the shackles of hell, yet it was a movement largely comprised of Northern, white, well-educated men.

Sounds beautiful, correct — this abolitionist movement?"

"Of course," I answered.

"But," he said, "on the other hand — the hand that a so-called Garveyite would choose to see — these same white men are simply undoing the damage that they themselves caused."

He paused and picked at a scone.

"I keep trying to understand what's pulling me into this," I said. "This obsession that Garvey seems to have with convincing all coloreds to leave America and return to Africa is too simpleminded for me to digest. It in no way takes into account the complexities and deep roots that coloreds have in this country."

"I know what's pulling you into this," he said. "You can't enjoy any personal success while the overwhelming majority of black America lives under segregation. Not even as a highly educated man. You're really no different than Du Bois in that regard."

"Yes," I said, "and I want my future children to live in an integrated country. None of this Garvey separatism. I need to know how far he's willing to go — if and how he plans to destroy Du Bois and the NAACP."

"Indeed," Gold said. "But perhaps this

young Hoover is the dangerous opposition of both men."

"Perhaps. But like Du Bois, my mission is to stay right here in America and right the wrongs of the past, not cut all ties and pretend the ugly past never happened."

He poured me a fresh cup of coffee.

"Let's get one thing very clear," I continued. "My reason for spying on Garvey is quite different from Hoover's. His distrust of the man is likely due to the simple color of his skin. Hoover and the greater BOI probably have a similar distrust of Du Bois for the same baseless reason. But I believe the government and Garvey may be equal threats to Du Bois and his agenda. Becoming an agent is the only job that affords me the opportunity to learn the intricacies of both threats."

"All of this requires quite a bit of presuming on your part."

"In short," I said, sipping, "I will be spying on the Bureau."

"Repeat that."

"I look at this as an opportunity to spy on the Bureau. No colored in history has had access to the type of information or individuals I'll have access to. What other prominent coloreds are on the government's watch list? Maybe I'll find out."

"Fascinating," he said. "They hire some young graduate — thinking he's a greenhorn — and that student fools them all."

"I can only fool them if I can first fool Garvey."

"Well, the Bureau sicced you on Garvey. Now find out whom they've sicced on Du Bois. Find a way to get this agent to open up to you about what he's trying to find out. Then secretly share the info with Du Bois himself. Now you truly are spying on the Bureau."

"It will all hinge," I said, "on the quality of information I can glean from said agent."

"Information gathering is the name of the game," he said. "That reminds me, in terms of Garvey info, I recently read that he is trying to purchase his first ship, the *Yarmouth,* I believe it was called."

"Why a ship?"

"Sounds as if he's up to something big," he said.

"Well, I'll certainly find out about this and more. My objective is to be a floater of sorts, to develop relationships with men close to Eastman, Johnson, and Garvey. It won't be easy. I do find it a bit presumptuous of Hoover to think that Eastman, Johnson, and Garvey should all be shadowed because they are supposedly part of the same socialist world. The fact is they likely all live in completely separate worlds. I guess he figures all suspected communists are part of some grand conspiracy against the government."

Professor Gold began rummaging through his desk drawer. I poured myself a little more coffee to warm my cup.

"Before I forget," he said with a smile, "because you're going to be in New York, I'm sure you wouldn't mind going to hear Du Bois speak."

"You cannot be serious," I replied enthusiastically.

"Well, as you know, Du Bois has recently returned from the Pan-African Congress in Paris. He's to speak in front of a private gathering of NAACP donors and various politicos at a town house in Manhattan — the Upper East Side. The gathering is scheduled for August twenty-sixth."

"This is true fate."

"It'll be an intimate, very exclusive affair — difficult to get on the guest list, but I'll contact Phil Daley, a close friend who gives money to the NAACP. He likes to give money to causes he believes in, and his family roots are deep in the abolitionist movement. I'll make sure he gets you in. Just get yourself to this address. He's to speak in the evening at seven."

He handed me a slip of paper with the Manhattan address written down.

"There's a novel I'd like you to have," he said, standing. "Come."

We walked into his adjoining library, and I scanned his collection of novels. He climbed his rolling ladder and ran his index finger along a top row of hardbacks. "Here it is," he said. "Have you ever heard of *The Secret Agent* by Joseph Conrad, the great British novelist?"

"No."

"It was published in 1907 and is set in 1886 London. It is a political novel that deals with exploitation, espionage, terrorism, and anarchism." He placed the book in my hand. "Considering what you're about to face, it's quite apropos."

"Thank you," I said, studying the cover of the book.

"Come, let's take a walk," he said, heading for the doorway. "The sun is just coming up and you know how I love morning light on the autumn leaves."

Several minutes later, with Muddy practically leading the way, we approached the guesthouse where Loretta and I had lived.

"Place is not quite the same with you two gone," he said. "It just sits here — empty.

I'll have to find me another graduate student to rent it to."

I ran my hand along the house's outer surface. It was a log cabin, built in the early eighteen hundreds — a very warm, cozy place.

Later that evening, Mary made my favorite meal — chicken and dumplings. Hers were the best I'd ever had. Whenever Loretta and I were in the company of the Golds, they treated us as if we were their own children. They had only one child, a daughter who lived in Missouri. No grandchildren.

After finishing dinner and talking to Mary awhile, I washed up for bed, but not before Professor Gold loaded me up with several newspapers. And though I had an early train to catch, I was up late into the night reading copies of the *Negro World, Crisis, Messenger, Guardian,* and *Defender.* At about two in the morning I finally retired for the night, albeit for a short four hours.

Loretta greeted me at the front door of the West Philadelphia home. As I walked in, I noticed that everything was packed in boxes. Both of us took a seat on the mauve velvet, walnut-framed settee. I was relieved, but not surprised, that she had managed to sell the house while I was in Washington.

Unbeknownst to her, the Bureau had arranged to have all of our items, from both Vermont and Philadelphia, moved to Harlem as soon as we secured a house. All we needed to do was get ourselves to Harlem. Now I just had to sell the idea to her.

I adjusted my posture, as the old coil springs squeaked beneath us, and began the lie. "I have been given a great opportunity to work in Harlem."

"Harlem?" she asked with surprise.

"A gentleman, who was at the commission meetings in Washington, owns a civil engineering and land-use planning firm in New York City, and he's secured some lucrative contracts to build administrative buildings in several colored communities. He wants me to come work for him and open a new office in Harlem."

"This is completely coming out of left field. What about Washington?"

"Well, you don't spend three weeks in D.C. without meeting a host of fascinating individuals. This was unexpected but impossible to turn down."

"Nothing's impossible to turn down, Sid."

"I should say difficult. And the government work in Washington is still a possibility in the future, but work on the Pennsylvania Avenue Triangle won't likely start for at least a year, maybe even longer. Besides, with the wave of colored artists making their way to New York, Harlem in specific, this could be a blessing for you."

"I'm just trying to digest such a sudden and drastic change of plans, that's all. I'd been visualizing Washington for weeks. But I've never actually cared about where we move. You know that."

"There's nothing holding us back," I said.

She slightly nodded in agreement. "I've actually been reading about Harlem," she said. "Sounds like it's becoming the mecca for writers, poets, painters, and sculptors."

"So that's even more good reason."

"Sid, you don't have to try and convince me. Let me just soak up the change of plans for a second. It's not like I'm upset. I'm actually kind of excited."

"Okay."

It was quiet for a bit before she reengaged. "When were you planning for us to move?"

"I figured I would leave in three days, find us a short-term residence, and then you will join me in a couple of weeks. I will then arrange for our items to be moved. In the meantime, you can tie up the loose ends with the house and say all of your good-byes. Oh, and you'll need your father's Chevrolet for the next couple of weeks, but

I don't want you driving it to New York. I'll arrange to have it driven out when you leave on the train."

"I think this could really work, Sid. For both of us."

6

New York was a massive beast of a city — like nothing I'd seen before. Chicago paled in comparison to its enormity. I arrived at Grand Central Terminal, beautiful Penn Station and managed to connect to the Lenox Avenue Line en route to Harlem.

I got off at Lenox Avenue and 145th Street and hailed a taxi. I told the driver, "Please take me directly to a clean and relatively inexpensive hotel." Wasn't long before he'd turned onto 130th Street and pulled in front of a cozy-looking spot called the Sweet Tree Hotel.

I checked in, dropped off my luggage, and phoned the BOI, notifying them of my arrival and location, just as they'd ordered. Agent Speed was to be my contact and I was to spend the first few weeks just learning Harlem, getting my bearings.

I headed back out, spending most of the day just walking the streets — looking, smelling, absorbing the sounds. On one block I could smell cinnamon, nutmeg, and vanilla, which made me think of Momma's sweet potato pie. Each block brought with it a new aroma.

As I approached West 145th Street, the unmistakable scent of simmering black-eyed peas, smoked ham hocks, and fried onion began whetting my appetite. It was a warm August day, and people were out in force, many of them buying bananas, melons, and oranges from various fruit stands. I approached one that featured a variety of fruits I'd never seen before.

"What are you selling?" I asked the dark-skinned, bald-headed vendor manning the stand.

"All dis da good fresh fruit, friend," he answered with a thick Jamaican accent, his front teeth missing. "Dis guava from Jamaica. Din dis da hog plum and da June plum. You from U.S. like dis papaya. Yes?"

"Which is your favorite?" I asked.

"Okay, friend. Dis ones da mammy apple, and da star apple. Oh, and dis sea grapes. Maybe you buy dis sweet cherry, friend. All deez from Jamaica. All deez my favorite."

"I'll try some sea grapes," I said, handing him some change.

"Is good one. You like. Dank you."

I nodded as he filled a small brown bag. Walking away, I tasted one — salty and bitter. But I was hungry and continued eating them, puckering my lips and scrunching up my face as I headed down to a post office on West 133rd Street that the hotel attendant had mentioned. I secured a post office box and mailed some black newspaper subscription slips that I had taken while visiting Gold.

It was about six in the evening, and I was getting hungry. I headed back to the Sweet Tree, went up, and changed clothes.

When I came back downstairs, the female attendant at the front office told me I could grab some great ribs at a joint called Sonny's Pool Hall up on 134th. I headed over to Seventh Avenue and up.

The place was large and dark, but had only a few customers. I went to the back corner away from the pool tables and positioned myself so that I could see the front door — had done this all of my life. It wasn't long before a middle-aged waitress came over and took my order.

"What'll it be, Baby?"

"I'll have the 'Sonny's Bad Boy' with fries and a root beer."

"Aw right, Sugar."

They served the side of juicy pork baby

back ribs on a brown paper bag — no plate. It was one of the most enjoyable thirty minutes of eating I had experienced. I licked my fingers clean and gulped down what remained of my icy soda. A young man — early twenties — was hitting pool balls by himself. I walked over.

"Would you like to play a game?" I asked.

"Rack 'em," he said.

"All right. Name's Sidney."

"I'm Drew."

I racked the balls and grabbed a stick. He took the first shot and the game was on. It took him about five minutes to dispose of me, and he, of course, wanted to play a second game. I obliged. Sonny's started to get a bit busier as our game continued. Folks were filing in, ordering ribs, and having a grand old time. The volume in the joint had certainly gone up a few notches.

"Place usually fills up between eight and ten," Drew said.

All of a sudden, I got on a lucky streak, making every shot. When I knocked the eight ball in the far corner pocket, I heard a deep voice from about twenty feet away.

"I got next!"

I turned and could barely make out what seemed to be two well-dressed men in three-piece suits and fedora hats sitting at a table, engulfed in smoke. That combined with the darkness of the room and their coffee-colored skin made it difficult to make out their faces. But I could see the burn of their cigarettes. I squinted and looked through the smoke. One of the men stepped through the thick cloud and walked toward us. He slammed a ten-dollar bill down on the pool table and looked squarely at me.

"You game, pretty boy?"

I didn't say a word. I had quite a bit of cash on me, but it was for securing a brownstone, and I certainly didn't want to waste any of it on a pool game. I looked at him in his expensive suit. He was a tall, dark-skinned, angular man — about my height. Never having been one to resist a challenge, I reached into my pants pocket and took out two five-dollar bills. I then did the racking.

As my opponent retrieved a pool stick, Drew grabbed a seat at the next table. He looked on with angst. Chalking his stick, my opponent turned to his buddy in the distance and yelled:

"This shouldn't take long, brother! We'll make the party on time. You hear me, brotha? We gon' make the party on time."

I heard laughter through the smoke. Again, I ignored my opponent and watched as he broke with an aggressive shot. He knocked the five ball in the side pocket and then proceeded to miss his next shot after strutting into it. The man strutted like nobody's business.

My lucky streak hadn't waned, as I began holing every ball I hit. People from afar were whooping and hollering as I did my best impersonation of a professional. My opponent just stood there, cigarette hanging from his mouth, glaring at me. I lined up the eight ball and stretched across the table to make a difficult shot.

"Eight ball, corner pocket," I said.

And with that the game was over.

"Double or nothing," he immediately demanded.

"I'm through for the night," I said, knowing my luck would end.

I picked up the twenty dollars and turned to say good-bye to Drew. But he was nowhere in sight. I then attempted to shake my opponent's hand, but he didn't budge. He just stood there clutching his pool stick. I sensed a brewing hatred of me in his jaundiced eyes.

I brushed off his slight, casually made my way to the front door, and stepped out into the fresh night air. It was time to make my way back to the Sweet Tree.

■ ■ ■ ■

I woke early the next morning and did my usual hour of meditation and Kodokan exercises. After a good sweat, I washed up and headed over to the newsstand to pick up several papers. I then popped in to Snappy's Restaurant on Lenox for coffee, eggs, and toast. I opened a copy of the *Negro World* and read that Garvey was still in negotiations to officially purchase the *Yarmouth.*

With breakfast finished and the papers read, I decided to walk up Lenox Avenue from 130th to 145th. I wanted to experience every block, not knowing exactly where I was going or whom I might meet. It would allow me to get a feel for the engine of Harlem.

I stopped and had my wing tips shined by an old gray-haired gentleman. He talked nonstop about the city and made me promise to try his favorite joint on 144th.

"Best damn sausage in the world," he kept saying. "Damn near choked to death last time I had 'em. They the best now! I wouldn't lie to you, young brother."

As I walked along each block, I saw artists painting on corners, musicians lugging their packed instruments around — or playing — and poets reading their material. With the war over, thousands looked to be flocking here to take part in some kind of artistic awakening that was uniquely Harlem's.

A fellow in a convenience store on 145th told me to head over by City College of New York to find a brownstone. The man believed that I would like West Harlem.

"Ain't but a few coloreds be livin' 'round there," he said. "But they be the high-livin' types."

He told me that Eighth Avenue was an informal color line — west of it was mostly white. I decided to take him up on his suggestion. My feet were sore, so I splurged and took a short ride in a beaten-up, open-air taxi. I also wanted the taxi to drive by Marcus Garvey's office at the Universal Negro Improvement Association's headquarters. We headed south and then took a left on 135th.

"There it is," he said.

"So close?"

"Yep. Fifty-six West 135th."

I had walked right past the building earlier, not knowing what it was. My heart began to pound as we passed. There it was — Garvey's office. I had no intentions of stopping but just needed to see it. I wondered how soon I'd be able to penetrate those walls. Hoover's clock was probably ticking fast.

"Where is the City College?" I asked.

"138th and Convent."

"Take me to the neighborhood near there."

"Yes, sir."

He dropped me off on Amsterdam near the college. Walking east on West 140th, I noticed an available bow-front brick town house on the north side of the street. I approached the front door and a short, middle-aged brother was there to greet me.

"Come on in," he said. "Take a look around. Name's Paul Smith."

"Sidney Temple." We shook. "I can't believe my good luck. I don't even know where I'm at."

"You in the Sugar Hill section of Harlem."

"You the owner?" I asked, looking around.

"No, I'm one of the sales agents. I've been doing this here line of work for about fifteen years. Used to work for the Afro-American Realty Company."

"How many rooms does the place have?"

"Place has one big bedroom and another little one. But as you can tell, it's got plenty of space up in here."

103

I moved slowly around the living room. "So tell me about this company you worked for."

"Well, that company had been owned by Mr. Philip A. Payton, Jr. He was my boss. Hell of a man. Father of colored Harlem. Old Payton, Jr., had been buying up real estate and renting and selling to Negroes since 'bout 1904. But he died two years back."

"I'm sorry to hear that." I rubbed my hand along the front window seal.

"Before that company existed, white owners was refusing to rent or sell to colored folks. A whole lot of coloreds would be living just as fine as can be, but all of a sudden some white man would buy the building and start evicting folks — then renting those spots to whites. But Mr. Payton, Jr., changed all that. He started buying up Harlem properties and evicting the white folks."

Mr. Smith began laughing loudly. The idea that a colored man had turned the tables on white folks tickled him to death. I made my way to the master bedroom and he followed with a bit of a limp.

"After Mr. Payton, Jr., died, more Negro realty companies sprung up, and I was able to hook on with Jeffers Realty. They treat me real good, and they rent and sell to colored folks for fair dollars. Negroes is buying homes here in Harlem like you wouldn't believe. Folks with regular payin' jobs is even buying themselves a place. It's buying time in Harlem. Investment time."

"Well, I certainly like this place, especially these hardwood floors and freshly painted walls."

"If you look out the window there you can see the college to the south."

"Yes, I saw it on my way over." I approached the window and took a look. "Maybe Loretta can take some classes. She's my wife. We're not looking to buy right away. She wants to take her time picking a place to own."

I looked out at the large vacant field across the street, the City College in the distance. The field occupied about a quarter block. "Why is that field vacant and so shabby?" I asked.

"Oh, the City College been planning to develop that land for some five years. Nothin' but weeds and bushes livin' there now."

"Well, the view beyond it is pleasant. But I don't plan on spending a lot of time looking out the window. And this place has character. How much per month?"

"Well, most regular one-bedrooms in Harlem be goin' for about one hundred dollars a month. But this here Sugar Hill town house goin' for one seventy-five a month."

I wasn't sure if Loretta would love it, but it would suffice for the time being. When the moment arrived for us to actually buy a home, I knew she would don her love for all things romantic.

"When can we move in?"

"Well now, if I can get you to fill out this here paperwork, I'll take it back to the office and let you know by tomorrow. Ain't no one else in the runnin', so, I suppose you'll be the one gets it."

I took out two hundred fifty in cash and handed it to him. "I really like the place."

"Oh, no. I said one-hundred-seventy-five, Mr. Temple."

"The extra seventy five is for you."

He stood there wide-eyed for a moment. "All right then. Well, uh . . . well . . . okay . . . I'll have the keys for you tomorrow. Where are you staying?"

"The Sweet Tree."

"How does high noon sound?"

"Sounds good. Look here. You wouldn't happen to know of any small office space that might be available for rent in the area would you? I'm an engineering consultant and need a nice building to work out of."

"Indeed. More than I can count," he said, staring at the money. "Be happy to show 'em to you. Real happy!"

"I'd certainly appreciate it."

I spent the next few minutes filling out papers. All of the day's sights and sounds had put me in the mood to wash up and go hear some live music. With the town house secured, I'd notify Loretta and she'd soon be on her way.

I approached the jazz club at 132nd and Fifth Avenue, a place called Edmond's Cellar. The sign out front listed Ethel Waters as the night's headliner. I had never heard of her. I walked down a set of creaky, gummy, wooden steps toward the sound of a powerful female voice.

It was dark but not pitch black inside the stairway, the walls sticky-looking, like someone had painted them with syrup. Funky smoke and spills of alcohol had stained them as well.

The place got muggier and hotter as I reached the bottom step and prepared to enter the basement. My skin was becoming damp and my clothes clingy, but the music was clutching my chest and yanking me forward. *Damn the vexatious elements!* I thought. *This magnetic, avant-garde sound trumps everything.*

I made my way to the bluish light and entered a room that was filled to a capacity of about one hundred fifty, each patron seeming to hang on every word that flowed from the mouth of the powerful Ethel Waters. The tables were tiny, and there were several folks crammed onto a small dance floor. I felt like I was entering a closet, as the roof was quite low.

Squeezing through the sweaty crowd — some sitting, others standing — I grabbed a chair near the stage. A cocktail waitress immediately asked me if I wanted a whiskey or beer. I rarely drank the heavy stuff, as Loretta and I liked our wine with dinner on the weekends. But with the Prohibition amendment having been ratified back in January, I figured it was now or never. The amendment would take effect within months, so I ordered a dry whiskey.

I scanned the room. There appeared to be an alarming number of gorgeous, stunningly dressed colored women in attendance. Most of the men were middle-aged; quite a few were white. I wondered if any might be an agent whom Hoover had tasked to follow me during these first days.

Still scanning, I could see one sister off in

the corner groping a much older white man. I couldn't help but imagine his wife at home waiting up late for him in their upscale Manhattan apartment.

I downed the whiskey and absorbed the sound of Miss Waters's soft and sultry voice. I felt the whiskey racing through my blood, that tantalizing tingle in my body. For the first time in months I felt a release from all things toilsome.

But I still thought of Garvey. How could I get in? How much time was this young man Hoover going to give me? And had he yet assigned an agent to infiltrate Du Bois's world? Maybe my training buddy, Ellington, could be my go-to guy on all things Du Bois. I'd have to reconnect with him as soon as possible.

I ordered another whiskey. Ethel Waters began making her way through the crowd, and the two of us locked eyes. She was a tall, light-skinned woman and, based on her features, likely mixed. Her large, white-hooped earrings sparkled in the backlight.

She stopped and sang to me for a good minute as the crowd cheered and whistled. I couldn't help but accept the flirtatious gestures of the pretty woman in her twenties. Her band of four was providing a rhythm and beat that only enhanced her raw talent. The saxophone, bass guitar, piano, and drums were working the audience into a frenzy. I sat back and enjoyed several songs, letting the time pass while sipping my drink.

About two hours later I headed outside, walking briskly through a crowd of folks still waiting to get in. In the distance about fifty feet away and heading toward me, I saw the two men from the pool hall the night before. I put my head down and tried to keep them from spotting me, but to no avail. Just as I was about ten feet from them I heard my former opponent's voice. He walked directly in front of me, impeding my forward motion.

"Yo, hold up there, pretty boy."

I stopped and looked him in his face.

"Don't you know you always give a nigga a second game?" he asked. "This is Harlem, motherfucker, not Kansas."

This was a man who couldn't be reasoned with so I treated him as such, responding with, "I see. Well, shit, you must really need it." I reached in my pants pocket, digging for some cash. I attempted to hand him back his ten dollars, but he slapped it out of my hand.

"Nigga if I want my money I'll take it from yo ass."

I glared at him and then put it back in my pocket. "What the hell you wastin' my time for then?" I said. "Take it from me."

He sat on those words a second. Then he revved back and swung, but I ducked it, kneeing him instead between the legs and punching him in his Adam's apple. He fell to the ground, clutching his groin and gasping for air. No doubt I'd damaged his larynx. Eyes bulging, he began to convulse.

His friend kicked me in the ribcage with his wing tips. I felt a break. While dropping to my knees, I used the force of the fall to sweep my right leg through both of his, knocking him off his feet.

Before he could react, I rolled over on top of him, grabbing his neck with my left hand. I used my right to deliver two violent punches — one to an eye, the other to his nose. As the second one connected, I could hear the distinct sound of breaking nose cartilage. Blood spewed from his nostrils.

I stood up, clutching my ribs. Both men lay there moaning and immobile. Several onlookers had witnessed the event. I hobbled down the street, trying to catch my breath.

When I entered the Sweet Tree, the female attendant noticed blood on my shirt and how I was gingerly holding my ribcage.

"My heavens, what happened?" She approached and tried to help by lifting my arm and putting it over her shoulder.

"No," I said with a painful whisper. "That makes it worse. Do you have any aspirin?"

"Let me check. I'll bring you what I have."

I managed to climb the steps and enter my room. I slowly lay on the bed and tried to find a position that would best allow me to breathe. The attendant entered with a first aid kit. "I have aspirin, ointment, and an ace bandage. Can you sit up to take these pills?"

I took a deep, excruciating breath and sat up. I downed four pills, realizing they were barely going to minimize the pain.

"I need you to help me wrap the bandage around my ribcage," I said. "The break is on the left side."

"If it's broken, maybe we shouldn't wrap it."

"No, I have to," I said, knowing it would restrict my breathing but help limit the natural ribcage movement.

I stood and walked over to the mirror above the sink. She helped me remove my shirt and tie and began wrapping the bandage around the area. I was thankful that she was so patient, caring, and good with her hands. She finished wrapping and helped me back to the bed.

"I'll come by early in the morning to check on you. I'm leaving you a few cups of water and the bottle of aspirin. I hope you'll be okay."

"I'll be fine. Thank you for your help."

The night was endless. I didn't sleep a wink, barely sipping the night air as if sucking it through a straw. The only cure for a fractured rib was time and aspirin. I had plenty of aspirin but not a lot of time.

7

I took a taxi to Carnegie Hall in hopes of hearing Garvey speak at a mass meeting. It was nice to be out and about taking in the scenery along Madison Avenue after days of lying in bed and living on little white pills.

I had already headed over to 145th and Seventh where Paul Smith had showed me an available office space. It was perfect, so I'd signed the papers on the spot and contacted the Bureau, informing them of its location.

I had spent the past days tipping and sending a hotel janitor on daily errands, mainly to get me soup and any colored newspapers he could find. The more I read, the more I got a sense of why so many Negroes had been moving north.

The war had depleted cities of their industrial manpower, as millions of men went off to fight. Also, fewer folks from overseas had moved to America during the war, opening up good-paying industrial jobs in the North. And Northern life had to seem much more peaceful than the Jim Crow South.

Because of the race riots that were taking place all over the country, the summer of 1919 was being called Red Summer. Editorials about coloreds demanding their equality were cropping up all over the place. The anger over so many shootings and lynchings was on the rise.

As I had achingly rested in bed, I clipped a poem called "If We Must Die" from a Jamaican-born poet named Claude McKay that summed up this new, pervasive defiance amongst many coloreds. It began with, "If we must die, let it not be like hogs — hunted and penned in an inglorious spot." I was moved by his words.

I had never heard of this McKay, but he was obviously talented. I found his poem gripping and wondered who he aligned himself with politically — Garvey, Du Bois, or someone else. There were other bold remarks being made. One of the New York papers had reprinted an editorial that was originally written in a Kansas City paper — the *Call*. It read, "The New Negro, unlike the old time Negro, does not fear the face of day. The time for cringing is over."

As the driver continued down Madison and made a right on East Fifty-ninth Street, I thought about how Harlem was quickly becoming the epicenter for colored politics — perhaps throughout the world. Many American Negroes were expressing a willingness to embrace militancy in order to secure their rights. But that approach had been tried before.

Even back when John Brown led a group of slaves in an attempt to take back their freedom violently, it ended with his being hanged. Most of the slaves had no intentions of rising up and using violence as a means to break the chains of slavery. They knew they'd meet certain death. Most coloreds in the summer of 1919 probably felt the same way. They wanted to stay alive first, and if that meant continuing to make progress slowly, so be it.

We turned left on Seventh Avenue and approached Carnegie Hall. Brothers and sisters were lining the street. I wasn't sure whether I could even get in, but I at least wanted to soak up the mood. I opened the taxi door and stepped into a parade of energy. A teenager bumped up against me and shoved a leaflet into my chest, aggravating the muscles around my wounded rib.

"Take it, brother — take it!" he yelled.

"Marcus Garvey is putting the fear of God in the white man! He's our new king!"

Taking the leaflet, I was bumped again from behind, then again from the side, jostled around in the thick, loud crowd, unable to step a foot in any direction. I did manage to hold the leaflet very close to my face as I let the movement of the mob carry me forward like an ocean wave.

The headline of the leaflet read, GRAND REUNION OF THE NEGRO PEOPLES OF THE WORLD OF AMERICA, AFRICA, WEST INDIES, CANADA, CENTRAL AND SOUTH AMERICA AT THE FAMOUS CARNEGIE HALL — A RALLY FOR THE BLACK STAR LINE STEAMSHIP CORPORATION. The subtitle read, "Stocks will be on sale at this big meeting. The stocks in the Black Star Line are sold at $5.00 each and you can buy as many as you want and make money. Admission Free."

I found it interesting that Garvey was selling stock for a steamship corporation but still didn't officially own a ship. Luckily for him, he hadn't yet technically advertised the *Yarmouth,* hadn't specifically solicited money for that particular boat. It seemed unethical because the only money he actually had was likely coming from these investors. They were the ones doing all the buying. He was simply selling an idea.

As the mob came within ten feet of the Carnegie Hall entrance, we were told no one else would be allowed inside. They couldn't squeeze another body in.

"I'm not 'bout to buy any more of them damn stocks nohow!" yelled a man directly in front of me. "I'm here to get my money back for the damn stocks I done already bought!"

I tapped him on his shoulder, curious to hear why he was so angry.

"What?" he yelled above the ruckus.

"Why do you want your money back?" I hollered back.

"Because the ship that nigga Garvey's still tryin' to buy is sittin' over in the water and it's broke down! Damn sure ain't 'bout to make it to no Africa! Shit! This brotha's stealin' brothas' money! Like I said, he still ain't bought the ship nohow! I know niggas that been workin' on that cheap-ass boat for months, tryin' to get it ready to sell to some fool. But it ain't worth nothin'. And that's why them white folks is willing to sell it to him. Don't know why I let my old lady talk me into puttin' money in them damn stocks. I thought the fool already owned a bunch of ships and that I was just investing in a real company. You know, like puttin' money in Ford automobiles."

Suddenly, the idea hit me. If the ship Garvey was still trying to purchase was a lemon, what he would soon be in need of was an engineering consultant. I would sell myself as the man he could hire to oversee his ship's refurbishing and maintenance — someone he could trust to diagnose the problem, come up with a cost estimate, and make sure the mechanics he hired were qualified.

It was worth a try. For now, getting out of this angry crowd — angry at having been duped into parting with their precious cash or at being denied access to the speech of their newfound god — was my mission.

The next day I headed to Manhattan to hear Du Bois speak, arriving an hour early. Professor Gold's friend had left my name on a list, so I was able to go right in. It was a massive town house on the Upper East Side — probably twenty thousand square feet. I made my way to the gigantic main room where I found several people mingling. It was a mixed crowd. There were nine round tables set up for the guests. I counted eight chairs at each.

Walking past three serving tables covered with delicious-looking fare, I started to ask the heavyset chef hovering over the tables with a knife to slice me off a piece of the beef but figured I'd wait a few minutes. I found the table with my name card on it and took a seat, waiting for everyone to arrive.

A waiter came by with a tray of wine-filled glasses. I took a red and made myself comfortable. People were filling their plates and sitting wherever they chose, some on sofas, a few in the adjacent huge dining room, others at their respective tables.

It was an elegant setting with fine china and beautiful linen. I didn't know whether to eat or take photographs. The host — whoever that was — had extremely deep pockets. Wow! Du Bois and a fancy meal. What a treat. I could hear Garvey's voice ridiculing the setting and accusing us all of being uppity brothers.

I felt a tap on my right shoulder. I turned and saw a short, brown-suited old white man. He couldn't have been taller than five feet.

"Could you be Sidney Temple, the young engineer?" he said, with a thick New York accent — his teeth corn yellow. "The card in front of you says you are."

"I am," I said, standing to shake his hand. "You're Phil Daley?"

"Yes," he said.

"It's a pleasure to meet you. I can't thank you enough for this."

"You're worth it — at least according to that communist Gold. He says you love engineering and adore Dr. Du Bois. Please, let's sit. Where's the waiter?"

"He was just here."

He put his hand in the air, snapping his fingers to draw a waiter's attention. The man was a ball of energy. A waiter came running over.

"Coffee, please," he said. "Black. And I'd like some cubed sugar. Thank you, lad."

We watched the waiter scurry off and almost immediately return with a tray of coffee and sugar. Daley reached his stubby little fingers into the crystal dish, grabbing what seemed like twenty cubes of sugar before the waiter headed back to the kitchen again.

"Take a look around the room, kid. A bunch of folks not sure who to pledge their loyalties to — the NAACP, UNIA, or ABB. I say that jokingly, as I assume these men support Du Bois. But you wonder these days, with West Indians flooding New York and recruiting every Tom, Dick, and Harry in Harlem to join with them in their quest to lead your people to . . . to I don't know, heaven up high."

"I can't wait to hear him speak."

"Should be great, kid. I said all that because Du Bois *isn't* promising coloreds some golden stairway to a fantasyland. He isn't propping himself up as some savior or messiah. He's doing what he's always done — steadying the ship, chipping away at this race problem, preaching education, ensuring that all breakthroughs will be long-lasting."

He gulped down his entire cup before the waiter popped by again and refilled it. He was conversing with me, but I need not have been there, for he seemed just as willing to share his inner thoughts with a random busboy. He just had to get it out. Luckily for him, I was transfixed.

I recalled Hoover's initial request of me — to find out who was giving money to the NAACP. The Bureau would certainly want to know of Daley and his power. Telling Hoover about him would be a feather in my cap, but I wasn't about to offer him up.

I thought about how I could maintain a relationship with the wealthy little New Yorker. His knowledge of the key political players could be invaluable. As people began to take their seats around us, Daley ignored them and continued yapping.

Chatter now filled the entire house. We

made our way toward the buffet, and he continued talking as we stood in line.

"You know what I like most about the honorable Du Bois? He's about my height. You know most smart people are short, don't you?"

"I'm beginning to realize that."

"Ooh, they've got liver and onions," he said, licking his lips.

"You see the distinguished-looking man in the corner with the aides around him?" he asked, grabbing a plate and filling it with liver and onions.

"Yes."

"That is James Weldon Johnson — quite possibly the greatest living colored writer in America and soon to be executive secretary of the NAACP. He is growing the organization expeditiously — recruiting new members left and right."

I studied Johnson carefully while pouring some gravy on my rice. He was relatively tall and bronze-skinned — looked to be in his late forties. He had the presence of a senator or diplomat. He didn't look like the type I could easily get close to.

"You don't mind sitting with your plate in your lap do you, Sidney?"

"No."

"Good. Our table is filling up quickly and

I don't want anyone to interrupt our conversation."

We walked into an adjacent room that was filled with antique furniture and old European art. Daley took a seat on a black sofa, and I joined him. I guess he felt comfortable talking to me because of his previous conversations with Gold.

"Back to James Weldon Johnson," he said, trying to keep his plate from sliding off his lap. "His political influence in Washington is going to be pivotal in helping the NAACP have a voice. He will be lobbying Congress to help pass the Dyer Anti-Lynching Bill."

"That'll be one hell of a task," I said.

"Yeah. His presence in the South, speaking in favor of the bill, has already made him quite unpopular with the Ku Klux Klan. In fact, there are little Klan cells popping up in the North more and more, spawned, no doubt, by the growth of the NAACP. The more Johnson pushes for the bill, the more I fear for his safety."

"How far does the bill go?" I asked, taking a bite of rice.

"It seeks to make lynching a federal felony."

I watched him dig into his food and wanted to ask about Max Eastman but thought better of it. I didn't want to come off as some investigative journalist, and I figured if I was patient enough, he might just bring Eastman up on his own.

"I'm still thinking about your comment regarding Mr. Weldon Johnson's safety," I said.

"The current secretary of the NAACP — guy named Shillady — got himself beaten to a bloody pulp in Austin just a few days ago. By whom? A judge, for Chrissakes! Can you believe that?"

"Doesn't shock me," I said. "How could it?"

"Shillady was white."

"Oh."

"Now you can see why I fear for Johnson's very life if he becomes secretary."

"Some things are worth dying for," I said. "Maybe Johnson feels that this cause is."

"I'm sure he does. Let's get back to our table."

Plates in hand, we made our way back into the main room, which was full now, and took our seats. I looked around and couldn't believe what I saw. A young man sitting to our left, two tables over, was none other than Paul Mann, one of the agents I'd been in training with. *What the hell is he doing here?*

"Mr. Daley," I said, "you wouldn't happen to know who the gentleman in the blue suit is — the one with his legs crossed?"

"Ah yes," he said, cutting. "That is Paul Mann, the new sales assistant over at the *Crisis.* He's actually been put in charge of increasing our New England distribution. Brilliant lad. Columbia graduate. Recognize him?"

"I believe we met at a conference of some sort during college," I said.

So it was Paul Mann whom Hoover had sicced on Du Bois. I guess he figured that because there were so many whites involved in both the NAACP and the *Crusader,* he could use Paul. I had probably said two words to him during our entire training. As I recalled, Ellington hadn't liked him very much either. The guy was arrogant.

I scanned the rest of the room looking for someone else I might recognize. I was beginning to wonder just who else was or wasn't a spy; maybe I was surrounded by them.

Paul Mann and I finally locked eyes. "If you'll excuse me for just a second, Mr. Daley, the restroom calls."

Mouth full, he simply nodded while I kept my eyes on Mann, as if summoning him to join me.

A minute later, as I stood in the hallway

near the restroom studying one of the paintings on the wall, he obliged.

"You would almost swear this is a Rembrandt," I said, leaning in.

"I didn't know Hoover assigned you to some art aficionado," Mann snarkily said, as he studied a piece on the adjacent wall, neither of us openly acknowledging the other.

"Funny," I said. "But perhaps Garvey is just that."

"Your assignment is Garvey, huh?" he asked in his uppity, Ivy League accent.

"Yes. And yours?"

"Tonight's keynote speaker," he said.

"You know they're basically one and the same, right?" I asked, still looking at the painting.

"You mean enemy aliens? To that the answer is no. Du Bois is home grown. But enemy communists? Well, of course, the answer to that is yes."

"It's probable," I said, "that a lot of the people Du Bois and Garvey know cross paths with one another. Maybe some folks I meet might share pertinent info with me. Pertinent to you. Might help you do your job better. Help you dig in the right places."

"Maybe," he said. "At least I'm already in. Are you?"

"Not yet. But I will be soon."

"Then this is all a bit premature, don't you think?"

"Look," I said, "we're both new agents. And New York just might swallow both of us up. Why not help each other?"

"Uh, New York is home for me," he said, still stuck on that point.

"But colored New York ain't. And I know there's nothing you'd like more than to move right on up Hoover's ladder. So . . . when possible, I'll help you if you help me. I take it you're working at the *Crisis*?"

"Indeed," he said, both of us still eyeing our paintings.

"What is the best time for me to reach you there? You know, to tell you I'm hungry. I love eating at a restaurant called Snappy's."

"Very well," he said, beginning to walk away, "I'm usually free from eleven to one." He stopped and turned, finally looking at me. Then, with a smirk, said, "But you still have to get in."

With that he returned to his seat and I did the same, only to have Daley start right up. "I tell you what, kid, I'm a chartered member of the Civic Club. So are Mr. Johnson and Mr. Du Bois. You'll have to come down one day as my guest — get to know folks."

"I'd be very thankful for such a privilege."

A redheaded gentleman stepped to a podium at the front of the room to address the audience. The room grew quiet.

"Ladies and gentlemen, it is time for me to introduce our guest for this evening. He is the author of the groundbreaking and internationally celebrated book *The Souls of Black Folk*. He is credited with playing a major role in the formation of the NAACP and is the editor of America's preeminent colored news magazine, the *Crisis*. He has been called the most important colored voice since Frederick Douglass. Ladies and gentlemen, please give a warm reception to Dr. William Edward Burghardt Du Bois."

Du Bois had been sitting in a different room, out of sight. He entered and approached the podium. He was not a tall man, but walked very upright, with much confidence, and was impeccably dressed — distinguished-looking. He appeared much younger than his fifty-one years, wearing a well-groomed goatee and exuding a charisma that swept through the room. He had lost all of his hair on top and kept the dark ring that was left cut very short. It made him look professorial.

The guests stood in applause for quite a

spell. It was a magnetic moment — one I would never forget.

"Thank you very much," he said with humility. "Thank you."

I took a peek at Paul Mann as he impersonated a loyal employee. I wanted to walk over and hit him right between the eyes, but who was I to knock a man for being an informant. I was guilty of grotesque hypocrisy.

"Thank you," Du Bois said again. "Please . . . sit."

A hush came over the room. Du Bois gathered himself and opened what looked like a leather folder. You could hear a pin drop.

"We are returning from war," he said. "The *Crisis* and tens of thousands of black men were drafted into a great struggle. For bleeding France and what she means and has meant and will mean to us and humanity and against the threat of German race arrogance, we fought gladly and to the last drop of blood; for America and her highest ideals, we fought in far-off hope; for the dominant Southern oligarchy entrenched in Washington, we fought in bitter resignation. . . ."

The entire room was captivated — hanging on his every word. I had already read this portion of Du Bois's lecture in a May edition of the *Crisis.* He was reading from his own editorial entitled "Returning Soldiers," but listening to him say the words live was like hearing them for the first time.

"But today we return. We return from the slavery of uniform which the world's madness demanded us to don to the freedom of civil garb. We stand again to look America squarely in the face and call a spade a spade. We sing: This country of ours, despite all its better souls have done and dreamed, is yet a shameful land. It lynches. And lynching is barbarism of a degree of contemptible nastiness unparalleled in human history. Yet for fifty years we have lynched two Negroes a week, and we have kept this up right through the war. . . ."

His words were shaking me, putting me into a transcendent state, allowing me to forget about my achy rib. Everything was coming into focus.

"This is the country to which we Soldiers of Democracy return. This is the fatherland for which we fought! But it is our fatherland. It was right for us to fight. The faults of our country are our faults. Under similar circumstances, we would fight again. But by the God of Heaven, we are cowards and jackasses if now that that war is over, we do not marshal every ounce of our brain and brawn to fight a sterner, longer, more unbending battle against the forces of hell in our own land. We return. We return from fighting . . ."

After the reading, Du Bois went on to speak for several minutes. I wanted to walk up to the man as soon as he finished and offer my services for free. But I realized my contribution to his cause would forever go faceless. My work was to be done in the shadows, without recognition or appreciation.

8

It was now September fourth, the day I'd been longing for. As I sat and waited for Loretta to step off the train, my broken rib throbbed. Earlier that day I'd mailed an anonymous letter to Du Bois, informing him of Paul Mann and a few other items.

Dear Dr. Du Bois,
It has come to my attention that the gentleman you recently hired as a circulations assistant, Mr. Paul Mann, is an informant for the Bureau of Investigation. You would be well served not to out him, as knowing his identity and whereabouts will serve you well and prevent the Bureau from planting any further informants within your organization for the time being. Telling him only what you don't mind the government knowing will also keep the Bureau at bay. Thank you for the leadership you

are giving to the American Negro. The prosperity of your association is critical, and it is important for you to know that there are many of us working behind the scenes to protect the movement.

Sincerely,
The Loyalist

From this point forward I intended to write such letters. I would keep him one step ahead of Garvey and the government as best I could. What I actually intended to solicit from Agent Mann were details about what Hoover was asking him to look for. I figured he just might share such info if I volunteered what Hoover was asking me to focus on. But it was going to take time to build this type of relationship.

Loretta stepped off the train in a pink sundress looking more vibrant and beautiful than ever. Seeing her was sure to be the medicine I had been missing. I had no intentions of letting her see me in pain. I wanted her to feel at ease, safe, and inspired to paint something beautiful.

"Hello, my love," she said. I didn't say a word but grabbed the sides of her face with both hands and gave her a long, warm kiss.

We entered the town house just before sundown. All I had installed so far were a bedspring and mattress. The rest of the place was so empty our voices echoed.

As we made our way into the master bedroom, Loretta tried to act interested in the interior aesthetics, but she was more interested in touching and holding me. The feeling was mutual. It was as if we had just met, both feeling the magnetic force of physical attraction.

She grabbed my shoulders and kindly guided me backward toward the sheetless mattress. I lay down as she slowly climbed on top of me, straddling me in a squatting position, lifting the bottom front side of her sundress and holding it in her mouth, lips gripping it tightly.

She put her hands on my upper chest, using it to press against and maintain her balance. She aggressively unzipped my slacks with her left hand, never bothering to pull them down. Fondling my hardness with the same hand, she used the tip of it to pull her white cotton panties to the side and put me in her.

The warm thrust immediately relieved all of my pain, and I reached for the back of her head, pulling it down with my right hand — palming it as the tips of her hair tickled my nose. I put my hands under her dress, clutching her hips in an attempt to slow her movement, but her thrust only became more aggressive.

She sensed my release and put her right fingers in my mouth. I softly bit down on them as the two of us climaxed for what felt like everlastingness.

The next morning her father's Chevrolet Baby Grand arrived from Philadelphia while she was still asleep. Because of my injury, I still couldn't do my Kodokan routine, so I drove over to the post office. The smoothness of the ride likely spoiled me forever, and the slick automobile blended right in with the rest of Harlem's finest.

Waiting for me in my mailbox was a copy of the *Chicago Defender,* arguably the leading colored newspaper. In it was their "Weekly Comment" regarding the Carnegie Hall meeting I had tried to attend. I sat behind the wheel and read it.

Such meetings as that of the Marcus Garvey one Monday night, Aug. 25, in Carnegie Hall are more harmful than helpful to the Race. We say Marcus Garvey because it would appear that he alone is the whole association. In the first place, the man who got himself misquoted in all the white dailies of Tuesday morning, Aug.

26, is not an American citizen. Our Race, it is true, is struggling hard here for justice, but the fiery little man who wants to start a Black Star Line to Africa will find conditions almost as bad in his own country, where he might better center his activities. His organization, too, is composed mainly of foreigners, and certainly does not represent one iota of the American Race man. Our people will not be frightened into quitting their fight for equality, but we can well dispense with the help of a man like Garvey.

Next, I headed over to my new office on 145th and Seventh. A Bureau employee was there finishing up. Dressed as a handyman, he showed me the layout and explained what was what. Two phones had been installed, one for everyday business, the other for Bureau communications only. And they had separate lines in case Hoover or Speed tried to contact me while I was on the business phone with a client.

Several wooden chairs and a desk had also been delivered. It was a small office, but of good quality. I was amazed at how freely the Bureau was willing to spend its money on all things that concerned spying on so-called enemy aliens like Garvey. Whatever I needed to enhance the effectiveness of my mission was granted. And the office itself was expensive — especially considering it was only a front business, a home base and cover for me.

But it was smart to have such an office because it would give the appearance to greater Harlem that I was independent, and Garvey himself would surely be more suspicious of an unemployed man coming to beg for a job. If and when I did go to work for Garvey, greater Harlem would simply see it as another of my many contracts.

I called the Bureau, which had much information to share. A secured post office box had been set up for me under the code name Q3Z. It was located at a different post office from the one I'd been using. One of their couriers would be delivering sealed telegrams and money addressed to that box, so I was to check it regularly. I was to phone in all newsworthy messages by dialing the Bureau's telegraph office. An operator would transcribe my message, and it would soon be read by Hoover, then filed away. The Bureau wanted all brand-new info in writing.

Two men from Davis Brothers' Signs were out front putting up a small placard with my business name on it. It read: TEMPLE

CONSULTING. That was all — no specifics about the type of consulting. Since I would rarely be there and solicit only the work I was interested in, it was important not to advertise loudly and lure more folks in than I could help.

I would market the business as an engineering and land-use planning firm. I would do no labor but offer consultation to any interested developers, builders, architects, or property owners who needed my service. Being strictly a consultant on such matters was not only something I was comfortable with, it would also allow me to come and go freely. It would allow me to provide a legitimate service and build an actual client base. I figured that when I left the Bureau, I could keep the business, assuming it created revenue.

Today I planned to make my first attempt at visiting Garvey's office. But first I was going to pick Loretta up and take her to breakfast. She wanted to spend the afternoon soaking up the Harlem art. It would still be days before our furniture and other items arrived, so there was little to do around the house.

We sat in a booth at Snappy's and talked while enjoying our oatmeal and coffee. She was still melancholy about her father but at the same time anxious to see the new city.

"I wish I was an early riser like you," she said. "The idea of getting up at five every morning is dreadful."

"The good thing," I said, "is that it gives me a chance to get three hours of work done before you even wake up."

"Do you think we can make a habit of meeting for breakfast like this? It will give me a chance to connect with you every day, at least briefly."

"I don't see any reason why we can't."

"Thanks for letting me snoop for a bit across the street," she said. "The paintings being done in the class over there are some of the best I've ever seen. The instructor is a woman from France. She said she teaches the class two days a week and that there are other classes being taught by foreign artists all over Harlem."

"Wait until they see your work."

"You know what I need, Sid? A bicycle. You can have the car. And you won't have to pick me up all the time if I get one. I either want to ride out in the open and feel the Harlem wind on my face or walk wherever I go. If I see something that interests me — a particular painting or a group of artists gathering — I want to be able to stop and take a look. I want to ride all the way down to Central Park — explore this whole damn city."

"What kind of bicycle?"

"I want one of those new sleek-looking ones that I saw some of the girls riding back at Middlebury. I think they're made by Worksman Cycles. Will you get me one?"

"That's the least I can do. You deserve it. We'll go look tomorrow."

"How do you like your new office?"

"Well, remember the man from D.C. who I said I'm working for? He owns a firm here in New York City."

"Of course, silly. That's the entire reason we came to New York."

"Sorry — I didn't mean to insult your intelligence. I've just got too much on my mind. Anyway, as you already know, his intention was to have me open up this office here in Harlem for the purpose of doing consulting on the planning and building of several major Harlem building projects."

"Let me guess. They're now minor building projects."

"No, the projects are just being put on hold for a bit. But it's nothing to worry about. He's paying me a salary, and any contract I secure is bonus money. Right now he wants me to secure a job that involves, in essence, coming up with a detailed plan for refurbishing a large cruise ship that's docked here in Harlem. Based on my recommendations, the owner would then hire the contractors and mechanics to do the job."

"Think you'll get it?"

"Yes. There are very few engineering consultants in Harlem. I have to submit my portfolio to the owner and hope that he likes it; the owner happens to be Marcus Garvey."

"Marcus Garvey? I keep hearing more and more about him. New president of the NAACP, right?"

"No, he started a different organization — not the NAACP."

"Why does he own a ship of all things?" she asked.

"Beats me."

At least I'd managed to bring Garvey's name up to her. Now, my being seen with him as his engineer wouldn't draw her suspicion. Besides that, Loretta's head was a bit in the clouds when it came to the political world. She was a voracious reader, unless it had to do with current politics. Luckily for me, the art world and fiction were the beginning and end with her.

We finished breakfast and parted, Loretta still insisting on spending her day walking. As I made my way over to 135th and approached the Universal Negro Improvement

Association headquarters, I noticed about ten young colored men lining the sidewalk, rehearsing some type of march.

I passed them, parked, exited the car, and stood at the front steps of the UNIA office, watching the rehearsal take place from about fifty feet away. The longer I watched, the more I began to realize that these men were being put through a military-style training session by a man who looked to have a background in the Army.

They were holding wooden rifle stocks and learning how to maneuver them while marching. Most looked as if they'd never handled guns. They were all wearing jeans, white T-shirts, and black boots.

Out of the UNIA office walked a tall, stoic-looking man — mid thirties — pristinely dressed in a black suit and tie. His skin was lighter than mine. "God bless them young men," he said to himself, shaking his head in disbelief, as he watched them train.

He was saying it half jokingly as the men struggled to grasp the rifle manipulation that their instructor was demonstrating. Several of the youngsters were dropping their rifles.

"Enough to tickle you, ain't it?" he said, smiling at me. "Them men right there are the first recruits of Brother Garvey's African Legion. Got a lot of work to do. Don't you think?"

I smiled and didn't answer him. I was fascinated with the idea that Garvey was literally starting his own army. This would certainly raise Hoover's antenna.

"I'm Reverend James Eason."

"Nice to meet you," I responded, shaking his hand. "Sidney Temple."

"Those boys training over yonder ain't the only ones. Brother Garvey has hundreds of ex-fighting men from the war who are fixin' to start training soon."

"I see."

"Pleasure to meet you, young brother. You must be here for the assistant editor position."

"No."

"Not here for the *Negro World*? There are about five young men in suits sitting inside waiting to be interviewed."

"I'm actually here to talk to someone about the *Yarmouth*."

"Regarding?"

"I want to offer my services. I own an engineering and land-use planning firm here in Harlem. But I have a particular expertise in rebuilding engines."

"How do you know Brother Garvey?"

"I don't. I'm just looking for contracts and simply need work. I was told at the Carnegie meeting that the *Yarmouth* could use some engine refurbishing."

"And you think you can fix it? Several men have already tried — white men at that."

"For the right price, yes," I said with confidence. "I'll fix it."

He began laughing. "Oh, the young brother says he can for the right price. All right — all right. Brother says he ain't gonna be doing nothing for free. I hear you. Amen!"

I laughed with him, realizing that he took my money demands as a sign of self-confidence. I figured the money demands would help throw off any suspicion.

"Brother Garvey still hasn't purchased the ship yet. Still negotiating. But the sale should go through any day now. I tell you what, young brother, I'll talk to him this evening. You have any credentials? Marcus will want to see your résumé."

"I do. Here's my portfolio."

I handed him a folder that included copies of my two degrees, letters of recommendation, and several jobs that had been fabricated by the Bureau. Let's just say my résumé looked outstanding, replete with contracts I'd supposedly filled while in graduate school. I did do some impressive work while in Vermont during the summers — mainly reassembling auto engines and assisting with the design and construction of several roads and bridges — proving my engineering prowess, but not to the extent that my résumé suggested.

"How long have you been a pastor?"

"Oh, about fifteen years. I am currently the UNIA Chaplain General. Before joining Garvey, I was pastor of the AME Zion Church in Philadelphia."

"Get out of here!" I said. "My wife's late father, Reverend Barry Cunningham, was the pastor of the Westside Baptist Church in Philadelphia."

"Hold on now!" he enthusiastically said. "Just hold on, youngster. Brother Cunningham was *my* people! I knew B. C. well. We prayed together and attended many a meeting with one another. Had heard of his passing. May he rest in peace . . . and it is certainly a pleasure to meet you, brother."

We stood there shaking hands. I liked him immediately. And though I used the word *brother* occasionally, I'd never heard anyone use it this much, not even a pastor.

There seemed to be a genuine goodness emanating from him. But I could say for a fact that Loretta's father would never have joined Garvey. He'd been a staunch NAACP supporter.

"Look here," he said, "I would love to meet your wife and personally offer her my condolences. Can the three of us meet for coffee? That will also give me a chance to get back to you about Garvey and the *Yarmouth;* he actually intends to call it the *Frederick Douglass.*"

"I would love that. I'll talk to Loretta. And here is my card. It has my office number on it. You can reach me there during the day."

"I'll call you and we'll set up a time and place. You like apple pie?"

"Yeah."

"Good to hear. Know a great spot."

Two days later, my office was fully operational and I was quite comfortable. I had heard from Reverend Eason earlier that day and was told that he had to leave town for two weeks. He apologized and said we'd have to meet for coffee later. When we did eventually meet, I wasn't going to take Loretta because I wanted to avoid discussing the potential *Yarmouth* hire in front of her. Plus, any discussion of my bloated résumé or lies I might have to tell about pledging allegiances to Garvey's radical ideas would only raise her suspicions.

I dialed the BOI and readied myself to use clear diction and speak slowly. The telegraph operator answered.

"Code and location please," she said.

"Code name . . . Q3Z . . . stop. Harlem, New York . . . stop."

"Cleared. Proceed for input."

"Initial contact, Garvey official . . . stop. Name: Reverend James Eason . . . stop. Spelled: E-A-S-O-N . . . stop. Previous pastor AME Zion Church, Philadelphia . . . stop. Current UNIA pastor . . . stop. Submitted portfolio . . . stop. Eason, Garvey to discuss my portfolio . . . stop. Eason and I to discuss my potential employment . . . stop. Seeking work on Black Star Line's *Yarmouth* . . . stop. Garvey training own army . . . stop. Name: African Legion. End."

9

Fourteen days had passed. I sat in Snappy's reading the *New York Times,* sipping my morning coffee, and waiting for Loretta to meet me for our usual nine o'clock breakfast. Two days earlier I had been sitting in this same booth during lunch while Agent Mann had eaten at the booth behind me.

"How are things at the *Crisis?*" I'd asked, our backs to each other.

"Normal business," he'd replied. "However, Du Bois seems to correspond quite a bit with some of New York's more influential Jews. I'm trying to see if a Jerry Silverman is funding him. Silverman may be a member of the Communist Party."

"Good," I'd said, laughing on the inside. "I may have something for you next month. I think I may get a job with Garvey's Black Star Line. Perhaps I can find out who's funding him. Maybe the two have common donors."

"Yes. Communist Party donors."

"By the way, what's your code?"

"6W6," he'd said. "Yours?"

"Q3Z."

Mann had left shortly thereafter and I'd informed Du Bois in an anonymous letter about the Bureau's tracking of Silverman. The Bureau sure was hell-bent on linking them to communism.

Loretta still hadn't arrived for breakfast so I continued reading the paper. I came across an editorial that examined how Attorney General Palmer was beefing up security in an attempt to deal with the growing threat of Bolshevism. He was arresting even more folks.

According to the editorial, yes, the Communist Party was beating the drum for an overthrow of the U.S. government, but it wasn't a crime to be a member, thus it wasn't grounds for deportation under the Constitution.

The waitress came by and refilled my coffee. Through the window I could see Loretta riding up on her yellow bicycle, lugging her backpack. She parked it and walked in with a bright smile on her face.

We sat and had breakfast for an hour before I headed over to Cookie's Coffee to meet Eason. It was a spot near the UNIA.

He was there, waiting for me at the front door when I pulled up, standing with another gentlemen. He approached with a bit of urgency and we shook hands.

"Nice to see you again, Brother Temple. This here is Brother William Ferris."

"Good to meet you," I said, shaking the studious-looking, cocoa brown fellow's hand.

"Look here," said Eason. "Marcus can meet with you right now. He'll be in the office for another hour. The condition of the *Yarmouth* is number one on his mind right now. The purchase became official four days ago. We have some insurance matters to settle, but things look good. Come on, we can walk."

We made our way toward headquarters and I braced myself for the much-anticipated encounter.

"Listen," he said, "if you're not busy tomorrow, you wouldn't mind driving Brother Ferris and me down to Greenwich Village, would you? A friend of ours has invited us to lunch. He wants us to meet Claude McKay, a poet friend of his who's about to embark on a sojourn abroad. It's short notice and I apologize, but that lovely ride you just pulled up in certainly has room for the three of us."

He laughed, watching my reaction. I knew he was asking because he wanted to feel me out a little more. What better way than to take a drive into the Village?

"I'm free," I said. "Let's do it."

"Amen!"

We entered headquarters and stepped into what seemed to be nothing more than a very large, high-ceilinged, wooden-floored living room with desks occupying almost every inch of it. In fact, the entire building was most likely a converted three-story town house. But a very busy one. Colored office clerks, male and female, were sitting at desks typing and answering phones, probably selling Black Star Line stock.

We made our way through a hallway and passed a room that housed a large Linotype machine, used for producing and printing newspapers. We then headed up a set of stairs toward the second floor. One word best described the entire UNIA scene: *busy.*

"Brother Garvey's office is on the third floor," said Eason.

The air in the building looked smoky, which was odd because no one was smoking. Perhaps it was simply the window light illuminating the floating dust being kicked up by all of the scrambling, hard-at-work feet.

When we reached the third floor, the powerful presence of Garvey seemed to be coming through the closed office door. Eason knocked and a young woman answered.

"Oh, Brother Eason," she said, with a thick Jamaican accent. "Come on in."

She pulled the door open for us. Sitting there behind a desk, talking on the phone, was a hefty, thick-mustached, ebony-skinned man. His clothes hugged his squatty torso tightly. He wore a thickish-looking dress coat — perhaps corduroy or velvet. I couldn't tell if it was deep purple, dark blue, or black. He had a striped tie on, and I could see that the golden vest he sported was indeed velvet. As he engaged in the phone conversation, his powerful voice filled the room.

Reverend Eason reached his hand out to the secretary. "How are you, Sister Ashwood?"

"Very good, Reverend. He'll be off the phone in just a minute."

"This here is Brother Sidney Temple, and you know Brother Ferris. Sidney, this is Miss Amy Ashwood."

"Pleasure," I said.

"Reverend Eason!" said Garvey, hanging up the phone. "Come. Introduce. Please."

"Marcus," said Eason, "this is Mr. Sidney

Temple. Sidney, Mr. Marcus Garvey."

"A fit, finely dressed young man," said Garvey. "And so well educated. Or so I've read. Please, sit. Sister Amy, can you go see to it that I receive the first copy of the *World* as soon as they print it in a few hours?"

"Yes, right away," she said.

"All right then, Sidney," said Eason, "Brother Ferris and I will see you tomorrow at Cookie's Coffee around noon."

"Okay."

The three of them exited as Garvey and I sat alone in his office. There were stacks of old *Negro World* newspapers along all four walls. Two wooden desks helped fill the large room, Miss Ashwood's to the left, Mr. Garvey's right in front of me.

It was evident that he was a printer by trade, as his desk was covered with articles that he was situating on large, blank sheets of paper, arranging them appropriately, giving each a headline. He was, in effect, designing the final look of the paper before it went to print. Once he was finished, I assumed that an operator would take Garvey's blueprint, retype the articles into the Linotype, and make sure the finished product was designed accordingly.

A large typewriter sat on Garvey's desk along with copies of the *New York Times,* the *Times of London,* and various other national and international papers. Carbon paper and typewriter ribbons were scattered all over Miss Ashwood's desk, which was just as cluttered and also equipped with a beautiful, black Underwood typewriter.

"Ahh, Mr. Vermont!" he bellowed, as he continued arranging the articles. "A gorgeous portion of New England. But not a lot of Negroes running around the Green Mountain State."

He still had his attention on the articles. I was busy staring at the man, marveling at his dynamic voice and heavy Jamaican accent. I was also still studying his office. One item in particular caught my attention. Resting on his desk was a large, shiny machete. It was intimidating, to say the least, and looked old.

"This is next week's paper," he said, thumbing through some pages. "Producing a newspaper is never-ending labor. I've been working in the printing business my whole life. I got my first apprenticeship at my godfather's printing business in St. Ann's Bay when I was thirteen. So while the other boys were hacking away in the sugar cane fields, I was learning a trade. That's why that sharp symbol is sitting on my desk — to remind me to push ahead, never go backward toward the sugar cane fields where the white man worked the Negro like a dog. Cotton was to America as sugar cane was to Jamaica. Both are reprehensible productions."

Garvey held up what looked like my résumé. "Let me be very clear up front. I don't make a habit of doing one-on-one sit-downs with people I don't know. My time is precious. If I weren't truly concerned about the condition of my ship, I wouldn't be meeting with you. It's safe to say that your timing is impeccable. So, let me take a look here. You run an engineering consulting firm. Impressive, but how does that qualify you to work specifically on ship engines?"

"If you look further," I said, "you'll see that one of my areas of expertise is mechanical engineering."

"An extensive background for such a young man. What service does your business offer?"

"Clients hire me to assess and then advise."

"I must tell you that I have several mechanics working on my ship as we speak. They claim it has leaky boilers."

"Perhaps, but it's important to find out if anything else is malfunctioning. Besides, if it's only leaky boilers, fixing those shouldn't be a problem. Something as simple as that shouldn't be taking this long."

"I concur completely," he said, eyes still on my résumé. "Now if I can just get you to convince Captain Cockburn of that. The *Yarmouth* will never be fit to chug off if he has his way. But he has his boys working hard. Whether or not they're making any progress is another thing altogether. They certainly don't have your education."

"Thank you," I said.

"I myself was schooled in London — Birkbeck College. I never received a degree, but what I learned on my own surpassed anything any college could have ever taught me. Some of these Negroes walking around with their fancy university degrees nailed to their foreheads for everyone to see make me sick. Attending a college does not make a man educated. So tell me, what do you know of me?"

"I know that you own a ship and that it needs work," I said. "I also know that you're head of this UNIA, and I've read an article or two about your association. But in short, I know little. I'm not a political man."

"Sometimes," he said, "the less a man knows about you, the more useful he can be to you."

Garvey hadn't made much eye contact with me. He kept his head down, reading my résumé. There was a vanity to the man that was overwhelming, plus an obvious insecurity about his education.

"I have been in this country for three years," he said. "I watched those colored soldiers march up Fifth Avenue as people lined the streets to welcome them home from that white man's war, and I can honestly say, American Negroes need a different kind of education, a street one. They had no business bleeding in that white man's war. The street education I received in Jamaica was enough to teach me that."

I now knew it was going to require a Herculean effort to convince him that I didn't hold any strong political beliefs that opposed him. The only way I could curry favor with him was to become a piece of clay he could mold. It would be similar to the buffoonish role I'd played with Hoover.

"Is there a Mrs. Temple?" he asked.

"Yes."

"I intend to wed the little lady who just left this office. She helped me start the UNIA. And now, it's beginning to thrive. As soon as we can get the *Yarmouth* in mint condition, it will set sail — first to the West Indies, and later, to the Motherland. We will ship and trade goods and provide leisure travel for our people. They won't have to travel as second-class citizens anymore, and if they so choose, can see the Caribbean, Europe, and Africa."

He sat there with such pride. His intentions to sail to Africa were obviously sincere.

"Please don't think I've forgotten why you're here, Sidney. I want you to come visit the ship and survey the work that's being done. We will then sit down and you can tell me if you feel it's sufficient or whether there need to be changes made — changes I would hire you to make, assuming I agree with your recommendations. Reverend Eason likes you. That's enough for me right now. He's a smart man — smart enough to part ways with the NAACP and join me. He's provided great counsel to me regarding that idiot assistant district attorney — Edwin Kilroe.

"Kilroe has done everything possible to derail my business ventures. He's an evil, Irish-Catholic S.O.B. You'd think he'd be more kind to me considering my own Catholic faith. And I certainly know who brought me to his attention. Ever since I met W. E. B. Du Bois when he came to Jamaica four years back, he's felt threatened by me, and I know he's in cahoots with Kilroe."

He was still looking down and seemed unaware that he was saying more than he should. As far as he knew I could have been from the NAACP. I could have been from Kilroe's office. And, of course, I could have been a government spy. But then again, maybe he didn't care — was comfortable with me going right back to these people and sharing what he had said. Perhaps he was revealing so much of his inner thinking because he wanted to gauge my reaction. But I showed none. What I really believed was that he couldn't help himself — had so much pent-up frustration that it just poured out of him, regardless of his company. He had gotten my attention with this Kilroe individual. I would need to find out more about him.

"The fact that you are not from New York is a good thing," he said. "You've spent all of your adult life in Vermont of all places — hardly a hotbed for black politics. You could call that place 'Whiteville.' But you're not tainted by all of these ambitious, unethical New York coloreds. You're at the perfect age to begin learning — forming your political philosophy."

He hadn't even asked where I'd grown up, failing to realize or even consider that I, like most Americans of color, was from a ghetto. He'd instantly formed an inaccurate opinion of me.

"I will have the reverend ring you once I decide when to have you survey the *Yarmouth*. Right now I must ready myself for Chicago. That pathetic newspaper editor, Robert Abbott, has been attacking me in the press. He has Chicago Negroes thinking I'm trying to swindle them out of their money."

Garvey began intensely writing, as if noting something he wanted to remember. "This," he said, "coming from a man who makes all of his money advertising ways for our people to lighten their skin and straighten their hair. When I finish with him, no one will buy his paper, though it will be aptly named. His paper is the *Chicago Defender* and he'll be doing nothing but defending himself against me."

He looked up at me with a slight look of displeasure. "It has been good meeting you, Mr. Vermont."

I stood, reached across the desk, and shook his hand. His grip was firm and quick and he immediately returned to his writing. I exited his office, made my way down the steps, and headed for my car. Then I drove to the office and phoned the BOI telegraph operator.

"Code and location please," she said.

"Code name . . . Q3Z . . . stop. Harlem,

161

New York . . . stop."

"Cleared. Proceed for input."

"Initial contact with Marcus Garvey . . . stop. Marcus Garvey officially purchased ship four days prior to today . . . stop. Ship name is *Yarmouth* . . . stop. Spelled: Y-A-R-M-O-U-T-H . . . stop. Marcus Garvey currently reviewing Agent Q3Z resume . . . stop. Marcus Garvey not satisfied with current *Yarmouth* engineers . . . stop. Agent Q3Z to survey condition of *Yarmouth* per Garvey's request . . . stop. Date of requested survey still unknown . . . stop. Update on said survey forthcoming. End."

10

Eason and Ferris were there waiting outside of Cookie's the following day when I drove up. And before I could even get out, they walked up and hopped in. I noticed a familiar face getting into a car across the way. It was Agent James Wormley Jones. We began to move and he followed.

"You're gonna take Broadway quite a ways," said Eason, "until you get to Thirteenth Street. We're heading to 138 West Thirteenth Street. The brother that invited us to lunch, Brother Hubert Harrison, helps edit the *Negro World.* But he mostly be out in them streets, up on that soapbox, hollerin' to the world. Ol' Hubert is the one who showed Marcus how to preach from that box."

"So what is it you do, William?" I asked Mr. Ferris, who was sitting in the backseat. I was asking, but my eyes were on the black vehicle behind us with agent Jones inside.

Why the hell is he tailing me?

"I like to refer to myself as an author, minister, and scholar," answered William. "I also help edit the *Negro World* for Mr. Garvey."

"Brother Ferris is being way too doggone humble," said Eason. "This is a man who graduated from Yale in . . . What year, Brother Ferris?"

"1895."

"That's right," said Eason. "Then the brother received a master's degree from Harvard in journalism. Ain't a lot a Negroes runnin' round them schools. Only man I know as smart as Brother Ferris is Hubert. Hubert been around plenty of white folks."

William was smiling, amused by Eason's praise of him. He was a distinguished-acting man, and now I knew why. His voice was quiet, his stature small, and his disposition gentle. He started telling me more about his background.

"After Harvard," said William, "I wrote a book, *Typical Negro Traits,* in 1908. I also worked with Willy Du Bois and the Niagara Movement."

"You took part in the Niagara Movement?" I asked.

"Yes. It called for opposition to racial segregation, and it was also a movement

designed to push back against the philosophy of Booker T. Washington, who was
angling for accommodation, pushing for
Negroes to accept and make the most of
their weak position within the American
social system. First meeting took place near
Niagara Falls. It was one heck of a group —
led by Du Bois."

"Willy Du Bois started out as such a
strong brother," said Eason. "It was
Booker T. who most fighting brothers and
sisters saw as weak, submissive, and passive.
But after Booker T. died a few years back,
aggressive Negroes thought Du Bois would
become even louder, more defiant. I remember when he once said so powerfully, 'We
want full manhood suffrage and we want it
now . . . we are men . . . we want to be
treated as men . . . and we shall win.' Du
Bois had folks in a frenzy."

"He certainly did," said William.

"But the way I see it," said Eason, "— and
this is only me talking — Brother Du Bois
softened after Booker T. passed. There was
an important, very brief moment immediately after Booker's death that needed to be
seized by Du Bois. But it was not. That left
a big hole for another strong, outspoken
leader to fill. And that's when Garvey
stepped into that void. Colored folks was

clamoring for a powerful, almost instigative voice."

"Instigative?" I asked, still eyeing Agent Jones in the rearview mirror.

"Yes," continued Eason. "Don't get me wrong, I was with the NAACP, and God as my witness, I love and respect Brother Du Bois. But I'm in a fightin' mood, not a political mood. Brother Du Bois is a master at that political game. I want to scream, not whisper — want to jump, not sit down — want to run, not walk. Brother Garvey is the one in a screamin', jumpin', and runnin' kinda mood. Can I get an amen, Brother Ferris?"

"Amen."

I listened closely but wanted to ask Eason what good screaming did if a man was screaming the wrong message — what good jumping did if he continued to hit his head on the same old concrete ceiling — what good running did if he was heading for a cliff? I held my tongue.

Eason's poet friend and three others were already sipping their sodas at a table right in the middle of the restaurant when the three of us entered. Eason casually led Ferris and me past the patrons. They appeared oblivious to our entrance. Still, the seven of us were the only coloreds in this particular eatery, and it was standing room only.

"You're late," said a coffee-skinned man in a gray suit fitted nicely to his compact build. He was smart-looking with his thick-rimmed eyeglasses and sounded refined with his West Indian accent.

"Brother Hubert Harrison, it's nice to see you," said Eason, as the two shook and we took our seats.

"What in God's name were you thinkin' havin' us meet here?" asked Eason, who was sternly surveying the place.

"This wasn't my idea," said Hubert, turning and pointing to the well-built man sitting to his left. "Blame it on the genius poet. This is who I was telling you about. This is Claude McKay. And these two spooked cockerels are my friends Clarence Jolly and Oliver Mayberry."

Wearing slacks and a white T-shirt, the mustached McKay just sat there grinning from ear to ear, as if he were pleased as all get-out that he had chosen a place that would make most coloreds more than uncomfortable. In the case of Oliver and Clarence, he'd certainly done just that.

"Not gonna be no trouble in this place now is there?" asked Eason.

"That's what I was wondering," said Clarence.

"Me too," said the fidgety Oliver.

Mr. McKay, who looked to be in his thirties, bent over chuckling. I couldn't help but see the playfulness in his personality. It was as if he had set the entire event up as a ruse.

"They know me here," said McKay, still giggling. "You're in Greenwich Village." His Jamaican accent was slight. He put his arm around Oliver's shoulder and then lightly pinched the back of his neck. "Don't worry, my West Indian brother. I've eaten here before."

"Good," said Oliver, scanning the place along with me, except I was looking for Agent Jones.

"You boys need a hanky to wipe the sweat from your brows?" McKay asked. He offered a white handkerchief to Clarence, who declined. McKay chuckled again.

"Do you know that woman there, Claude?" asked Oliver. We all slowly turned to a table about ten feet over to the left. A well-dressed old woman was staring at us as if we'd stolen something. She had an irksome look on her face, completely ignoring the younger woman across from her — perhaps her daughter.

"Uh, I believe she's the wife of the local police chief," McKay said. "He's a cantankerous old boar. Can't stand coloreds comin' up in the local diners."

Oliver looked at him with trepidation. All of us but Clarence figured McKay was pulling Oliver's leg.

"Reckon we ought to head on out of here," said Clarence. The woman stood and walked toward the back of the diner.

"That might not be such a bad idea," said McKay, now displaying a panicked expression. "She prolly headin' to the payphone to ring up that old cob roller a hers. He mean as all get out! Liked to had me up in jail last month."

Oliver panicked. "I'll go first," he said, standing to head out.

McKay grabbed the back of his suit jacket, pulling him back in his chair. "Sit yo skittish-actin' self down. That old petticoat done gone to the washroom. She ain't studyin' us, fool!" He began clapping his hands demonstratively and laughing out loud.

So this was the man who'd written a poem that had colored America in awe? "If We Must Die" was making him famous, yet his playfulness and acting prowess made him equally suited for the stage.

"Look here, Claude," said Hubert, "this is Reverend James Eason." The two finally shook hands.

"And who are these two distinguished-lookin' gents?" McKay asked.

"This is William Ferris, a good friend of Hubert's and mine," said Eason. "And this is my new friend, Sidney Temple." There were more handshakes all around as, again, I casually looked to see if Agent Jones was anywhere in sight.

"Hubert said ya'll came all the way down here just to meet little ol' me," said McKay. "That truly is a shame."

"No it ain't," said Eason. "That poem you wrote got everyone over at the UNIA worked up, feelin' good, stickin' they chests out."

"You done made Negroes proud, Claude," said Hubert. "I must have wept the first time I read them words. 'If We Must Die' is 'bout to start a revolution."

"Nah," said Eason. "The revolution done started. 'If We Must Die' just the battle cry. Brother Garvey's army is trainin' and marchin' to it. They puttin' the words into action — ready to die today, tomorrow, or the day after."

"The NAACP is *also* fond of your poem," said William.

"Ah, shoot, they ain't 'bout nothin' but kowtowin' to white folks," said Eason.

"Now wait a minute, Reverend," said William. "Willy Du Bois's essay, 'Returning Soldiers,' is coming straight from the same place as 'If We Must Die.' Mr. McKay here and Willy are both talkin' about fighting. Fightin' is fightin'."

"You see it that way, Claude?" asked Hubert.

"Yes I do. Angry Negroes just ain't in the mood for the NAACP right now, that's all."

"Hard to put politics aside, though," chimed Eason.

"Du Bois's *Souls of Black Folk* is what initially stirred me politically when I first came to America," said McKay. "I know how Hubert here feels about Du Bois. He's already written about the brother's supposed fall from grace."

"Indeed," said Hubert. "The editorial was called 'The Descent of Dr. Du Bois.' For him to have the audacity to ask us Negroes to put our grievances aside while the war was going on, and fight alongside the white man, really riled me up."

"I don't agree with Willy's position on the war," said William, "but I know where he was coming from. What he was asking us to do was help win a war that would decide whether every American — colored or white — would even have the chance to take another breath."

"But the grievances he was asking us to put aside included lynching and segregation," said Hubert. "Those are more than just grievances. And the lynching certainly continued during the war. The white man didn't put anything aside."

"Yes," said William, "but not everyone here at home pauses during a war abroad in an effort to show a united America. A pig shall act as a pig. But Willy could argue that if we had lost the war, the five of us might not be sitting here talking about anything, including lynching, segregation, or beautiful poetry."

"So we helped the white man win a war so he could continue to lynch us?" asked an angry Hubert.

"At least now we have a chance to change his mind," said William. "That's what Willy would argue. Besides, you don't think the victorious Germans would have been happy to take the American white man's place in hanging our colored behinds? And you have to understand something, Du Bois has a long-term plan and vision for the Negro — not an immediate one. I simply don't share his patience. Why else do you think you and I are on the same team, Hubert?"

"Well," said a joking Hubert, "I'd rather

be hung by a German any day."

We all laughed as the hostess approached. "Excuse me, gentlemen," she said, "but is one of you the driver of a gray Baby Grand that's parked across the way?"

"Yes," I said.

"Well," she said, "we were just informed up front that it's parked in a no-park zone. Would you be so kind as to move it? Sorry to interrupt."

"Certainly," I replied, getting up. "Be right back, gentlemen."

They all nodded as I headed out. Parked right behind me was Agent Jones. As I approached he rolled down his window. "Take your time opening the door," he said. "They can't see us from this vantage point."

"Didn't know your job was me," I said.

"How good is your memory?" he asked. "I need names. Or I should say, Hoover needs names. Other than Mr. Eason, of course, who you messaged in already. I'm assuming one of them is him."

"Yes," I answered, pretending to read the street signs.

"We both know you're parked just fine," he said, a pen and pad in hand. "Names?"

"Why the hell are you following me? Hoover doesn't think I can handle this?"

"Just doing my job. You need to get back

inside. Names?"

"Hubert Harrison, Claude McKay, William Ferris, Clarence Jolly, and Oliver Mayberry."

"Good," he said, writing. "Excellent recall. Hoover should be impressed." He started the engine and drove off. I headed back inside, my mind racing, knowing I needed to stay in agent mode. But I was angry at having been followed.

"Welcome back," said Eason. "Get it handled?"

"Yes," I said, sitting, preparing myself to memorize any pertinent info.

A young, redbone waitress approached the table. "Will you three gentlemen be havin' a soda as well?" she asked.

"That sounds just fine," said Eason, looking at William and me for approval as we both nodded yes.

"And I think we can go ahead and tell you what we want to eat, too," said Hubert, his West Indian accent seeming to thicken. "Ya'll ready to eat, ain't you?"

"Uh-huh," we all said at the same time.

"I want some of them pork chops I see over yonder," said Eason. "Them there at the table behind you, darlin'. The one that big jowly lookin' man gobblin' up like they 'bout to run away from him."

She turned to look and we all laughed under our breaths. He was a very big, round-faced white man in a tight brown suit and suspenders. Looked to be in his mid fifties. He was sitting by himself, looking down at his plate, and eating some fried pork chops about as fast as humanly possible.

"Look like he 'bout to pop!" said Eason. "Better get that big ol' man a bucket of Epsom salt, or better yet, get yourself ready to call them ol' stiff-collectors down at the morgue. Fidna have to roll him up on outta here. God bless that man!"

Our entire table broke into muffled giggling.

"All right," she said, smiling. "You better quit."

McKay was clapping his hands and grinning from ear to ear, trying to hold down the volume of his laughter. Luckily the café was filled with the sounds of chatter and clanking dishes.

"We call him Mr. Regular," she said. "He be here every day. That's the special he's eatin'. It comes with green beans and mashed potatoes and gravy, too. And you, sir?" she asked, turning to me, still smiling from Eason's comment.

"Is the special as good as it looks?" I said,

still eyeballing the fat man as he licked his lips.

"Sure is," she said. "About the best thing you can get."

"Then I'll have the pork chops too," I said.

"Yeah," said William, "me too."

"Uh-huh," said Hubert.

"Make it seven," said a still-giggling Mc-Kay.

"All right then," she said, walking away.

"You ain't right, Reverend!" said Oliver, still laughing.

"Back to your earlier point, Hubert," said McKay. "Is it possible that you and I and our West Indian compatriots — Garvey included — simply haven't acknowledged that the American Negro truly sees himself as part of America's disparate tapestry? Maybe they're conditioned to seek the justice that was never afforded their American ancestors — however long that may take."

"Perhaps," said Hubert. "All I know is the battle line has been drawn between this West Indian and Dr. Du Bois. Besides, those of us from the West Indies seek the same justice."

"But we haven't always sought it from the American white man," said McKay.

"Speak for yourself, you Jamaican," said

Hubert. "My homeland of Saint Croix was sold by Denmark to these United States two years ago."

"My point exactly," said McKay. "Two years ago! Any grumblings you and your ancestors had were directed at the Danish — mine at the British."

"Well, things have changed in the last two years," said Hubert.

"But we weren't born into this tangled culture," said McKay. "You know my beliefs, Hubert, especially about the war. But I'm just playing devil's advocate. One can argue that whether we want to accept it or not, many Negroes in this country desperately wanted to fight in the war and defend what they believe is their nation. They didn't need Du Bois's permission. They must believe there is something to fight for and defend."

"What?" asked Hubert.

"The very thing that made you and me want to leave the Caribbean and come here. Whatever that ethereal quality about this place is."

We all paused to think about what McKay had just said. I knew that slavery also had deep roots in Hubert and Claude's West Indies, but it could be argued that, by 1919, race relations had become more fluid there than they had in the United States. It made me wonder why they ever desired to leave home and come to a place that was perhaps less accepting of Negroes. I figured it was indeed that intangible thing McKay had referred to — that which colored soldiers were willing to fight for.

"I just wish Du Bois would act like his old self, that's all," said Hubert.

"It sounds like the battle line has been drawn in your mind, too, Reverend," said McKay.

"You doggone right. And it ain't drawn in no sand neitha! Du Bois may be my fellow American, but I'm with Hubert on this one."

"Ain't it supposed to be in your thinking ways to always have forgiveness on the mind, Reverend?" said William. "Like I said, Willy Du Bois has fallen out of favor with me a little too, but it doesn't run so deep. I just have a preference for Garvey, not a disdain for Willy."

"You feel the same way, Sidney?" asked McKay.

"Well, I don't know much about Du Bois," I replied. "I think I'll hold off on offerin' anything up 'til I learn some more. I'm sure Reverend Eason will teach me all I need to know."

"Yes," said Eason, "I got a lot to teach

you, young brother. And when I'm done with you, I'll get to work on William here, 'cause he done forgot some things."

"I most certainly have not," said William. "It's just that I've known Willy Du Bois for years. During the Niagara Movement, we would read . . ."

"Stop," said Eason. "Don't make me mad up in here now, William. I don't care how many books you done read. I know some things from livin'. I got one of them done-lived-a-lot educations. Done learned some things ain't in them books."

McKay laughed as Eason and William stared at each other with a playful seriousness — as if they'd argued about similar things a thousand times before.

"Boy I tell ya," said McKay. "It's being in the company of good-natured gents like you that makes me think twice about going to London."

"How long will you be abroad?" I asked.

"Well, I'm not certain at this point. Unless London has good hog food like Harlem, it'll probably be a short visit. You know, all this talk about colored and white and I forgot to mention, I owe a big debt of gratitude to a white friend of mine over at the *Liberator* named Max Eastman. If he hadn't published my poem I'd still be unknown."

The name Eastman drew my attention as I continued listening to the table talk. We sat there for another hour and discussed politics as if it were all there was in the world. And McKay expressed his desire to go it alone rather than join up with Garvey, despite their recruitment. McKay wasn't all that pleased with Garvey's seeming rejection of socialism. I was just hoping Garvey wouldn't reject me.

11

By the time I got home after dropping Eason and Ferris off at UNIA headquarters, it was late. Hoover would certainly want to know that I had met the man whose poem had been published by Max Eastman, but the last thing I wanted was for McKay to have agents following his every move. Still, now that Jones had the list of names, I had no control of it.

I was hoping Hoover would lose interest in Eastman the more entrenched I became with Garvey. I liked McKay very much. Perhaps I was already falling victim to item number one on any spy's don't-do list — letting friendship get in the way of the mission.

But the folks at the *Liberator* were harmless and in no way a threat to what was important to me. However, when it came to those connected to Garvey, I had to follow through. My loyalty was to Du Bois, and I

could let nothing get in the way of that —
not even the charisma, charm, and persua-
siveness of Reverend Eason.

When I opened the front door, Loretta
greeted me with glasses of wine. We sat in
the living room drinking and listening to
the blues music emanating from the Columbia Grafonola that had been her father's. It
played the vinyl so smoothly. The two of us
took in the soulful sound of Marion Harris's
"A Good Man Is Hard to Find." Loretta's
father had been a savant when it came to
music. He was a collector of jazz and blues
records, so we inherited some wonderful
vinyl.

Loretta had been here less than three
weeks, but already the town house had a
warm, cozy feel to it. She had such a touch.
Her paintbrushes, palettes, and canvases
filled a section of the living room. Several
large cloths, used to rid her hands of excess
paint, hung from a beautiful wooden easel
and displayed a rainbow of colors, adding
to the room's décor. Art books lined the
shelves.

Professor Gold had given us an endless
supply of old literature from his massive
library. Most of the classics were included.
Many of the books were stacked on the
floor, as we lacked the proper shelf space.

Our living room reminded me of a cross between Picasso's studio and Walt Whitman's writing and research nook.

Several crates sat against the wall by the front door, as Professor Gold had also shipped cases of red wine to us. He had been storing wine in his cellar for years. With Prohibition looming, I suppose he wanted to make sure Loretta and I could properly entertain guests. Besides, he and Mary no longer drank much.

As we sat on the brown Chesterfield sofa, with its high arms and deep-buttoned leather upholstery, I rested my feet on the cherry wood coffee table. Loretta had lit four candles, setting a dark and romantic tone.

"A gentleman came by the house today," she said, sipping her Sangiovese. "I wrote his name down."

She reached for a slip of paper on the coffee table. "Here it is. His name is Dale Meeks. He said he was visiting on behalf of the Black Star Line. He asked me several questions."

"Like?"

"He wanted a few reference telephone numbers for some of the jobs you listed on your résumé. He also asked if I knew about any volunteer work you may have done for

183

the government."

"That's odd. What did you say? Did he actually have you look at my résumé?"

"No. Before he could even pull it out I made it clear that I hadn't a clue about any telephone numbers or job details. I told him to come back when you were home."

"I don't know what made him think you could answer such questions," I said.

"Did you list the Washington training session you attended on your résumé?"

"Not for this particular job," I said. "Did you happen to mention it to him?"

"I already told you I said nothing, Love. But maybe someone from the Black Star Line was also at the training session. And because you didn't list it, they simply wanted to double check."

She was sounding a little tipsy from the wine and trying to connect some non-existent dots.

"You think so, dear?" she asked, resting her head on my chest.

"No. Pretty sure no one from there was in attendance. Whatever the case, it's probably best to avoid even mentioning the word *government* around these people."

"Why?"

"Because . . . being a new business . . . perhaps the Black Star Line folks are a little distrusting of the government. Maybe they're worried about them prying into their affairs."

"They shouldn't be so worried if their *affairs* are in order," she said, sipping.

"True. But still, it's probably best we keep my training session between the two of us for the time being."

"Okay," she said, "but just so we're clear, I didn't mention the training session because I didn't know if you were okay with them believing you had any job interests outside of Harlem. I figured you wanted them to think that the *Yarmouth* job was the only one you were focused on. You want this job, right? Did I do the right thing, Love?"

"Of course. You always do."

If she had so much as stuttered when Mr. Meeks asked about government work, I was certain Garvey would reject my application. Eason had probably ordered the visit, knowing I'd be with him all day. It was clever of Meeks to visit my wife while I wasn't home and use the arbitrary "government volunteer" phrase to see if she'd slip up.

I experienced an overwhelming urge to tell her about my being an agent. I briefly entertained the thought that she would be able to keep the secret. She had always shown an ability to keep our business private. But then the truth hit me. If I told her, she would demand that I get out, and there was no doubt about it. She would never, in a million years, accept being part of some double life.

The song ended and Loretta walked over to change the record — obviously enjoying Marion Harris, because she put on her other hit song, "After You've Gone," which was a much slower and more intimate tune. Many people thought that Marion Harris was colored when they heard her bluesy voice, but she was a white woman.

"Why can't we have a telephone installed?" Loretta asked, returning to the couch. "I'm not comfortable having strange people visit me here at the house."

"I don't want a telephone because folks from every consulting job I take will be calling the house around the clock. This way they can only reach me during the day at the office."

"But what about me? What if I want to call family or friends?"

"Sweetheart, it's just better this way. Trust me. You can always use the telephone down the street. Most folks don't have a telephone in their house anyway. They can't afford it."

"Will you dance with me?" she asked in a sexy voice, standing and pulling me up, which I allowed.

"Oh — you're feeling that music — and the wine. I'd love to."

We held each other and danced slowly, falling deeper in rhythm with every step.

"How much do you love me?" I asked.

"More than you can imagine."

"I can imagine a lot."

"Then beyond the universe," she said. "It can't be quantified."

I rose early as usual and did my Kodokan before heading to the office. My phone conversation with Agent Speed was brief. He wanted to follow up on the list of names Agent Jones, code name 800, had given him.

"800 is just following you around until you pop your cherry, Q," he said.

"Well I don't like being followed," I replied. "And it's not Q, it's Q3Z."

"Look, you'll be Q to me. Thanks for the list."

After he hung up, I read several newspapers, scouring for info. I was interrupted around noon when Eason phoned and said he wanted to stop by and see me before he left for Chicago. "I've got someone else I want you to meet," he said.

"Come on by," I replied. "I'll be here 'til five."

A few hours later Eason and his friend Reverend Adam Clayton Powell, Sr. were sitting in my office.

"Reverend Powell's the man who's gonna keep your little firm in business," said Eason. " 'Cause no matter how much Brother Garvey agrees to pay you, it won't be enough."

"I can use all the business I can get," I said.

"Brother Powell is raising money to build the new Abyssinian Baptist Church. It'll be the biggest church in New York."

"Is that right?"

"Indeed," said Powell. "We've actually already purchased the land. But seeing the project through will require some expertise in several areas. Right now I'm dealing with the city, and I have to obtain certain building permits before we can even break ground. Now, I understand you're an engineer, but what services does your office provide?"

"Well, engineering is such a wide field. My strengths are in the areas of electrical, mechanical, and structural engineering. But I mainly assess and advise."

"Assess and advise?"

"Yes. For instance, I do land assessments, and it sounds like that's what you need right now. I can also consult with the architect during the planning phase and then work in cooperation with the construction manager throughout the building phase. I'll make sure the building is strong enough and stable enough to resist structural loads like gravity, wind, snow, rain, earthquakes, earth pressure, and temperature. Wait. I'm getting ahead of myself. Before we begin building, we'll have to excavate the land. Do a lot of digging. And I can operate a steam shovel with the best of 'em, Reverend Powell."

"Those big ol' machines that move tons of earth?"

"Mm-hmm. Learned to operate 'em during college."

"Ain't but a handful of Negroes in America with them kinda technical skills," said Eason. "Praise God for that education."

Sitting in my chair, I felt proud for a second, almost sticking my chest out before continuing. "What is the city's main concern, Reverend Powell?"

"We've been told we can't build but so high and that the ground in certain areas is unstable. The land needs to be surveyed. I need someone who can assist a team in getting it ready for the city to give us the go-ahead. Matter of fact, I just need a right-hand man who understands measurements, zoning, land cultivation, and numbers."

"Amen," said Eason. "You, Brother Powell, are a man of the Word, not numbers. Ain't that right?"

"Right. And most of all, I would like to have my go-to man be colored. So far, all of the individuals involved are white folks, from the city licensing officials to the real estate agents and so on."

Looking at Powell, I could have sworn he was white himself. But he wasn't. He was colored, and looked to be in his fifties. His dark-rimmed eyeglasses, buttoned-up almond-colored suit, and wavy hair gave him the look of an aristocrat. His burgundy waistcoat was more distinguished-looking, and perhaps of a thicker cloth, than the vests the average Harlem man was sporting — more British perhaps. And though I wanted it for myself, it was certainly more appropriate for a man his age.

"Brother Powell gonna need someone involved he can trust," said Eason. "Lotta money being invested. And though God is watching over him and his congregation, the devil also has a vested interest."

"Amen," said Powell. "The congregation has given generously with their tithing, and I don't want to let them down. They're willing to be patient as long as the end result is a marvelous place of worship. I've told them that this is at least a three-year project. I've had visions of building a church since my Yale Divinity School days."

Reverend Powell was beaming with pride. He crossed his legs and I noticed one of his freshly polished patent-leather shoes. The man was refined, both in dress and demeanor.

"I've always marveled at beautiful architecture," he added. "My intention is to have the church built in a new Gothic and Tudor style. The architect I'm hoping to hire shares my taste. He's the renowned Charles Bolton, but he doesn't come cheap. If all goes well I want stained glass windows and Italian marble furnishings. It will be a grand undertaking."

"Where will it be?" I asked.

"On West 138th. Right next to Liberty Hall."

"Look, Brother Temple," said Eason, "splitting your time between the Black Star Line and the Abyssinian will be good for your health. Besides, even I can only handle small doses of Brother Garvey at a time."

"Hold on now," said Powell. "I'd like to see what the young man knows before we get too far ahead of ourselves."

"I'll offer my services on a trial basis for

the next month," I said. "We'll see where it goes from there. How does that sound?"

"You are a God-fearing man, correct?" asked Powell.

"Both me and my wife."

Eason jumped in. "I done told you 'bout his wife, Brother Powell. She from Philadelphia — the late Reverend Cunningham's daughter."

"That's right. You did tell me that. Very well then, Sidney. I'm meeting with a representative from the Buildings Department on Friday. His name is Henry Burns. He can better explain the obstacles that are standing in our way. And it'll give you a chance to see the property. Can you be there?"

"Count on it."

"Good. Maybe once you and Burns get better acquainted, I won't have to deal with him anymore. That will be your job."

"That's what my business is here for."

"I need to spend more time preparing my sermons anyway."

"What is the story behind the church's name?" I asked.

"Oh, it's a story we're proud of. Back in 1808 some Ethiopian sea merchants had moved here and were attending the First Baptist Church in Manhattan. They were asked to sit in a different section from the whites. But they refused to. They weren't accustomed to segregation. They left and started their own church where folks were free to worship openly. Abyssinia is simply another word for Ethiopia."

"Ain't that something," said Eason, standing. "Well, look, I hate to end our little visit so fast, but I need to get up out of here." His eyes peering down, he flicked his suit jacket just below his left shoulder, removing some lint. "Chicago is calling. You know where the *Yarmouth* is docked, right, Brother Sidney?"

"Yes."

"Why don't you go by and introduce yourself to Captain Cockburn tomorrow. I done told him about you. And feel free to inspect things. Brother Garvey's ready to fire all them boys down there anyhow. He's done pegged 'em as a bunch of amateurs. You ready, Reverend?"

"It was a pleasure," said Powell, standing to shake my hand.

"Likewise," I said.

After they left I finished my sandwich and headed out. My destination was a telephone booth on Seventh Avenue. Weeks earlier I'd filled an empty can with coins and put it under my car seat. Now they'd come in handy because I was going to call Professor Gold. Just needed to tell him I was fine.

"I'm glad you're adjusting to the city," he said, "and that your evening with Phil Daley went well. How was it hearing Dr. Du Bois?"

"It was one of the best nights of my life. I can't thank you enough. But listen, Professor Gold, I'm phoning you from a paying booth, as I'm of the assumption that the Bureau is periodically listening in on my conversations at the office. Why wouldn't they ensure their investment?"

"You're probably correct, Sidney. Better safe than sorry. I certainly don't ever want any men in suits visiting me out here in the woods."

"Don't worry, Professor Gold. You're the one person in my inner circle who doesn't exist."

I smiled into the transmitter and heard him snicker through the receiver. I also felt the gnawing stress pain in my upper stomach coming on again.

"Mary feels the same way about me," he joked. "All I have is the dog."

"I pity you."

"Listen, you should also be careful with the sidewalk telephones. If anyone were to follow you, they could wait until you hang up, then dial the operator, claim they'd been accidentally cut off, and have the call reconnected."

"Good to know."

"I was a spy in my former life," he said.

"A magnificent one I'm sure."

"Quite average, actually."

"In all seriousness," I said, pressing the right side of my abdomen, "I don't think the Bureau knows anything about you."

"They don't — at least nothing beyond my being one of your many professors. I spoke to President Tanenbaum about the conversation he originally had with a Bureau agent regarding you. Only academic performance was discussed and a letter he had written to the Army on your behalf. Interesting that they looked into all of your records, public statements you made in the newspaper, and your high school history but never looked into your college living situation — at least as far as we know."

"Even the smartest of us overlooks something significant at one time or another."

"That is and will always be a fact, Sidney."

"I will try not to let too much time pass before contacting you, and I look forward to the day when we can sit down and discuss all of this."

"Well, Sidney, I'm sure with you on the

job Dr. Du Bois and the NAACP's future is in good hands."

"Let's hope. It certainly won't come without great sacrifice."

"I'm just glad to hear you're well."

"I am, and send my best to Mary. Good-bye, Professor Gold."

"Good-bye, Sidney, and stay safe."

12

I laid eyes on the *Yarmouth* for the first time and knew I had my work cut out for me. It looked to be in terrible condition. Walking through a light rain that had set in, I studied the old vessel and couldn't help but wonder why it had ever been purchased. If impressing Garvey meant getting this rickety boat up and running, my days as a spy might be short-lived.

The ship had been floated, its water pumped out, and it was on a dry dock supported by blocks. Making my way past the many hands attending to its every nook and cranny, I saw men trying to remove excessive growth that was covering the hull.

I approached a skinny young man who was on his knees near one of the deckhouses replacing some damaged wood. I asked him where I could find Captain Cockburn, and he told me that he hadn't seen him in days. I made my way to the engine room below. I figured if leaky boilers were the problem I'd take a quick look.

Not only was the room empty, it was filthy. There were tools lying around everywhere. After about an hour of tinkering around and getting myself filthy, I discovered that two of the boilers were badly corroded and someone had made a poor attempt at welding several fissures together. They should have known that the rusty steel surrounding the fissures was too eroded to repair.

I couldn't be certain, but it looked like a section of bulged boilerplate had been removed and replaced with a much thinner patch — sloppy work to say the least. The *Yarmouth* needed new boilers — an expensive proposition that Garvey likely wouldn't want to hear. But how much pressure the boilers could take depended on how many passengers and how much cargo he intended to carry to Cuba. Any excessive steam pressure could cause the boilers to explode.

With Garvey and Eason in Chicago for about a week, it gave me a chance, later in the week, to meet Captain Cockburn and further assess the vessel. Even when Garvey did get back into town, he was busy dealing with other matters. But I managed to explain the boiler problem to Eason. He said that Garvey was adamant about not replacing them, so I ended up spending the next few weeks doing the best repair job I could manage.

Finally, in mid-October, while sitting in my office with Reverend Powell — going over some logistics regarding the Abyssinian — Amy Ashwood phoned and said that Garvey wanted to see me at the pier immediately.

Within thirty minutes I arrived and he was already there, standing with his hands on the railing, looking out at his docked *Yarmouth*.

"Mr. Garvey?" I said walking up from behind.

"Ah, good, you're here, Sidney," he said, not looking at me, his eyes still on his boat, only a few deck hands scuttling about. "I want to discuss those boilers you repaired."

"Okay," I said, positioning myself to his right, my eyes also fixed on his *Yarmouth*.

"Did you do a good job?" he asked.

"Yes."

"Well then, why do you now want to replace the boilers? I received the estimates you gave to Eason. Are you telling me that your patch job will not actually suffice?"

"It will not suffice for long," I said. "You need new boilers."

"What you're suggesting will cost as much as an entire new ship. And with the ridiculous salary Captain Cockburn has negotiated for himself, this is no time to spend where we need not spend."

I studied his big rickety ship and was certain he'd grossly overpaid for it, a reported $168,500. I believed it was worth no more than $30,000.

"You have all this education," he continued, a strong wind kicking up. "If I can get you the proper supplies, can the problem be sufficiently repaired?"

"It's not likely," I reluctantly responded, knowing the move could put my entire employment in jeopardy. But I knew he was a smart man and would be able to sniff out any sort of kowtowing on my part.

"I pay you to fix. So . . . fix! I just fired all of those idiot Negroes masquerading as mechanics and now you're bringing bad news just two weeks before we're scheduled to launch my baby in front of thousands of proud and anxious brothers and sisters."

"My deepest apologies, Mr. Garvey."

He looked up at the gray sky, as if calculating something. "If we had more of our people qualified to captain boats, I could have told Cockburn to go fry an egg. He used his leverage much to his advantage."

He began gripping the railing tightly. "And this bad boiler news comes in the middle of my having to go back and forth to the office of that jackass of a man, Edwin Kilroe. He is without question the most reprehensible assistant district attorney in America. He can't even disguise his revulsion of the darker race."

"Perhaps it can make this one trip to Cuba," I said, knowing if the boat sank he'd at least know I'd warned him. "But I strongly suggest replacing the boilers before any future voyages."

"Now that is much more encouraging news, Sidney." He pointed his chubby finger at me, looking at me for the first time. "That we can do."

He pulled a paper from his coat pocket and began studying it, the wind flapping it about. The man never seemed to stop doing something. And his disregard for what he was saying, when he was saying it, and whom he was saying it to was alarming.

"Yes," he said, slapping the paper, "Kilroe may be trying to stop progress, but he's got another thing coming if he thinks he's got this proud West Indian pegged. There are four million Negroes around the world pledging their allegiance to my UNIA. Four million! Feel free to repeat this?"

"Four million," I repeated, knowing the figure was dramatically overblown.

"Good, Sidney. You know nothing but science, but our world is a political one. These pale-faced imposters like Dr. Du Bois and his flock will do anything to stop me . . . those who must use the darkness of the skin under their fingernails to prove their Negroness."

He folded up the paper, put it back in his pocket, and pulled another from a different pocket. He was obviously juggling different ideas and allowing me in on his thinking. He was preoccupied to say the least.

"I'm a very dark, proud man. And you, Sidney, you fall somewhere in between. But you're at least very brown, like this Paul Robeson — this very popular football sportsman. Where does he run with that ball?"

"Rutgers University."

"I see. Rutgers for Robeson — Harvard for Du Bois."

"Birkbeck for Garvey," I said, watching him study the paper, wishing I could read it myself.

"I read that Mr. Robeson," he said, "is an admirer of Du Bois. In fact, many men are choosing to follow this Harvard man. But there's a simple choice for our people to make when comparing that mulatto excuse for a leader to me: Which way forward? Can you say it?"

"Which way forward?" I repeated.

"That's right. Garvey or Du Bois?"

"Garvey," I said.

"Where's your conviction? Perhaps you would be more comfortable working for him?"

"Only if he has a big ship for me to work on."

He smiled but stayed on the paper. "Ever the professional you are, Sidney — thinking of the job at hand only. Good. And I didn't hire some white man to fix my boat. I hired you. All we need is each other. And all you and I need is Africa. The white man can have America."

"He already does," I said.

"Right. But Du Bois and his stolid group of intellectuals are keeping the colored man lazy. Having him believe that if he just goes and receives the white man's education he can perhaps become president someday. President of the white man's own country! Foolishness!"

I shook my head, trying to convince him that I agreed with his sentiment.

"Look at that ship," he continued. "It is mine."

"It most certainly is."

"To be used for international trade, Sidney. The Negro won't have to depend on whites to exchange goods anymore. We can also allow Negroes to visit Africa on a shorter route, avoid going to Europe first. But as for now, I just want your assurances that you can ready it for launch in two weeks."

"You've hired me to do a job, Mr. Garvey, and it's a job I'll do."

I listened to him go on and on about Kilroe some more, along with a myriad of other topics, before he finally ended the conversation by saying, "Come by tomorrow morning at eleven sharp, Sidney. I want to show you something."

Back at my office an hour later I was heavy into a phone conversation with Speed. He wanted some details about Mr. Garvey and was chomping at the bit. I'd already decided to share only what I felt like sharing.

"This will be received quite well here in Washington," said Speed. "What else you got?"

"Garvey," I said, "wants me to attend all future sales meetings, along with his lawyers.

He claims he doesn't want to make another offer on a vessel without quote, 'a man like you present.' "

"This is strong," said Speed. "Shit. Real strong. Pays to be colored I guess."

"Excuse me?"

"Nothing, Q. It's just that none of our white asses can get within ten miles of that Jamaican bastard, that's all. Continue."

"Garvey is also establishing other businesses along West 136th Street with the help of his real estate friend, a Mr. Jimmy Pope. Pope is securing several buildings."

"Give me the names of the businesses," said Speed.

"One is the Universal Restaurant. There will be a Phyllis Wheatley Hotel and a Booker T. Washington University. Then there's a tearoom and an ice cream parlor."

"A fuckin' tearoom?" said Speed. "Let me guess . . . they're gonna serve African tea? Pardon me while I laugh my ass off."

"You still writing?" I asked, bothered by his disrespectful tone. "Or do you want me to send all this in a telegram?"

"Go ahead, Q. But a fuckin' tearoom!" He laughed. "Go ahead."

"He wants me to assess the electrical wiring throughout all of these facilities at some point."

"Good, that means access. Hold on one minute, Q. Our boss would like to speak with you. Just continue filling him in. And be sure to send a telegram detailing the names of these businesses after we get off the phone here. Okay?"

"Got it," I said, surprised that Mr. Hoover was getting on.

"Hold on, Q. Here's the boss."

"Q3Z?" said Hoover, his somewhat youthful voice reminding me again of our age similarity.

"Yes, sir," I calmly answered. "This is Q3Z."

"You brought up a name I see written down here, a Jimmy Pope. What other names did Garvey mention?"

"A Mr. Edwin Kilroe," I said, knowing I wasn't going to bring up anything Garvey had said about Du Bois. "He's the assistant district attorney."

"And?" said Hoover. "Take me inside the conversation. He must have gotten into the race thing. He prides himself on having an us-against-them mentality."

"I see," I said, laughing on the inside at the hypocrisy. "Mr. Garvey claimed that he was being targeted by Kilroe as a lawbreaker because of his growing popularity, his black power. Garvey said he'd shout 'Africa for

206

the Africans to the hilltop,' in spite of Kilroe's threats."

"Is that right?" said Hoover in a somewhat challenging tone.

"Yes," I continued. "Garvey said the following: 'Kilroe wants to convince the world that I'm stealing from my own people — that I'm soliciting funds for my Black Star Line, then using those same funds to start other businesses.' Garvey also said the following: 'This problem with Kilroe started as most of our people's problems do. One of our own betrays us.' "

"Who betrayed him?" asked Hoover.

"Garvey said he did the good deed of hiring a fellow Jamaican to be one of his auditors, and when the books became too complicated for him to handle, he began making far too many mistakes. Garvey accused him of mismanagement in front of an entire committee. The nameless auditor was offended and resigned before Garvey could fire him."

"At least that's his version," said Hoover. "Where does Kilroe come in?"

"The disgruntled auditor then sought revenge and turned the books over to Kilroe. But Garvey claims that if anyone mismanaged the books it was the auditor . . . not him."

"How convenient," said Hoover.

"Garvey," I continued, "said he was called down to Kilroe's office for a scolding. He said Kilroe threatened him with jail time if he didn't clean up his books and begin acting as an honest broker. But Garvey then said to me, 'We'll see who wins this little war because I don't lose.' "

"Well this is good work, Q3Z," said Hoover. "Sounds awfully defensive about his books. Speed says you are meeting with Garvey in the morning."

"Yes. He wants to show me something."

"Exactly what time is the meeting?"

"Eleven."

"And is the meeting to take place at his office?"

"Yes," I said, curious as to why he cared so much.

"You're in a unique position now, Q3Z. Try to inform Speed as soon as possible about the details. And again, good work."

Later that evening, when the sun went down, I left my office and headed for Broadway en route to Greenwich Village to pick up Loretta from an art class. I was heavy in thought about tomorrow's meeting when I heard a loud siren behind me.

It didn't take me long to realize I was being asked to pull over by a policeman. I hadn't been driving very fast or swerving.

Once we'd both pulled to the right of the street, he rolled up about a foot behind me, his headlights illuminating my entire cabin. I probably waited a good five minutes before he finally decided to approach my left door.

"Where you headin'?" he asked, pointing a flashlight directly in my eyes.

"Greenwich Village, Officer," I said, squinting but not lifting my hand to shield the light.

"Where you comin' from?" he asked.

"Harlem, sir."

"You live in Harlem?"

"Yes."

"You don't sound like you're from Harlem," he said, still blinding me with the light, so much so that I couldn't make him out. "How long you been there?"

"A few months."

"Ah," he said. "That explains it. Can I see some identification?"

"Certainly," I replied. "It's here in my coat pocket."

"Go ahead and slowly get it out."

I did as he asked and handed it to him while he kept the light on my eyes and held up the card.

" 'Sidney Temple,' " he read aloud. "Says here you were born in Chicago."

"Yes. But I grew up in the Milwaukee area."

"Well," he said, handing me back my card, "I don't know about Milwaukee, but New York City has some understood boundaries that most new coloreds have to be schooled on. I'm sure you understand where I'm coming from?"

"I was actually recently in Greenwich Village, sir."

"Well you're not in Greenwich Village yet but you certainly are in Manhattan. And your vehicle should be heading toward Harlem, not toward the Village. We try to keep things in their place in New York. Day codes have their place and night codes have theirs."

"I see."

"Good," he said, lowering the flashlight a bit, but still not enough for me to make him out. "So you won't mind turning this thing around and heading north?"

"I'm just picking up my wife and driving straight back to Harlem."

"Look, Mr. Temple, maybe you've had some dealings with some of our less experienced officers who don't seem to follow these codes with the kind of discipline us veterans do, but coloreds know to take the subways at night. Your wife will have to catch a ride with someone in the Village tonight, take the subway, or you can pick her up at sunup."

I clenched my jaw and fought back the rage that was boiling up inside me. I couldn't tell him I was with the Bureau because I didn't know who the hell this officer was. He might out me to Garvey if he ever saw me around him. It wasn't likely but still too risky.

"There's just no exception you can make here?" I asked. "My wife will be waiting for me."

"Look, Mr. Temple. I know this is not the South, but we still try to keep folks organized, the races separate, particularly at night. It makes things run smoothly, that's all. Now please! Move along."

As I casually began to drive forward and turn around, the rage returned. I drove slowly away and managed to wait until the squad car was no longer in my rearview mirror before I allowed myself to blow off some steam by hitting the steering wheel and cursing the insane cultures Loretta and I were caught between.

As far as I knew Du Bois was the only one fighting all this madness with cool saneness.

Only when I envisioned myself as something of a soldier in Du Bois's army — a peaceful army that would nevertheless blow people like this police officer and his boundaries and codes to kingdom come eventually — did I manage to tamp down the rage and refocus on getting through this one night.

Fortunately, Loretta had given me the phone number of the studio where she was studying. It was at someone's home. I didn't want her taking the subway at night, so I figured I'd drive back to the office and try to reach her and come up with an alternate plan.

As soon as I tracked her down and began to speak, something told me not to tell her about the policeman. Didn't want to upset her. Instead I told her that the car wouldn't start and that I was in the process of trying to fix the problem. I told her that it might take me several hours and asked if she had someone who could drive her home tonight. Luckily, a French friend of hers named Ginger was more than happy to do just that.

13

I parked facing west on 135th about a half block from Seventh Avenue. UNIA headquarters was a little more than half a block east from there. It was the only available parking I could find. My appointment wasn't until eleven, so I had about forty-five minutes to kill. I decided to stay in my car for a while and study one of the several railroad maps I had in my briefcase. I was quite enjoying daydreaming about chugging along through the Rocky Mountains, visiting some faraway city like Denver, Colorado.

I studied the various Missouri Pacific Railroad routes for about five minutes then grabbed a different map. Noticing how packed my briefcase had become, I removed the other maps and placed them under my seat.

As I reached down, I glanced to the left and saw a colored man, dressed like a regular deliveryman in all white, standing behind a black ice cream truck parked on the south side of 135th facing east. It was a typical delivery truck with a high rising outer shell over the bed. JOHNSON'S ICE CREAM CO. was written on the side of it.

The man had caught my attention because he was looking back and forth in both directions up and down 135th. I also noticed a heavyset colored man sitting in the front passenger's seat smoking a cigar.

My attention was drawn back to the deliveryman as he continued watching folks walk past him. Why wasn't he unloading the truck? I had no reason to be suspicious of the man, but I kept an eye on him nonetheless. Empty parked automobiles lined both sides of the street, but he wasn't focused on them, so he didn't see me.

Finally, there was a break in the foot traffic, and the sidewalks were empty for a moment. Just then the man opened the back doors of the shell and a man calmly hopped out. He was also colored. The deliveryman hopped back in the driver's seat and started the truck. As he turned to his left to check for oncoming automobiles, he spotted me.

I tried to pretend not to see him, but it was too late. He stared directly at me with these lazy eyes. His was a haunting face I could never forget. I gave him a nod, but he didn't respond. Instead he made an immediate hard left turn, driving and heading his truck in the western direction I was facing.

He pulled up right beside my Chevrolet, and the heavyset passenger scowled at me through his cigar smoke. The driver leaned forward and did the same. I froze, not knowing how to react. After about ten seconds of them sizing me up, they drove away.

The man who'd hopped out of the shell was now standing against the brownstone across 135th from me. He was nervous-acting. It was as if he was afraid to move. Was he preparing to rob someone?

With no pistol on me and not a policeman in sight, I didn't want to stick around to find out. Besides, it was time for me to get to my meeting. I casually exited the car and began my walk east. All the while, I wondered what had just happened. I knew the three were up to no good, but I certainly didn't want to involve myself in their mess.

I crossed Lenox Avenue, approached the UNIA brownstone, and quickly entered. Once inside, I walked past several busy staff members and headed upstairs. Just as I approached Garvey's office, out walked Amy

Ashwood.

"Marcus is ready for you, Sidney. Go on in."

I entered the office and found him busy at his desk writing. Just as I was sitting he said, "Tell me which play I'm quoting from, Sidney: 'Farewell the neighing steed and the shrill trump, the spirit-stirring drum, th' ear-piercing fife, the royal banner, and all quality, pride, pomp, and circumstance of glorious war!' "

"Othello," I answered.

"Good, Sidney. The Brits adore their Shakespeare. But I ask: Why should the English have a monopoly on pomp and circumstance?"

Garvey stood and walked to the wall directly behind his desk. He reached up and grabbed a narrow vase-shaped item that was hanging horizontally on the wall by a leather string. It had African-looking beads on it. He then turned and showed it to me.

"You like this?" he asked.

"It's beautiful."

"It's a long gourd that you might see hanging from the belts of the Maasai people of Africa. They use them for storing water on long treks and also for storing milk, which will often curdle and turn into a sort of cheese. The Maasai also use them for storing cow's blood, which they extract from the large vein of the cow's neck. The white man has his canteen, we have our gourd."

He turned it upside down and out spilled a set of keys. He then walked over and unlocked a closet door, opening it and removing a hanging black suit bag. He unzipped it and revealed a stunning Victorian-style blue military uniform with gold trim and epaulettes.

"If you are going to be in my employ," he said, "you need to see what we are all about. You need to soak it up. You agree?"

"Yes."

"I will soon show the world the Negro's version of pomp and circumstance — giving them a grand show and parade like they've never witnessed."

He spread the uniform over his desk and then removed some items from the closet's top shelf, also setting them on his desk. There was a plumed bicorn hat, a ceremonial sword, and plumed helmet. Napoleon himself would have been proud. I guessed that somewhere in the recesses of his mind Garvey fancied himself a man plucked from the era of the French Revolution or before. I had never seen anything so grandiose in person and assumed he'd picked the items up during his stay in Europe.

"My African Legion soldiers will also wear similar blue uniforms — not with such grand hats like mine, of course. All of this is for special occasions only. I like to spend most of my time dressed in regular suits, but none of mine are as fine as those you wear, Sidney."

"Thank you."

"But make no mistake, my African Legionnaires will dress in uniform around the clock. They will also carry rifles, for symbolic purposes of course, as the pins have been removed. Here, I'll show you."

Again he walked to the closet, removed a rifle, and proceeded to show me the mechanics of the gun. I felt his presence smothering me as if being forced to partake in something I'd rather not. I found myself wanting to shove him away — anything just to create some space for myself and not feel cornered. He held the rifle sideways within a foot of my face so that I could examine it.

"You can see here where the pin is supposed to be."

"I see."

He set the rifle on the desk and began admiring his display of items.

"You're probably wondering why I have such things — why I have Legionnaires and such?"

"I must say, I am curious."

He spread his arms like wings. "Why all of this, you ask?"

We both stared at the assortment covering the desk. He then picked up the dress sword and began running his right fingers along the blade.

"I'll tell you why. It's important for any sovereign state to project an image that says, 'We can protect ourselves.' The French have done it — so has Germany and Italy. But, of course, I must express my admiration for what the Irish are doing as we speak. They are doing more than posturing. They are fighting the British right now — shedding blood."

"I can certainly feel," I said, "that you're projecting a powerful and bold image, Mr. Garvey."

"It was only when Americans began to project an image that said, 'Listen, King George, we will fight back,' that the king took notice."

"I've seen the men training," I said.

"The message our Legionnaires are sending is this: 'We, as a Negro unit representing Africa, are very well organized and willing to fight back.' "

"I'm sure the message is being heard loud and clear," I said.

"Just the smallest possibility of a threat must be projected, Sidney. President Wilson must be forced to pause and take notice. Symbolism is paramount."

Garvey walked around and stood behind his desk. Facing me, he held the dress sword tightly and began slowly swiping at the air as if he were in a duel.

"You know who John Brown was, correct?"

"Yes, the white abolitionist."

"Right," he said, continuing to slowly swipe at the air. "They tried to kill him with a dress sword just like this one. I do believe you could kill a man with this. You'd have to use quite a bit of force though. Agree?"

"Probably."

Though he was standing behind his desk, it felt like the tip of the sword was no more than a couple of feet from my face, and I was growing quite uncomfortable.

"You probably know this, Sidney, but Brown was stabbed by Lieutenant Israel Green. He thrust his sword into Brown's abdomen. There couldn't possibly be anything more painful than having a blunt instrument thrust into your belly."

He made a stabbing motion, extending his right arm straightforward, holding the pose for a moment.

"You see, Sidney, Lieutenant Green forgot to exchange his dress sword for his battle saber."

He continued casually whipping at the air.

"When he stabbed Brown, the dress sword bent. But Green was undeterred and used it to hit Brown on the head over and over. There was plenty of bleeding before Brown was knocked out and fell to the ground."

Finally, Garvey stopped and froze. He then began gathering up all of the items, walked over to the closet, and put them away.

"WHERE'S GARVEY?" screamed someone from downstairs.

Garvey and I were both startled by the angry shouts we could hear through his open office door. Miss Ashwood walked in shaking her head.

"There's a man downstairs hollerin' and askin' for ya," she said. "I told him you were busy, but he started kickin' the desks and lookin' in all the offices. Man done lost his mind, Marcus!"

Garvey stormed out, making his way to the top of the staircase and down to the second floor. I followed close behind.

"WHERE'S GARVEY?" a voice rang out again. "I WANT THE MONEY BACK I GAVE HIM FOR THAT DAMN RES-

TAURANT!"

I saw a colored man down below kicking a desk and slamming his fist down. Staffers were ducking and hiding behind desks.

"WHAT IS THIS?" shouted Garvey.

The man looked up and casually walked toward the stairs. He locked eyes with Garvey's. I immediately recognized him as the man who'd been hiding in back of the ice cream truck earlier. I noticed he was holding a gun at his side. In the blink of an eye he raised it and fired four shots at Garvey, hitting him in the head and lower body — knocking him off his feet. Blood sprayed against the railing and wall.

Miss Ashwood screamed several times and then quickly rushed to his aid, covering his body with hers, while others downstairs began struggling with the gunman, trying to snatch his pistol away. But he wrestled free and ran for the door.

Garvey was now covered in blood, and I was sure he'd met his fate. Instinctively, I bolted down the stairs and gave chase. But I didn't need to run far because a patrolman was already pursuing him down the block heading west toward Lenox. How in God's name had a police officer arrived on the scene so quickly?

I stopped running and surveyed the entire

scene. The gunman didn't even make it to Lenox before the patrolman tackled him. I approached, breathing heavily, as the patrolman held him facedown — hands behind his back.

"I've got him," he shouted.

I still found it too strange that the policeman had been on the scene so soon. It was as if he had been waiting outside for him. The entire incident struck me as a setup of some sort.

As I watched the patrolman walk the shooter to his police mobile, I looked up and couldn't believe my eyes. Slowly driving by and looking squarely at me were the two men in the ice cream truck. I headed straight for the patrolman and tapped him on the shoulder.

"What is it?" he asked.

As I was about to point out the truck, something told me not to. I couldn't help but wonder if the patrolman was part of their scheme, so I froze. One thing Momma had always told me was not to trust the police.

"Nothing," I answered, as the two men glared at me and drove away. "It's nothing."

If this was a setup that the patrolman was in on, and I was the only one who could connect the two men to the shooter, I'd better keep my mouth shut. I stood there with several other UNIA clerks and secretaries — many of them crying — as the gunman was being hauled off to jail and Garvey was being transported to the Harlem Hospital. It had all happened so fast.

14

Later that evening I sat in the hospital waiting room with Eason, Hubert Harrison, and William Ferris. There were probably twenty other UNIA officials sitting around and pacing the hallways as well. Garvey had survived — defying the gunman or whoever had sent him.

"He was likely paid big money by someone," said Hubert. "Just dumb enough to think he'd get away with it. And the cowardly thug who paid him will make sure he doesn't talk."

"You think it's that simple?" I asked.

"Maybe we should find out who this coward is," said William.

"We don't hunt thugs down," added Eason. "Let the hooligans act like hooligans. We're high-minded men."

"Principled!" said Hubert.

"But make no mistake," said Eason, "this will all come to the surface in due time."

"Right now," interjected William, "I feel like taking action — principles be damned!"

"Listen," said Eason, "whoever the coward is will only see Garvey's legend grow. His power will reach unfathomable proportions. And I'll tell you why, brothers. To the millions who already see him as a hero, they'll now see him as bulletproof — an ethereal figure who can't be slain. They'll call him Black Moses with more conviction than ever."

Hours later I opened my front door and waiting for me was an empty house. I went into our bedroom and took off my shoes, suit jacket, dress shirt, and tie. It felt good to relax in my undershirt, pants, and socks.

I headed into the kitchen and grabbed a beer from the icebox, then entered the main room and put a record on. Bert Williams's "When the Moon Shines on the Moonshine" never sounded so good, so I turned it up loud, which helped to erase all of the ugliness from that day. Williams was one of the only colored singers who'd ever been recorded. I'd been waiting for years for that to change, but to no avail.

Sipping my beer, I grabbed my Joseph Conrad book, *The Secret Agent,* from the adjacent bookshelf and headed for the couch to relax and read. I wasn't five minutes into it before Loretta knocked at the door. I was glad she'd made it home in time for us to share a drink and talk. She had a habit of forgetting her key.

"Coming!"

I hustled over and answered. Then I froze because standing there wearing a dark green suit was the lazy-eyed ice cream truck driver. He was holding a gun at his right side. Sensing my uneasiness, he gave me a slight grin and searing glare — cigarette dangling from his mouth.

"Sometimes fools are just in the wrong place at the wrong time," he said.

My heart was pounding as I stood there defenseless, searching my racing mind for a series of moves I could make. The stare-off between us seemed to last forever — the music and voice of Bert Williams still blaring. I dropped my eyes, focusing on his gun, noticing his shooting finger tickling the trigger.

He took the cigarette from his mouth with his left hand, extending it toward me — the hot end pointed at my face. I looked at the tobacco slowly burning five inches from my mouth, wondering if he would singe me with it. I froze, studying the ash up close, as if through a magnifying glass — the center

227

of the burn pulsating like cooling lava.

"I'm offering you a pull from my last cigarette. That's nice of me. Go on — take it."

I didn't move an inch. The grating, throaty sound of his voice was unsettling.

"That's wild tobacco you're looking at — best in Harlem," he said. "They roll 'em special for me — fresh — down on La Salle Street — Friday mornings. We spent hundreds of years picking the shit — God knows we the ones ought to take pleasure in smokin' it."

He slowly and creatively flipped the cigarette with his long fingers — the butt now facing me. I gently took it from his hand, put it in my mouth, and smoked for the first time — inhaling a thousand thoughts. It was the only thing prolonging what seemed like my inevitable fate — buying me a few more seconds.

"I never got your name," he said.

"It's Sidney."

"Sidney and Sleepy . . . sharing a cigarette. Who woulda thought it? They call me Sleepy 'cause of my eyes."

We continued staring each other down as I handed the cigarette back to him. You could cut the tension with a knife.

"You see, Sidney, we have a problem. The

Negro we sent in to get Garvey was crazier than hell. We knew that. We just needed to drop him off and make sure he went inside. Simple, don't you think?"

I nodded.

"And when we saw you earlier that day sittin' in that beautiful Chevrolet, we knew you'd seen too much — knew you could connect us three. But we didn't think no mo 'bout it. We never figured you was headin' to Garvey's office. But when Jumpy and me came back by there, much to our surprise, who was standing there with that policeman — hovering over him and that fool who can't shoot straight?"

He took a deep drag from the cigarette and blew the smoke directly at me.

"You!" he said.

I tried to keep an eye on the gun through the thick smoke.

"You see the problem, Sidney?"

"There's no problem."

"I could tell when I first saw you earlier this mornin' that you was one of them nosy niggas. You'll keep snoopin' 'round 'til me and Jumpy is done with. You probably think some high-up man sent us to do the job and you won't quit 'til you find out who. But maybe it was just us three simple niggas who thought the whole thing up. You think?"

"Maybe."

"But you see . . . my gut be tellin' me you won't quit 'til you got the answer. And with you runnin' round out there in them streets — knowin' what you know — Jumpy and me will end up dead at the hands of Garvey's boys, or in jail like that crazy fool who can't shoot straight. And we can't have that."

I noticed him fingering the trigger again and knew time was running out. Anticipating him raising the gun to shoot me, I attempted to slam the door. But my anticipation came a hair too late, as he had raised the gun just in time to get the barrel jammed between the door and frame.

I tried to press the door shut, but the barrel was still jammed. He fired a shot, hitting some bottles of wine against the wall. I clutched the doorknob with my right hand and jammed my right foot against the base of the door. With my left hand I grabbed the gun barrel, forcing its angle upward. He fired again, hitting the ceiling.

Using every bit of strength I could muster, I dislodged the barrel and slammed the door. I then locked it at both the knob and chain, as he began violently kicking. I raced to the bedroom, rushed to the bed, and reached under the frame for my pistol. I could hear the door-wood splitting — breaking open.

Pistol secured, I made sure there was a bullet in the chamber and that the magazine was full. Operating on complete instinct, as if moving to the rhythm of Bert Williams — his music still providing the soundtrack to this violent scene — I rushed to the bedroom entry, stopped, and took aim at him from about twenty feet away.

Just as he was stepping through the splintery, dangling front door, I fired and hit him in his left arm — spinning him around like a top and knocking the gun out of his hand. He gathered his balance and retreated.

I rushed to the door, picked up his gun, secured it under my belt, and carefully pursued him. I noticed blood on the front porch and began following some drops down the stone stairway — then along the sidewalk.

It was very dark out with only a few dim streetlights in either direction. Of those, several weren't working. Still, I saw him laboring along in the distance and gave chase. He began to run, but I was rapidly gaining on him. I crossed Convent Avenue, approaching the section of 140th that began to curve southward.

Now about two blocks from home, I stood

in the middle of the street aiming my pistol at his silhouette. I heard the faint sound of an automobile, then the elevated roar of an engine. Two gunshots rang out, but the bullets missed me. I turned, and in an instant, a Cadillac Roadster was upon me.

I dove out of the way, barely escaping with my life and managing to get a quick look at the driver's face. It was his heavyset partner, Jumpy. Luckily for me he wasn't a very good shot. The car sped up and came to a screeching halt about a hundred yards in the distance. Sleepy jumped into the passenger's seat and the car accelerated, careening as it turned the corner and disappeared.

I stared into the night sky trying to catch my breath for a minute. Then I turned and headed home, walking briskly. After about a block, I heard the engine again behind me. I stopped and looked directly into the car lights. Just then Jumpy hit the gas and sped toward me.

Running as fast as I could, I looked for an alley, but saw nothing except continuous brownstones lining both sides of the street. I ran onto the sidewalk but knew that wouldn't suffice. They were quickly gaining.

I wasn't about to possibly lead them back to Loretta, so I ran right past the town house. As the wind pressed against my face, my eyes began to water. Two more shots were fired at me — one bullet nipping my shoulder.

The vehicle drew within what felt like twenty feet of me. I couldn't be sure because I was moving too rapidly to turn and look. Angling to the left, I saw the vacant field that the City College had yet to develop.

Just as the Cadillac was about to hit me I dove out of the way, landing on a pile of gravel, badly skinning both hands and the side of my face. The automobile screeched to a halt.

I got to my feet and moved through the field. The farther into the open space I ran, the darker it became. I was out of breath and needed to stop running. Knee-high in weedy grass now and not sure if they were following me on foot, I stopped.

Perhaps they had decided to drive around the block and meet me on the other side. Or maybe one was following me on foot and the other was driving around the block.

Looking back and forth, I couldn't see a foot in either direction. Facing in the direction I had just come, I lay down on my stomach in the thick, high grass, practically burying myself in it. It was silent and I would be able to hear the faintest sound of them approaching.

Quietly breathing, I clutched my pistol, knowing I still had seven bullets left in the magazine. I heard footsteps and then whispering.

"Move slow," one said.

"Can't see a damn thing," said the other.

"He can't see nothin' either. Just keep quiet and move slow."

Now there was nothing but the sound of my rapid heartbeat and their feet mashing down the vegetation. My eyes were slowly adjusting to the dark, and I could make out their bodies about thirty feet away. They were heading right toward me.

Knowing I had only a few seconds before their eyes too would adjust to the dark, I lifted my head just above the weeds, poked my right arm through the thick brush, and took aim at Sleepy. My shooting hand trembled like it was freezing. Such are the nerves of a man who's never killed.

With his head as my direct target, some ten feet away now, I fired, then delivered two shots to the body of Jumpy before he could react. Rushing to my feet, I ran to them.

Sleepy lay lifeless while Jumpy gasped for air. I stood directly over him, contemplating whether to let him live — wanting to — but knowing his intention would always be to kill me.

"Who sent ya'll to kill Garvey?" I asked.

He was choking on his own blood, trying to answer me. He finally forced one powerful word out.

"God!"

Pointing the gun at his face, I turned away and fired two shots. And just like that I had become an entirely different man.

15

My God, how the time passed. I'd been in Harlem for a year now. As I stood in Madison Square Garden marveling at the thousands who were packed in to hear Garvey speak, I reflected on how living a double life had actually become routine.

I'd spent each day dividing my time between the Black Star Line business and the Abyssinian Church construction site. I filed weekly reports to headquarters, and Hoover seemed pleased with the progress I was making. Learning the details about Garvey's day-to-day activities — his motives — was enough for him.

He was convinced that I'd gained Garvey's trust and that no white agent could ever have gotten so close. I was just pleased to be getting paid by the government to keep an eye on Garvey for Du Bois — at least that's the way I continued to rationalize it. I'd written and mailed more anonymous letters to Du Bois, keeping him informed about the intentions of his West Indian nemesis.

But the past year had seen Garvey's image grow to a level that I never could have imagined. I witnessed him becoming an even bigger threat to Du Bois by the day. The Bureau now believed Garvey's UNIA to have some five hundred thousand members — far fewer than Garvey's claim of four million but still an ever-growing and alarming number.

The year had seen Garvey marry Amy Ashwood, only to quickly separate from her and begin living with another one of his West Indian secretaries — Miss Amy Jacques.

Much controversy surrounded that relationship, as Garvey had not divorced his wife. But none of it concerned me. It simply provided entertaining chatter between Reverend Eason, Hubert Harrison, and William Ferris on our nights out at Snappy's Restaurant. The gossip was filled with amusing details about Garvey's personal life.

I found it ironic that men who were so loyal to Garvey took such delight in joking about his habits — his quibbles over certain foods, his insistence on selling his likeness to adoring crowds for outrageous prices, and his obsession with collecting fine pottery.

Sprinkled in with my routine that year had been visits with Professor Gold's friend, Phil Daley. Daley had taken me to the Civic Club on several occasions, a fancy place on Twelfth Street near Fifth Avenue, where many intellectuals — both white and colored — gathered and discussed politics.

I hadn't met Du Bois, but visiting the Civic Club gave me an opportunity to keep abreast of his agenda. "Garvey is becoming more and more dangerous," Daley had said. "Du Bois feels like he's undermining all of the diplomatic work the NAACP has spent years doing."

The year also brought with it a new home, a massive one at that. Loretta had wanted to stop leasing and buy, and she was determined to find something of quality to invest in. For weekends on end we drove the streets looking at various neighborhoods.

She asked every person we met where the safest place in Harlem was to live. We kept getting the same answer: Strivers' Row, which we came to know was an aristocratic area in West Harlem — fairly close to where we'd been living and very close to the land Reverend Powell had purchased for the future Abyssinian Baptist Church.

Strivers' Row consisted of four rows of town houses, two bordering the north and south sides of West 138th, the other two bordering the north and south sides of West 139th. The entire community was nestled in between Seventh and Eighth Avenues. The homes attracted well-paid professionals or "strivers." The colored folks who lived there had supposedly "made it." In fact, most were involved in the fields of law, medicine, the arts, and even architecture. I was likely the only government spy.

We purchased a stunning four-bedroom place for $8,000 — a good chunk of Loretta's inheritance. But she could not have been more impressed with the design and security of the place. There was one room in particular that she believed would be the perfect painting studio. The first day the sales agent allowed us to see inside, Loretta found the upstairs master bedroom, walked out onto the Juliet balcony, and looked out at the view.

"Daddy would have loved this place," she said, "the walnut flooring throughout, the magical, high ceilings. There's just something stunning about the dark wood, white wall contrast everywhere. Simple and clean."

"But it's way too big," I replied. "A king

would be impressed."

"We'll fill it with children. Besides, I can't think of a better way to turn our money into a lot more . . . well . . . money. And we could live here forever."

"*Our* money?"

"Stop it, Sidney. Yes, *our* money."

The window framed her beautifully. She put her hand up to the glass and seemed to dream for a moment.

"This will be my escape," she said. "This is where I will close out the world and feed my soul."

And now, many months later, I had just taken the route from Strivers' Row to Madison Square Garden, avoiding the massive UNIA parade that had taken place. It had begun at 135th Street, made its way through the heart of Harlem, then down the long stretch of Seventh Avenue. It was all part of the UNIA's first International Convention of the Negro Peoples of the World that Garvey had organized.

Eason had asked me to take part but I'd made a habit of not being involved in any of Garvey's grand, public, ceremonial events. I worked with him behind the scenes only. It was my tireless work that made Garvey see me as a loyal UNIA man, but many folks around town — including Reverend Powell

— simply saw me as Harlem's engineer — a man who didn't let political allegiances get in the way of those he served.

Earlier that day, before leaving for Madison Square Garden, I'd spent the morning getting a haircut and purchasing some supplies for Loretta. I walked through the front door at about noon carrying several cans of paint. As I approached Loretta's studio, I saw the usual cast of characters — around ten, all but two of them colored. Loretta had been hosting a weekly gathering of local painters for months. I stopped at the doorway before entering.

"People think the shadows illustrate something evil about America," said Peter Monday in his high-pitched voice, as he stood over his painting, pointing out its various features.

"I see lots of pain, Peter," said Ginger Bouvier, a French woman who'd been in New York for two years. "*Plus de douleur que je peux supporter.* More pain than I can bear."

"The shadows are insignificant," added May Baxter, a tiny copper-skinned women in her forties. "One would be better served focusing on the faces themselves, the joy emanating from each as they delight in tearing off their shirts."

Tony Binn was the youngest of the group — probably no older than eighteen. "The smoke reminds me of a painting I saw at a show last month," he said. "The artist's name is Stuart Davis, and the painting was called *Newark.* Has anyone else seen it or even heard of Davis?"

Everyone shook their heads no except Loretta. "When I saw Davis's *Newark,*" she said, "it hurt me. I can still see it vividly. I see an emerging burst of blood near the center of the painting. The blood is beginning to fill a dormant riverbed. Perhaps it's blood from the city's slain innocent. They've been slaughtered in masses in the adjacent barn or shack by an army of evil occupiers. It makes me recall the bloody images Gustave Flaubert's novel *Salammbô* created in my mind."

Her words took everyone by surprise and seemed out of place for the otherwise casual mood. And she was describing something they'd never seen. It was as if she'd been thinking about the obscure Stuart Davis painting for days and was offering up far more analysis than the group was prepared for. Her words simply confirmed to me that she was still able to go to dark places on a whim — especially when it came to the issue of death. But did she see darkness where there was none?

"Hmm," said Tony Binn with a confused look. "I didn't see any violence at all in Davis's painting."

"They had all of the colors you wanted," I said, interrupting.

"Thank you so much, Love," said Loretta.

"J'ai besoin d'un bon monsieur de faire les choses pour moi," said Ginger.

Loretta translated. "Ginger said she needs a kind gentleman to do such things for her."

"Thank you," I said.

"Yes, I know I am a lucky woman," said Loretta. *"Oui, je sais que je suis une femme très chanceuse."*

"Your French is getting quite good," said Ginger.

"Thanks to you, Oh Wise One of a thousand tongues," said Loretta, beginning to joke a bit, her arms moving about. "All of the greats speak French. Maybe I'm preparing to become a world sensation — a Suzanne Valadon, if you will. *Oui,* Ginger?"

"*Oui.* A master of canvas and language. A savant. *The* . . . Loretta Temple."

The two stood, giving each other a hug and then a kiss on the cheek. They had developed a deep friendship and had considerable respect for each other, Ginger's effusiveness having certainly rubbed off on

Loretta.

Ginger was not married, had an abundance of wealth, and exhibited much more independence than the average American woman. She was quite the painter herself and had even taught at the University of Paris. Her fascination with colored artists and Harlem life was what had brought her to America — a sabbatical of sorts.

"Suzanne Valadon?" said Ginger, sitting back down. "*Non, Loretta, vous serez mieux que sa.* You will be better than her."

Ginger rarely held her tongue about any subject, even in front of men, and there was never enough wine on hand for her. But she was a delight. Her willingness to show public affection toward Loretta, regardless of whoever was around, had been good for my wife. And with me rarely at home, it was helping her recover. Ginger also taught a weekly Impressionism class in Greenwich Village, made up of about twenty students, most of them white, and Loretta was enthralled by it.

"I'm off to the office," I said, purposely not mentioning the fact that I was actually heading to Madison Square Garden.

"Oh, Sidney," Loretta said, grabbing something from the desk, "will you do me a favor and drop these invitations off on your way. I've invited a couple of the neighbors to the party. Both live here on The Row."

"Who?" I asked as she handed me two cards.

"Dr. Louis T. Wright and Vertner Tandy. Vertner is the architect. You two will have plenty to talk about. I met them both at the Strivers' Row Homeowners Committee meeting last week."

"Ah, Loretta," said Ginger, "only one week 'til your birthday. You must take her shopping, Sidney."

"Yes," I said, smiling. "I must. Listen, Loretta, Reverend Eason will also be attending."

"Wonderful. He promised to show me some of his drawings. Make sure you remind him to bring them."

Later I did just that, as I stood with Eason near a tunnel entryway directly behind the stage that he and an entourage of UNIA officials would soon speak from.

"I don't think your wife will be impressed with my artistic skills," yelled Eason over the noise of the crowd.

"But she thinks you can do no wrong," I countered.

"I hope all these Negroes packed in this hotbox feel the same way about Marcus," he shouted. We both looked up into the sea of black faces — slowly panning back and forth. "God knows one of these riled up folks may have been sent here by the devil. The same devil that sent George Tyler."

Shortly after Tyler had shot Garvey that past year, he'd apparently jumped to his death while in jail. That fact merely added to our suspicion about who'd sent him to kill Garvey. As for me, I wondered who'd sent Tyler, Sleepy, and his heavyset partner.

I tried to avoid speculation, as it could have been anyone. But all of us had become paranoid ever since — constantly looking over our shoulders — flinching at the slightest clang or pop. UNIA staff members had received several other threats over the phone and each time had notified the police. But it became apparent that the men in uniform had a strong hatred for Garvey, seemingly not caring if he was assassinated.

I was learning that being colored and contacting the police for help didn't go together — especially if it involved one Negro threatening or harming another. New York was like the rest of the country in that regard. Harlemites spoke openly about how the police would just as soon we all dispose of one another.

I'd spent a good part of the year trying to forget about how I'd disposed of Sleepy and

Jumpy. I'd actually left them lying there in the weeds, and out of pure nervousness, had driven their Cadillac as far east as possible before walking back home that night. I'd cleaned up the glass from the broken wine bottles, replacing them with new bottles so the bullet hole in the wall didn't show.

When Loretta arrived, I lied again, telling her that someone had tried to break in earlier that day while we were both gone, hence why the door was practically split in two and barely hanging on the hinges. The news only deepened her desire to move.

The next day I sent an anonymous letter to the local coroner, and the bodies were removed some days later. Not one time during the months following the incident did a police officer come by our neighborhood and question people about their deaths. They were just two more dead Negroes to them.

"I often wonder," yelled Eason, "if we need even more young brothers protecting Marcus."

"Probably!" I shouted back.

The past year had seen Garvey step up security. Marcellus Strong was his headman and the leader of a handful of armed bodyguards assigned to Garvey. There were also at least ten African Legionnaires surrounding him at all times. In fact, moments before Garvey entered Madison Square Garden, a policeman tried to approach him and couldn't get within fifty feet. A message had to be relayed to Garvey.

The police department had gotten used to such inconveniences. They'd grown tired of the UNIA leader and his outrageous processions that covered the streets whenever he made a simple trip to a department store or museum. Anytime Garvey went for so much as a walk to a fruit stand, he was sandwiched between an army of men. Anyone attempting to take a shot at him, as Tyler had, would at best only be able to hit one of his officers.

On top of this, ever since the shooting, UNIA headquarters had been surrounded with African Legionnaires. It would have been difficult for the president of the United States himself to get into the building. Garvey was easily the most protected Negro in America — from sunup to sundown.

"I wish you had seen the parade," shouted Eason. "I can't imagine there will ever be a more spectacular scene. Thousands lined the streets — many of them white — just to take a look at the spectacle. White folks ain't never seen that many Negroes in one place. We done scared 'em to death! I bet it's the biggest parade in New York history. Had to be over four hundred automobiles took part, and I ain't lyin' to ya, brother."

"Where was Garvey's automobile positioned?"

"Near the front, just behind several policemen and their horses. But listen. It was our marching band, the choir, and uniformed Legionnaires that made it special — made it a truly colorful event. There was such harmony, and everyone marched with amazing unity. And the Black Cross nurses, dressed in their white robes, looked beautiful. I'm tellin' ya! You needed to see it, Sidney."

"I caught a glimpse of it," I yelled.

"What?" he screamed.

"I said I caught a glimpse of it — the very end of it."

"Well, it was true history. And there were so many banners and flags representing UNIA members from different states and countries. If it's true that there are four hundred million Negroes in the world, it felt like every last one was there today lining the streets. All in all it was as if royalty were parading through New York. But what we're seeing right here is just as spectacular. Ain't no doubt. This here rally is a monster."

Again we surveyed the crowd of about

twenty-five thousand. The energy in the building was more ferocious than anything I'd ever witnessed. It was at that very moment that I truly recognized the power of Marcus Garvey.

"Time for me to take the stage," shouted Eason.

I remained standing near the tunnel entryway as he joined the other UNIA dignitaries — many of them from other parts of the world. There had to be a few hundred of them — some dressed in regular suits, others in traditional African and Caribbean apparel.

All of them took their seats on the huge stage that had been built for the special event. It was a high platform surrounded by uniformed African Legionnaires. I knew that Madison Square Garden wasn't built to hold that many people. Not only were all of the stadium seats occupied, thousands sat in chairs on the massive stadium floor. Many others stood in any available spot they could find. Garvey's organizing committee had spent months preparing for the parade and rally, and boy had they delivered.

I found myself studying certain individuals in the crowd. One man seated directly in front of the stage about twenty rows back kept reaching into his coat pocket. I walked toward the side of the stage to get a better look. Again, the man reached into his pocket.

I nudged one of the Legionnaires and pointed at the shifty man. Two Legionnaires began to make their way toward the twentieth row. But the man removed his hand and simply pulled out a five-inch wooden stick with some fabric wrapped around it. He unrolled it and revealed a tiny red, black, and green flag. Those were the official UNIA colors, and the man had made the flag himself. Still, the Legionnaires took his jacket, searched it, but found nothing. These kinds of false alarms had become the norm for those of us surrounding Garvey. But it was better to be safe than sorry.

16

The stage was now completely full and a band began to play. I stared at Garvey in his academic cap and gown of purple, green, and gold. I figured he wore such a gown because of the insecurity he felt when comparing himself to the more academically accomplished Dr. Du Bois.

I wondered why a man without any degree to speak of would have the audacity to dress as such. I continued staring at him, wondering how insane he actually was and what wild exhibitions of his I'd have to endure in the future. His act was far too ostentatious for my taste.

The band continued and my mind began to wander. I recalled sitting in a meeting that past June that Hoover had called — the only one I'd been summoned to attend that year. Agent James Wormley Jones was also ordered to be at the New York gathering. There I learned that he'd been training

Garvey's African Legion soldiers in Newport News, Virginia.

Also present at the meeting had been my old training buddy Bobby Ellington along with Taylor Knox, the racist agent from training. He was sitting between Agent Speed and Paul Mann, who gave reports on Du Bois and James Weldon Johnson. We were told that Agent Mann was now exclusively assigned to Du Bois and Johnson. Of course, through my talks with Daley, I knew the facts about Du Bois. Mann only knew what lies Du Bois had fed him. But that didn't stop him from spouting platitudes to Hoover at the meeting, the same ones he'd already told me about at Snappy's. The two of us had met several more times over the year, but now he had the boss's ear.

"Mr. Hoover, Du Bois is likely more dangerous than any Negro in America," said Mann. "He's as familiar with the intricacies of our government as any man I've ever met. You'd think he'd worked within the president's cabinet. Given enough time, he's more than capable of building his NAACP into the most powerful communist organization in the world."

"I'm mainly concerned about his ability to raise money via the Bolsheviks," said Hoover, still not looking a day older than twenty-one. "Follow the money, Agent Mann."

"Of the two, Garvey's attracting a more dangerous element," said Speed. "According to Jones's reports, it's only a matter of time before blood is shed on a grand scale."

"He's broken no laws," I said.

"Yet," Speed countered.

"They're one and the same — Garvey and Du Bois," said Hoover. "One's more calculating and diplomatic; the other more arrogant and grandstanding. But they're both on the same team. They're both communists trying to build organizations powerful enough to overthrow the government. God help us if they join forces. And the Bolsheviks have enough money to bankroll them for a century."

"Garvey's no fool," said Jones, "but some of his Legionnaires are foolishly searching for a fight — a physical one — and Garvey will ultimately have to be held accountable for their actions."

"Again, as we sit here today, he has broken no laws," I said. "I'll be the first to report it when he does. That's what I think I've been assigned to do."

I was knowingly speaking boldly — telling them what I really thought — because I knew they needed me. I'd gotten so close to

Garvey, and the odds of any future agent doing so were bad.

"As long as you're not covering anything up, Temple," said Speed, standing to confront me — pointing his finger.

"How dare you question me!" I replied, also standing.

"There's shit all around him," said Speed. "All you have to do is help him step in it."

"Easy, you two," Ellington interjected, rising and positioning himself between us.

"We want him sitting in a courtroom with shit on his shoes," said Speed. "Shit we can use to send his ass to jail. There's no way in hell he's building that empire on the up-and-up."

"I'll do my job; you do yours," I said. "It's not my fault Garvey would never let the likes of you within a mile of him."

Speed just stood there huffing and puffing, his bald head getting redder by the second, the veins on his temples pulsating. I stared directly at him.

Taylor Knox, with his racist behind, hadn't said a word, but he patted Speed on the shoulder as if congratulating him for scolding me. I think he was simply Speed's assistant at this point and Ellington was Hoover's.

"Are his sales documents in order, Agent

Temple?" asked Hoover. "Those proving his ownership of the ship?"

"I have never been able to gain access to those documents," I answered, calmly sitting again, regaining my composure. "But he's been negotiating the sale of two more ships. One is a steam-paddle ship called the SS *Shadyside,* and the other is a yacht — the SS *Kanawha.* He may even officially own them at this point."

"I've recently been added to Garvey's publicity committee," said Jones. "The odds are long, but it may afford me an opportunity to look at the books — at least a better opportunity than Temple."

"Jones might be right," I added, "but I don't think those books are ever leaving Garvey's office."

"Where does he keep them?" Hoover asked.

"He keeps them locked in his office. I've purchased equipment for the *Yarmouth* before and had to turn all receipts in to his secretary, Miss Jacques. She logs everything in a large book then places the receipts in separate envelopes. I saw where she stored all of the items — in a padlocked file cabinet behind his desk."

"Question," said Speed. "Where does she log the thousands of dollars being given to

Garvey by all of those foolish followers of his? Huh, Temple?"

"In a separate book."

"What would it take for you to gain access?" asked Hoover.

"It'd be next to impossible. But he's asked me to upgrade the entire electrical system throughout UNIA headquarters soon. I'll have access at that point, but he'll have to be out of the office and have no one manning the door. What are the odds?"

"Make it work, Temple," said Hoover, "even if it's months from now."

"I'll do my best, but he has two men in particular that split time overseeing security detail. If one is at Garvey's side while he's out and about, the other is heading up security at the offices."

"Tell me about them," Hoover ordered.

"The first is William Grant who just might be the meanest son of a bitch I've ever met. The other is Marcellus Strong. Both are more than willing to give their lives for Garvey and are highly trained strongmen. I've seen Grant beat one man to within an inch of his life. He's a war veteran from the West Indies who heads up the Tiger Division of Garvey's African Legion. He trains his Legionnaires military style."

"Yeah, we've had words about my training

tactics on more than one occasion," added Jones. "He's a monster of a man. I'll vouch for that."

"Again," said Hoover, "make it work. You've been trained to handle such men, Temple. I know it may take some time, but we need to see those sales documents."

"I can also confirm what Temple is saying about the *Shadyside* and *Kanawha,*" said Jones. "From what I've heard, he's raised thousands by recently mailing out adverts, boasting about these specific boats — getting folks to invest in them."

"The question is," said Hoover, "did he officially own the ships when he began soliciting funds for them? Does he even own them as we sit here today? What we need is to compare these adverts with the official bills of sale for these two ships."

"I'm not sure the adverts had dates on them," I said.

"Well if they did, and that date precedes the date of the official sale, Mr. Garvey has a major problem. We must get access to those documents."

"Garvey is sloppy," said Speed. "We knew that before you two came on board. It's just a matter of time before his ambition forces him to slip up. And when he does, don't try to catch him."

"Why should we believe Garvey will continue to trust you, Agent Temple?" asked Hoover.

"Because the first successful voyage of the *Yarmouth* was a feather in my cap. He credited my mechanical work for its safe return. And that first voyage was vital in Garvey's eyes."

"Why?"

"He wanted his followers to actually see something tangible — something grand — to make them believe in him like never before. He wanted to make the first launch a big to-do. And it worked. There were thousands of folks gathered at the pier, cheering and crying when they saw the *Yarmouth* for the first time. As Garvey stood there with them and watched the boat sail off into the distance, the cheering and crying turned to silence and almost worship. The crowd saw Garvey as the man who was going to take them from hell to heaven. I was standing there. His power was real."

"But the second voyage was a disaster," said Speed. "According to your own report, Temple, Garvey had a cargo full of whiskey aboard when it began to capsize a hundred miles from New York. You reported that he had to call the coast guard to help him save it from sinking. And this was in the middle of Prohibition laws going into effect. He didn't blame you for that mess?"

"No. He blamed Captain Cockburn, who ignored my advice and refused my consultation. The whiskey trip was to be the *Yarmouth's* second official voyage. I had adamantly advised against it from the beginning, telling Garvey the ship was in terrible condition. And at first, Cockburn agreed with me. But I think he cut a side deal with the distillery and suddenly changed his mind, telling Garvey the ship's condition had miraculously been improved. Again, I told Garvey not to ship out. But he did. And when the voyage failed, Garvey knew I was one of the only advisors he could trust. My good standing was sealed. Garvey had me attend to the ship afterward and a third voyage was a success. The ship has since returned from the Caribbean. In fact, Cockburn has been fired and a new man, Hugh Mulzac, is now the first officer of the *Yarmouth.*"

"What was Garvey doing with all that whiskey anyway?" asked Speed. "Tell Mr. Hoover what you told me on the phone."

"Trying to get it out of the country before the Prohibition laws went into effect," I said. "He'd made a deal with a distillery to ship it to Havana for them."

"He seems to be involving himself in more business than he can ultimately handle," said Hoover. "He's getting in over his head, and that's a good thing for us. Stay on top of it. Thanks to the telephone numbers Agent Jones has been able to wire to us, we now have both his office and home phones tapped."

"That won't bear any fruit," I said. "Garvey never discusses business over the telephone. Ever! He always assumes the authorities are listening."

"Well then," Hoover replied, "that makes it doubly important that you gain access. Now, Agent Mann, Du Bois is clearly more involved in international affairs than you can handle alone, with his attending these Pan-African conferences in Europe and all. We want you to stay put, but you'll soon have company. We intend to place another agent within his NAACP as soon as possible, perhaps one with some foreign relations experience. We need to know what's being discussed at these conferences — what his detailed plans are and perhaps the names of those helping to fund him."

"Any names of potential Du Bois funders we can gather will serve us well," said Speed. "If those Reds get wind that the United States government is aware of them

261

funding a communist sympathizer, we can put the fear of God in them. They may be proud foreign communists, but they don't want us to know their names. They'll close their checkbooks faster than you can say boo, and perhaps that will help dry up Du Bois's funds."

Upon hearing those words I knew why I had to stay in the mix. Listening to Hoover and Speed talk about Garvey made it clear that they feared him for the wrong reasons. They thought he was a communist. He wasn't. They thought he wanted to overthrow the government. He didn't. He simply wanted to be solely responsible for the plight of the Negro and part of that meant crushing Du Bois. So what I'd already known was being reaffirmed — both the Bureau and Garvey were Du Bois's enemies.

I continued listening as Hoover told me that the government's interest had cooled on Max Eastman. I was to focus exclusively on Garvey, which was good news because I didn't have to shadow Claude McKay, who'd just returned from overseas and been hired by Eastman to edit his *Liberator*. Hubert Harrison, Eason, and I were spending quite a bit of time with the poet down in Greenwich Village talking politics, and I would have hated having to share any of it with Hoover.

A roar came over the crowd and my attention was drawn back to the present, back to the Madison Square Garden stage. Garvey had finally been called to the platform and was accompanied by several aides.

They walked him to the podium and, before heading back to their seats, referred to him as "Your Majesty," something that made me sick to my stomach. He had to wait at least five minutes before the screaming crowd quieted down. That gave him time to take out a perfumed handkerchief, breathe into it for a while, and gather his thoughts. According to Eason, he'd been doing this for years.

"I have sent a telegram of greeting to Eamon de Valera," Garvey began. "He is the president of the Irish Republic. The message said, 'Please accept sympathy of Negroes of the world for your cause. We believe Ireland should be free even as Africa shall be free for the Negroes of the world. Keep up the fight for a free Ireland. Signed, Marcus Garvey, President-General of the Universal Negro Improvement Association.' "

The crowd rose and gave a thunderous applause. Garvey waited for the right moment and then shouted, "We are the descendants of a suffering people. We are the descendants of a people determined to suffer no longer."

As the crowd roared, I panned the adoring faces again. It was as if they saw God in him.

"We shall now organize the four hundred million Negroes of the world into a vast organization to plant the banner of freedom on the great continent of Africa. We have no apologies to make and will make none. We do not desire what has belonged to others, though others have always sought to deprive us of that which belonged to us. We new Negroes — we men who have returned from war — we will dispute every inch of the way until we win. We will begin by framing a Bill of Rights of the Negro Race with a Constitution to guide the life and destiny of the four hundred million. The Constitution of the United States means that every white American would shed his blood to defend that Constitution. The Constitution of the Negro Race will mean that every Negro will shed his blood to defend his Constitution. If Europe is for the Europeans, then Africa shall be for the black peoples of the world. We say it, we mean it."

There was no doubting that he meant it. And there was no doubting that he believed

America belonged to whites. Du Bois would strongly disagree, and so would I. But the screaming audience seemingly concurred with their Black Moses. He was clearly framing what it meant to be a separatist.

"Wheresoever I go," he bellowed, "whether it is England, France, or Germany, I am told, 'This is a white man's country.' Wheresoever I travel throughout the United States of America, I am made to understand that I am a nigger. If the Englishman claims England as his native habitat and the Frenchman claims France, the time has come for four hundred million Negroes to claim Africa as their native land."

The noise rose to a pitch so loud that my bones rattled. Garvey had the audience by the throat, and he could do with them as he wished. I wondered if Du Bois stood a chance.

17

After Garvey spoke I headed home, even though the event was scheduled to continue well into the night. I was looking forward to some quiet time with Loretta and couldn't drive fast enough. Approaching Strivers' Row, I recalled the last letter I'd sent to Du Bois back in July. It was very much to the point.

Dear Dr. Du Bois,
Please know that the Bureau of Investigation is planning on placing a new agent inside the NAACP. He will tout his foreign affairs expertise. His job is to make a list of all possible communist donors you may have. I don't presume to know if you have any, as that is not my concern. Just be mindful of keeping your donor list top secret, and be on the

lookout when hiring new staff.

Sincerely,
The Loyalist

I approached Strivers' Row's Seventh Avenue gate, and Ivan, the uniformed young man who stood guard and let tenants in and out of the back alleyway, gave me a wave.

"How are you, Mr. Temple?" he asked, pulling the gate open and letting me drive through.

"Real good, Ivan. Thanks for asking."

I parked, got out, took off my gun and holster, then placed it under the car's hood. I'd made a habit of doing such, knowing I could never let Loretta see me with it.

I'd also purchased another pistol and had placed it in a secure spot in my upstairs closet. I'd cut away several slabs of wood to create a storage place under the closet floor. Along with the pistol, I'd stored an extra magazine, several boxes of bullets, and an extra holster.

I closed the hood and headed inside. As I walked down the hallway, I could hear Loretta and Ginger — mainly Ginger, her voice so theatrical, her words so enunciated. Even when she was speaking English, it felt like French.

I slowed my walk, stopping several feet

from the doorway. I should have entered the room and let them know I was home, but instead I eavesdropped.

"He was a disgusting man, Loretta. I detested him in the end. And to think, for six years I thought of him as a prince of sorts — a charming, honest gentleman."

"I want nothing more than for you to find true love again, Ginger."

"True love? I cannot have it again, as you say, because I never had it to begin with. The next time will be the first. But it matters not. Because I will never marry again. A man's nature is to sleep with this woman and that woman. They cannot help it. Besides, Olivier only married me because he knew of my father's wealth. *Dégoûtant!* Disgusting!"

"You're only twenty-nine, Ginger. Have faith. And you're beautiful."

"Oh? I don't feel beautiful."

"You have what so many women want. You're tall, have such satiny skin, and have the eyes — or better yet, the overall face — of a modern-day Cleopatra. You're stunning, Ginger."

"*Vous êtes trop aimable.* You're too kind. Though I must say, I'm constantly being asked if I'm Egyptian. Are Egyptian men less promiscuous than French? Why do I even bother asking such a foolish question? Of course they are. But if I'm not mistaken, Cleopatra was actually Greek. Maybe I'll travel to Athens."

"Maybe you will meet an American."

"They haven't the artistic souls of French-men. They bore me. I am not referring to colored American men. Colored American men have a natural soulfulness. They have an artistic quality to them that is born out of overcoming years of mistreatment — of having to reach down deep and find creative ways to distract their minds from all the ugliness. Your husband — your Sidney — is encouraging your art. It's lovely."

"I'm home," I said, casually approaching the doorway. "Hello, Ginger."

"*Bonjour,* Sidney."

"I'll let you two continue your visit," I said. "I have to go down the street and make a telephone call."

"Why don't you two have a telephone installed in this gigantic castle?" asked Ginger.

"Sidney doesn't want people from work calling the house late at night," said Loretta.

"It's a man's world," said Ginger. "*Il est un monde d'hommes.* I repeat everything in French, Sidney, so your wife can better pick up the language."

"I see. Well, carry on, you two."

Moments later I parked on Seventh Avenue and phoned Momma. She had just turned sixty and hadn't been feeling well. I dialed the operator and waited for the connection. After several rings she picked up.

"Temple residence," she said with a raspy voice that worried me.

"It's Sidney, Momma."

"Hi, Sugar."

"You feelin' any better?"

"Oh yeah, Sugar. Momma's fine."

"Did you get that money I sent you?"

"Yes, Sugar."

"Your voice is cracking, Momma."

"Oh . . . I've just been havin' a little trouble breathing, Sugar. That's all. Don't you worry about me. You been sleepin' any better?"

"Yeah," I said. "The doctor prescribed me some barbital pills. I just take one at night and sleep like a baby."

"Sure am glad to hear that."

"Listen, Momma, and listen real good. I've done spoke to Professor Gold, and you remember the little place Loretta and I had on his property?"

"Uh-huh."

"Well, I want you to go stay there — at least for a while. The clean air in Vermont

270

will help heal your lungs. I don't think it's good for you to live in the city anymore — not Milwaukee *or* Chicago, and definitely not New York. You need a slower pace. And with you not having to work no more, it'll be real good for you."

"Now, Sugar, you know I got my sister real close by."

"Now, Momma, Aunt Coretta's in Chicago, and ain't goin' nowhere. Besides, you don't see her but about once a year. Loretta has already agreed to come help you pack and take the train with you — help you get situated. You can get rid of what you don't need."

"But, Sugar, what's Momma gonna do out there all alone?"

"But you're all alone now. And this way you'll be closer to us. Besides, the Golds are like family. They'll visit with you every day and take you into town when you need. And if you wanna work, they have plenty of gardening and cleaning you can do."

"I just don't wanna be that far away from Coretta, Sugar. Darn well goin' on seventy, and she ain't doin' so good. Don't know how much longer she's got."

"What if Aunt Coretta moved with you?"

"Well, I'd have to think on that, Sugar."

"You'd be able to take care of her then."

271

"Let me think on it."

"Okay. But I'm serious about this now."

"I know you is. Momma appreciates that. Tell me about your new house, Sugar."

"It's a big ol' four-bedroom place."

"What's it look like, Sugar, the neighborhood, the house? Paint a picture for Momma."

"Well, Seventh and Eighth Avenues run north and south. 138th and 139th Streets run east and west. Strivers' Row is basically a block that includes those four streets."

"Is there a good church nearby?"

"Yes, Momma."

"All right. Just wanna make sure you two are attendin' service, that's all."

"Anyhow, we live on the southern side of 139th. That's row three. It shares a private back alleyway with row two."

"Ooh, you got your own private alleyway?"

"Yeah. If you're headin' north on Seventh you turn left and enter through a big old black iron gate. Ours is the fourth place on the right. 'Course I'm talkin' about entering through the back."

"I can't wait to see it, Sugar."

Momma and I talked a little longer, and I did my best to explain to her what Harlem was like. I was hoping she'd soon be able to see it for herself.

I returned home to find Loretta alone in her studio, hard at work.

"Can I give you a bath?" I asked.

"Yes."

Moments later I sat in a wooden chair just behind the tub in the middle of our all-white washroom. Loretta was relaxing with her back to me — seemingly in a daze. The only sound was that of me dipping a white cloth into the soapy water before running it along her neck and shoulders. I then scrubbed her fingertips one by one — the cloth absorbing different shades of caked-on blue paint.

"I should be washing your hands," she said, grabbing mine, turning them, and surveying my oil-stained palms. "I want you to start using gloves when you're in that engine room. You need to protect your beautiful hands, Love."

She interlocked her right hand with my left, leaned back, and we kissed, just above her left shoulder.

"Turn your body around and face me," I said.

She turned around, her hips splashing water over the side of the tub in the process. Looking into her eyes and marveling at her damp, buttery-looking skin, it took all of the restraint I could muster not to undress, ease into the water, and have my needs satisfied. But this wasn't about me.

"Lie back."

Her head rested against the opposite end of the tub, and she continued eyeing me. Her chin was barely above water, and I could see portions of her nakedness through the suds. I reached into the warm water and grabbed her feet, pulling them toward me. Taking the cloth, I began washing her feet.

"What did I do to deserve this?" she asked.

"You said yes to me three years ago."

I dropped the cloth back in the water and began caressing and massaging her arches and heels, then moved on to her toes.

"Why don't you ever talk about work?" she asked.

"Because when I'm with you I want it to be all about you."

"But I want to know how you spend your days. Do you spend most of the time at the new church site or on the ships?"

"At the church site and with Reverend Powell at his office. And at my own office."

"And with Mr. Garvey, right?"

"No!" I snapped, stopping the foot rub.

"Jeez . . . I just asked."

"You know I spend no time with him. None! I barely even know him. He's into political stuff I don't concern myself with.

When it comes to the contractual work I do for the Black Star Line, I just go directly to the pier, do my work, and leave."

"All right. Keep rubbing."

"Listen," I said, massaging her feet again, "Reverend Eason's the only one affiliated with the UNIA that I'm close to, and that's because of his connection to your father. And we share mutual friends."

"Like who?"

"Just people. People you don't know. Just like I don't know many of your new friends."

"Was Reverend Eason at that parade today? It was quite a spectacle."

"You saw it? I thought you were here working all day."

"Ginger and I went and had lunch. I've never seen so many people. All of the flags and colors, the men dressed in military uniforms. What does it all mean? And why are so many men and women following Mr. Garvey?"

"He's a powerful speaker from outside the United States. They've never seen anyone quite like him. But most parades do draw crowds."

"Not like that."

I tried to get a sense of what she might be thinking. She was more curious than usual, and I wanted to change the subject.

"Am I rubbing too hard?"

"No. You know, the more I hear about Mr. Garvey, the more I don't like him. Ginger thinks he's a hateful man. Why is Reverend Eason so pleasant and Mr. Garvey so . . ."

"Like I just said, I don't really know him. Just like a Coca-Cola deliveryman doesn't know the president of Coca-Cola. I just have a contract to work on his ships."

"Sorry. I'll let it go. Last thing I'm trying to do is upset you."

"It's okay. I'm not upset."

"Good," she said, closing her eyes. "That feels so amazing."

"Am I the best at it?"

"I don't know. You're the only one who's ever rubbed my feet."

"Hey!"

"I'm just pullin' your leg, silly," she said. "You're so thoughtful. So kind."

I grabbed her ankles and began sliding my grip down to her calves.

"How's that?" I asked, massaging.

"So good."

After a minute or two I leaned forward, sliding my hands around from her calves to her thighs. Again I massaged, but with broad strokes under the warm water.

"Magic hands," she said.

Moments later, her eyes still closed, she

276

took my right hand and slid it farther under water. Running it along her inner thigh, she placed it where she wanted. I needn't rush now, as we were in perfect rhythm. I wanted this to be entirely about her.

18

I was about to leave the office and make my way to meet Mr. Daley at the Civic Club when the Bureau phone rang. Much to my surprise it was Hoover, and I'd never heard him this upset.

"What in God's name was all of that African garbage marching up and down the street the other day?" he asked. "The pictures and reports we're getting in to D.C. are disgusting. Your telegram didn't quite do all of that African pageantry justice, Q3Z."

"It's simply a symbolic exercise in black unity," I said. "That's all at this point."

"Well it flies in the face of everything America stands for. And we won't have it. This is the U.S. Not some damn monkey Africa. Stay glued to that sonofabitch, you hear? I want his colored rear end behind bars. He's lucky the legal system has its protocol. I'm trying to remain patient."

"I'm on top of it," I said, sick to my stomach at his unabashed racism.

"He's scaring real Americans to death with all this wild, primitive behavior. Parading down the damn streets of *our* America. And it makes me look bad. Attorney general is irate! These damn photographs! Look like a bunch of rabid animals. Why can't they be more like you, Q3Z?"

"I don't know how to answer that, sir."

"Don't. But make no mistake. He's taking his cues from commie Russia about how to start a revolution. Over my dead body, you hear?"

"Yes."

"Harlem," he angrily said, "is becoming just what I feared it would with the likes of Garvey and Du Bois and the rest of these commies stoking the flames of hate. It has become an inferno of black madness."

Minutes later I drove slowly enough to make out the face of the man driving about three cars behind me in an Auburn Beauty-Six Roadster. It was blue with black fenders. It seemed that every left or right turn I'd made, the vehicle had followed. I was heading to the Civic Club to meet Daley, something I had no reason to keep secret, but still, if I was being followed — why?

I was now driving south on Fifth Avenue with Central Park to my right. As long as I continued on Fifth, I would eventually hit the Civic Club at Twelfth Street. But I made a right on Fifty-fifth Street instead. I sped up and made a quick right, weaving in and out of traffic until I'd lost him.

An hour later I sat with Daley in a large, smoke-filled dining room at the Civic Club, surrounded by dark wood panels, thick chairs, and scholarly looking men. It was about six in the evening and the place was filling up quickly. Ideas that would affect all of colored America were hatched here and often by white men. Yet, the place embodied integration like no other, and I felt very much at home.

"What exactly is it like being associated with Garvey?" asked Daley, sipping his coffee. "I can't imagine. Why even bother being linked to him?"

"I'm an engineer. I don't let politics get in the way of making a wage. Some of us can't afford to be so selective. Some might ask why I'm associated with the Abyssinian Church — you know — some who have a disdain for religion."

"Reverend Powell and Garvey are hardly viewed in the same way — by the overall general public, I mean."

280

"Look, it's a job, okay? How many white ship owners do you know who'd be willing to hire me? The answer is none. And how many colored men do you know who can afford to turn down a job? Let us not forget the difference between you and me, Mr. Daley."

"I just worry for you, that's all. Garvey has a lot of enemies."

Daley raised his eyebrows at me as a waitress set down a thick steak in front of him. It looked like it'd barely been cooked, and he'd ordered no bread, vegetables, or potatoes to go with it. Just a big, fat, greasy, raw-looking steak. I wasn't eating but was enjoying a hot cup of coffee with milk and sugar.

"Can you believe," he said, chewing his steak, "that Garvey named himself Provisional President of Africa at the convention he held?"

"No. I can't."

"Does he not understand that Africa is an enormous continent with over forty countries, each seeking to reinstate its own unique political, tribal, and ideological beliefs? Why would they want to rid themselves of one foreign ruler, only to gain another?"

"They wouldn't," I said, sipping.

"He does the continent a tremendous disservice with his proclamation. I was also dumbfounded to learn that he has never even been to Africa."

"He hasn't?" I asked.

"No."

I took a sip of my coffee and observed the entire room. There had to be at least fifty men in the place, and at each table, groups were engaging in fervid conversation.

"Is that who I think it is?" I asked.

"Who?"

"At the front door, walking in with the other two men."

"Ah, yes. That indeed is Dr. Du Bois. I must introduce you this time . . . once he's been seated."

"Can I ask one favor?"

"Certainly."

"I'd rather you not mention my work with Garvey's Black Star Line."

"Done!"

I watched as Du Bois and his two colleagues — one colored, one white — walked over and sat at a far corner table. He was dressed impeccably in a brown suit with a golden tie.

"Come with me," said Daley.

He led me through the dimly lit room, and we made our way toward the back corner — the muted light from the lamp above Du Bois's table serving as an orangish spotlight on the political giant. I was surprised at how calm my nerves were. It was as if I'd been destined to meet the legend.

"Willy, how are you?" asked Daley, as the two shook hands.

"Very nice to see you, Phil. I'm doing well."

"I'd like you to meet a good friend of mine. This is Sidney Temple. He's intricately involved in the planning phase of the Abyssinian Church. He's an engineer."

"That's marvelous. It's a pleasure to make your acquaintance, Sidney."

"It is truly an honor, Dr. Du Bois," I said, shaking his hand.

"You two sit," said Du Bois.

"Good to see you, Elmore," said Daley, sitting. "How are you, Carl?"

He shook the two gentlemen's hands and I followed suit as Du Bois engaged me.

"Mr. Temple, I do believe the development and completion of that church will do more for Harlem in the way of symbolism than just about anything I can imagine. And in corresponding with Reverend Powell, he feels the same way. I wish you all the success in the world."

"Thank you," I said. "With several architects being attached at different points, my part of the undertaking will likely take at least three years to complete."

"Willy," said Daley, "I think it's safe to say that Sidney here has staked out his place as a member of the Talented Tenth. He graduated last year with a master's degree from the distinguished Middlebury College. With honors."

"Outstanding," said Du Bois. "Wish more of our people would get traditional educations. They need to learn more than basic farming, carpentry, and home economics. May Booker T. Washington rest in peace, and may his Tuskegee Institute continue to thrive, but our people are more than industrial laborers. Need to develop their minds."

"To do so," said Daley, "would certainly mean attending so-called 'white institutions.' The loud voice of Marcus Garvey is still ringing in my ears — saying your people should steer clear of such places."

I could see Du Bois's mind wandering. He calmly lit a gold-tipped Benson & Hedges cigarette and took a puff as the four of us waited for him to break the silence. Finally, he sipped his coffee and continued.

"My good friend James Weldon Johnson

makes a habit of stating our NAACP creed. It's as follows: The only possible end of the race problem in the United States to which we can now look without despair is one which embraces the fullest cooperation between white and black in all the phases of national activity."

"I profoundly concur," I excitedly said.

Du Bois continued. "As you well know, friends, Marcus Garvey and I don't agree on anything, save our support for the Dyer Anti-Lynching Bill. I'm doing my best not to engage in a public war of words with him. I fear such a sparring match would only embolden him and his impetuous followers."

"Hearing the sound of his own voice is enough to embolden Garvey," said Daley. "He wants nothing more than for you to treat him as your equal. And engaging him would suggest just that to the greater public. You're doing well to stay silent."

"But for how long?" asked the dark-chocolate-skinned Carl. "With every divisive word he utters, a new person joins the ranks of the UNIA rather than the NAACP. We may be losing this war of words."

"As it relates to the masses today . . . perhaps," said Du Bois. "But with respect to the clairvoyant minority — those of us sitting here included — the higher ground is ours. And through humility, patience, and a well-thought-out, well-crafted agenda, it shall remain ours."

"I heard that Mr. Garvey railed against you at Liberty Hall after your return from Paris," said Daley. "In fact, he's rather preoccupied with bringing your name up *whenever* he speaks to his throng at Liberty Hall."

"The mere mention of Liberty Hall," said Du Bois, "reminds me of Garvey's fascination with Ireland's struggle for independence. He named his paper, the *Negro World,* after the *Irish World.* And he named his Liberty Hall after the Liberty Hall in Dublin. But I would like to remind my Jamaican counterpart of something: When it comes to the Irish, no people in the world have gone with blither spirit to kill niggers — from Kingston to Delhi and from Kumasi to Fiji — than they."

Daley and I sat there chatting a bit longer before heading back to our table. I felt so empowered — so much more attached to Du Bois. Shaking his hand and looking him in the eye had given even more weight to the work I was doing. It further strengthened my support for him and allowed me to feel his indignation toward Garvey. The

Jamaican's rise was obviously weighing on the Harvard man. But not enough to deter him. In fact, after that evening I was more certain than ever that Du Bois had the strength and vision to carry us home.

Later in the week I left Snappy's and headed to my office, having just heard Agent Mann go on and on about Du Bois's travel habits. Apparently he was out of town all the time. "He's lecture happy," Mann had said. "I think his ego is much like you explained Garvey's being. Except Du Bois is constantly pandering to the Jews. He's addicted to the applause, too. Damn commie."

I was glad that I'd survived the meeting without slapping him. But when I walked into my office a few minutes later and picked up the Bureau phone, Speed sounded like he wanted to slap me.

"Don't go stickin' your damn chest out like you're some colored Harlem king all of a sudden, Q!" he'd said. "You're in deep with Garvey, but that doesn't mean I'm not your damn boss still."

"Where is all of this coming from?" I asked.

"I told you to get back to me right away on this latest ship purchase Garvey's got up his sleeve. That means right fuckin' away."

"It's all still in limbo. I told you that."

"Limbo my ass! Don't go getting *colored-comfy* with all them Harlem Jamaicans now. You work for the Bureau of Investigation. I need some sales data soon. None of this limbo shit. Got it?"

"As soon as it presents itself . . . yes. What good is it for me to give you names of ships he isn't going to buy? I'm waiting for him to make an actual offer on one first. I don't want to waste your time."

"I'm just staying on top of you. It's my job. How's the family?"

"Good. Actually, I'm throwing a birthday party for my wife tomorrow."

"All of colored New York gonna be there? Do you need me to bring some water-melon?" He laughed real hard. "Don't answer that, Q. Just fuckin' with you. Who's invited?"

"Mostly her artist friends. Real simple. And, I beg your pardon, but there will be plenty of whites in attendance."

"Is that right? A mixed crowd? Sounds mighty revolutionary. Mighty Bolshevik-like. But, I know you have to be a man-about-town and keep up appearances with her. You're a successful Harlem consultant, right? What time's the party?"

"Eight."

The following evening I stood in front of our bedroom cheval glass adjusting my blue tie as Loretta sat on the bed putting on her red high heels.

"How many wineglasses do we have?" she asked.

"About fifteen. But we have plenty of paper cups. We'll put the glasses aside for your closest friends."

"Is that a new suit you're wearing?"

"Yes."

"You mean to tell me you bought me this beautiful red dress for my birthday and bought yourself a suit also? You're not supposed to buy yourself a gift on someone else's birthday."

"I spotted that dress months ago and purchased it last week. I bought this suit today. I don't own one that's this shade of gray. Besides, I had to have something special to wear for your party."

"Like I always say, I've never seen a man spend that much time in front of the mirror. In fact, I've never known anyone, man or a woman, who loves clothes as much as you."

"Stop," I said, thinking about the latest cash delivery I'd received at my office from the Bureau courier. Hoover was paying me well.

"But you do look good," she continued in a flirtatious voice, her eyes cutting up at me real sharp as she sat there still putting on her heels.

"Sweetheart, do you see that little box on the end table?" I asked, tilting the cheval glass so that I could see my entire body and continue adjusting my tie.

"Where?"

"Top of the end table on my side of the bed."

"Yes."

"Can you open it and hand me my cufflinks?"

She stood, walked over, and opened the box.

"Sidney?"

"Yes."

"These aren't cufflinks. They're earrings. Oh my gosh. They're absolutely stunning."

"Happy birthday again, my dear." I'd spent almost every last cent I'd made on them, but she was worth every penny.

"You outdid yourself, Love." She approached and hugged me from behind as I continued with my tie — both of us looking into the mirror.

"Look at us," I said. "We're not a bad-looking couple. Either that or this mirror loves us."

I moved aside so she could see herself trying on the earrings. Backing up and sitting on the edge of the bed, I admired her beauty. She looked even more stunning in the dress than I'd imagined and would certainly be the belle of the ball.

I stood out front under one of the graceful trees that lined both sides of 139th Street greeting guests and pointing them in the right direction as they arrived, all the while hoping each was as loosely committed to the new Prohibition laws as Loretta and I — at least for the night.

As a gust of wind swept through and blew the leaves above me, I turned to look at the front door. Loretta and Ginger were standing there accepting gifts and exchanging pleasantries with one friend after another.

It was as if they'd all known each other for years. She'd created an entire separate world that didn't include me. The realization took me aback for a second. But I quickly caught myself. Who in the hell was I to have such thoughts? Besides, these strangers were all so polite, each having practically uttered the same words upon shaking my hand: "My, what a stunning place you have here."

Later, with most of the guests now in attendance, Eason and I stood in the dining room — he with a cup of coffee, I with a glass of red wine. Mamie Smith's "Crazy Blues" was playing. The tune filled the house and everyone was having a grand old time.

I was just happy finally to be playing music by a colored singer. Other than Bert Williams, W. C. Handy, and a few others, Mamie was one of the only colored artists to have a record, and her bluesy sound was far different from anything else available. I loved Handy, but he was a composer. Mamie was actually singing. Before her, folks had to go to the cabarets to hear such music. But it was 1920 and Mamie had finally broken through.

"Brother Sidney," said Eason, dressed in a black tuxedo, "I know you just walked in from outdoors, but I been standin' here for a while, and that's about the fifth time Peavine done played that same record."

"Is that right? Hold on a second."

I walked over to the Columbia Grafonola and approached Peavine. He was a nineteen-year-old young man, tall like me, but more stringy. He worked as a security guard down at the UNIA. He loved music and fancied himself a future musician. I'd taken a liking to him, even though he seemed to have his head in the clouds more often than not.

"Peavine," I said to him, "how many times you gonna play the same song? They've done heard Mamie about five times."

"Yeah, but ain't she something?" He flashed a big smile.

"Yes, but you need to play somebody else."

"How 'bout some Bert Williams, Mr. Temple?" He thumbed through the records. "Some W. C. Handy?"

"You can't just play the colored singers, Peavine. If you do, we'll be hearing the same songs over and over."

"You ain't got Bert Williams's "Somebody Else, Not Me" in this stack, Sidney?"

"No. I can't stand that song. He talks all the way through it."

"You right."

"Besides, we've only got one song by Mamie, one by W. C. Handy, and one by Bert Williams in that whole stack. That ain't enough music to be playin' all night."

He finally pulled a record out — proudly — as if he'd found a missing jewel, and then damn near shoved it in my face. "Here. I'll play some Marion Harris and the Louisiana Five."

"Good."

"Oh, Mr. Temple." He flipped the record and blew on it. "I saw your Chevrolet when I walked up. Love that *au-to-mo-bile,* sir!"

"Maybe I'll give you a ride in it someday if you can manage to stop playing Mamie over and over again."

"Ooh-ee! What I wouldn't give for a ride in that beauty."

"Just try to focus on switching the records, Peavine. You *are* gettin' paid for this."

He smiled, danced to what was left of "Crazy Blues," and began admiring the crowd. He seemed to be having more fun than anyone. It was as if he hadn't heard a word I'd said. I shook my head and walked back over to rejoin Reverend Eason.

"Peavine's got me worried, Rev."

"It's about time you started calling me James," said Eason.

"Okay, *James* . . . Peavine's got me worried."

"He just a bit slow, that's all. And too damn happy."

"Happy, I don't mind," I said. "It's the slow part I'm worried about."

"I've been surveying the room, Brother Sidney. There ain't a single man or woman without a glass of that devil's grape juice in hand."

"It's a party, James. Didn't Jesus himself

partake?"

"Perhaps. His words have been examined and interpreted exhaustively. Still, I shall abstain. The coffee's doing me just fine."

"What about a cup of whiskey? I have a few bottles stashed away upstairs for a rainy day. Bought 'em when I first got to Harlem."

"Lord no."

"Good. They might be worth a lot someday."

"Suckers better be worth more than yo soul, brother."

"God bless you, James." I shook my head, smiled, and held up my wine. "Yep, we're all goin' to hell."

I looked over toward the door and watched folks stream in. One face took me aback. There stood that racist sonofabitch Taylor Knox from Baltimore training. I couldn't believe he had set foot in my house.

19

Agent Knox had been in my house for no more than five minutes before I made my way over to him near the stairwell. James was now chatting with Peavine near the china closet and the party was in full swing.

"What in the hell are you doing in my house?" I asked, his oily, alcoholic-looking red nose appearing puffier than ever.

"Is that the way you welcome a fellow . . . you know . . . into your home?" Knox said, smiling real big.

"You damn sure weren't invited," I said, both of us with our backs to the stairwell now. "What kind of shit is this anyway? You're gonna blow my damn —"

"Easy, Q. Speed invited me. Said it was going to be a multiracial affair, and boy was he right." He scanned the place. "Looks like a lot of loosey gooseys up in here. The Red type, so to speak."

"Try," I said, "not to talk with that stupid

Southern drawl. This is New York. And these people are my wife's friends. She's trying to raise her profile as a New York painter. She has to be very social. But I'll have you know . . . one of Garvey's top men is here. You idiot!"

"Don't worry, Q. I'm playing the role of the gentleman who owns the building where your office is located. Mr. Bob Hannity. So, you see, why wouldn't we be friends? Why wouldn't a man like me get an invite?"

"Did Mr. Hoover . . ."

"Hoover don't know anything about this. Besides, he don't spend every second of the day worryin' about Harlem. He's busy with an entire fuckin' country of Reds, boy. Nah . . . Speed and me set up this little visit. So, relax. I'm just here to . . . take roll . . . so to speak. See how the niggers get down."

"You better watch yourself," I said, both of us standing nearly shoulder-to-shoulder, looking out at the crowd, pretending to be cordial.

"What are all these commies drinking by the way?" he asked. "That wouldn't be the jail juice would it?"

"What, you gonna round them all up and arrest them? They're artists. You can't expect me to be in New York undercover and not allow my wife to function in her world. They all brought their own wine. Besides, I can smell the much heavier stuff on your breath."

"Your wife isn't going to be a problem, is she?"

"You're the damn problem! Her high profile will allow me to keep a low profile while being in the thick of things. Everyone in Harlem knows I'm an engineer. That's what matters here. Not these people."

"You don't mind if I sorta make the rounds, do you, Q? See if I can get a feel for things, maybe meet someone I can put on the list?"

"I want you to leave."

"Five minutes, Q."

"Make it two. I need to get back to Mr. Eason. I'm sure you're familiar with the name."

"Indeed."

"And again, try to speak like you're from New York if you can. You own a building here, right?"

"Don't you worry, Q. I can fake-talk real good like a Yankee."

"Two minutes."

I squeezed my way through the crowd and headed back over to James, trying my best to cool off. Telling Speed about the mixed crowd had been a mistake. Of course he'd taken it as his opportunity to send a white agent into Harlem to check on me. But I wasn't in trouble. I was in too deep now and Speed knew it.

"How you holding up, James?" I said.

"Doin' just fine. Just standin' here soakin' it all up."

"Good. You look mighty distinguished in that tux, James — like a man who's indeed been named UNIA's Leader of American Negroes. Congrats again."

"Appreciate that. Maybe now I can get Marcus to comprehend the unique thoughts that us American-born Negroes have — to appreciate our specific aspirations — the complexities of our roots."

"Takes time, James. He's focused on his ships for the time being."

"Speaking of ships, I'm starting to feel like the *Yarmouth* may be being used simply to fool folks into investing their money."

"That's a lot of fools, James."

"I see no signs of them boats being used for anything more than propaganda — that or for shipping whiskey out of the country for a suitable fee. You can't tell me that those poor folks down in Alabama invested in the *Yarmouth* so it could ship alcohol to Havana. They ain't nothin' but ships-for-show."

"You really believe that?" I asked.

"Yep."

"I've never heard you question Marcus this way, James. You losing trust in him?"

"Not in him, but maybe in the way business is being done. Marcus has a lot of no-good people pullin' at him — tellin' him to do this and that with the funds."

"Ships-for-show, huh?" I asked, taking a look over at Knox who was now conversing with a group of young gentlemen.

"For show!" he repeated. "But Marcus needs to watch how he's handling business overall. Someone from Kilroe's office actually mailed Marcus a letter telling him that their office has been receiving information from an informant who works at a high level within the UNIA."

"Why would someone in Kilroe's office potentially out someone who's giving them confidential information about Garvey?"

"Who knows? Could be a colored man who loves the UNIA but happens to work in Kilroe's office. Could be a cleanin' man simply overheard a phone conversation Kilroe was having, or a mailroom brother who saw a strange Negro talking to one of Kilroe's assistants."

"That's a lot of could be's, James."

"Or, maybe Marcus just made the whole

thing up because he wants to scare every-one around him into actin' right. Marcus will do anything to ensure loyalty. Whatever the case, Marcus is more worked up than ever. He's suspicious of everyone in his im-mediate inner circle, including me."

Again I eyed Knox who was casually mak-ing the rounds, working my nerves with every step he took. I tried to focus on what James had just said. It made sense in terms of why I'd been being followed. Now if I could just shake Knox loose maybe I could enjoy the party.

"If Marcus isn't making it up," I said, "was there any evidence in the letter that proved Kilroe's office had private information about Marcus?"

"Marcus said there was. He said that the letter included information about potential UNIA transactions that were only discussed during our private meetings."

"But there were always at least twenty folks at those meetings."

"Uh-huh. But unfortunately, you was one and so was I."

"Do you think Marcus has a good idea who it is?" I asked.

"Brother Sidney, I don't know. All I know is that Marcus and Kilroe are at war, and it's personal."

"You think Kilroe had Marcus shot?"

"Yes. 'Cause I think Tyler was crazy. Why else would he have walked in screamin' and hollerin' before he shot Marcus? You can get a crazy man to do anything. And Kilroe got him to shoot Marcus."

"Crazy he was," I said, furious that Knox was now conversing with Loretta over by the front door. I was boiling inside, but had to keep cool.

"And," continued James, "Kilroe could have easily promised Tyler a hefty sum of cash and a guarantee of walking out of jail. If Tyler was as crazy as he seemed, he'd a believed anything."

"But Kilroe would've known he couldn't guarantee that to Tyler — a free walk out of jail. There were too many eyewitnesses."

"Exactly. So he got rid of him as he'd planned to all along. Think about it, brother. We're supposed to believe that Tyler jumped to his death while being walked from his jail cell? I don't buy it. He was pushed to his death and I know it. Never be able to prove it, but I darn well know it."

As I glared at Knox chatting it up with my wife and Ginger, I thought back and wondered what would have happened had I gone down to the police station immediately after Tyler had been arrested. What if I had demanded to see the patrolman who'd arrested Tyler? What if I'd explained to him exactly what Sleepy and Jumpy looked like — what the truck they'd been driving looked like? Would that have prevented me from having to kill them?

"Kilroe's a no-good son of a gun," added Eason, my mind still racing through the past.

Maybe Tyler, Sleepy, and Jumpy had been paid by Kilroe to get Garvey. And perhaps that specific patrolman had been paid by Kilroe to arrest Tyler immediately after the shooting, with Tyler, as Eason suggested, having been told he'd get off. And could it have been that Kilroe not only hired that patrolman but a few other corrupt officers — the ones who possibly threw Tyler to his death while in jail? If that arresting patrolman had been in on it, it's a good thing I hadn't visited the station and told him what I'd seen.

I wanted to make sense of that day, but it was all too messy. Besides, Tyler and company could have been working independently or been hired by someone else altogether. Maybe the patrolman had simply been in the right place at the right time and made a legitimate arrest, foiling Sleepy and Jumpy's ill-planned attempt to whisk Tyler away. Anything was possible. I just found it ironic that I had killed two men whose aim was to murder Garvey — a man I vehemently opposed but certainly didn't want to see dead.

"Not to change the subject," said James, interrupting my reverie, "but I ain't never seen so many white folks in my life. Surprised these pale brothers and sisters didn't set foot in Harlem, see all them Negroes on the streets, and scoot on back down where they came from."

"You need to quit, James."

"I mean to tell you, Sidney!" He pretended to loosen his tie as if it were choking him. "Startin' to get a little worried up in here."

"Quit," I jokingly yelled, laughing at his playful demeanor.

"But seriously, Sidney, you don't actually think it can ever be this way — so colorly blended — out there on them mean streets? You do know this here is just a fantasy — a sample of what can never be?"

"Go ask Loretta," I said. "She doesn't live in our political world. She sees people as people, as most artists do. That's why I always ask you not to bring up the color thing around her, James."

"And I don't. I love the sista. But you see,

304

I know better. These white folks is rare. They the exception to the rule. The rest of 'em out there is doin' the devil's work."

"Loretta doesn't see it that way."

"Good. May God continue watching over her."

"Look, however hard it is for you to believe, she is a woman of color who actually hasn't had to wrestle with being colored. Her father put a wall around her. Can't we have some of those types who exist among us — however naïve it may sound?"

"No," he said.

"No? Why not?"

"Because the ugly hand of bigotry will find her eventually and slap her right across the face."

"She just wants to paint, James."

"Our entire movement is rooted in a belief that colored folks should separate themselves from whites. Yet here you and I stand in the middle of a big ol' mix-pot party. It's too ironic. It's unfair to Marcus. It's also dangerous."

He took a deep breath — then held up his cup of coffee.

"But tonight is not about us," he continued. "It's about your wife. I'll get back to thinking about Africa for the Africans tomorrow."

"I'll drink to that. Because until we get to this 'all-black society' — the one with an imaginary fence around it that Garvey often speaks of — we have to live in this one."

"Amen."

I cared deeply about James and knew he was slowly losing faith in Garvey. And regarding the issue of race, I wanted to make him come around and see things my way. But I wasn't in a position to express "my way" to him — at least not yet.

"Ya'll tryin' to hide from the rest of us?" asked an approaching Claude McKay — his hair straighter than I'd last seen it — his maroon three-piece suit more expensive-looking than most.

"How you doing, Claude?" I asked. "I'm glad you got my invite."

"Well ain't this something!" added James. "Great to see you, Claude."

"What a house, Sidney. Am I actually in Harlem or back in London?"

"Thank you, Claude."

"I want you both to meet my friend Max Eastman," he said.

"I didn't really think you were going to bring him," I said.

"Of course," he said. "As I mentioned, he wants to meet the painter. He's here some-where. There . . . the tall white gentleman in the grayish-brown suit by the front entrance. He's flirting with the stunning woman in the blue dress."

"That's Ginger," I said, all of us looking.

"Ol' Max is at it again," said a smiling Claude. "He has a way with the ladies. And don't be fooled by his mop of white hair. My boss is still in his thirties."

I watched Eastman and Ginger conversing and could see Knox making his way over to them. Claude's boss was here to possibly help Loretta, and I had to make sure Knox didn't mess it all up, he with his obvious agent look and stupid talk. Plus, he probably didn't yet know it was actually Eastman, a man high on Hoover's enemy list, and wrongly so.

"Excuse me, gentlemen," I said. "I see the landlord of my office building over there about to leave. He has a car he wants to show me that I may purchase for Loretta. Told him I'd take a look before he heads home."

Before they could even respond I was pushing through bodies. Just before Knox was able to reach Eastman, I cut him off.

"You won't believe this," I said with a pressing tone.

"What?" Knox frowned.

"This could bring Garvey down tonight.

Come with me. Now!"

As we made our way back toward the dining room, I glanced over at Claude and James who were fully engaged with Peavine. "What's the news?" Knox asked, following me through the kitchen toward the back door.

"I'll tell you outside," I said. "This is too sensitive."

Outside, we approached the rear end of my vehicle and stopped. I looked up and down the dark, quiet alleyway. There wasn't a soul in sight.

"You know which major law Garvey has finally broken?" I asked.

"Of course not. Tell me."

"Neither do I, you stupid sonofabitch! That's why I'm still undercover and putting my life on the line every single day. Unlike you."

"What the fuck are you —"

"Shut your damn mouth!" I said, pointing my finger into his chest. "You're putting my entire mission in jeopardy because you're playing damn games. And if Hoover indeed doesn't know about this little solo act, you probably don't want me telling him. I know he wouldn't approve of this. He wants Garvey far too bad and I'm his ticket, not your country ass."

"Look, nigger," he said, slapping my finger away, "I'll do what the —"

Before he could finish I slapped him across his face. He stumbled but fisted up and swung real big, missing by a foot, as I ducked. I grabbed him by the knot of his tie and pulled him into three heavy, right slugs, the last of which put him on the ground.

"Get your ass outta Harlem!" I said, as he squirmed around.

He spit some blood. I knew he was hurt.

"Those people in there," I said, pointing to my house, "are my wife's friends. Except for a few. Do you understand me? This is *her* night!"

He rolled up into a seated position and tried to right himself.

"I'm a man, just like you. And this is my house, not some playground you can just show up to whenever you'd like. Now sit there as long as you need to. And when you can manage, walk your ugly behind over to the gate and Ivan will let you out. But do not come back inside my house. If you do, so help me God I'll break every bone in your body."

He nodded.

"The boys back in D.C. don't need to know you got your ass whipped by that nigger named Sidney tonight. That would be quite the embarrassment for you. Just go on back and tell them that all is well with Q3Z."

I stood there a bit longer, then made my way back inside, rejoining James and Claude, who were now conversing with Loretta, Ginger, and Max Eastman. The music seemed a bit louder — the house a bit fuller.

"The world will change when the artists take over," said Ginger, who was obviously a bit tipsy at this point.

"I agree," said Mr. Eastman.

Ginger was stunning in her blue dress, pearl earrings, and pearl necklace. Her hair was in a bun and she was also wearing a clear beaded necklace around the top of her forehead with a blue gemstone hanging from the middle of it — practically reaching the middle of her eyes.

"It's nice to finally meet you, Mr. Eastman," I interjected. "Sidney."

"Call me Max." We shook. "The pleasure's mine, Sidney."

"Wonderful," said Ginger. "Now we've all met. So! All of you! Come! Let me show you the birthday girl's contribution to changing this crazy world we speak of. *Ce monde de fous!*"

We all followed her from the dining room to the studio down the hall.

"Ta-dah!" said Ginger, walking through

the doorway and pointing at the pieces along the floor as we all filed into the studio. "Only peace can come from taking in such beauty."

"Indeed," said Eastman. "This is the beautiful thing about art. A painting cares not about the color of the hands which grip the brush that paints it."

"Oui," said Ginger. "It cares not about the color of the man who stands before it, staring with appreciation."

Ginger and Eastman stood arm in arm as if they'd been a couple for years. In fact, one would have found it hard to believe they'd just met, considering the difficulty they were having keeping their hands off one another. Their unfettered behavior made me laugh on the inside.

"Each piece tells a different story," added Claude. "I see abstracts and realism. Many painters choose one form and stick with it. You're truly talented, Mrs. Temple."

"Thank you," said Loretta, beaming with pride as I held her hand. "If only my paintings were as rich as your poetry. Sidney has told me all about you, Claude."

"Don't go tellin' no lies 'bout me, Sidney. I'm just a simple poet."

"Simple you are not," said Max, gulping down the rest of his wine. "You're one of the greatest!"

Max's charm and confidence were serving him well in the case of Ginger. She released his arm, walked over, and picked up one of the paintings.

"This is my favorite. *Magnifique!*"

It was a painting of a nude man and woman interlocked like a pretzel. Their skin was olive-colored and the backdrop powder blue.

"Why your favorite?" asked Claude.

"Because it says no inhibition," said Ginger. "It says two in love is one. It says you can have all of me because I surrender. *Je me rends!*"

Ginger smiled and looked directly at the blushing Mr. Eastman whose face was growing more pinkish by the second. Claude discreetly patted his boss on the back, and the two raised their eyebrows at each other. Without speaking it, Claude seemed to be jokingly saying, *Aren't you lucky, boss!*

Eastman took the painting, studied it, and then passed it along to Claude. Claude handed it to Reverend Eason who had a puzzled look on his face.

"Lord have mercy!" he said.

The entire room laughed as James turned the painting from side to side, looking at the bodies from different angles.

"You like it, James?" asked Loretta.

"Boy, I mean to tell ya! Hope you done asked for your forgiveness, girl."

There was more laughter as James handed it back to Ginger.

"There is no sin," she said, "in admiring the beauty of the naked body, Reverend. An artist must be free of the hindrances that plague greater society."

"I ain't mad at ya!" he responded in a high-pitched voice — raising his hands to suggest his innocence.

"Good, Reverend. *Bonne.* I am happy. *Je suis heureux.*"

"Call me James, sister. And in the case of Sister Loretta's painting, God never created anything more beautiful."

Loretta walked over and gave him a hug. "You're far too kind, James. I know it's not your taste."

James took out a handkerchief and began dabbing the moisture on his forehead, raising his eyebrows. He was still slightly taken aback by the painting but was also trying to be a bit funny.

"I just wanted you all to see the beautiful work the birthday girl is creating," said Ginger, walking over and returning the painting.

"Well, Mrs. Temple," said Max, "you

certainly have enough work on display here to do a showing. When and if you decide to do so, maybe we could give you some coverage. Readers of the *Liberator* would certainly be interested in learning more about you. We can send Claude here to do a write-up. What ya say, Claude?"

"I'd love to. I'd actually like us to start covering some of the Negro theater and jazz also. There seems to be something rooting up here in Harlem — a colored renaissance of art and music, you might say. I'd like the *Liberator* to be on the forefront of featuring burgeoning artists such as yourself, Loretta."

"I'd be more than honored. Whenever Ginger thinks I'm ready for a public showing. She's the renowned one."

"You're ready now," said Ginger. "*Maintenant!* We will put it together. But today it's time for the birthday girl to dance. It's time for all of us to dance."

Ginger took Eastman by the hand and led him out of the room. I took Loretta by the hand and followed. Making our way into the crowded living room, Ginger took charge, walking over to the Columbia Grafonola, ignoring Peavine, and turning the music down.

"Can I have everyone's attention," she

said, tapping a wineglass with a spoon repeatedly. "We are all gathered here tonight to celebrate the birthday of my dear friend Loretta. *Mon bon ami!* And what a beautiful gathering we have here. You have all come to know Loretta over the past year in your own way, just as I have. So we all know what a warm, considerate, and passionate woman she is. And we're all delighted to be in your new, beautiful home, Loretta and Sidney. The fun is just beginning. But enough of my bad English. Please join me in song before we continue the festivities."

"HAPPY BIRTHDAY TO YOU . . ." she began to sing. "EVERYONE!" she shouted as we all joined in, raising our cups and glasses.

As the song ended, there was whistling and light cheering all around before Ginger spoke up again. "NOW LET'S DANCE!"

She turned the music up very loud as folks scurried about, some setting their drinks down on end tables, others on the living room mantelshelf. Everyone then coupled up and began dancing to "Blues My Naughty Sweetie Gives to Me" by Ted Lewis and his Jazz Band.

"Are you happy?" I asked Loretta as we shuffled our feet and twisted to the tune.

"I'm happy and in love."

I took her hand and spun her around. Hardly a soul in the place wasn't dancing. I even saw Reverend Eason standing to the side with his coffee, bobbing his head and having a ball. Claude was dancing with a gorgeous redboned girl, Ginger with Max, and they were certainly the most flamboyant. It was a sea of white and black moving as if they hadn't a care in the world.

"Ginger certainly seems to be enjoying herself," said Loretta, leaning in to make sure I could hear her.

"So does James," I said.

I pulled her close to me so we could hear each other above the noise. Her arms were wrapped around my neck, mine around her waist, as we casually dipped from side to side and circled to the rhythm.

I watched Max pinch Ginger on the leg. She took him by the hand and led him through the crowd toward the stairway. They made their way to the second floor, presumably en route to one of the guest-rooms.

"By the way," said Loretta, watching them as well, "Ginger is sleeping here tonight."

"By herself?"

"Stop it, Sid. Yes."

"Whatever you want. It's your birthday."

316

20

After a few months of relative inactivity, December brought with it a more than usual amount of snow. Several of Garvey's entourage had been called to a meeting at UNIA headquarters where Black Star Line business was to be discussed. I was sitting at a large conference table by myself, waiting for Garvey and company.

Two Legionnaires were keeping guard at the door. One of them was Peavine, who stood at attention with great discipline — following orders much better than he had at Loretta's party. As usual, the two Legionnaires made it impossible for anyone not connected to the UNIA to enter the room.

In walked a young lady with a platter of cheese and crackers. She placed it at the head of the table where Garvey always sat. She also placed beside it his customary carafe of fresh mango juice. Whenever his mango juice arrived, I knew the meeting would start within five minutes.

I began the countdown, and just like clockwork, in walked everyone. Many removed their snow-covered overcoats and hung them on the rack next to the door before taking their seats.

Two of Garvey's accountants and one of his lawyers were present, as well as John E. Bruce, Orlando Thompson, Hubert Harrison, William Ferris, and Reverend Eason. His two top security men were also there — Marcellus Strong and William Grant — one sitting to his right, the other his left. Both were built like prizefighters — tall and husky.

"I called this meeting," said Garvey, pouring his glass of mango juice, "to discuss the idea of purchasing a ship that will be used as a luxury cruiser for our people. No more of these broken down war boats. We must secure a vessel that will allow our people to travel abroad in style. The *Kanawha* is a decent yacht, but we need something much more grand."

He took a drink of his juice and savored it. He certainly didn't share it with anyone — ever. The juice was his and his alone. So were the cheese and crackers, but he always waited for the meetings to end before eating them.

"It may take more time than I'd like," he said, sipping again, "before our people can begin moving to Africa permanently. In the meantime, we shall provide them with a cruiser that will at least let them visit the motherland. Speaking of visiting the motherland, as you all know, Elie Garcia is in Liberia now and sends promising news about the land development negotiations taking place with President C. B. D. King."

I couldn't help but wonder where "our" people were going to get the money to take such lavish trips abroad. Amidst the poverty that existed throughout colored America, it seemed foolish to be conjuring up such schemes.

"This is good news," said the tall, angular John E. Bruce. "Folks are ready for it. They need it — to be able to travel without being told to sit in this section or that."

Bruce, in his sixties, was a veteran journalist who'd helped Garvey gain footing in Harlem. He acted as one of his main advisors and was famous for having once written bold words about the white man. "If they burn your house, burn theirs," he'd penned. "If they kill your wives and children, kill theirs." Garvey leaned heavily on Bruce for advice.

"Shall we mention this search for a luxury

steamer in the *Negro World*?" asked Hubert.

"It may be a bit premature for that," said William.

"Correct," added Garvey. "It's premature. But listen, Hubert. I must commend you and William in front of everyone here for the job you're both doing with the paper. You're the best editors in New York."

"It's mostly Hubert, sir," said William.

"Nonsense," said Hubert. "It's you."

"Back to the business at hand," quipped Garvey. "I've got my eye on several boats, but want to make sure they are properly appraised before we make a bid on one. It's in the best interest of Black Star Line stockholders that we broker a fair deal. And as you are all aware, I will be taking an extensive trip to the Caribbean in February to raise money. That leaves you, Orlando, two months to try and negotiate a purchase before I depart."

"Yes, sir," said the bookish-looking Orlando. "In fact, I wanted to know if you think it may be in our best interest to hire an outside brokerage firm."

"That may not be a bad idea," said Garvey. "But who?"

"Now hear me out here, Marcus. Just hear me out. There's a broker . . . a Mr. Anton Silverstone . . . who comes highly recommended. Word on the street is he's known for being fair to colored folk."

"What is this you speak of, Orlando?"

"Well . . . now . . . he's a white man. A Jew."

Garvey placed both hands on the edge of the table, scooted his chair back, and stood. He began slowly pacing. Orlando nervously tapped his pencil while the accountants pretended to shuffle some papers.

I stared straight ahead at the door near Peavine, who seemed quite pleased with his special post, one likely assigned to him because of the high praise James and I had given him during discussions with Garvey.

It seemed to take forever but Garvey finally rounded the table and took his seat again. But before another word was spoken, Amy Jacques walked in and approached Garvey. She whispered something in his ear. After about twenty seconds, she finished and exited.

Garvey sat there stewing over whatever news had just been delivered. So far this had been a meeting filled with nothing but tension. Such was life around Garvey. Distractions always got in the way of business — hence the many UNIA undertakings left undone.

Garvey pointed at Peavine and the other

Legionnaire.

"You two!" he yelled. "Leave!"

Peavine quickly exited and the other guard followed.

"Well," said Garvey. "It seems our snitch has finally been pegged — at least one of them. Yes . . . there is a snitch among us."

The room was painfully silent. Those five words, "at least one of them," had hit me like a truck. Ever since I'd heard that an alleged informant had been feeding Kilroe's office information about Garvey, I'd assumed I was safe. But now my heart raced.

"There's nothing worse than a double-crossing, no good, evildoing snitch," said Garvey. "Their fate be damned!"

Suddenly, all of the lights went out and we were in the dark. It was a reminder of the electrical work I'd yet to do. Perhaps I should have prioritized better.

After about ten seconds the lights returned. Garvey scanned the room, then took a deep breath before speaking.

"Of course, when I say there's a snitch among us, I mean among us in the broader sense — not among us here at this table. All of you are my closest confidants."

A huge relief came over me, but I just sat and watched as Garvey sat there thinking. I'd never seen him so enraged.

"Strong," he said, "the snitch is having lunch as we speak with someone from Kilroe's office. They're at a place called Webster's in Manhattan. Take care of this. You and Grant are excused."

"We'll need someone to drive," said Strong. "Gerald and Elmore, along with several Legionnaires, took all the Fords to retrieve Prince Mutato and his entourage at the Waldorf. They'll be back shortly."

"We don't have time," said Grant.

"Then we'll have to find a guard with an available vehicle," said Strong. "Let's go."

"We don't have time for that," said Garvey. "And do you think I want some random Legionnaire to witness your handling of this? One of them might also be a snitch. This is in-house business. You must get to this Webster's immediately. Reverend Eason can drive you."

"In what?" asked Eason. "I have no transportation. Can you drive, Sidney?"

"Yes."

"Do you know where Webster's is, Sidney?" asked Strong.

"No."

"I do," said Eason.

"Very well," said Garvey. "You direct Sidney where to drive, Reverend. The four of you go. Now! Before he leaves."

We stood, grabbed our overcoats, and exited. I was relieved to be out of the room, even though I had no idea exactly what we were being tasked to do.

With snow covering the ground, each step I took en route to my car left a three-inch-deep footprint in its wake. I looked ahead to my right and noticed the prints that Eason and company had left in front of me.

After about twenty steps I looked back at the various footprints behind us. It was as if they were following me. All of the footprints were a metaphor for what my life had become — following and being followed.

The prints reminded me of the many young, loyal teenage men Garvey had tailing various members of the UNIA. These ambitious youngsters were willing to do anything to curry favor with him. At least one had done just that by following this so-called snitch to Webster's Restaurant.

The falling snow was difficult to drive in, and it showed no signs of relenting. We made our way slowly down Park Avenue. No one said a word. Strong and Grant sat in the backseat and Eason was up front with me pointing the way.

I took a left on East Fifty-second Street and found a parking space across the way from Webster's. We waited. I was eager to see the snitch come walking out. Who was he?

"Turn the engine off," said Strong. "When he comes out, I'll get out. You three just wait here."

We waited about twenty minutes before we saw two men exit — one white, one colored.

"It's Pope," said Strong. "I knew that nigga was no good."

"Quick," said Grant. "He's 'bout to get in his car."

Strong got out, walked across the street, and approached the two men from behind. The three engaged in conversation for a bit before Strong grabbed the white man's briefcase, opened it, and began rummaging through the papers inside. He read a few of the documents, then put them back inside, closing the briefcase and handing it to Pope.

He shoved the white man in the chest, the force knocking him to the ground. He just sat there, afraid to get up. Strong then grabbed Pope by the collar, led him toward us, opened the door, and shoved him in the backseat.

"Drive," said Strong, snatching the briefcase from Pope and handing it up front to James.

I found my way back to Park Avenue and

drove north until we got to 135th Street.

"Park near the pier," said Strong.

I thought about what was to come. Eason hadn't said a word. I knew that Strong and Grant were able to sense any disloyalty and would easily sniff me out if I showed the slightest bit of uneasiness. Their commitment to Garvey was stronger than anyone else's within the UNIA.

"This is good," said Strong as I peeked at him in the mirror. "Stop."

"Good ol' Pope," said Grant, shaking his head and putting on some thick black gloves as I parked. "How many leases did you help Marcus secure? He credited you for helping him get that restaurant. He probably figured you knew more about real estate than just about anybody in Harlem."

"I'm gonna ask you one time," said Strong, also putting on his black gloves. "Who do you work for?"

"I've been acting independently," said Pope, sweating through his shirt.

Strong revved back and landed a heavy punch across Pope's face, likely breaking his jaw. He then grabbed him by the arm and began pulling him out of the car.

"Ya'll come with me," said Strong to the three of us.

We stepped into the blizzard, walked to

the front of the car, and watched Strong deliver several blows to Pope's ribs and face. He fell to his knees and gasped for air.

"Please!" said Pope, extending his arm up to defend himself.

"You gotta choice," said Grant, joining in. "You either tell us . . . or you will die today."

Blood was pouring out of Pope's mouth onto the snow.

"I'm independent," he said again.

Grant kicked him in the face, thrusting him back. It was a violent kick that could have easily killed him. He now lay flat on his back.

"Who?" yelled Strong.

It took every ounce of will not to intervene, but I decided to wait a bit longer. I knew this could just as well have been me bleeding on the ground and figured it was about at this point where I'd confess if it were.

"M . . . I . . . D," whispered Pope.

"What's that?" asked Grant, getting down on one knee and placing his ear near Pope's mouth.

"Military Intelligence Division," whispered Pope as his eyes rolled up into his head.

"And you been feedin' information to that son of a bitch Kilroe, huh?" asked Strong.

"I ain't never met Kilroe," whispered Pope. "I just dealt with someone in his office. That man you saw me with."

"So," said Grant, "you the one who told Marcus's sorry bookkeeper to turn them files over to Kilroe? What was that no good nigga's name again?"

Pope just lay there.

"Huh?" shouted Grant, kicking him in the ribs.

"Uriah!" cried Pope.

"That's right," said Grant. "It was Uriah the one turned them books over to Kilroe. Claimed Marcus was cheatin' 'em out they money. What'd you offer Uriah to turn them books over — a guarantee that he wouldn't go down with Marcus? Well, it's you who's goin' down."

Strong bent over and grabbed Pope by the front of his shirt with both hands — lifting him to his feet — holding him up, his useless legs dangling. He was one more punch away from Heaven or Hell.

"Never liked you," said Strong. "If I ever see your face in Harlem again . . . better yet . . . in all of New York, you're a dead man. Dead! You hear me?"

Pope could barely muster up the energy to nod his head yes, but did.

"Any other snitches from the MID working for Marcus?" asked Strong. Pope nodded no. His face was so swollen I could hardly recognize him. "You been writin' a hell of a lotta snitch-ass letters to your bosses, I'm sure. That's a mighty busy hand you got. A naughty one! You right-handed?"

Pope nodded yes. As Strong continued holding him up, Grant grabbed his right hand and began breaking each of his fingers by bending them back violently until they touched the top of his hand. Pope shrilly screamed for mercy but Grant continued. Eason and I couldn't help but cringe.

Grant finished his barbaric act, and Strong threw Pope to the ground. He lay there curled up like a baby. I looked down at all the blood covering the snow like splattered red paint on one of Loretta's abstracts.

"You can go on and tell them white devils at your MID to come and get me," said Grant, huffing like a rabid animal. "Tell 'em to come and get this tiger! And tell every other snitch in Harlem you know that Marcus can't be touched. No one can get close to Black Moses! He has a shield of well-trained soldiers surrounding him. Every single one of my men — hundreds — are trained to kill if need be."

Grant stepped back and held his arms out to the side. He kept them extended, then began slowly circling, looking into the distance.

"YOU HEAR ME, SNITCHES?" he screamed. "COME GET THIS TIGER!"

I could see Pope still breathing and was glad they hadn't killed him. Still, the event shook me fiercely. It jolted me into realizing how extremely careful I'd need to be from this point forward.

21

Winter quickly passed. It was April of 1921. I'd been getting more pressure than ever from Hoover to check Garvey's files. With Garvey still in the Caribbean, I decided to try my luck. Strong had joined him on the escapade, Grant left behind to man the offices. He had Legionnaires from his Tiger Division patrolling the building day and night.

I began by rewiring the office lights on the first two floors, which took me the better part of two weeks. Before I could begin work on Garvey's office upstairs, I had to get Grant to unlock the door. Not an easy task. He and I argued back and forth over the matter.

"Why do you need to get into Marcus's office today?" he'd asked. "Just leave that room untouched until he returns. This is not about trust, Sidney. No one, including myself, is trusted by Marcus to be in that office when he's gone."

"But Marcus himself asked me to rewire the lights throughout the building — including his office. He was adamant about it."

"You need to wait until he returns."

I didn't accept his demand, and finally, through much technical talk and persuasion, he relented. But I did have to agree to allow one of his men to oversee my every move. Amy Jacques was also traveling with Garvey, but I was hoping she'd left the documents in the file cabinet.

It was about seven in the evening. With several bags of electrical equipment, lightbulbs, and two Autographic Kodak cameras in tow — one provided by the Bureau — I made my way up to Garvey's office. Waiting for me was Grant and one of his young Legionnaires, Clayborn.

"Leave the door cracked," said Grant, unlocking the door and pushing it forward. "How long is this gonna take? Hours . . . days?"

"That depends on the various problems I may encounter. The whole building has glitches throughout. One from another room may be affecting the power in Marcus's office, and vice versa."

He frowned. "Well Clayborn here will make sure you don't miss any . . . *glitches.*"

Grant left the two of us alone and headed downstairs. I entered, set my bags down, and grabbed what I needed. I climbed the ladder and began replacing old electrical wiring, sockets, and lightbulbs as Clayborn just sat there eyeing me. He was a huge young man, seeming to take up most of the wall next to the office door, which remained slightly ajar.

After working for about two hours, I stepped down from the ladder and took out a pot roast sandwich and a bottle of root beer from my bag.

"Sorry," I said, sitting, unwrapping the paper from the sandwich, and taking a big bite.

"It's okay, Mr. Temple," said Clayborn, his voice very deep.

"You ate supper yet?" I chewed big, knowing that by the mere size of the youngster, he liked to eat.

"No."

"If I'd remembered better, I would have thrown a sandwich and soda in for you. Maybe tomorrow night."

"Tomorrow night?"

I nodded. "Office needs more new wire than I'd anticipated. Also need more new sockets, some larger ones." I guzzled down some root beer. "Whole building's system was jerry-built back in the Stone Ages it seems. Yeah, this here's a two- or three-day job, considering I can't be here 'til night-time. Got other contracts I have to attend to."

"Everybody knows you stay real busy, Mr. Temple."

He spoke to me with such reverence, reminding me that my stature within the organization was, at least, perceived to be one of importance.

"Tell you what, Clayborn, I'll bring supper for both of us tomorrow night. You like pork ribs?"

"Yes, sir." He lightly smiled.

"What's your favorite soda? You like root beer?"

"Orange soda."

"You got it."

I finished eating and sizing him up. I imagined he could easily fall asleep right in that chair if given a certain number of barbital to aid him along a bit. And I had a whole bottle full in my bedside drawer.

The next night I arrived with all of my equipment, a bottle of orange pop, a bottle of root beer, and two orders of juicy pork baby back ribs from Sonny's Pool Hall. Clayborn and I ate before I got to work. Didn't want the ribs to get cold.

"Best ribs in Harlem, ain't they?" I asked.

He just nodded and licked his saucy fingers. Then he took a big swig from his bottle — the orange soda inside mixed with three of my mashed-up pills.

I left my food there on the desk and climbed the ladder. "You go on and finish eatin', Clayborn. I need to get started."

"All right. Thank you for the supper, Mr. Temple."

"You're welcome. Brother gets hungry just sittin' up here all night waitin' on me."

"Yes, sir."

Clayborn was a nice kid — very respect-ful. He wore the extra, extra large Legion-naire uniform with much pride.

It took about thirty minutes before he was sound asleep in his chair. But I had to make sure no one was roaming the hallways. Staff members worked well into the night — well past ten. And ever since Garvey had left on his trip, Grant had remained a permanent fixture at headquarters. He actually slept in one of the offices downstairs. The last thing I needed was for him to come barging in while I was knee-deep in Garvey's books.

Whatever information I found would need to be photographed, as removing anything was out of the question. If the books showed that Garvey had indeed officially owned the

Shadyside and *Kanawha* when he began sending out flyers soliciting folks to buy stock in them, we'd be back to square one.

The Bureau had some of the flyers in their possession. The date on them read "May 20, 1920." So if the dates on the official sales receipts for the *Shadyside* and *Kanawha* preceded May 20, the Bureau would be out of luck when it came to charging Garvey with mail fraud.

I walked over, opened the door, and made sure the hallway was clear. I could hear staffers below and wasn't sure where Grant was. I'd have to be quick. Returning the door to its barely-open position, I used all of my strength to scoot Clayborn directly in front of it — making it next to impossible for someone to enter. If Grant did return, he'd only be able to yell at Clayborn for sitting in front of the door, giving me time to return to the ladder.

I approached the wall behind Garvey's desk and removed the Maasai gourd that was hanging there. I turned the gourd upside down and out spilled the keys.

I looked over at Clayborn who was definitely out cold. I tried one key after another on the top drawer of the black file cabinet. Finally, I found one that worked.

I opened the drawer and saw three thick

books. The first book listed the names of thousands who'd invested their money in the Black Star Line — not what I was looking for.

I opened the second book and realized it was a transactions book, so I began flipping page after page. There were transactions documented as far back as 1916. Near the back of the book I found final sales transactions listed for both the *Shadyside* and *Kanawha*. Someone had written down April 19, 1920, for both. I took one of the cameras from my bag and photographed the page. Now I needed to match that date with actual receipts.

I looked again in the top drawer, but there was nothing. I found the key that opened the middle drawer. In it were what looked like hundreds of large envelopes. They were packed in vertically, so tightly I couldn't pull any of them out.

I found my screwdriver and wedged it in between a few, managing to create enough space to get my fingers in and pull some of them out — actually tearing a couple in the process, and sending a few flying across the room.

I heard footsteps in the hallway so I shut the drawer, rushed to Clayborn, and scooted his chair away from the door again. I quickly picked the envelopes up off the floor, shoved them in my bag, leaped toward the ladder, and climbed up as fast as I could. If Grant were to see Clayborn asleep, so be it. That would be the end of his short career in the Tiger Division.

But the footsteps passed and there was silence again. I waited a few seconds, then climbed down and struggled to position Clayborn back in front of the door. His wooden chair was on the verge of breaking.

Returning to the file cabinet, I pulled as many envelopes out as possible and stacked them on the desk. I'd never sifted through a pile of anything so fast in my life. Each envelope had something different labeled on it: "Laundry Service," "Ford Automobile Purchase," "1920 International Convention," etc. One caught my attention. It read: "Nemesis."

I opened it and found several handwritten letters. I quickly read through a few. One was addressed to Madam C. J. Walker — an entrepreneur who'd made her fortune by developing and marketing a hugely successful line of beauty and hair products for colored women. She'd recently passed away.

The letter began: "Dear Madam C. J. Walker, I'm writing to you regarding one W. E. B. Du Bois. As you know, he has done much to disrupt my Africa-centered agenda. This Du Bois is a white Negro who is dead set on destroying the purity of the race. The fact is this Du Bois is not like you and me, Madame Walker. Too much white blood flows through his veins."

Garvey went on to thank Walker for her past loyalties and asked for her continued support of the UNIA. The letter was certainly disturbing, but there was another that seemed far more important — one that Du Bois would like to see. It was written as a questionnaire, and a scribbled note at the top read: "To be typed and directly sent at the appropriate time to the United States Attorney General, Alexander Mitchell Palmer, and all members of the U.S. Senate." Another scribbled note read: "Letter to be sent as a last resort, to avoid deportation or imprisonment."

The first paragraph explained the purpose of the questionnaire. It read: "I write to you as the recognized leader of Africans across the globe. And I believe America's race problem can be solved quite swiftly and permanently if given the proper attention and resources — and most of all, if assigned the proper leader.

"I ask that you help me in my endeavor to be officially named by the United States

Government: 'Director of African Repatriation.' I wish to act as the sole director in immediately removing all colored Americans back to their native Africa, to Liberia. Colored America as a whole will certainly follow my orders — especially if given your endorsement. They have grown quite weary of other colored leaders, specifically one W. E. B. Du Bois."

I was stunned by Garvey's ignorance and presumptuousness, as well as his willingness to sell out his own people, if need be, to save his own hide — exemplified so clearly in the line I just had to read once more to be sure: "Letter to be sent as a last resort, to avoid deportation or imprisonment."

If granted such preposterous authority by the government to *remove* all coloreds back to Africa, millions against their will no doubt, Garvey would be ordering utter chaos. He was banking on them being racist enough to grant him such power. It was my worst fear. Just the thought of my family's future resting in such a man's hands gave me chills.

The questions that followed were written in a manner that could only build his case. He asked the readers to explain why they did or didn't agree with questions like: "With the further intermixing of coloreds and whites certainly in America's future, is it not time for Africans to return to Africa? Please explain why or why not."

At the bottom of the page was Garvey's signature and a line that read: "Please sign and date here and mail to UNIA headquarters." I took one of the cameras from my bag — the one Loretta and I owned — and photographed the letter.

Refocusing on the remaining stack of envelopes, I finally found one labeled "Black Star Line Vessels." I opened it and there they were — several receipts for the *Shadyside* and *Kanawha*. Payments had obviously been made periodically over a one-year period. But two receipts had statements attached that listed April 15, 1920, as the date of final payment for both respectively. The bottom of both statements read: "Outstanding Balance: $0.00." There were also two official certificates that verified ownership of both ships.

So Garvey had indeed taken ownership of them a month before mailing out the flyers. I wondered if he had done so by coincidence or on purpose — fully aware of the law regarding the mail service. Either way, he was safe — for now.

With the Bureau camera now, I photographed all of the documents, then managed to get the envelopes back inside the drawer, move Clayborn again, finish my work, and avoid a confrontation with Grant. I made sure the office was clean and packed up my equipment.

On my way out I woke Clayborn and told him he needed to try to stay awake on the job. I told him I wouldn't tell Grant as long as he could avoid falling asleep in the future. With his eyes barely open, he nodded in agreement and we both exited.

I headed straight for my office and sent a telegram to the Bureau explaining my findings regarding the ships. Of course, a courier would be sent to retrieve the camera in order to confirm my findings. Hoover would likely be impressed with my skills as a photographer but disappointed with what the pictures revealed.

Later that week I was sitting in my office and received a call from Agent Speed. He was in an angry mood.

"Did you receive my telegram?" he asked.

"No. At least not yet."

"That's 'cause you're never in your damn office."

"Garvey doesn't spend his time in my office."

"Very funny."

"I wasn't trying to be."

"Well . . . seeing as how I managed to catch you by telephone, ignore the telegram when you get it. I'll just tell you now."

"Okay."

"You're to be commended for the investigative work you've done, Q, but I'm not calling to sing your praises. We just received word from Agent 800 that suggests Garvey's publicity committee has recently printed thousands of circulars for a new ship. The photograph they were ordered to use displays a ship called the *Orion*. But apparently Garvey has sent word for the committee to scratch the word *Orion* out and replace it with the *Phyllis Wheatley*. Does Garvey own the *Orion* as we speak?"

"I know for a fact that he doesn't. A Jewish man named Silverstone has been hired by Garvey to broker a deal for that ship. Those negotiations are still under way."

"So these circulars may go out well before the *Orion* is purchased. Stay on top of this. Agent 800 will handle confirmation of when the flyers are mailed out. You handle when the sale officially goes through."

"I'll notify you immediately when it does."

"Stay safe, Q."

I hung up and thought about those words. I knew that staying safe for a man of color was wishful thinking to say the least, regardless of the circumstances and surroundings. In fact, ever since my cousin's murder, I'd always felt the fleetingness of life.

I reached in my briefcase for the *New York Times* and thought about the church service Loretta and I would be attending this Sunday. Maybe that was the one exception, being inside a church. Yes. Looking back, it was the only time I'd ever felt truly safe.

We arrived at 242 West Fortieth Street just in time for service. We were Reverend Adam Clayton Powell's special guests. It was a lovely church, but I could see why they needed a much larger place to worship. There were hundreds packed in tight. We sat in the front row, as Powell began by thanking a long list of donors and members.

"And thanks to Sister Lolita Jones Jackson. God bless your soul, sister. Sister Jackson has been so diligent in her fundraising efforts, working tirelessly into the night for weeks on end. Won't you stand, sister?"

Ms. Jackson was a round, middle-aged woman and looked beautiful in her yellow dress and hat. The congregation gave her a big hand.

"And I'd like to recognize a young gentleman whose tireless efforts in helping us with our future church in Harlem have been God-sent. We're lucky to have such a well-educated, meticulous-minded engineer willing to represent us when it comes to meeting the city's building codes and zoning demands, and all that other confusing stuff that the Good Lord needs to explain to me . . ."

There was laughter from the congregation and several "Amens."

"But the Good Lord don't have to explain it to me 'cause he sent a young man by the name of Sidney Temple instead. I've had the opportunity to introduce many of you to him over the past year during his many visits to my office here at the church. He's a big part of the building team we've assembled. He's been a guiding hand in the development of our soon-to-be new place of worship. And he's here today with his lovely wife, Loretta. Mr. and Mrs. Temple . . . won't you stand?"

We stood to a big round of applause.

"Praise God," said Powell.

We sat and I wondered if the "Good Lord" would forgive me for the double life I'd created. After two years in Harlem, all of it filled with lies and secrecy, it was probably a good thing I was finally sitting in a house of worship. I closed my eyes, and for the first time in my life asked Him to forgive me for whatever sins I'd committed or was about to commit.

I rose extra early and did my Kodokan exercise in the living room. Loretta was still asleep. Balancing on my left foot and kicking my right leg repeatedly, I thought about the photographed letter I'd mailed to Du Bois. I was sure the *Crisis* editor would take great stock in learning that Garvey had designs on seeking the government's endorsement of his repatriation plan.

I was hoping such a letter would further inspire Du Bois to ramp up his efforts and weaken the Garvey movement. Perhaps it would assist in keeping him one step ahead. In terms of keeping him one step ahead of Hoover, I hadn't met with Agent Mann at Snappy's in months because he was constantly reneging on me, leaving me guessing what the Bureau's latest Du Bois agenda was.

Now doing a series of spinning kicks, I stopped and saw Loretta sitting at the bottom of the stairwell watching me.

"How long have you been there?" I asked.

She smiled. "Long enough to see what I like seeing."

"You're up so early. Can I cook you some breakfast?"

"Go ahead and finish your exercise. I'm enjoying watching."

"I'm finished," I said, taking a towel and wiping my face.

She stood. "Guess what, sweaty boy."

"What?"

"I'll have some help moving your mother and aunt to Vermont."

"What do you mean?"

"Ginger wants to come with me. She's always wanted to visit Canada, so once we've gotten them settled in Middlebury, the two of us are planning to visit Montreal, Quebec City, and maybe Halifax."

"I'd be worried sick about you. Is this safe?"

"Of course it is." She made two fists and frowned. "We're two tough broads."

"Oh . . . okay, okay . . . listen to you . . . with your *bad* self."

"That's right." She put her hands on her waist and tilted her head to the side. "You want some of this, big fella?"

I just smiled and wiped some more sweat from my brow.

"Ah, before I forget," she said, playfully clapping her hands once, "where did you put your railroad maps?"

"They're in the Baby Grand . . . under the seat . . . on the driver's side."

"Why there?"

"I don't know. I took them out of my briefcase one day and never put 'em back. Guess I just like having 'em there now."

"Well, I'd like to borrow one, Mr. Temple."

"Halifax is so far east. You're going to have to purchase a Canadian Pacific Railway map. You two can probably connect with that train in Montreal. I'll find out. You planning on taking the New York Central to Chicago?"

"Yes."

"Map is under the seat. Just make sure you put it back when you two get home."

"Yes, sir!" she sarcastically said, saluting me.

"Before you go, let me teach you some of these kicks. Come here."

She approached with her fists up again as if she were about to attack me. She then pretended to reenact the routine I'd been doing, playfully kicking her right leg at me.

"You better quit before you fall and hurt yourself," I said, grabbing and hugging her as we both chuckled.

She was so happy. I imagined the disapproval Garvey would have of her fully integrated life, her belief that she could live amongst her white friends and travel anywhere without reservation. She would never want to live in a separatist society. Nor would I. My aim was still crystal clear. Absolute freedom was the only answer and the dream had to have a chance. Du Bois had to win out.

22

The house didn't feel the same with her gone. But I stayed plenty busy. I received a telegram at my office that read, "This is Zeus. Meet me at the site of my worst hangover at nine tomorrow night."

Those were the only words written down, but it was enough for me to realize the sender was Bobby Ellington. I searched my mind trying to remember the story he'd told me back during training. He'd talked about a graduation trip, about a spot down in the Tenderloin District where he'd gotten drunk. *Where was it?* "Ah," I said aloud to myself. "The Kessler."

Ellington was waiting inside when I arrived. I'd made sure I wasn't followed, but the meeting was still risky.

"How are you, Bobby?" I asked, sitting down.

"Good, Sidney. I'm only in New York for two days and I'm not getting paid for it. I asked for the time off so I could come see you. The Bureau thinks I'm visiting my brother in Boston."

"Now you got me worried."

"Can I get you two something to drink?" said an approaching waitress.

"Do you care what we drink, Sidney?"

"No."

"We'll take two lemonades for now," said Ellington.

"They'll be right up," she said, walking away.

"Why in the world did you contact me?" I asked.

"I wanted to talk to you about Garvey still being in the Caribbean."

"It's a huge fundraising campaign he's on," I said. "He needs money to build his dream colony in Liberia — the one he wants all us colored folk to return to eventually. I've received word that he's being swarmed by massive crowds wherever he goes — Jamaica, Panama, Costa Rica, etcetera."

"Well, if Hoover has his way, Garvey may be there permanently. He's working with immigration authorities to deny Garvey's reentrance."

"There will be no stopping him from returning," I said. "Trust me. He'll pay folks off if need be, or he'll take a submarine if necessary."

"Submarine?"

"In fact, he just did that," I said. "Authorities were trying to keep him away from Colon, Panama, so he traveled underwater."

"Shit. Well, when he is able to return, assuming it isn't in a submarine, what ship is he due to travel on?"

"The *Kanawha*," I said. "It was being repaired in Havana for weeks but it's now heading for Kingston to retrieve him."

"I just wanted to confirm that it was indeed the *Kanawha* he was due to return on. We got a disturbing tip out of our Florida office. It strongly suggested that several Cuban mechanics were paid handsomely by members of a radical organization out of Jacksonville to rig Garvey's cabin with explosives. Explosives powerful enough to kill him and his party."

"What?"

"But," said Ellington, "officials at the Bureau ignored the tip. They completely turned a blind eye to it — claiming it couldn't be verified. Now I don't know about you, but I didn't get in this business to ignore potential assassination attempts. People may want to see him fail, but do you want him dead, Sidney?"

"No. Well, let me think about it. No."

"Here you go, gentlemen," said the returning waitress, setting two glasses of lemonade on the table. "What can I get you two to eat?"

"I'll have the ham sandwich," said Ellington.

"Make it two," I said.

"They'll be right up."

"Listen, Sidney. I'm not accusing the Bureau of some conspiracy to have Garvey murdered, but ignoring this news is troubling. Now, the tip may be part of a ruse to send agents on a wild-goose chase. God knows we've had our fair share of those, but it could very well be valid."

"It sure could."

"You still have time to do something about it — to stop it."

"You're a good man, Bobby. I knew it from the minute I met you."

"You seemed unsure just now when I asked if you wanted to see him dead."

"I just think he's devising dangerous plans for our people," I said.

"Where do you come down on this war that seems to be brewing between Du Bois and Garvey?"

"You're aware of that?" I asked. "I thought everyone at the Bureau saw them as one and the same."

"I'm not part of that 'everyone.' I think Du Bois is continuing the fight that was born during the abolitionist movement, and it's unique to American coloreds. I'm assuming you support Du Bois."

"You're correct," I said.

"Then you won't like this bit of information. I wouldn't be surprised if the Bureau nails Dr. Du Bois soon for violating the Mann Act. The new agent working at the *Crisis* is claiming that Du Bois has crossed state lines with a young woman, not his wife, on more than one occasion. Agents plan to follow him whenever he travels in the future."

"But I've heard from my friend, a Mr. Daley, that Du Bois simply travels to his speaking engagements occasionally with a young secretary who handles all of his publicity affairs. That's no crime."

"But the agent claims he can prove that the two have a romantic relationship. He claims he can take photographs."

"I doubt it."

"Listen, Sidney. The Mann Act makes it a crime to transport women across state lines 'for the purpose of prostitution or debauchery, or for any other immoral purpose.' It's that last clause — 'for any other immoral purpose' — that gives the government a hell

of a lot of leeway. They're legislating moral-
ity by claiming that adultery is just that —
immoral."

"Du Bois and adultery. I doubt it."

"The agent claims —"

"I got it," I quipped, upset at the very
thought of any of this.

"Okay." He sipped his lemonade.

"Du Bois aside, I'm curious for other folks
in perhaps different situations. What else
falls under this huge umbrella of 'any other
immoral purpose' — or are they making it
up as they go?"

"How about romantic relations between
colored men and white women? The boxer,
Jack Johnson, was arrested for violating the
Mann Act back in 1912. And the woman he
crossed state lines with was his companion.
He even married her later that year."

"Ah, but she was white . . . hence 'any
other immoral purpose.' I got it. This is
unbelievable, Bobby."

"I know. And don't expect any of these
practices to change now that Warren G.
Harding is president."

"You said you had one foot out the door."

"I'm thinking about going to law school.
I've applied here at Columbia."

"Law school in New York, huh? Will you
practice here too eventually?"

"I'd like to return home to Ohio and practice. I want to help folks who can't get a fair shake. Meanwhile, I feel the need to get out of Washington."

"Well, don't leave too soon. I may need you."

"I'll stick around a bit longer."

"Good."

He reached into his coat pocket, pulled out a slip of paper, and slid it across the table.

"Here is my parents' telephone number in Hudson. If I do get into Columbia, you can always track me down by calling them. I'm assuming you won't be getting a home telephone anytime soon?"

"No," I said, picking up the slip of paper. "It's all I can do to protect what little life I do have from the Bureau."

"You know, Sidney, they may not be listening in on your conversations from the office at all. Then again, maybe, just maybe, they are."

"Too much of a risk. So it looks like I'll be calling your parents in Ohio in order to get in touch with you here in New York. Strange is this life of mine."

"Just don't lose touch, Sidney."

I drove to the office contemplating whether

or not I should let Garvey meet his possible fate. After all, I'd killed two men before. Still, I knew there was a difference between having to kill and choosing to kill. One makes you a survivor, the other, a murderer. And what about Miss Jacques? She would also be in the cabin. I knew I had to notify someone of the potential danger. Just how was another question.

I couldn't go directly to Grant and tell him about the possible assassination plot. He'd want to know how I'd learned of it, and I'd be putting a target on my chest as someone privy to top-secret information. UNIA members would never trust me again.

I decided to stop at a telephone booth on Amsterdam Avenue and call UNIA headquarters. It was well past eleven p.m., but I knew someone would be there. Dialing the numbers, I tried to formulate what I'd say, but the telephone only rang once.

"UNIA," said a female voice that I recognized. It was Cindy, and I knew she'd take the message seriously.

"Yes," I said in a deep, well-disguised Southern voice — trying to sound like a white man. "This is officer Role Coleman of the Jacksonville Police Department in Florida."

"Yes," she said.

"We understand that Mr. Marcus Garvey is currently in Kingston, Jamaica."

"Yes."

"He's to board the *Kanway,* right?" I asked, purposely mispronouncing the name — my Southern drawl growing even deeper. I'd never performed like this before. "How you say the name of that ship, darlin'?"

"Kanawha," she answered.

"Got it! We have reason to believe he may be in some serious danger if he boards the *Konway,* whenever it arrives in Kingston. We've contacted the authorities in Kingston about a possible attempt that may be made on his life, but they haven't cooperated. Of course international affairs are outside of our jurisdiction, so we depend on the local authorities to handle this, but they're not. Buncha no-good, lazy sons a bitches!"

"Yes, please continue," she anxiously said.

"You writin' all this down, darlin'?"

"Yes."

"Please be thorough. I would strongly suggest that you have Mr. Garvey's security team sweep the entire ship before he boards — particularly his cabin. There may be explosives on board. His team should also clear the ship of all its personnel and search them thoroughly. Send word immediately."

"I will, officer. Thank you."

"There are a few of us lawmen out here who care about doing the right thing. Some local men here in Jacksonville, part of a dangerous operation, may likely be behind this. We're still investigating. I'll contact you if we find any further information."

"I'll send word immediately. I must go. Thank you again."

She hung up and I stood there holding the telephone, analyzing what I'd just done. I then hung it up and walked to my car, contemplating my next move. I had to inform Du Bois of the Bureau's intentions — of possibly nailing him violating the Mann Act.

What in the world was I doing? On one hand I was helping Garvey stay alive; on the other, preventing Du Bois from possibly going to jail. If my conscience wouldn't allow Garvey to die, I'd have to accept that his agenda might never be curtailed and I'd failed in accomplishing my objective. Though I was banking on his eventually being charged with mail fraud or some other illegality, perhaps death was all that could truly stop him. Maybe I'd made a grave mistake.

Driving home, I thought about the many ships Garvey had purchased. Every single one was in terrible condition. How I'd managed to help get any of them up and running was hard to believe. And what was he doing with all these lemons anyway? He wanted to do something specific with the Black Star Line but was only managing to create a big financial mess. And to somehow think that all of this was going to lead eventually to transporting people back to Africa was preposterous.

With Loretta now back from her trip, the two of us relaxed in bed before going to sleep for the night, each of us with a book in hand. It was as if the candle lanterns on each of our night tables were tucking us in, providing just enough dim light to keep us awake for a few more minutes.

I looked over to see what she was enthralled in and saw that it was *The Picture of Dorian Gray* by Oscar Wilde. I was beginning *The Thirty-Nine Steps* by John Buchan. Part of the opening paragraph took hold of me. Writing about his main character, Buchan penned, ". . . I couldn't get enough exercise, and the amusements of London seemed as flat as soda-water that has been standing in the sun. 'Richard Hannay,' I kept telling myself, 'you have got into the wrong ditch, my friend, and you better climb out.' "

I could have easily replaced the name Richard Hannay with Sidney Temple. My mind wandered back and forth from Hannay's world to my own. Garvey was finally returning from Kingston aboard the *Kanawha*. I didn't know whether or not my warning had been heeded, and I'd likely never find out. I certainly wasn't going to ask anyone traveling with Garvey if they'd found explosives on board. Perhaps I'd learn what took place in due time without inquiring.

I turned the page of my novel, trying to refocus on Hannay's London flat behind Langham Place but could think only about Du Bois and the newest anonymous letter I'd sent him. I'd made it very clear that the Bureau was trying to catch him violating the Mann Act and had outlined all the details involved. I warned him to be concerned only if what he'd been accused of doing were true.

Whether or not it was true didn't concern to me, as those matters were a man's private, personal affairs. My focus was on the job at hand, and it felt empowering to be doing just what I'd set out to do — protect Du Bois from both the Bureau and Garvey.

"Are you gonna read much longer?" asked

Loretta, setting her book on the end table.

"No, I'm finished for the night."

"I hope your mother and aunt are adjusting to their new little home. Ginger and I had such a fantastic time moving them in, and the four of us took daily long walks around the grounds. The maples looked more beautiful than ever. And your mother told me she intends to take that walk every day."

"That would be good for her."

"The entire trip was a joy, hopping from train to train in order to get to some remote town on time just so we could then catch another connecting train to get to the next city. Is that confusing enough?"

My mind was elsewhere, but still I answered: "Yes."

"But I'm dying to show you Canada now. So picturesque. Once we left Quebec City, the trip really became a visual odyssey. It was an event just trying to figure out how those engineers managed to carve through so much thick, woodsy, mountainous terrain in order to stretch the railroad all the way to Halifax."

"We must go. I'd love to see it. Which town did you enjoy the most?"

"Believe it or not, it wasn't in Canada. It was Portland, Maine, of all places. We passed through it on our way back to New York and slept at this delightful place called The Inn at St. John. It was quite charming, completely Victorian in décor . . . the ocean so close, the clean, crisp air. Delightful. It was as if that little inn was made for you and me. I felt such a connection to you while staying there. And now I know why."

"Why?"

"I'll always remember The Inn at St. John as the place where I first knew."

"Knew what?"

"Well . . . you know I went and saw Dr. Wade today, right?"

"Yes."

"Well . . . are you ready to be a daddy?"

I just lay there staring at her. The news caught me completely off guard. I had not granted myself the time to even think of such a possibility. I realized how consumed I'd been with work — how detached I'd been from Loretta. But the news got my heart racing.

"Don't pull my leg, Loretta."

"No, I'm serious. I'm several weeks along. Toward the end of the trip I began feeling a bit sick to my stomach. So I scheduled the doctor visit upon our return and today I received the news."

"Oh, my God," I said, reaching over and

touching her stomach.

"You happy, Love?"

"I'm the happiest man in Harlem. Why didn't you tell me earlier?"

"I wanted it to be the last thing you heard today before falling asleep. Maybe tonight will be the first time in a long time that you sleep through the night without tossing and turning, a night in which you'll have nothing but wonderful dreams."

"I need that. Body has grown too used to these damn pills and the doctor said not to take more than one a night."

"Listen to him."

"I can't believe I'm going to have a son."

"Hey! I want a girl."

"Then one of us will get what we want."

"That's right."

"My God, you've made me a happy man, woman."

"I can tell."

"I love you, I love you, I love you," I said, kissing her repeatedly. "I'll be right back."

I hopped out of bed with the youthful exuberance of a five-year-old and headed downstairs to make us both some hot tea. I returned to find her smiling from ear to ear. We sat in bed sipping from our cups and coming up with possible names for our future child. It was hours before we fell asleep. What a night!

23

On a Saturday in July, Lennox Avenue was bustling with colored artists displaying paintings, playing instruments, and reading poetry along the sidewalks. Rife with the smells, sights, and sounds unique to Harlem, it was the biggest street festival I'd witnessed since arriving two years earlier. Thousands, it seemed, walked up and down the avenue, taking in the art while snacking on everything from fresh fruit, peanuts, and pastries to caramels, dried sausages, and Cracker Jacks.

Loretta and Ginger led the way as Peavine and I talked about his family and ambitions. I'd invited him along for the day because I'd sensed something missing in the young man's life. He seemed to be drifting along aimlessly, only latching on to Garvey's movement out of happenstance.

"Touching brass jumpstarts my heart," he said, the two of us stopping in front of an ashy-handed trumpet player who blew hard enough for even lower Manhattan to hear him. "I want to be him, Mr. Temple. Look at him with his eyes shut, his right fingers dancing, and cheeks 'bout to pop. He's feelin' somethin' we ain't — traveling somewhere we ain't been — a place only that horn can take you."

"Maybe you can play like that someday."

"I need to go to Chicago. I need to learn from these new cats, Joe King Oliver and Bill Johnson. They done brought a style of music up to Chicago from New Orleans — this thing called Hot Jazz. I heard 'em play here in Harlem last year. I ain't been the same since."

"What would it take for you to move to Chicago?"

"Ah, Mr. Temple, I sleep at a different spot every night as it is. I got me a livin' system. Ain't got no livin' system in Chicago."

"Where's your family?"

"I been livin' on the streets since I was twelve . . . some eight years now. Ain't got no family. This music done become my kinfolk."

We continued listening to the trumpet player, then squeezed our way through the thick cluster of onlookers before catching up with Loretta and Ginger about a half block down. We gathered around a young poet who was reading his poem with the kind of experienced voice reserved for a man twice his age.

Folks clapped with enthusiasm. I stood in line and purchased a copy, learning that the young man's name was Countee Cullen. The poem was entitled, "I Have a Rendezvous With Life." I couldn't help but think of my favorite poet — my friend, Claude — who was preparing to head overseas again — to Russia. This time I wondered if he'd ever return.

The four of us continued on, walking past several restaurants, the food on full display and being sold from carts right there on the sticky sidewalk. We stopped again to watch several painters at work. Placing my hand on Loretta's belly and lightly rubbing, I looked up and around, north and south, trying to take it all in, wishing all of colored America could take part in this rare moment of collective freedom and gaiety.

The sounds of brass and banjos. The smells of fried catfish, buttery collard greens, and banana pudding. The sights of ebony old men with canes, young brown girls chewing bubble gum, jubilant cocoa couples walking hand-in-hand — an angelic array of Harlemites bathing in a sea of artistic tranquility.

A huge part of my job that Hoover and company simply had to accept was playing the so-called "waiting game." There was no speeding up the clock either. Undercover work is a slow, tedious grind. In situations like mine, the agent's sole task is to remain intimately attached to the target. The Bureau wanted Garvey bad and knew he was stepping into a trap, but his step was a big, slow one, and he hadn't been snagged yet.

We had to be one hundred percent certain that he'd broken the law before any move could be made. And more time meant more one-on-one meetings with Garvey, my least favorite thing. The tension was always suffocating. But here I was — again — sitting in the office I'd searched just a few months back. I could hear Speed's recent words ringing in my ear.

"I don't care if you have to sit in his office all day and discuss the fucking unique and varietal shapes of African Pygmy dicks! You stay in Garvey's lap, Q! We're close here to nailing the fucker."

I watched Garvey studying an elaborate architectural drawing of the future UNIA headquarters he intended to construct in

Liberia. Leaning against the wall behind him were rolls of drawings that hadn't been opened yet. I assumed they were sketches of other buildings, ones that would serve as the original landmarks of this undeveloped city he was dreaming up.

"Sidney, you ever read Edward Wilmot Blyden?" he asked, running his hand along the drawing, trying to flatten it out. As usual, he wasn't making eye contact.

"No," I answered.

"He is the father of Pan-Africanism. He, like me, was born in the West Indies. But he moved to Liberia and actually became editor of the *Liberia Herald.* At different points he was the Liberian ambassador to France and Britain and was the president of Liberia College. He is my hero. You have any heroes?"

"My mother."

"Why not me?" he asked, placing coins on each corner of the stubborn paper to keep it from rolling back up.

"Well, I . . ."

"Don't bother answering that. I know you're a careful man. You're still studying me. Take your time. It took me years to decide that Blyden was my champion. Perhaps when I die you will crown me your king."

"The fact that I'm sitting in this chair should tell you how certain I am that you're the most powerful Negro in the world."

"Well, then! Enough said on that topic. Do you think we are wise to be in negotiations to purchase this boat, the *Orion*? Is it a quality ship?"

"I think it's in decent condition, but with limited access, I've only given it a brief inspection. When will you take official ownership?"

"Soon, but the U.S. Shipping Board is being difficult. Cyril Briggs and his African Blood Brotherhood have convinced them that I don't have the funds. Anyway, you do realize it's more grand than our other ships?"

"Yes, it's a luxury ocean liner," I said. "I toured more than *just* the engine room during the brief time I was allowed aboard."

"Yes, a luxury boat, which means it will not be used for transporting goods, although that is a critical part of this shipping business. Negroes from America to Jamaica to Africa need to be able to trade products with one another exclusively. We must cut out the white man. Fend for ourselves."

"So you see the *Orion* as the first ship you'll use to begin ferrying folks back to Africa?"

"Yes," he said, jotting something down on the elaborate drawing with a pencil, examining it as if he were the architect himself. "But, Sidney, nothing is coming easy these days. The powers that be tried to make it impossible for me to reenter the country. Now they're making it difficult for me to stay here. And the number one culprit behind all of this is that mulatto, Du Bois."

"I didn't realize he was part of the powers that be," I said.

"Come again."

Realizing I had instinctively countered his point with sarcasm, I quickly walked my comment back.

"Du Bois only wishes he were part of the powers that be. But God knows he's willing to kiss whoever's rear end in order to become so."

"Good point, Sidney. Nevertheless, who knows what lies he's feeding the government about me. One of the reasons I respect Blyden so much has to do with his statements about these yellow types of people. Blyden died years ago, but were he alive today, he'd have plenty to say about Du Bois and Cyril Briggs — two white Negroes of the worst sort. They're both likely behind this movement to have me thoroughly audited."

"But Briggs, like you, is from the West Indies. Correct?"

"And I'm not proud of that fact. He's a fool. He keeps trying to convince me that Marxism should be the ideology we adopt. Nonsense. Capitalism will be the economic system under which we govern in Africa very soon. But we must mobilize quickly. The government is squeezing me from all directions."

I could sense his uneasiness and urgency, an awareness that his movement might finally be going under. He turned and reached for another one of the drawings. He began unrolling it, positioning it directly on top of the other. Again, he placed coins on its corners.

"Sidney, it's important for the man who's examining my dream boat to feel the same conviction about our Africa agenda as I feel. Such conviction will guide the work you do."

"Understood. I will inspect it thoroughly. I hear everything you're saying. I feel Africa in my bones."

"You know, Sidney . . . I was treated like a god wherever I traveled in the Caribbean. Thousands swarmed me at each and every stop. And now I return to America, only to be challenged by these second-rate Negroes like Cyril Briggs, A. Philip Randolph, and

Chandler Owen. But I'll show them all the reach of my power."

"Your power cannot be questioned."

"And it will be on full display in a few weeks, once our second International Convention of the Negro Peoples of the World begins. I understand that Du Bois is readying himself to leave for France soon again. So while we're having our convention, he will be attending the second Pan-African Congress. That is a convention of dreamers. Ours is a convention of doers. Where would you rather be?"

"Here, of course. I'm a doer."

"I know this," he said, scribbling something on the drawing. "So was Blyden. And he knew the dangers of having uppity white Negroes like Du Bois in power. When speaking about the importance of all Negroes returning to Africa, Blyden once said, 'The Negro leader of the exodus, who will succeed, will be a Negro of the Negroes, like Moses was a Hebrew of the Hebrews — even if brought up in Pharaoh's palace — no half-Hebrew and half-Egyptian will do the work.' He also said, 'When I am dead, write nothing on my tombstone but . . . *He hated mulattoes.*' "

"He made himself clear, didn't he?" I said.

"And I will make myself clear. I've said

374

this before. Du Bois is not a real man of color. He is a little Dutch, a little French, a little Negro . . . a mulatto. He is a monstrosity."

He still wasn't looking up, but just in case he could see me, I nodded my head to suggest I agreed. But my hatred for Garvey had never been more intense. I wanted to reach across the desk and pummel him. Instead, I just glared at him as he continued making notations.

"Du Bois's NAACP will soon go under," he said.

"I hope so. But why?"

"We are pulling members away from him one by one. And now we must go for his big fish. Du Bois is only as strong as the top men around him. William Pickens is one of those. He's a Yale man. I've learned that he is unhappy with his pay. I will offer him a cabinet position."

"How can he help?"

"He was a professor of foreign languages. We could use a man of his ilk, especially when we land in Africa and begin reaching out to Europe, Asia, etcetera, building relationships with world leaders. I will make Pickens an offer he won't refuse. Money is a powerful thing."

"Sounds promising."

"The UNIA contingent I sent to Liberia is laying the groundwork for all of us to move there soon. Cyril Crichlow is heading things up on our behalf. I am offering up a loan to the Liberian treasury. But we must raise money. Getting folks excited about this new ship and going to Liberia will be the key to raising enough funds for the loan. And this Liberian excitement will also be the key to keeping the Black Star Line afloat. I think the two million dollars we've proposed will do the trick?"

"That's a lot of money."

"Well, it can be raised. I raised quite a bit in the Caribbean. Now we must double our efforts. Besides, if Charles D. B. King, Liberia's president, thinks he's going to secure the millions he's seeking from the American government, he's a fool. And why would he even consider taking money from them? Such a deal will only stifle their independence."

"So you're saying you'll give them two million to develop Liberia in exchange for them allowing you to bring Negroes from the West Indies and America there to be a part of this development?"

"Indeed. It goes hand in hand. Millions of proud returning Negroes, anxious to work, raise families, and purchase goods will only boost Liberia's overall economy. And we shall go soon, develop a massive plot of land near Monrovia, and live like we were meant to live. It's all here on these architectural drawings."

"I see."

"And who will be the lead engineer of all of this, you might be wondering?"

"Well, you'll want the very best. I know that."

"You, Sidney. You will oversee the construction of this new African city — this Negro capital of the world."

I paused at the thought. "I'm humbled by your suggestion, sir."

"You know, I've been asked on more than one occasion if I actually expect to take all of the millions of Negroes in the West Indies and America back to Africa on my ships. And I always say, we were all brought here on big, filthy, ugly boats, but we shall return on big, clean, beautiful ones."

He moved his face very close to the drawing and frowned. Something he saw was unsettling. Taking his pencil, he drew a big X through a portion of it.

"Doesn't this idiot of an architect know that I want a much larger office? These measurements are incorrect. Such a miniature office isn't fit for the Provisional

President of Africa."

He took a ruler from his drawer and slammed it on the desk. He then placed it above the portion of the drawing he'd crossed out. I'd never seen him so focused, so engineer-like.

Running his pencil along the ruler, he began changing the measurements of his future office. With his nose damn near touching the drawing and his focus squarely on the ruler, he began speaking slowly, as if doing so would help him concentrate.

"All through the previous century," he said, "coloreds from America made attempts to return to Africa. Paul Cuffe sailed into Sierra Leone with several Negro families in 1816. But what I'm proposing is moving every family. And I don't believe President Harding will be opposed to such an exodus. He seems to be a decent white man, and I think it's important that the UNIA begin to project a pro-U.S. government image."

"Why now?"

"Let's just say I believe President Harding, if given the choice, would choose me to represent colored America over Du Bois. And the more I denounce communism in favor of capitalism, the more I denounce Du Bois's integration platform in favor of separation, the more likely it is that our movement can gain the support of the new president."

I adjusted in the chair and crossed my legs as he continued with the pencil and ruler.

"Also, Sidney, perhaps the government will call off the dogs . . . the authorities that seem dead set on forcing me out of the country. And, of course I actually believe in capitalism and separatism."

I couldn't believe it. He was actually admitting that he was willing to kowtow to the government to save his hide. Didn't he understand that forcing them to accept integration was the brave thing to do — that it was, in effect, standing up for Negroes, not selling them out?

I found it laughable and naïve that after all the negative things he'd said about white America and the government, he now believed that cozying up to the president was going to keep officials from getting rid of him. I wanted to tell him he was a marked man and that there was no getting around it. I also wanted to know more about his newly professed respect for the president.

"What about Harding strikes you as decent?"

"Well, as you know, Harding said, 'Race amalgamation there can never be.' This is certainly in conflict with Du Bois's views and directly in line with mine. So I believe Mr. Harding and I see this race issue in the same light. And, like me, he is not afraid to say what he thinks publicly."

"But didn't the president also say that both races should stand against social equality?"

"Yes. And he is right. We cannot be socially equal to the white man in his country. In his American society, he makes the societal rules. He sets the agenda. We must establish our own society."

"We're well on our way."

"In the meantime," he said, still drawing the proper measurements for his office, "I must stay out of trouble, both here and abroad. I got myself in a bit of a pickle with British authorities while in Jamaica. They were upset over what I said at Liberty Hall before heading to the Caribbean. Do you remember what I said about the British Colonial Secretary?"

"You mean your comments about Winston Churchill?"

"Yes. I am testing whether or not you pay attention to my speeches."

"You said something along the lines of him being the greatest Negro hater in the British Empire."

"Good! Very good! I went on to say that he was appointed because of his willingness to carry out that savagery and brutality among the darker and weaker races of the world through a system of exploitation that will bring bankrupt Britain the solvency she so much desires."

"Right. I remember."

"When the British authorities confronted me with the quote, I denied having said it. Unfortunately, my words had been printed in a very peculiar place — in my own paper, the *Negro World.*"

I immediately let out a bit of a laugh. Garvey abruptly stopped drawing, as if making sure he'd actually heard me. But he didn't look up. He simply stared at his pencil for a second, then continued drawing. Somehow I think he intended to tell the story in a funny way and didn't mind my reaction. Nevertheless, I quickly regained my composure.

"And, Sidney, what doubled the matter is Churchill himself had supposedly read my words. So I was told. Not a pleasant encounter with those authorities to say the least."

"I'll bet."

"This Churchill oversees these various colonies — these slave plantations if you will. He sickens me. Great Britain may think they own my native Jamaica. They may believe they own beautiful Sierra Leone, but they are wrong on both counts."

"Sierra Leone borders Liberia, correct?"

"Yes. Why else do you think British authorities fear me gaining a stronghold there? They want to keep me as far away from Sierra Leone as possible. They know my presence will embolden the natives. They remember 1898, when the natives rose up and fought the British for their independence."

"The Hut Tax War. I've read of it."

"You please me very much, Sidney. So well informed. Hundreds of British soldiers and hundreds of natives were killed in that war. But, of course, the natives were ultimately crushed, their leader, Bai Bureh, captured, and almost a hundred of his close confidants hanged by the cowardly Brits."

"Maybe the British authorities think you're the new Bai Bureh."

"All I know is they fear me. I'm sure they pay close attention to everything I say. I've made it crystal clear to them how much I intend to fight against British colonialism. It's evil. It must be eradicated. And I'll continue to say so publicly."

"Amen," I said.

And I meant it. Garvey did occasionally

say things I agreed with wholeheartedly. But Du Bois felt the same way about British colonialism. What colored man with a pulse didn't?

"Counter to that," he continued, "here in America I must take a different course. When it comes to speaking out against the U.S. government, those men in Washington will be pleased to know I'm turning over a new leaf. No more agitating the powers that be, especially if such actions threaten our goal of heading home to Africa with me at the helm. Time to play nice."

But how long could he play nice once he was arrested and thrown in jail? I saw that day coming very soon.

24

With Loretta now several months along, I tried to think of ways to lighten her load a bit. I decided to take her to a Broadway play. *Shuffle Along* was premiering. I'd gotten the tickets from Phil Daley, who'd intended to use them, but another event required his attendance. Loretta was very much looking forward to getting out of the house and seeing the much-talked-about musical.

As we entered the 63rd Street Music Hall, I marveled at the well-dressed patrons funneling through the foyer and into the theater, all of them white. Loretta was so lively, so happy, and walking with great anticipation. It was as if she were made for showy events like this. And I certainly felt handsome in my black tuxedo.

"How do I look?" she asked.

"Stunning. I love you in black. But you're beautiful in all your dresses."

We had presented ourselves at the box office, and now, with stubs in hand, we started toward the entryway of the orchestra. Approaching the usher, I couldn't help but notice the quizzical look on his face. He stopped us.

"May I see your stubs, sir?"

I handed them over and he eyed them, obviously trying to confirm that we were heading in the right direction. He handed them back and, with a bit of a frown, pointed us toward our seats.

"You're in the second row," he muttered. "Right orchestra. The two seats on the end."

"Thank you," I said.

Taking Loretta's hand, I led the way to our seats. The theater was just about full, and loud with chatter. I was overcome with pride to see so many pouring in to see a Negro musical. Presenting all black faces on stage performing a play written by people of color was a first for Broadway.

"This is a splendid scene," Loretta said, taking her seat.

"The play is getting rave reviews," I said, easing into my chair. "How are you feeling?"

"Wonderful."

"I mean, how are both of you feeling?" I reached over and discreetly touched her stomach, which was now showing a bit of a bump.

"We're fantastic."

"Can I get you anything?"

"Just hold my hand," she said, giving me a big smile, as I took her hand in mine.

"It should be starting in about ten minutes. Oh, I forgot to mention something. Claude sent word that the *Liberator* hasn't forgotten about you. Max Eastman still intends to do a write-up of your work whenever you do a showing."

"How thoughtful. I wonder how much Ginger has to do with that?"

"Is she still seeing him?" I asked.

"We tend to avoid the subject. His divorce isn't finalized."

"What? He's married?"

"Yes," she said. "So to speak."

"So to speak?"

"Max never wanted to get married. He doesn't even believe in marriage, according to Ginger."

"Then what does he believe in?"

"Bolshevism and Russia," she whispered. "He intends to go very soon."

"So does Claude. Hmm. Both he and Claude in Russia. Interesting."

The woman seated next to Loretta began looking at her as if she wanted to strike up a conversation. And she did.

"Pardon me."

"Yes," said Loretta.

"Do you happen to know how long the play has been running?"

"I read that it's been up for about four months."

"Oh. My husband and I love Eubie Blake," said the middle-aged woman.

"So do we. My husband raves about him."

"Well, you two make a lovely young couple."

"How kind of you. Thank you very much. I hope you enjoy the play."

I noticed the usher approaching us, still with that same frown. An older gentleman accompanied him.

"Excuse me, sir," he said. "This is the theater manager, Mr. Loving."

"Yes," I responded. "How can I help you?"

"Well," said the stuffy manager, "you must understand, sir, we don't allow coloreds to sit in this section of the orchestra. I must ask that you and your wife sit in the special section at the left rear of the orchestra."

I turned and saw a tiny designated area where about twenty coloreds were seated. Granted, they were orchestra seats, but they were very far back.

"Pardon me?" said Loretta. "We have

tickets for these seats. Show them, Sidney."

"Don't bother," said the manager. "We've seen your tickets. We kindly ask that you follow theater protocol and make your way to the colored section."

My heart fell into my stomach. I'd tried to avoid ever letting Loretta experience such embarrassment. But I knew she'd eventually come face-to-face with the sting of racism. I always wanted her to see me as her protector, someone who wouldn't allow anyone to talk down to me. But here it was, and the look on her face hurt me more than the manager's request itself.

"These are our seats," she continued. "I don't understand."

"Please," said the manager, as many in the audience looked on and whispered. "The show is about to commence."

I felt glued to my seat. I felt heavy and a bit dizzy. I felt powerless. And at that very moment I knew like never before why I'd agreed to be a spy. I knew that the cause of my work was to see Du Bois's dream of complete integration come to fruition and never to be treated like a dog again. I was experiencing a seminal moment. I could hear Garvey's voice in my ear. "You shouldn't be in that white theater anyway, Sidney! We must start our own theaters!"

But I wanted to be in *this* theater seeing *this* show. I wanted my wife to continue her conversation with the lovely woman next to her. I wanted to experience *Shuffle Along* up close. But America wasn't willing to let me. I thought about my unborn child and committed right then and there to doing everything in my power to make sure he or she could sit in these seats someday. Fighting back the anger, I squeezed Loretta's hand and led her out.

"Come on, sweetheart."

She felt very light, as if there was no strength to her. As we entered the foyer, I turned and looked into her empty eyes. Directly behind us walked the manager and usher. *Would turning and hitting one of them square in the face do anything to relieve her pain?* I wondered, but then realized that my being in jail for years would only hurt her and leave my baby without a father.

"Sir," said the manager, "the entrance to the colored section is straight ahead to the right."

"We're fine," I said, still walking, the two of them following. "I think we'll pass on seeing the show from the slave quarters."

"Now please calm down, sir. At least we've begun allowing you-all to sit in the orchestra. It was only the balcony before, and before that you weren't even allowed in."

"Well praise God!" I hollered, the two of us stooping just before exiting the building. I stiffened my back. "We surely thanks you, Massa!"

"Why, I beg your pardon, sir!"

I leaned forward and in a fit of rage yelled, "Well then go ahead! Beg!"

"Excuse me?" said the manager, confusion on his face.

"Beg me to pardon you."

There was silence as he and the usher stood there gawking at us. The foyer was empty save for a few more ushers scuttling about. I waited for him to reply but didn't hear a peep.

"That's what I thought. You can't bring yourself to beg a nigger for anything. You're the worst kind of man. You're not the type to whip us down South, but you're perfectly fine running a so-called 'fine establishment' in uppity New York City that treats colored folks like garbage."

"Sir . . . please," he calmly said.

"No! I respect a man holding a sign in front of him that says he hates Negroes more than I respect you — a phony who hides behind a nice suit and fancy surroundings. You just don't want anyone to know you're a bigot. We're in New York, not

Alabama. There's no law forcing you to follow this protocol. You *choose* to continue enforcing such barbaric rules."

He stood there, beet red, along with his young sidekick. Somehow it was apropos that we had come to see a play entitled *Shuffle Along,* because that was exactly what we intended to do, rather than see the musical from the cheap seats. We stepped out into the night air and, with our spirits broken but pride still intact, shuffled along.

Driving home, I tried to imagine what Loretta was feeling. I recalled her birthday party and how I'd tried to explain Loretta's upbringing to James. I knew she'd been shielded from discrimination her entire life, living in an upper-class colored community, encountering whites only while attending institutions that supported equality of the races.

"Are you okay?"

She nodded yes. But she wasn't okay. Her father had succeeded in creating a unique reality for her, but in doing so he'd also created a very fragile soul. Of course, I knew she could ultimately survive the ugliness that existed out there, but how much would it change her?

"I love you, Loretta," I said, thinking of the latest letter I'd sent to Du Bois.

"I love you too," she quietly said. "Let's just get home. I'll make us some tea."

I nodded, my mind still on the letter. After what had just happened inside that theater, I wondered if I was actually doing enough to keep Du Bois one step ahead of Garvey. The letter had been brief.

Dear Dr. Du Bois,

Please know that Marcus Garvey has every intention of offering one of your top men, William Pickens, a job offer he can't refuse. He has learned that Pickens is unhappy with his pay there at the NAACP and intends to lure him away from you by offering him a cabinet position and a lot of money. He also intends to begin pulling your top members away one by one and believes this is the way to weaken the NAACP and strengthen the UNIA. Finally, please be aware that Garvey intends to make his Back to Africa plan come true by offering President Charles D. B. King of Liberia a two-million-dollar loan.

Sincerely,
The Loyalist

Glancing again over at Loretta, I thought of her future. I knew there'd be no more private school walls or liberal college fences to protect her. Her interpretation of the world was being challenged. However naïve it was, I loved her rosy optimism. I wanted to protect it. Millions of well-to-do white girls were afforded it. Why not her? I didn't believe that she had to experience man-made ugliness in order to be a true artist. Life itself provided enough natural pain, like the death of her parents.

"I'll drive by Fats' and get us some of that cake you like," I said, trying anything to lift her spirit just a tiny bit.

"Okay."

I wondered if she no longer saw me as her knight in shining armor, the one who could do anything, even convince the racist theater manager to buck the rules and allow us to remain in the second row. Her admiring me was, in many ways, all I lived for. In the recesses of my mind I knew that even my becoming an agent was so that I could make possible a pathway to ascend to some impressive position in society — one that no other Negro had occupied.

"Cake and tea sounds good," I said. "And I'll read to you."

She nodded yes as I continued driving, observing the many colored men walking the night streets, most of them very poor-looking, lumbering along as if they had the weight of the world on their shoulders, wondering where to turn for some relief from the mighty grip of oppression. They were me and I was them.

But I was in denial in a sense, trying at times to pretend that I didn't have colored skin. I had no desire to be a king as Garvey did. I just wanted to be free to rise as high as my ability and ambition would take me, and for Loretta to have no limitations placed upon her. I never wanted to pause and take the time to realize my true position in American society, that of a second-class citizen. Death would be better than accepting such a role.

25

October 21, 1921, turned out to be a day I'd never forget. James, Hubert Harrison, William Ferris, and I were sitting inside the machine house atop a gigantic steam shovel at the future sight of the Abyssinian Church, eating doughnuts and drinking coffee. We sat on the left side of the car frame with our legs hanging over.

It was early in the morning and none of the contractors had arrived yet to continue the excavation that had been going on for months. With nearly a quarter block of freshly dug dirt surrounding us and the sun barely peeking over the brownstones of West 138th Street, William opened a copy of the *New York Times.*

"Don't you be bringin' us no bad news this early in the mornin', William," said James, nibbling on his doughnut. "Gosh darn *New York Times!*"

William looked up and we all surveyed

the various large mounds of freshly dug soil — some of which looked like fifteen-foot pyramids. The morning mist had dampened the ground, and we could smell the earth.

"I tell you what," I said. "It looks like it may take another two years before this project is finished."

"Gotta build it right," said James. "Build it strong."

"You see how the landscape drops down over yonder?" I said. "This big ol' steam shovel we're sittin' on is at ground level. But the other half of this lot is already about fifteen feet deep. They've gotta dig this whole lot deep enough for a church basement."

"You know how to operate a scary monster like this here, Sidney?" asked Hubert.

"Yep. But it takes a team of folks. Three. The engineer, fireman, and ground man. The engineer operates the shovel."

"That'd be you?" Hubert asked, taking another doughnut from the brown paper bag.

"Mm-hmm. And if one of you wanted to be the fireman, you'd be in charge of tendin' to that big boiler at the back of the house."

They all three leaned back and stared at the large boiler as I reached into the bag and took the last doughnut.

"Good golly," James jokingly said, chewing with his mouth open before I continued.

"You'd have to stoke the flames with coal and maintain just the right amount of pressure, enough to provide the steam needed to power the movement of that long dipper stick and heavy bucket out front. You reckon you're up for the job, James?"

"Think I'll stick to preachin' if you don't mind."

"I think that'd be good," I said, taking a big drink of coffee. "For all of our sakes."

"You done good on helpin' Reverend Powell out on this," said James. "He a good man. One of the best. Sho nuff! You've done the Lord's work on tryin' to get this here church built. And believe me, your reward is comin'."

"I cannot believe my eyes," said William, staring at the newspaper. Something had obviously caught his attention and he handed the paper to James.

"What in the name of the good Lord do we have here?" asked James, setting his cup on the car frame, taking the last bite of his doughnut, and pulling the paper close. "I said don't you bring me no bad news this early, William."

"What does it say, James?" asked Hubert.

"It says that President Harding just gave a speech in Birmingham, Alabama. The headline reads, HARDING SUPPORTS NEW POLICY IN SOUTH. A subtitle reads, NEGROES ENDORSE SPEECH."

"But continue reading, James," said William.

"It says, 'Marcus Garvey, President General of the Universal Negro Improvement Association, sent the following telegram to President Harding yesterday congratulating him on his speech on the Negro question as delivered at Birmingham, Alabama.' "

"That's what I thought it said," quipped William, angrily taking the paper back from James. "I just wanted to make sure my eyes weren't deceiving me. I thought I saw Marcus's name on that paper."

"Marcus's telegram reads just like this," said William: " 'Honorable Warren G. Harding, President of the United States. Please accept heartfelt thanks of four hundred million Negroes of the world for the splendid interpretation you have given of the race problem in today's speech at Birmingham. The Negroes of the world at this time, when the world is gone wild in its injustice to weaker peoples, greet you as a wise and great statesman, and feel that with principles such as you stand for, humanity will lose its prejudice and the brotherhood of man will be established.' "

"Jesus," said Hubert.

"I can't believe my ears," added James.

"Wait," said William. "The telegram goes further saying, 'All true Negroes are against social equality, believing that all races should develop on their own social lines. Only a few selfish members of the Negro race believe in the social amalgamation of black and white. The new Negro will join hands with those who are desirous of keeping the two opposite races socially pure and work together for the industrial, educational, and political liberation of all peoples.' "

"Is that all?" I asked.

"Believe it or not, no," said William. "He writes further: 'The Negro peoples of the world expect the South of the United States of America to give the Negro a fair chance, and your message of today shall be conveyed to the four hundred millions of our race around the world. Long live America! Long live President Harding in his manly advocacy of human justice! I have the honor to be your obedient servant.' "

"Wow," I said.

"He then signs off," continued William, " 'Marcus Garvey, President General, Universal Negro Improvement Association and Provisional President of Africa.' "

"Did he really say, 'I have the honor to be your obedient servant?' " asked Hubert.

"Mm-hmm," said William. "God as my witness. I wouldna believed it myself were it not right here in bold print. And in the *New York Times* at that."

James grabbed the paper from William, slapped it with the back of his hand, and then threw it off the steam shovel.

"Marcus done miscalculated here," said James. "Dr. Du Bois, Mr. Weldon Johnson, and the rest of the Talented Tenth will use these words against him like none he's spoken before. They will use it as a rallying cry for American Negroes — those born here — to unite. And I don't say 'American' lightly. American brothers and sisters won't go for this. I won't go for it."

"Neither will I," said William. "The last straw."

"Absolutely not," said Hubert. "Unacceptable."

"Ain't no Negroes raised in America ready to talk about being obedient to no man," said James. "To God, yes. To a man, no. This a cryin' shame."

As the conversing continued, I recalled the conversation I'd had with Garvey. And though he'd told me of his plans to begin pushing a pro government agenda, never did I expect him to be so barefaced about it.

"He's toadying to authorities," said Hubert. "But he's overreaching. It's too big a switch. One day he's railing against the government, the next he's kissing their rear ends. It makes him look scared, desperate, and weak."

"Tell you what," said James. "If I was President Harding and received a letter like this from Marcus, it would only make me more suspicious of him. It'd surely make me think he's up to somethin'."

"Isn't Marcus smart enough to see that?" I said. "What's he thinking being so obvious — showing his hand so foolishly?"

"I'm through trying to figure out what he's thinking," said William.

"What Marcus has forgotten to realize," said Hubert, "is that the very thing that made so many follow him was his brashness — his willingness to stand up to the white man and be ever so combative, even threatening."

"Instead," said James, "he's now saying, 'Look at me. I'll be a good Negro, one you ain't gotta worry about, as long as you let me be the leader of these millions of ignorant colored folks.' But he's got one problem. We ain't ignorant."

"Well said," injected William.

"And," added Hubert, "perhaps he should shelve his fantasy of being king of Africa. He should try focusing on being servant of his people here in America and in the West Indies. Be a servant, not a king!"

"Look here," said James. "This is just between us, but I have officially parted ways with Marcus. I just haven't done so publicly . . . yet. I'm going to start my own movement — one focused more on the American Negro."

"When will you inform Marcus?" I asked.

"When the time is right. He can already smell something fishy when it comes to my challenging him in meetings and such."

"He also can't stand the way so many hang on your every word," said William, "or how they scream and shout with approval when you speak at Liberty Hall. I could swear they cheer louder for you than they do for Marcus. And he detests it. I can see it in his eyes."

"Listen," said James, "when I do get this movement up and running, I want all three of ya'll to be a part of it."

We all just nodded, our thoughts still on the article. If James, Hubert, and William were any indication, Marcus had finally found a way to bite the hand that was feeding him. His top supporters were now falling off.

Later in the day I found out that Speed had also read the *Times* article. Of course, it had struck him in a much different way.

"I've got to hand it to him, Q," he said. "Appealing directly to Harding. Does he think we're fucking stupid?"

"Yes," I said.

"Watch yourself, Q!"

"Then tell me," I said, "what's his angle?"

"He wants to keep the races separate so he can build his movement in the shadows, away from us with the guns and laws and prisons. He wants to buy time, enough time to build up his damn global army. Enough time to turn those empty toy guns into loaded rifles. He wants a bloody war of the races. He wants to kill, just like the Bolsheviks killed the czars. We're the motherfuckin' czars! Don't you see, Q?"

"Does that *we* include me?"

"Sure, Q." I could see him rolling his eyes through the phone. "Why not! Listen. What you, my colored friend, need to be concerned with, is stopping his damn revolution."

"I'm doing my job," I said. "Always have. I'm focused on the *Orion* purchase, just as we've previously discussed."

"He's now got every colored in the world thinking he's in with the president. Slick sonofabitch! Coloreds will see this *Times* article as some sorta meeting of the minds between two leaders. Damn Africans are too ignorant to know the difference."

"I think you're misjudging coloreds as a whole," I said. "You don't know enough about us to make such claims. Stick to bashing Garvey, not the entire —"

"You know what I mean, Q. Not your type."

"My type?"

"Look, Garvey and Du Bois have already shown that they're communists. But now, with this letter, Garvey somehow expects whites to think he's an America lover? Talk about lurching."

"Just don't insult my people. We are not a monolith."

"Mono-what?"

"Never mind," I said.

"What Garvey's actually doing, Q, is showing the Russians that he's organized, that he can gather all the coloreds of the world up and hand deliver them to the

Bolsheviks in their quest to take over the world."

"Du Bois as well?" I asked.

"Of course. He's targeting the uppity ones, though . . . the ones with money and education. Hell, Du Bois left for France today according to 6W6."

"Is 6W6 going with him?" I asked, pleased that Du Bois knew exactly who Mann was because of my handiwork.

"No. He's not going. But this trip of Du Bois's comes after he attended a fundraiser just the other night at James Weldon Johnson's house where a bunch of commies got together to help raise money for some colored poet's trip to Russia. A Mr. Claude McKay."

"Is that right?"

I knew about the event already from Hubert, who'd actually attended.

"Got the list of commies in attendance right here," he said. "C77, as you know, is attached to Mr. Johnson."

"Who's on the list?" I asked. "Maybe I'll recognize one who's also in with Garvey."

"Well, I know you know one. Hubert Harrison was on the old list that 800 gave us way back when you were first getting in. Remember your lunch down in Greenwich Village way back when?"

"Of course," I said, feeling a bit stuck. "I see Hubert Harrison around a lot. But he stays busy editing Garvey's paper."

"Well, he was there with Du Bois at the fundraiser, Q. Also there were Walter White, Jessie Fauset, and a Rosamond Johnson. Any ring a bell?"

"No, just Hubert," I said, already aware that he'd attended only because Claude had insisted.

"Also on the list," he continued, "is a Mr. Heywood Broun, a Mr. John C. Farrar, and a Mrs. Ruth Hale. Bunch of these folks are white at that. There's definitely a Red takeover in the works, Q."

"Good work by C77, though."

"Yeah. He didn't attend but actually sent the official invitations out for Mr. Johnson weeks ago. Bunch of Reds raising money to send their propaganda-poet to Russia. They need a real writer to take detailed notes and bring them back home. See . . . the Russians need the coloreds to accomplish all this evil shit."

"Again," I said, "none of the other names ring a bell."

"That's fine, Q. We know Hubert Harrison was there and it proves that Du Bois and Garvey are on the same commie team. Simple. One of Garvey's boys at a Du Bois,

Johnson fundraiser involving a trip to Russia! Case closed."

"Interesting."

"This all means stay connected, Q . . . even through these busy, upcoming holidays. It's all getting awfully convoluted. But there's Red all around us."

26

Christmas was a family affair that'd been a long time coming, as Momma, Aunt Coretta, and Loretta's cousin Ruth, were in town. We decided to invite Ginger and Peavine over as well, knowing they'd enjoy the big dinner Momma was fixing. Of course, all of Ginger's kinfolk lived in Paris, and Peavine had told me his story.

I hadn't eaten a bite all day, as I wanted to savor every bite of Momma's feast. Loretta and I sat next to each other across from Peavine, Ruth, and Ginger, while Momma and Aunt Coretta sat at opposite short ends of the table.

We were surrounded by charming decorations, most of which Loretta had made by hand, and the house smelled of cinnamon, burning wood, and pine from the Christmas tree I'd purchased. The ladies had gone above and beyond in decorating it. In fact, with Momma in town and a baby on the way, the house finally felt complete. Though it was mighty cold outdoors, it didn't concern us because we had several logs on the fire and were warm and comfortable with plenty of stories to share.

"This ham is magnificent," said Ginger. "You've outdone yourself, Mrs. Temple."

"Thank you, honey."

"And these biscuits better than any I done had," said Peavine, dipping a piece of biscuit in the gravy that covered his mashed potatoes.

"Aunt Coretta the one made them biscuits," said Momma. "Now, Loretta, you make sure you eatin' enough for you and that baby. Get you some more of them butter beans, collard greens, and sweet potatoes. Give that baby some strength!"

"Here you go, Miz Loretta," said Peavine, serving her some collards. "You want me to get you some more of this here turkey, Miz Loretta?"

"Sure, Peavine. Just a little. I want to save room for some of that pie."

"Love me some pie," said Peavine, cutting into the turkey and filling Loretta's plate.

"Good," said Aunt Coretta in her crackly, weak voice. "Got plenty of pie in there, baby."

"How many pies ya'll cook, Aunt

Coretta?" I asked.

"Well . . . we got two sweet potatoes with that butter crust you like, Sugar. And then we got one apple and a cherry."

"Ooh wee!" said Peavine. "Cherry pie the best!"

"Especially Aunt Coretta's," I said. "Melt in your mouth. Ain't that right, Momma?"

"Mm-hmm."

I was glad to see Momma looking so good. Her hair was a lot grayer, but she looked and sounded strong. Her skin was still supple.

I couldn't say the same for Aunt Coretta. She was completely gray now and seemed frailer than ever. Both she and Momma had always been thin women, but now Aunt Coretta looked tired and weak. I wasn't sure how much longer she'd be with us and was surprised she'd been able to make the trip. Then again, she loved traveling on trains and probably mustered up all the strength she could for the ride to New York.

"Tell me about livin' in Vermont, Momma."

"Well, Sugar, we been stayin' plenty busy. Before winter hit, we was spending most days workin' in the garden." She began buttering her biscuit. "Gotta wait for springtime before we can tend to it again. Love to work in that garden. But now, three days a week, we go into town and cook for them lonely old folks at Oaks Village. Some of 'em goin' on eighty years old, and plenty of 'em done seen their husbands or wives pass on some-time back. But they love to see us comin' to cook for 'em. Aunt Coretta don't always come with me 'cause she be needin' her rest. But I like it better when she comes."

"You like going, Aunt Coretta?" I asked.

"Oh yeah, Sugar. I be havin' to sit down mostly, but your momma don't mind."

"No I don't," said Momma, biting into her biscuit. "Long as she keep me company. It's one of the best jobs I ever had. Mrs. Mary got us them jobs."

"That's good, Momma. Mary and Profes-sor Gold are some good-hearted folks."

"Course . . . on Sundays . . . Aunt Coretta and I go to church service."

"But the Golds don't go to church," I said, cutting my ham.

"Nah, Sugar. But we done found us a good church in town. Ain't that right, sis-ter?"

"Mm-hmm," said Aunt Coretta, taking a bite of butter beans from her shaking fork. "Full a good, God-fearin' white folks."

Hearing that made me refocus on Garvey. Was he a God-fearin' man? I couldn't answer that. As I continued eating dinner and enjoying the conversation, my mind slowly drifted back into his world.

"I'm happy to be sharing Christmas here in New York with all of you," said Ginger. "You are beautiful people. And let me tell you something . . ."

I saw Ginger moving her mouth, but her voice was slowly drowned out by that of Garvey's. I heard him shouting from the stage at Liberty Hall. "When my enemies attack me, they are actually attacking you!"

I continued watching Ginger as if she were pantomiming. Then I watched Peavine and Ruth do the same. As the dinner proceeded, all around the table were hand gestures, laughter, drinking, and chewing. But it was only Garvey's voice I heard. I could no longer be completely present among even my family and friends, no matter how hard I tried.

In January of 1922 I took the train to the Connolly Hotel somewhere in Newark, New Jersey, and made damn sure I wasn't followed. There were more agents than usual at this particular Bureau meeting, probably ten or so. Some I'd never met, and most of them white, except for Agent 800 and a young man I'd seen around the UNIA offices before. I hadn't the faintest idea he was an agent and couldn't wait for the meeting to begin so I could find out why he'd been hired.

There was great intensity in the room along with a lot of cigarette smoke. The agents reminded me of slobbering bloodhounds about to be turned loose on a runaway slave. And much to my disappointment, Ellington was absent.

"Listen up," said Hoover. "This is the first meeting Agent Parker has attended. He's been in Harlem for several months. Agent Temple, you and Agent Jones have probably seen him around."

We both nodded yes.

"His code name is 22X. Don't forget it. Welcome, Agent Parker. You should know that Agent Jones goes by 800 and Agent Temple's code is Q3Z. Now that you've seen their faces, remember their codes."

"Yes, sir," said Parker.

"Have you managed to ease into things without any hiccups?"

"Yes, sir. I'm part of a small planning committee Garvey's assembled. We've been tasked to help him write a philosophical manual for a major college he intends to build in Liberia."

"Interesting. Stay on top of it."

"Yes, sir."

"Well, gentlemen, this is it," said Hoover, holding a piece of paper. "We've got him. Is the man who received this circular in the mail willing to testify to it?"

"Yes," said Agent 800. "I've known of his unhappiness with Garvey for months now. His name is Bo Tremble. He's completely disconnected himself from the movement, but he's still on their mailing list. He says he's invested hundreds and hasn't received any return on it from the Black Star Line. Let's just say we have an angry man on our hands."

"Good," said Speed. "Anger is good in this case. It strengthens our hand. Agent Sloan, we're going to let NYPD take the lead on this. But your team will accompany them and make sure they don't flub it up."

"I'm on it," said the bone-thin Sloan, taking a big drag from his cigarette.

"Let's not get ahead of ourselves," said Hoover. "We've still got some bases to cover. So you say hundreds have received these papers via the mail services, Agent Jones?"

"No. Thousands have."

"And, Agent Temple, you're one hundred percent on the sale of the *Orion* having not gone through?"

"One hundred percent."

"I'm dumbfounded," said Sloan. "How could he be so foolish as to scratch the name *Orion* out and replace it with *Phyllis Wheatley* before actually buying it?"

"Because he'd promised his people a ship named the *Phyllis Wheatley*," I said. "He had to make them think he was making good on his promise. No one would have invested in a ship they'd never heard of called the *Orion.* This move was about raising money. But the name being blotted out is beside the point. Even if he'd advertised it as the *Orion,* he'd be in trouble. He doesn't own it."

"We'll need to find more men and women willing to come forward and testify," said Hoover. "The more we can get to come forward with actual envelopes addressed to them, the stronger our case will be. Now . . . Agent Jones, has infiltrating Cyril Briggs's African Blood Brotherhood borne any fruit?"

"Yes. Many UNIA defectors have joined Briggs's ABB to spite Garvey. They each claim he owes them wages, and they're willing to testify in court."

"Well, they're about to get their chance. We'll make the arrest tomorrow."

■ ■ ■ ■

The next day I engineered the big steam shovel like a man on a mission to do something good for the community. I wanted to lose myself in the work of building a beautiful church — to convince myself that such a deed would keep God from punishing me for the lies I was steeped in. With busy men all around me laboring in ditches and shoveling dirt into the back of trucks to be hauled away, I waited for the moment when James would likely approach the site with the news that Garvey had been arrested.

"More coal!" I yelled to the fat fireman, trying to make sure he could hear me over the loud engine.

"Yes, sir!" he shot back.

After about an hour of moving dirt I heard a loud voice yelling my name.

"Brother Sidney! Brother Sidney!"

I turned to my left and just as I'd imagined, James was standing in the distance beyond the ditch along with William and Hubert.

"You fellas take a break!" I yelled, motioning for my men to shut the shovel down.

I took my gloves off, jumped down, and circled around the ditch. They were standing there stone-faced.

"What is it?" I asked.

"They got him," said James. "The police done arrested Marcus at his home."

"For what?" I asked.

"We're waiting to find out," said Hubert. "We just learned of it from Miss Jacques. Everyone over at headquarters is in a fit."

Before I could say another word I saw, of all people, Ginger, running toward us. "Oh my God, Sidney," she said, approaching out of breath. "Loretta told me you were here. She's in the car. You must come immediately. She's very sick."

"Go!" said Hubert.

"I'll get in touch with ya'll later," I said, turning to head for the car with Ginger following.

"I'll come with you," said James.

Ginger, James, and I sat in the hospital vestibule awaiting word on Loretta's condition. I had been hopeful that she was simply going to deliver several weeks early, but when the doctor made me leave the delivery room I couldn't help but begin to worry.

"God is watching over all this," said James, putting his hand on my shoulder.

"*Oui,*" added Ginger. "Don't worry, Sidney."

I sat there with my interlocked hands pressed against my mouth. James had seemingly forgotten all about Marcus having been arrested and had given me his undivided attention.

The doctor finally came out. Immediately, I rushed to meet him halfway. I tried my best not to assume anything but could feel my heart pounding through my chest.

"How is she?" I asked.

"Mr. Temple, your wife is resting. She's going to be fine."

"Oh, God, thank you," I said, taking a deep breath and exhaling my relief. I turned to Ginger and James who were sitting about ten feet behind us and gave them an encouraging look. They too breathed sighs of relief.

"Can I see her?" I asked, turning back to face him.

"Mr. Temple, unfortunately there is some very bad news."

"Yes."

"The baby didn't make it."

I didn't respond. In fact, his words didn't even register.

"Mr. Temple?"

"Yes."

"The baby was stillborn."

It had been my cousin, Aunt Coretta's son, who'd had a knife driven through his stomach during that far back summer. The doctor may just as well have done the same to me rather than deliver this news of my dead child.

I stared into his blue eyes. He appeared no older than forty, a handsome white man with a full head of dark brown, thick, wavy hair and an angular nose. There was a compassion emanating from him and he never looked away. Somehow, some part of me that I wasn't in control of gave me the strength to ask him one more question.

"Was it a boy?"

Perhaps he knew the unique joy a man feels upon having a son because he hesitated before answering.

"Yes."

27

I finished dinner at Mr. Daley's Manhattan town house and made my way down the dark alleyway toward my car. It was mid-June and foggy. In fact, fog had been hovering over the whole of New York City for days on end, which suited a man in my condition just fine. I didn't miss the night stars or day sunshine and had no need for blue sky. Life was blue enough.

I'd been spending every day on the steam shovel, trying to dig my way out of hell. Garvey had managed to post bail the day after he'd been arrested and now, in what seemed like a pure act of defiance against authorities, was on a fundraising tour of the country.

His trial hadn't been set because there were several snags in the way, one being that Agent 800's star witness, Mr. Bo Tremble, had changed his mind and wasn't willing to testify against Garvey. The more agents scoured the country in search of disgruntled Black Star Line investors, the more they were being met with resistance. The trial would be set eventually, but when exactly was up in the air.

Still walking in the dark fog, I could hear nothing but the sound of my hard soles hitting the pavement. I thought about Loretta. She was at home with Ginger, painting and trying to get through the sadness that lingered. Our French friend had practically moved in, which was good. I didn't want Loretta to spend any time alone, and she was getting more work done than ever.

James had also been spending quite a bit of time at our place. He'd been instrumental in helping us through those first few days after leaving the hospital. The prayer he offered on our first night back home was certainly welcomed. The three of us sat in the living room, holding hands as he called on the man above.

"Let us pray," he'd begun. "Heavenly Father, Lord of us all, we humble ourselves in your presence here today. Lord, who knows all things, You know the pain these young people are feeling here today. Lord, who knows all things, You know the reasons that we don't yet know. Lord, who knows all things, You care about even the sparrow that drops from the sky.

"You see the whole picture that we can't see. Bless this young couple in their grief. Comfort them. Place your loving arms around them and provide relief. Help them to go forward with ever more faith that someday all suffering will be eased, all confusion will be made clear, and death will not triumph. Comfort them, we pray. These blessings we ask in the name of Our Lord and Savior, Jesus Christ. Amen."

Those words had soothed our souls. And now I was thinking only about getting home and soothing my mind with a glass of wine. Reaching into my coat pocket for my keys, I heard a deep voice call out my name.

"Good evening, Agent Temple."

Startled, I stopped and turned to my right where I saw only the silhouette of a man standing against the wall about ten feet away.

"Excuse me?" I cautiously asked, squinting my eyes, trying to make more of him out.

"Quite a night, wouldn't you say?"

"Come again?"

"The fog. It makes for quite a night."

"Sure . . . I guess. Sure."

"It lets a man hide from all the madness out there. At least for a while."

"Who are you and why did you call me Agent Temple?"

"Who I am shouldn't concern you. What I *know* should."

Again I tried to make out his face a little better through the darkness but couldn't. I wasn't about to move an inch for fear that he was here to kill me. I did have my pistol and was prepared to draw it at any second but chose to use words instead of bullets for the time being.

"What is it you think you know?"

"I know you're fucked unless you do exactly what I say."

I let those words sink in, realizing I was in no position to argue. I figured he was already holding a sidearm and that any attempt I made to reach under my coat for mine would be thwarted.

"I'm listening," I said.

"Good. Real good. How's Mr. Garvey doing?"

"Fine, I presume."

"Now, Agent Temple . . . you must realize you're in no position to play dumb with me. We both know that Mr. Marcus Garvey is a no-good snake of a man. And now he's laughing at the officials who arrested him. He has no intentions of ever going to prison over some trumped up charges of mail fraud. It's already been six months. So the way we see it, he'll have to be charged with something far worse to ever be put away for any significant amount of time."

"Who is this 'we' you speak of?"

"I thought I covered that. It doesn't concern you."

"What do you want from me?"

"You think a powerful man like that is going down for simply misusing the mail service? Use your head."

"Using the mail service to defraud folks out of their money is a serious crime."

"Trust me. It'll take something more attention-grabbing, something he can be directly connected to and can't wiggle out of or blame on someone else."

"Like?"

"Like violating the new Prohibition law."

"I've worked on his ships as an engineer. He's done no such thing."

"The documents I have in this briefcase suggest otherwise. They link him directly to Eddie Adams, one of the most notorious bootleggers, murderers, and outlaws in America. Adams was killed last year, so he certainly won't be around to deny such a connection."

"You've fabricated these documents?"

"Yes. They prove that Garvey was rum-running, using his ships to transport the stuff from Cuba to Florida, then working with Adams to make a load of dough."

"And?"

"And the fact that Garvey has been consumed with purchasing ships ever since Prohibition went into effect makes it all the more plausible. It further explains why his financial books have always been a mess. These documents are his death knell."

"You'll never be able to make it stick."

"No, I won't. You will. The documents will soon be planted in his office."

"By who? By me?"

"You catch on quick."

"I'll do no such thing."

"My guess is you will."

"I won't."

"Look. We know you've been an agent with the Bureau since 1919. We know everything about you. We also know that he trusts you."

"How have you come to such conclusions?"

"The United States Federal Government is an awfully big place. We've got a spy or two embedded in several departments. The BOI is no exception. You'd be amazed how many so-called loyal Americans will squeal on the government for the right amount of dough."

"Go on."

"Our inside man says your boss, Hoover, is too young for the job — that the Bureau is growing too fast — that too much is slipping past the wide-eyed George Washington University grad. Our man also tells us that Garvey is too smart for your boss."

"Your inside man couldn't be an actual agent."

"Of course he is. And he's very thorough. I have a photograph of the contract you signed. Several were taken. It proves you're an agent. You certainly wouldn't want Garvey to receive one. As you know, he's got a man or two working for him who'd be more than willing to tear you limb from limb. Oh, and remember that nice picture you took shaking Mr. J. Edgar Hoover's hand? It's such a nice picture of you two. He's a household name these days. Seen his face in the papers on more than a few occasions."

"I've heard of him."

"Still playin' dumb, huh? Our man took a nice picture of that picture as well. That's kinda funny. A picture of a picture."

"Where are the photographs of said contract, etcetera?"

Without missing a beat he took a step

forward and slid an envelope across the pavement toward my feet. I took a careful step forward and picked it up.

"Of course you can't see them in the dark," he said. "But I'm confident you'll recognize your pretty face and signature when you get home later and have a look. You look good holding up your Bureau badge, too."

"If you've got spies throughout Washington, why don't you have one working within Garvey's UNIA?"

"We do. But he can't do the job I'm asking you to do. He can't get close enough to the so-called Black Moses. That's what makes you unique."

"Why don't you just let the Bureau do its job?"

"We have. For years. Where has that gotten us? And now it may take another year for this trial to ever come about, if at all. We need him off the public scene now. And I'm assuming you do too. Why else would you have become an agent?"

"What, a Negro can't be an agent simply because he wants to be an agent?"

"No."

"White men do it every day."

"Such are the ways of the world."

"I see. Tell me who you're with."

"Look, you stubborn son of bitch! Maybe I'm with the Communist Party. Why don't we go with that? They certainly have reason to hate that Jamaican pig. Then again, so do a lot of organizations. All I can tell you is that I'm simply someone you're going to have to deal with. You can call me Timekeeper. It'll prove to be fitting."

"Somehow I don't think you're representing the Communist Party."

"Why not? Don't tell me it's because you believe, as your Bureau does, that Garvey himself is a communist. Anyone paying attention knows that Garvey spouts nothing but anti-communist rhetoric. He's a capitalist to the bone. He's certainly on the Communist Party's enemies list."

"Sounds like you've just tipped your hand."

"Not by a long shot. I'm just paid very well to know a lot. Look, trying to figure out who I'm representing is a complete waste of time. I promise you."

"All right, Timekeeper, if I were to agree to do it, how much time would I have?"

"I'd say get it done soon. And soon means soon."

"Then?"

"There's a number in the envelope I just gave you. When you've done the work, call it. Once we've received word that the evidence is in place, I'll notify my contact within the police department. Oh, I forgot to mention that. Don't bother contacting the NYPD. We've got several of their boys on our payroll. Besides, many a man in uniform would like to see Garvey's black ass hanging from a tree. With his parading around town surrounded by all that African pageantry, chaos in the streets all the time. Disgusting."

"How do I know you're not with the NYPD yourself?"

"Why don't you try and find out?" he asked, threateningly. "I don't exist. Don't you get it?"

"Give me the documents."

"You know, Agent Temple, sometimes a man is just stuck. Don't fight it. Make things easy on yourself and all will return to normal. Of course, you could tell your bosses that your mission has been compromised. That would certainly end your assignment. And who's to say there'd be any future ones for a colored agent like you?"

"Garvey going down for rum running would also end my assignment. What's the difference?"

"You're right. Your work on this assignment's going to end soon one way or another. But one scenario leaves your life at risk with Garvey's men. Another leaves you a failure who turned himself in to the Bureau with the job left undone. But the last leaves you looking like a topnotch agent who took part in the takedown of a government enemy who was illegally selling liquor."

"How would the latter play itself out?"

"Once you've planted the evidence, tell your bosses that you suspect Garvey of rum running, that you're trying to find evidence and may be close to something. Then, over the next few days, while they wait to hear back from you, the police will get the proper warrant, go in, and take control of the scene. When they find the evidence and make the arrest, your bosses will know that your original suspicions were right. Hell, they'll think you're the best agent they've ever had. Your fate will be sealed."

"I seriously doubt that."

"That's because you haven't thought it through yet."

"I'll say it again, give me the documents."

He slid another envelope toward me and I picked it up, knowing I would never do what he was suggesting. It wasn't in me. But I hadn't come this far just to quit either. I wasn't about to go running to the Bureau and admit that my mission had been compromised. That would effectively end any chance I'd have of continuing to spy on Garvey if he avoided prison. Du Bois would then be on his own and at the mercy of any schemes Garvey had up his sleeve. The NAACP boss was already rapidly losing popularity among the colored masses, while Garvey's image as a defiant, uncaged tiger was still soaring. I'd have to figure something out.

"Don't overthink this," he said. "You don't owe that foreign son of a bitch a damn thing. His time has come."

"Have a good night," I said, turning and slowly walking away.

"You be careful now, Sidney."

I walked into the house at about ten o'clock with both envelopes in hand and made my way down the hallway toward Loretta's studio. She and Ginger were sitting at their respective easels working on distinctly different-looking paintings. Ginger's was a portrait of an old Native American woman, Loretta's a piece she'd been working on for weeks, one she claimed was her interpretation of Heaven.

I chose not to interrupt them and headed straight for the kitchen where I poured myself a glass of wine — one of the last bottles we still had left. I walked out to the back porch and took a seat on the steps. Setting my glass down, I calmly opened one of the envelopes and pulled out the pictures I was hoping not to recognize. No such luck.

One was a clear photograph of the contract I'd signed back in 1919. Another was of me shaking Hoover's hand, and a third was of me standing beside him, holding up my official Bureau badge. For the record, it was a badge they never allowed me to take home.

I took a big drink of wine and sat there for an hour just thinking. It felt like the walls of Harlem were finally closing in on me.

28

I spent the next few days mulling over my options, none of which put my mind at ease. And with Garvey still traveling the country, I tried to pretend the Timekeeper didn't exist, tried to fool myself into thinking he might never show his face again. But deep down I knew better. I needed someone to help me plan my next move. I needed to see Ellington.

I made my way into The Kessler on a Friday in late June. It had become a habit for me to look over my shoulder, to flinch and reach for my gun whenever anyone made an unexpected move.

The scruffy-faced Latin man staggering near the front door raised my eyebrows, but as I walked by him, he asked for some spare change. I handed him a nickel and made my way inside past several tables. It was nine o'clock and the place was about half full. I spotted Ellington in the back corner and hurried to his table.

"There you are," he said, sipping his straight black coffee.

"Good to see you, Bobby."

I sat down and gave the place another once-over. If someone was following me, he hadn't entered the place yet.

"Make a note of whoever walks in," I said.

"What is it?"

"I think real trouble has found me. I don't even feel comfortable using the street phones anymore."

"What do you mean? Where did you call my folks from?"

"I was meeting with a friend, a Reverend Powell, at his office. When we were finished, he stepped out and let me use his private phone. I called your folks and then you."

"How are you in trouble?"

Before I could answer a waitress approached. "What'll it be?" she asked.

"I'm fine with coffee for now," said Ellington, pointing to his cup and asking me with his eyes if I wanted the same. I nodded yes and let him do the talking. "One more coffee, ma'am."

"You bet," she replied, scurrying off.

Again I scanned the entire place.

"Look, Bobby, I've been approached by a man who's demanding I frame Garvey for rum running. He's threatening to blow my cover if I don't plant some incriminating evidence. He calls himself the Timekeeper. He says his organization has one of our agents on its payroll."

"Shit."

"He has photographs of my contract. He has pictures of me shaking Hoover's hand."

"Damn. I'm surprised you're telling me."

"The way I see it, if I can't trust you, I can no longer trust myself. A man's instincts have to mean something in this world."

"I've got your back covered," he said, taking a sip.

"Too bad I have no idea who's on the take."

"A dozen faces are running through my mind. Agent Speed, Paul Mann, Knox, Long. Could be Agent Peterman out of the New York office, or that son of a bitch Truffle. But those two are focused on other New York assignments."

"What about Sloan?" I asked.

"He's only worked in New York. Couldn't have accessed your file."

"Right," I said. "Same with 800."

"You've gotta get out. Garvey finds out and you're toast."

"You mean give up on everything I've been working for? I'm closer to Garvey than ever. He survives this trial and remains in power, Du Bois and the NAACP won't stand a chance. I can't have that son of a bitch setting the course for us all."

"What? How can you be thinking about that right now?"

"Because it could very well define how I'm able to live the rest of my life. Garvey's message can't be allowed to take hold. It means everything."

"Is it worth losing your life over?"

"I said *everything*. But hang on. We certainly can't assume that anyone associated with Garvey would kill me. They might make sure I never walk again, but . . ."

"But they *might* kill you and make sure no one ever finds your body. People disappear all the time without the police ever being able to prove who got rid of them."

"Perhaps it isn't until a man is willing to actually die for something that he truly begins to live."

"You're fuckin' scarin' me, Sidney."

"Look, an America that includes full integration and absolute social equality is the only country I want to live in. I want to feel the way you feel."

"How's that?"

"At peace, dammit! And worth something."

"Man, Sid," he said, lowering his head, shaking it as if those words saddened him.

"Free from having to spend every second of the day thinking about the color of my skin."

The waitress approached and sat my coffee down. She then tended to an old gentleman three tables down, toward the front of the restaurant.

"Finish what you were saying," he said.

"Sounds like a dream, I know, but I feel obligated to do everything within my power to help that dream become a reality." I poured a bit of milk in my cup, then a little sugar. "And it's within my power to remain the eyes and ears of the NAACP at this critical moment in history. Within *my* power. So far I've managed to keep Du Bois well informed of both Garvey's and the Bureau's intentions."

"What are you talking about?"

"I've been sending Du Bois letters, anonymously signed of course."

"So that's what you've been up to all this time? I'll be damned."

"Now you know."

"So if you're dead set on saving the NAACP, are you actually considering planting the evidence?"

"Of course not," I said, taking a sip. "I'm

not a damn criminal. I'm just trying to buy some time, hoping this trial will start soon. Garvey is already guilty of something real and I trust he will pay the price."

"But is this Timekeeper willing to wait?"

"He's gonna have to."

"If you go to the Bureau with this they'll dismiss you immediately."

"What if there is no spy inside the Bureau? What if it was Hoover who sent the Time-keeper as an insurance plan in case the trial fails?"

"No. Get that out of your head. I know how he views you. He thinks you're ethical to a fault, the kind of man who'd quit if blackmailed. And what would he have to gain from that?"

"Why would he assume I'd just quit?" I said. "He might think that any Negro with a good-paying job at the prestigious Bureau would do anything to keep it."

"All right, Sid, just for argument's sake, let's assume it is Hoover."

"Let's do."

"He's damn sure smart, definitely enough to fool me. Shit . . . enough to fool every-one in the Bureau for that matter. Play it out."

"First of all," I said, "it may not just be Hoover. He may be following orders from above. Several folks may be behind this."

"Okay. Go."

"Hoover knows if Garvey does go to prison for mail fraud he'll have no use for me anymore anyway."

"Perhaps."

"No," I said, "not perhaps. You and I both know he's only using 800 and me to get Garvey. He'd never have me spy on a white man or simply work out of the offices in Washington like you did."

"Guess I just don't wanna believe that."

"Believe it," I said.

"Continue."

"But," I said, "Hoover figures if Garvey walks, they'll need a backup plan, and the rum running evidence is just that. He could never just come straight out and ask me to break the law. So he sends this Timekeeper to make up a story about an inside man. It's just a ploy. He figures if I do plant the evidence, it was a brilliant plan. If I don't, at least he tried."

"Why wouldn't he wait to see if Garvey beats the mail fraud charge before sending him?"

"Because," I said, "he doesn't know how long I'll be around. He knows I'm as far in as I'm ever going to be. I'm in the perfect position right now. He knows I've gained access to Garvey's private files before. He knows that 800 is in real deep too, but has no chance of pulling off such a plan."

"Hoover always said 800 was doing an outstanding job, that he was a key reason why this mail fraud case has real legs now."

"He is," I said. "800 has been masterful, but he doesn't sit around in Garvey's office talking about Ibsen and Shakespeare like I do. It's about accessing and planting the evidence in those intimate files."

"By the way, just how close are you to Garvey?"

"Only close in terms of being a core member of his business affairs team. He meets with me one-on-one quite a bit and philosophizes. But I'm certainly not privy to any intimate affairs. For instance, I know he's rapidly building his own secret service, but I have no idea who's a part of it. I have no idea what goes on in his private world."

"And that's the world that really matters."

"Ultimately, yes," I said.

"Back to this theory of yours. So if it is Hoover, and you were to go in right now and tell him about the Timekeeper, what would happen?"

"Since the trial is still looming, and he knows I might be needed if Garvey eventually walks, he'd probably say, 'Sidney, call this Timekeeper and set up a meeting. Then lie to him and tell him you've planted the evidence. When he leaves the meeting we'll have some agents follow him and take him into custody.' That's what he'd probably say. They'd then pull off some fake arrest. The entire thing would just go away and I'd be back on the job."

"You think he thinks you'd be dumb enough not to wonder about the Timekeeper's associates, not to assume they'd still be out there ready to go to Garvey with your contract?"

"Yes, I think he thinks I'm that dumb. I think he thinks Negroes in general are that dumb."

"So if you truly believe all this, why not just go in to headquarters?"

"Because it's more likely that —"

"That this Timekeeper has nothing to do with the Bureau, and if you go in you'll simply be dismissed because they can't have an agent working for them whose cover has been blown, whose contract has been shown to Garvey. It's that simple. They can't risk having Garvey's men beat you into submission, having you rat out Agent 800 and everyone else involved. The entire operation would be in jeopardy."

"In that scenario, you're right," I said,

looking at the front door. "There's also another colored agent. His code name is 22X."

"So he'd be in danger too."

"If you say so."

"You know, Sidney, maybe this guy's with some radical Southern outfit."

"Maybe. But that hardly narrows it down. How many of those are there? Too many to count. What's the word on that former assistant district attorney, Edwin P. Kilroe?"

"I only know what you informed the Bureau of some years back, that he and Garvey had been at each other's throats."

"Maybe he has a hand in this," I said.

"It's plausible. But all of this guessing will only drive you mad, Sidney."

"I just can't allow this Timekeeper to get in the way of protecting Du Bois."

"The fact that you've been anonymously spying for him all this time makes sense. Before I left the Bureau, something had become quite clear. Every attempt Hoover and company made at trying to get Du Bois failed. No names of potential Du Bois funders or, as Speed called them, 'Reds,' could be gathered. Agents could never nail him for crossing state lines with a young woman either. You protected him."

"And I must continue."

"You're crazy, Sid."

"I also sent Du Bois a picture of a letter I photographed. Garvey wrote to several senators and the attorney general asking if they'd give him the authority to lead us all back to Africa — Liberia to be specific. I don't know if Garvey ever actually sent the letter, but still, I sent the photograph to Du Bois. I also warned Du Bois of Garvey's plan to loan Liberia two million dollars."

"Maybe Du Bois forwarded this information to the right person in Washington. It could explain why the State Department recently proposed giving Liberia a five-million-dollar loan. Secretary of State Hughes even has the support of President Harding. Of course, Congress will have to approve it."

"But," I said, "is the proposal officially on the table?"

"Yes. But I'm not sure when it's to be voted on."

"If they vote yes it might very well end any chance Garvey has of brokering a deal with Liberian officials. You're right. Perhaps Harding and Hughes are doing it in exchange for Liberia's cutting off negotiations with Garvey, further weakening his promise of Back to Africa. He doesn't deliver on that promise, he loses credibility."

"To think you could be behind all this, Sidney."

"To think."

"Now I just wish you'd get out."

"You sure got out at the right time. How are things going at Columbia?"

"Challenging. I pray I can get through all the muck."

"While you're at it, pray for me and wish me good luck."

The next day the headlines in all the colored papers read, GARVEY MEETS WITH KKK'S IMPERIAL WIZARD. The news sent shockwaves through the streets of Harlem. Even the most ardent supporters of Garvey were taken aback by this move. And as I sat in my office with James and Reverend Powell, I tried to imagine how he'd ever be able to explain it.

"I'm dumbfounded," said Powell. "No self-respecting leader has ever pulled such a reprehensible stunt. I believe my entire congregation will find Mr. Garvey's sit-down in Atlanta with that enemy of a man the last straw. It can't be explained away either."

"He's been traveling the country for months," James said. "And according to his telegrams, things have been going well. His visit to California was a bang, and everyone figured he'd take the South by storm as well. But this will cause a different kind of storm. To actually concoct some crazy idea of meeting with the Imperial Wizard of the Klan is a shock to the system. I couldn't have imagined it in my wildest dreams."

"He's strategizing somehow," I said. "He must have a new idea."

"It sickens me," James said. "I think it's just his last attempt at convincing Washington that he's no threat to the white man."

"It'll have the opposite effect," said Powell. "Folks in Washington will be suspicious. It reeks of a *he's-up-to-something* move."

"You right," said James. "White folks, especially those who fear Marcus, will think it's a good ol' case of an enemy tryin' to get to know his opposition a little better — up close and personal, if you will. Mm, mm, mm! This just boggles the mind. My God, what an overreach. Discretion has never been Marcus's greatest strength."

"We'll see how he's received when he gets back to Harlem," Powell said, folding one of the newspapers and standing. "You ready to get to the prayer breakfast, Brother Eason?"

"Let's hit it."

"I'm sorry the conversation turned from

the church to Garvey," I said as James and I stood.

"It couldn't be avoided," said Powell, the three of us walking to the door. "This morning, every restaurant, barbershop, and church in Harlem is filled with chatter about this news."

We stood in the doorway, both of them with their backs to the street as I looked out.

"Speaking of the church," said Powell, "I'm quite pleased with the progress we're making. Thank you for all your hard work, Sidney."

"You're welcome."

"Loretta doing all right?" asked James.

I heard him but the car parked across the street had my attention. In it sat the Timekeeper. He looked squarely at me and put his thumb up, obviously asking if I had done the job yet. I subtly shook my head no.

"No?" asked James. "Her spirits were sure up last time we spoke."

I watched the Timekeeper drive away and drifted off for a second.

"Sidney?" asked James.

I just stood there.

"Everything okay?" Powell asked. "Look like you've seen a ghost."

"What is it?" James asked, this time grabbing my shoulder and jarring my limp body.

"Sorry, James. I was . . . I was . . . Loretta is doing just fine."

"Good," he said, releasing me. "Why don't you go home and get some sleep. I'll holler at you later this evenin'."

"Sounds good."

29

I was walking down the sidewalk toward UNIA headquarters with Professor Gold. We entered the building and walked right past several Legionnaires.

"Come in the conference room with me, Professor," I said.

We walked in and sat down. In walked a young woman carrying Garvey's mango juice.

"Think I'll have a taste of that," said Professor Gold.

"No!" I abruptly said. "It's for Garvey's meeting."

"Can I stay?" he asked.

"You'll have to step out when they arrive."

"I'll leave now. I want to stop and buy some fresh tomatoes and onions for Mary and Loretta from that street vendor."

Minutes later I sat there while Garvey held court as usual. The same group as always was his audience. But sitting at the opposite end of the long table from Garvey was W. E. B.

Du Bois.

"Why can't the two of us coexist, Dr. Du Bois?" asked Garvey, sandwiched in between Strong and Grant.

"You're a crazy man. That's why."

"Africa awaits this crazy man," said Garvey, sipping his juice.

"You'll never set foot in Africa. You're going to prison."

"If I'm so crazy, why are all of your NAACP boys leaving you and joining me?"

"Because you lie better than I do," said Du Bois. "I don't promise what I can't deliver. We may have to struggle for years to get what we want right here in America. No shortcuts. And that means, when it comes to you and me, one of us will have to win out."

"Fancy talk from a fancy fool. All that matters to me is Africa. Liberia."

"President King of Liberia and I," said Du Bois, "are much closer than you realize, Marcus. He knows not to take your stolen money. Our country will save Liberia from bankruptcy. I want to do what's in their best interest, you want to do what's in the best interest of Marcus Garvey. Why else would you meet with the Klan?"

"Because I'm not afraid of the Big Bad Wolf," said Garvey.

"The Klan hates the NAACP because of our

constant public outcries against them. You made some sort of deal with them."

"How so?"

"You probably told them you'd agree to destroy the NAACP in exchange for their allowing you to have free reign in the South. You want to continue selling worthless stocks to our most vulnerable Southern brothers and sisters, and you need the Klan to allow you to travel around freely to do so."

"How long has this devil, Sidney, been working for you?"

"What do you mean?" asked Du Bois.

"Tell him, Sidney."

"I don't know what you mean," I said.

"Mr. Garvey, who told you this?" asked Du Bois.

"My friend Bobby Ellington," replied Garvey.

Garvey stood and began walking around the table. None of the men in the room said a word. He stopped right behind me.

"This devil," he said, touching my right shoulder, "has been feeding you information about me for years. But now he's a problem of the past. And when I'm done with him, I will watch your white blood spill all over this table too, Mr. Harvard Man."

Garvey reached under his suit coat at the waist and grabbed the handle of a machete. He pulled it out and held it high in the air. With his eyes wide open like a man possessed, he took one violent swing at my neck.

"NO!" I yelled, sitting up in bed, my body covered in sweat.

"What is it?" asked Loretta, abruptly waking up and grabbing my arm. "What is it, Sidney?"

I sat there breathing heavily, gathering my thoughts. The nightmare had felt so real. And now that I was awake, my reality provided little comfort.

"Tell me," she said. "You're soaking wet."

"It was just a dream."

"Was it about the baby?"

"I don't remember."

She pulled me close. There was little left in life that felt decent or pure, so I clung to her in that moment. She felt so warm, so safe. I didn't want to think anymore. I wanted to let go and lose myself in her, to let that virtue she possessed wash over me.

I placed my hand behind her head and gently led it to the pillow. It was the first time we'd made love since losing our son, so passionately, both of us giving of ourselves completely.

I parked on West 138th Street and walked about half a block toward the construction site. It was muggy out, the sky was gray, the sidewalks were relatively empty, and the street traffic was light.

As I approached, I tried to imagine how the new church would look sandwiched in between the two town houses in front of me, one made of yellowish brick, the other of reddish. Once complete, the property would be nearly flush against the sidewalk, so close to the street that those driving along might feel as if they could reach out and touch the front door from their cars.

I took a moment to appreciate how the work was coming along. The concrete foundation had been poured; in fact it was barely dry. Now things would really begin to take shape. I sat my bag down and took out my camera. I wanted to capture this phase of construction then continue photographing at different stages until the project was complete. It might be nice to look back on someday. I clicked the camera a few times.

"Hello there, Sidney," said a voice I recognized.

I stopped and turned to my right. Sitting behind the wheel of a parked black Ford, smoking a cigar, was an olive-skinned man of about fifty. He had a gray mustache and was wearing a black suit, black fedora, and thick, dark-rimmed glasses. I couldn't tell if he was Italian or colored but knew he was the Timekeeper.

"Just stand there and try not to look directly at me," he said. "Keep your eyes on that church you've been working on. It's me, your friend, in broad daylight. You didn't think I'd disappeared now did you?"

"No."

"Good ol' Sidney. You think any of Garvey's boys are watching you right now?"

"Always a possibility."

"So you don't have any news for me?"

"No."

"Not good."

"I need more time. I haven't been able to gain access to his office yet."

"It's already late August. That means I've given you damn near eight weeks. I guess I didn't make myself clear enough that night. Why are you waffling?"

"Aside from the fact that I'm an agent, not a criminal, it's just what I said . . . I need more time."

"If you're telling me you can't frame that son of bitch because you're trying to hold on to your dignity, it's a little late for that. You're already a traitor to your race."

"I don't see it that way."

"You've already poisoned your soul. And don't think for a minute that you're any better than me."

I glanced at him then refocused on the site.

"Keep your eyes on the church."

"Why do you fear Garvey so much anyway?" I asked. "What exactly do you gain from seeing him out of power?"

"What have you gained by spying on him? Wasn't it your job to help bring him down? He's more powerful than ever."

"I'm just an agent who's been tasked to report on Garvey's actions."

"Then do what it takes to remain one."

"And you're wrong," I said, clicking the camera. "He's not more powerful than ever. He's in trouble with his own people now."

"That Klan visit won't change a thing."

I glanced his way again and saw him flick his cigar. "Look, the way I see it, outing me to Garvey does you no good. You need me to do a job for you. You need me to do it for you now, and you'll need me to do it for you tomorrow, or the next day, or the next month. You need me. Garvey walks away from this trial, you'll still need me . . . even more so."

"You think you're smarter than me? Think again."

"I'm just confident about how close I am to Garvey. No agent has ever gotten in so deep. That has value. You can't find anyone else who's able to get into his office — to find his hidden keys and know which one unlocks which drawer. UNIA headquarters looks more like a military base these days. Anyone but me would have a better chance getting into the Oval Office."

I knelt down, began rummaging through my bag, and took another quick look at him.

"You've got it all figured out, huh?" he asked, taking a drag from his cigar. "You better think about your safety."

"I'm just asking you to let the trial take place first, that's all. A little more time."

"This is the last time I'm going to pay you a visit. Forget about the trial. Do the job now or face the consequences. You hear me? That nigger ain't worth you losing any sleep over nohow."

"Your easy use of that word puzzles me. In looking at you I'm gathering you must have some Negro blood in you. But let me guess. You've always been able to pass?"

"I've just always known my place. I'm an American who wants to keep things just the way they are, and the organization I repre- sent intends to do everything in its power to protect real Americans."

"I'm a real American."

"Then prove it," he said, throwing his

cigar to the ground. "Plant the evidence and call the phone number I gave you. You're trying my patience."

He started the engine and drove off. I picked up my bag and headed for the site, still wondering how much longer I could get away with calling what I hoped was his bluff, not to mention how smart it was.

The next day Garvey took to the stage at Liberty Hall, fresh off his national tour. As I walked down the stairwell into the massive basement where all of the Liberty Hall gatherings took place, I saw Agent 800 standing near the bottom step with his arms folded. I joined him.

The place was packed to the rafters and everyone waited with bated breath to hear Garvey tell of his exploits. I took one look at the platform and saw that it was filled with several high-ranking UNIA officials, including Reverend Eason. And of course all of the typical grand ceremonial décor was on full display.

As Garvey stood and approached the podium, the audience erupted. He calmly waited for the cheering to die down, but sprinkled in were groans of disapproval. He held his perfumed handkerchief up to his mouth, collected his thoughts, and then began.

"Thank you! Thank you all! Please! Please! Be seated! Let me begin by telling you how proud I am to see you all taking part in this Third International Convention. It's good to know that the naysayers out there haven't managed to break our spirit."

There were mostly cheers, but the angry shouts could not be ignored. A battle of emotions was brewing.

"I want to respond to all of the fuss going around about my meeting with the Klan. Every paper I read seems hell-bent on misrepresenting the encounter. So let me set the record straight. As you all know, I've never been one to run from my enemies."

Quite a bit of the crowd stood at this point, but more than a few remained seated. I'd never seen so many of his supporters hold back their enthusiasm. But none of it appeared to ruffle him. He gripped the sides of the podium and spoke with great intensity.

"But the Imperial Wizard is not my enemy. He wants what's best for his people and I want what's best for mine. In fact, the Klan simply represents the invisible government of the United States."

Agent 800 and I looked at each other

upon hearing those bold words, each of us raising our eyebrows. We were probably thinking the same thing: Whatever good feelings Garvey had been trying to create between himself and President Harding's government had vanished into thin air.

"No . . . my enemies are over at the NAACP. They're over at the *Messenger.* They're all over Harlem. In fact, many of my enemies are sitting behind me on this stage. Don't think I'm blind to that fact. But I'll get to that in a minute."

He was referencing his executive council. None of them budged, but a hush came over the crowd. I was focused on James. Everyone in the building was aware of how outspoken he'd been about Garvey while he was traveling. But I was certain James welcomed the potential showdown. Several in the audience were probably behind him anyway. He sat there patiently as Garvey continued.

"Regarding this Klan issue. You are well aware that I've never had any intentions of joining the white man. That is the dream of that other so-called Negro and his ring of circus clowns over at the NAACP. And if I have no intentions of joining the white man, there's no harm in talking to them. Listen up! Let not my words be mixed up. America is theirs. Africa is ours. Yes, I said it. Print that, Mr. A. Phillip Randolph . . . Mr. William Du Bois! I said this in New Orleans and I'll share it with you: This is a white man's country. He found it, he conquered it, and we can't blame him if he wants to keep it. I am not vexed with the white man of the South for Jim Crowing me because I am black. I never built any streetcars or railroads. The white man built them for his own convenience. And if I don't want to ride where he's willing to ride then I'd better walk."

Disapproving hisses could be heard throughout. I wondered why he was going down this road, seemingly doubling down on his losing hand. A. Phillip Randolph had recently called him a "half-wit, low-grade moron," and the more he spoke, the more I wondered how many others would soon agree.

"Between the Ku Klux Klan and the NAACP," he said, "give me the Klan for their honesty of purpose toward the Negro. They are better friends of my race . . . for telling us what they are . . . and what they mean."

More hisses flooded the hall.

"This is my position," he said. "These are the facts. Those of you who boo me can join those backstabbing former members of my executive council who chose to resign. That's fine with me. It's time to clean house anyway. Time for a fresh start! Many members of my executive council chose not to resign. And there they sit."

Garvey kept his body facing the audience, but casually turned his head and glared at his council.

"And amongst them are men who like to badmouth me while I'm out of town. Well, I'm laying down the gauntlet right here and now. Any one of you can feel free to step forward and address this hall right in front of me."

With that, Garvey walked over and took a seat. Again, a hush came over the hall and everyone waited to see if anyone would step forward. They didn't have to wait long. James stood and approached the podium. Many cheered, others jeered, but my friend was more stoic and determined-looking than ever.

"I welcome this opportunity to address you, brothers and sisters," he said. "Please lend me your ears. The time has come to testify. For it is only God above that I fear."

"PREACH, BROTHER EASON!" shouted several throughout.

"GOD IS WITH GARVEY!" screamed a

man up front.

"THAT'S RIGHT, WE WITH GARVEY!" yelled others.

"*Loyalty* is a funny word," said James, his words being met with sprinkles of applause. "And loyalty is a two-way street!"

"GARVEY! GARVEY! GARVEY!" the chant began, but it didn't dissuade James. He waited for it to die down.

"I remember the days when the UNIA wasn't afraid to make it known that we were willing to combat any group, especially the Ku Klux Klan, in order to defend our rights as Negroes. They knew we'd be willing to use our fists if it came down to it. Some of us still feel this way."

"PREACH!" yelled several.

"I remember the sign that used to hang right out front that said, 'We are ready for the Ku Klux Klan.' And again, we were. But now we must come to terms with the unfathomable truth that our leader has met with the Imperial Wizard, an act that I cannot condone. You all know me. I speak for the U.S. brothers and sisters, and I was honored to be given the high-ranking position of UNIA Leader of the American Negroes. I thank you here publicly for bestowing upon me that honor, President Garvey. But I question your actions."

He turned and looked at Garvey. The stare-down lasted several seconds before the crowd began to yell and scream at James with disapproval. They didn't like seeing their president challenged, no matter the cause, and had never seen anyone speak out publicly against him, especially someone like James, who many argued was the second most powerful man within the UNIA.

"I speak only what is in my heart," said James. "And I will not resign as some of my colleagues have. I understand that you, Brother Garvey, have privately suggested to several delegates that I am not fit to lead the American Negro . . . that I am incompetent. I say . . . right here before this body . . . that it is your competence that should be called into question."

A collective deep breath could be heard from the throng.

"I request that you disprove this charge of incompetence in front of this convention's delegates. No more secrecy! I request a trial in the coming days, before this convention comes to a close. Let the international delegation decide my fate."

"YOU'RE FINISHED!" screamed someone.

"YOU'RE A TRAITOR!" yelled another.

"GARVEY! GARVEY! GARVEY!" the

hall began again.

My friend bravely stood there at the podium and waited for them to quiet down once more, but they didn't. In fact, Garvey's supporters would make sure those were the last words James spoke that night. He finally realized what he was up against and headed back to his seat.

I'd seen enough and headed upstairs to the exit. My God, how they shouted. So much so that the walls along the dark stairwell began to shake. It felt as if the noise was going to blow the roof off of Liberty Hall that night.

30

I arrived home around dinnertime later that night. Entering through the kitchen, I grabbed a sugar cookie from the counter and nibbled on it for a bit before walking into the living room.

I sat my briefcase down on the couch, loosened my tie, and noticed several suitcases by the front door. The house was quieter than usual. I stood there looking in each direction, absorbing the scene.

Turning to my left and looking up at the top of the stairwell, I saw the bottom of Loretta's legs. They were still. Then, as if on cue, she began to move. I noticed her black dress and high heels. Had I forgotten about an event we were supposed to attend? It certainly wasn't our anniversary or either of our birthdays.

She arrived at the base of the stairwell and looked directly at me, her face covered in tears. I wanted to run and grab her, but couldn't move.

"What happened?" I asked.

She held out some sheets of paper, waiting for me to come and grab them. I did, wondering if someone had sent news of a death in the family. But what I grabbed were two large photographs and a newspaper clipping. I took one look and recognized that the lie I'd been telling her for three years had finally come to an end.

"Where did you get these?" I asked, eyeing the picture of the official agent contract I'd signed.

"A man came by here and gave me these pictures and these press clippings. He said you've been an agent with the Bureau of Investigation since 1919. Is it true, Sid? The man photographed in that newspaper clipping is certainly the same man you're shaking hands with in the other picture. And you're holding a Bureau badge, for Christ's sake!"

"Give me a second here. I need you to try —"

"Please don't lie to me. The truth. At least give me that. The article says that man runs the Bureau of Investigation in Washington. And that's absolutely your signature."

"Would you hold on just a minute? Calm down."

"Is it true?"

"You're obviously already convinced that it is."

"Then tell me I'm wrong. Am I wrong?"

A dozen thoughts ran through my mind, but I was tired of lying. In fact, I was just plain tired.

"No," I said. "You're not wrong."

There was a long bit of nothing and then she asked, "How could you do this to me, Sidney?"

"Let me explain."

She put her hand up to keep me from saying another word and dropped her head. I'd never seen her this inconsolable. Her light cry turned to an intense, shaking one. I walked over and wrapped her up.

"It's not what you think, Loretta."

She began trying to break free, but I kept my arms locked.

"You let go of me!" she yelled, squirming away, the sound of her voice becoming nasal.

I released her and she took a big step back, slipping a bit on the hardwood floor. Her sadness had sharply turned to anger. Her eyes were cold, her nose runny.

"You've been lying to me, your mother, James, and on and on. Our life is a lie."

"Wait a minute!"

"Through it all, the loss of Daddy, moving your mother and aunt, buying this house, making new friends, losing our child, the one person I put my trust in was you."

"You can still trust me."

"There were even moments when the only reason I wanted to keep going was my love for you. And that was based one hundred percent on knowing I knew exactly who you were. That gave my life meaning. And now all of that is gone. None of what you did for me was ever about me. It was about fooling me so you could help yourself."

"That's not true. I love you more than anything. I'm doing all of this for us. Not for me. For all of us."

"Who is *us,* Sidney?"

"Our people."

"You could've told me."

"I had to protect you."

"Can you even protect yourself?"

"What?"

"The man who stopped by here may have something to say about that."

"Who?"

"He told me to give you a message."

"What?"

"He said to finish the job and call the phone number he gave you or things will get worse. What does that even mean for

God's sake, Sidney? Finish what job?"

"He wants me to frame Garvey."

"Or things will get worse? When did you think it might be okay to tell me our lives were in danger?"

"They're not."

"At least now I know why you never wanted to discuss your job, why you never introduced me to anyone, why we never got a house telephone."

"Never introduced you to anyone? You know James. You know —"

"STOP!"

Her shouting startled me. I looked over at the suitcases again and felt my heart speed up.

"Where are you going?"

"I waited until you got home before leaving because I wanted to find out that it all might somehow not be true."

"I said where are you going?"

"This house makes me sick. I can't think. I can't breathe."

"Then we will leave. We'll go to Vermont. Tomorrow."

"I'm staying with Ginger until I can decide what to do next."

"When are you coming back?"

"I'm not. We may go to Paris."

"You can't," I said, reaching out and grabbing her wrist.

"I can and I will!" she screamed, yanking her arm away.

"What about the house?"

"That's the last thing I care about. Do what you want with it."

"I've never heard you talk like this. Just listen to me. Calm down and let's talk about this. It's me. We've been through hell and back together. This is too much too fast. Please. We love each other."

"Don't mention love to me. Love is trust. Trust is love. There's nothing more to talk about."

Her glare was piercing. I'd watched her live under the cloud of her father's death for three years and had happily watched that cloud disappear. Now, all at once, it was back, but even darker. I realized she might never find her way out from under it this time.

We continued looking at each other until there was a knock at the door. She ignored it for a few seconds as I begged her with my eyes. Neither of us had any words left. After another knock she opened it and there stood Ginger.

"Are you ready?" she asked, her French accent never more pronounced.

"Yes," said Loretta.

Ginger stepped inside and didn't look at me. They each grabbed two suitcases as I took a deep breath and tried to grasp what was happening. Ginger quickly walked out, but Loretta stopped at the doorway. She turned and looked back at me, her blood-shot eyes telling me one more time how deeply I'd hurt her. Then, just like that, she was gone.

31

With the sun barely rising and most of Harlem still asleep, I sat in my office the next morning thinking about how I could have done it all so differently, without lying to her. But I'd thought I could pull the whole thing off without her ever getting hurt. And in the end, I thought I'd be okay living with the lie, especially considering I would have assured a better life for her and our children, a segregation-free one.

I watched the Bureau telephone on my desk ring and ring, knowing that if I picked it up it would put me right back in the middle of the mess, force me to deal once again with the web I was entangled in. I picked it up.

"Q3Z," I answered.

"Rise and shine," said Speed. "Shit, now I know when to catch you. You're a fuckin' early bird like me. What's the latest?"

"Eason is likely going to be forced out," I

471

answered. "Garvey doesn't trust him any-more. And you've heard about the KKK meeting, I assume?"

"All over the fuckin' papers. That calculating motherfucker is always . . . well . . . *calculating.* What's his angle on this, Q?"

"Can I get back to you on that? He's obviously trying to curry favor with a demographic powerful enough to raise eyebrows in Washington. I can hear those bigots now . . . telling D.C. to 'leave their well-meaning Negro alone.' You know? Your type of people, Speed."

"Fuck you straight to hell, Q. You're lucky Hoover needs your black ass."

"You see! There you go. Proving my point."

"Well, I don't hear you saying a damn thing solid. All I hear you saying is, 'It may be this and it may be that.' It's your job to find out his exact motive. Hell, I can sit around speculating and guessing."

"Give me a few days."

"Days, not weeks on this, okay, Q?"

"Got it," I said, hanging up the phone, knowing I wasn't going to lift a finger the rest of the day. I just wanted to think and stay out of sight. I reached in my briefcase and took out the slip of paper with the Timekeeper's phone number on it. He was probably waiting for me to call with the news that I'd finally planted the evidence.

Was Speed on the Timekeeper's team? Of course I wondered. But how would that change my position? Or was it Hoover alone sending the Timekeeper, keeping Speed and the others out of the loop? Or was it exactly as the Timekeeper had claimed — that his organization simply had a mole inside the Bureau that no one in D.C. knew about?

All I knew was that I had to look at this obstacle as one man. This game of chicken was between him and me. And this approach to thinking about it would allow me to focus because I wasn't about to quit. In fact I was beyond angry that the bastard had involved Loretta. I'd be damned if I was gonna give in to his demands now.

Hell, with her gone I felt a lot less fear. Besides, I just knew it was this Timekeeper's final play, and that I was still a man of too much value to whoever was pulling these strings. Outing me to Garvey served no one's purpose. However, part of me could see Hoover guessing that such a threat would have rattled my cage, for he was a man who thought me far too simple.

I walked in the house that evening and found a letter from Loretta on the dining room table. It simply read:

I have decided that the best thing for me to do is leave the country. Ginger was planning to move back to Paris in January, but she pushed it up as a favor to me. I don't feel safe here and I ask that you please try to understand. I'm taking control of my life and you must grant me that. I hope you haven't involved yourself in something you can't get out of, but please be careful. I will be leaving in a week. Please don't try to stop me, as it will only cause both of us more hurt. I have taken only what I need out of the bank and leave the house to you. Good-bye, Sidney.

The pain was too much, but I knew she was justified in not feeling safe, even though I figured she was. The Timekeeper had only made this move to scare me into thinking he might hurt her. He'd miscalculated.

I walked into her studio and saw that she'd taken all of her paintings. She'd left a few brushes, some cans of paint. An old blue dress shirt I'd given her to work in was resting on a stool. The sleeves were rolled up and it had splotches of paint all over. I picked it up, held it to my face, and just as I'd imagined, it smelled of her lovely perfume. All I could do at that moment was pray she'd come back to me someday. My gut told me she wouldn't. Still, I had to find the strength to respect her wishes.

I walked upstairs, found one of my hidden bottles of whiskey from years back, dragged myself out onto our bedroom balcony, and began to guzzle away my misery.

Looking out at the dimly lit street, I realized that whoever was watching me was, well, watching me. To them, the entire country was one big Harlem with no good hiding places for a man in my position. Besides, almost half of Loretta's financial worth was wrapped up in the house and all that was in it. I couldn't let her lose that, too, regardless of what was to become of us.

So, until I could sell it and head to God knows where, my intention was to keep working like a man is supposed to. I'd still make myself available to Garvey and I'd continue updating Du Bois as best I could. I would remain an agent until the trial and conviction. Then I'd be done.

After waking up the next morning with Loretta's paint-covered shirt in hand, I washed up and drove straight to the real estate office on 143rd Street and put the house up for sale. I learned that its value had appreciated considerably. Now I'd just have to wait for someone to make a fair offer.

And wait I did. Months went by as if they were one long, drawn out, miserable, lonely day with nothing but Loretta's absence permeating every second of it. There'd been no sign of the Timekeeper. Unfortunately, there'd been no sign of a buyer for the house either.

Speed, as usual, had done a lot of yelling through the phone, expressing how frustrating it was that everything was moving at a snail's pace. But he'd emphasized how sure the Bureau was about Garvey's ultimate fate. And he'd reiterated the fact that Hoover wanted me to remain in place, to continue operating out of the consulting front and working on the church. He'd expressed how pleased Hoover was with my positioning and how critical it would be for me to remain in Garvey's good graces if he managed to win his trial. According to Speed, Hoover had said I was "absolutely indispensable."

The fact that the Timekeeper hadn't shown his face in months after I hadn't succumbed to his approaching Loretta didn't seem to be a simple coincidence. There was no real ultimatum. He was going to wait for the trial like the rest of us. I kept hearing

Hoover's words: "absolutely indispensable."

I'd done a lot of planning, packing, and praying, none of which had put my mind at ease. I'd also managed to comb the entire house for the most irreplaceable, valuable items. I'd then taken them to a secure storage facility, one I'd hoped no one had seen me enter. Either way, it was money well spent for the time being.

I'd quit shaving, and as the cold winter weather set in, I'd begun to take on the look of a lumberjack posing as a suit-wearing engineer. I couldn't think of any good reason to worry about my appearance. In fact, I barely had any desire to brush my teeth and wash my socks. But I did.

I'd informed Speed that James had been officially voted out by the UNIA's convention delegates, expelled for ninety-nine years. He'd since done just as he'd said, started a rival organization. Meanwhile, both Hubert and William had cut ties with Garvey. They, along with most of Harlem's leaders, were still fuming over his visit with the Imperial Wizard. It had weakened him considerably, but he certainly didn't show it. Everything he said in the *Negro World* revealed a man more determined than ever to defeat his enemies and fulfill his promise of Africa for the Africans.

I'd been working closely with a man named Simpson Garfield, bringing him up to speed on the detailed information regarding the Abyssinian I'd compiled over the past few years. We worked from sunup to sundown, along with a slew of other architects, contractors, and advisors who had been brought on board. I was now part of a team of engineers. As I'd need to educate my replacement before moving on, I decided Mr. Garfield fit the bill. He was a short, coffee-skinned man in his forties from Boston, rather quiet, but very detail-oriented.

Because Liberty Hall was right next door to the Abyssinian, I'd run into UNIA members on a daily basis, especially when they were arriving at Sunday's big gatherings. I'd chatted with many of them on the streets, but Garvey had only sent for me once. Business matters seemed to be unofficially on hold while he awaited word on his trial date. Everyone knew it was coming. Lawyers on both sides were just getting their guns fully loaded. I did learn something significant during our one visit, however: I was still in good standing with him.

"Stay ready, Sidney," he'd said. "Stay sharp. When this trial is over we'll raise enough money to make the gods envious.

And with it we'll buy enough ships to deliver every Negro to Africa at once. Not to mention I can quadruple your salary. The U.S. government is kidding itself if it thinks cozying up to Liberia will somehow serve as an impediment to us ever gaining a foothold there. The government elites of both Liberia and America can sip tea and sniff each other's rear ends all day long. Harding can give them a billion dollars, but it still won't stop the common man, the Negro in the streets of Monrovia, from pledging his allegiance to the UNIA."

About a week before Christmas I drove James to the Grand Central Terminal. He was due to catch a train to Cleveland. Both he and Garvey had begun taking separate trips to various cities, speaking to large audiences and competing for their support.

If Garvey was due to speak in Baltimore, James would plan a speech there the following week. If James visited Philadelphia, Garvey did the same shortly thereafter. And so began their battle.

Traffic around the terminal was heavy, and it was getting dark out, but I weaved through the chaos and pulled alongside the curb to let him out. Suitcase-toting travelers were hustling in and out, flooding the sidewalk.

"Sure you don't wanna come with me?" asked James.

"Next time maybe."

"Next time will be New Orleans."

"Always wanted to see New Orleans. I may just do that."

"That reminds me," he said, reaching into his briefcase. "When you do make the trip down South, you'll have a new railroad map to study. Started collecting these a while back and didn't stop since I know how much you love 'em. Lord knows I done been to enough cities."

He handed me a stack of brand-new folded railroad maps. There had to be at least ten. I quickly began sifting through them.

"I mean to tell you, James. I sure do appreciate this. How much do I owe you?"

"Not a penny one. Consider it an early Christmas gift."

"This is one I've never seen." I held it up to read. " 'Canadian National Railway,' it says. I'll be darned."

"Picked that one up in Toronto. It's a mess of maps in that stack there."

"Can't thank you enough."

"You welcome, brotha. By the way, when is Loretta due back?"

"Not until January," I answered, putting

the maps in my briefcase. "I want her to enjoy Paris."

"Then I'll holler at ya'll when I get back." He opened the door and stepped out into the noise of cars, trains, and clacking shoes.

"You be safe now, James."

"Will do," he said, slamming the door.

On my way home I stopped by a tiny little spot on 137th called Tony's to grab a hot salami sandwich and a cup of hot cocoa for dinner, hardly a substitute for Loretta's pork roast or fried chicken, but very good nonetheless.

The folks at Tony's had become used to me stopping in around seven every night. After about a ten-minute wait, a young Italian woman named Sophia put my sandwich in a white paper bag and sat it on the oily-looking wooden countertop that separated her from the customers.

"Would you like me to double cup this cocoa for you?" she asked. "It's real hot."

"Yes, ma'am."

I hopped up from one of the five counter stools while she doubled it up and then handed it to me.

"You have a good night, Sophia."

"See ya next time, Mr. Temple."

Walking toward the Baby Grand, which was parked about ten cars down to the left,

I began sipping. I barely missed bumping into a youngster on a bicycle who was trying to avoid a pile of shoveled snow.

There was quite a bit of traffic on the street, but the sidewalk was clear. Just as I was opening the car door, I felt something hard press against my back.

"Don't move, don't say a word," said a voice. "That's a gun you feel. Just open the door, get in, and scoot."

He kept the gun pressed against me as I got in and eased my way over to the passenger's side. He then got behind the wheel. Two more men opened the back doors and got in, each pointing their guns at me.

"Give me the key," said the man behind the wheel. "And hand that shit to them."

I gave him the key, and he unlocked the ignition system. He then started the engine. As I turned around, the man sitting behind me snatched the paper bag out of my hand — then the cocoa, spilling a bit on me. He handed both to his partner and began patting my coat before removing my pistol.

"Any more of those?" asked the driver, eyeing my gun.

"No," I said.

We drove to the end of the block and he pulled over again. He got out, walked around the front of the car, and opened my door.

"Slide over behind the wheel," he said.

As I did, he got in and shut the door.

"Drive to your house," he said.

I headed up Seventh Avenue with both hands on the wheel. I'd never seen these three men before. As we pulled up to the gate, I saw Ivan standing there as usual.

"Don't try anything funny," said the man. "Which place is yours?"

"Fourth one down on the right."

"Can you see your back door from here?"

"Yes," I said, pointing to it. "Right there."

"I see. You have your porch light on. Good. Okay now . . . just do what you always do."

I gave Ivan my customary wave as he opened the gate and let us drive through. The alleyway had never been so quiet, never so still. It was dimly lit in spots, as there was a streetlamp behind every fifth house, but they were there mostly for effect, leaving the alleyway rather dark overall. I pulled into the carport behind the kitchen and waited for instructions. The engine was still running.

"Is this back entrance the only one?" asked the man, his gun resting on his lap but still pointed at me.

"No. Our front door faces the southern side of 139th."

"Why'd you use the back entrance?"

"We never enter from the front. All of the tenants use the alleyway and park in their carports. They all enter the alleyway from Seventh Avenue. That front door is only used for receiving guests."

"We're guests."

I slowly turned and caught a glimpse of the other two. Neither had said a word. They were sitting back with their pistols resting on their laps, their faces expressionless. All three men were colored, each about my size. They were dressed in dark three-piece suits, thick topcoats, their fedoras bigger than the typical ones.

"We just never park out front, that's all," I said, turning and staring straight ahead again.

"Where is that pretty wife of yours anyway?"

"She's in San Francisco. I'm to join her in a few months. She wants to make that home."

"Does that boy at the gate work there all day?"

"He works from seven in the morning 'til seven at night. Man named George works the overnight shift. He'll be relieving him soon."

"Can anyone just come and go through that gate?"

"No. Only tenants."

"Any more gates?"

"You mean as far as the ones that serve this block?"

"Yes."

"There are more along 138th and 139th, but they're for show only. They remain locked . . . unused. But there is another main one on the far-west end of this alleyway that opens to Eighth Avenue. I have never used it."

"This is an awfully nice place you got here. A secure alleyway, a private carport, and that sign by the gate said, 'Please Walk Your Horses.' Don't see no horses 'round here."

"All of these private carports were originally horse and carriage stables."

"Cut the engine off. Let's go inside."

32

I awoke several hours later throbbing in pain as I stared at the blurry living room ceiling through my left eye. The other was swollen shut. I began coughing up the blood that had poured into my mouth from a busted bottom lip. I rolled over and saw the three men sitting at the dining room table. They were smoking cigarettes and passing around a bottle of whiskey.

"Looks like he done finally come to," said one of them, taking a big drink from the bottle.

I noticed another approaching. He reached down and began dragging me over to the table. He picked me up, sat me in one of the chairs, and entered the kitchen. I barely had enough strength to hold myself up. My head fell back, then forward. I was so dizzy. I began sliding down in the chair until I came to a slouch, my arms just dangling to the side, my legs splayed open.

"I think he looks like he 'bout ready to listen," said the man directly across from me. I was able to make him out as the one who'd sat up front with me. "You ready to finally follow orders, Sidney?"

I subtly nodded my head yes.

"We didn't get a chance to properly introduce ourselves earlier," he said, flicking his cigarette ash onto one of Loretta's expensive dinner plates. "I'm Drake. This here's Cleo. And the man fetchin' you a glass is Goat. You sure do have a fine place here. And those are some mighty expensive suits in that closet upstairs. Hope you don't mind us leaving a mess. We had to . . . you know . . . sweep the place."

He put his hand on Cleo's shoulder and the two of them seemed to disappear in the smoke they were exhaling. I felt myself slipping in and out of consciousness.

Goat walked out with a glass and sat it right in front of me. He poured some whiskey in it and handed it to me. "Go on," he said, nudging my arm.

I took it in my left hand and guzzled it down, the burn actually soothing compared to the throbbing pain I felt throughout.

"Good," said Goat, sitting down in the chair to my left.

"I've got good and bad news," said Drake.

"Let's start with the bad. Your failure to deliver the evidence caused quite a problem for the boss man with his superiors. The good news: It has given them time to think things over, and now there's a new plan for dealing with Garvey. You hearing me?"

"Uh-huh."

"You see, they've learned that Garvey is promising big dollars to some top officials to make sure his stay in prison is a short one. And now, the way they see it, Garvey going to the slammer for rum running or anything else just won't cut it after all. His stay would be so short that he'd figure out a way to keep his Africa plans going from behind bars until he's released. And the boss man's superiors can't have that. Understand?"

"Yes."

"Do you like your superior, Mr. Hoover?"

"Sure."

"Is Mr. Hoover a smart man?"

"I . . ."

"Don't answer that. That wasn't one of the boss man's questions. It was just me being nosy. By the way, Mr. Banks sends his regards."

"Who?"

"Boss man! You call him Timekeeper. He said you kept on and on with the fuckin' questions. Did you find out anything?"

"Nothing important," I slurred, noticing my briefcase on the floor, all of the items dumped out, including my new maps.

"Mr. Banks doesn't like a lot of questions. In fact, he pays us very well not to ask too many, to simply deliver his messages and carry out orders. And in this case, he paid us to keep you alive."

"Why?"

"So you can kill Marcus Garvey."

Goat poured some more whiskey in my glass. I slowly picked it up and knocked it back, allowing the words *kill Marcus Garvey* to sink in.

"All you have to do now is convince us that you can do it. If you can't, there's no reason to keep you around. Ain't that right, Goat?"

"Right," he said, taking his gun and pressing it against my ear. "You done already embarrassed Mr. Banks with the big bosses. And now they don't know if they can count on him no more. So this here job's gonna get done one way or another. Garvey dies or you die. Long as one of those two things happens, Mr. Banks stays employed. And that's a mighty good thing for us."

"I can do it," I mumbled, the words a mere reflex from feeling like my brains were about to be blown all over the dining room wall.

"Good," said Drake. "But how? And can't no bullets be involved. If we thought he could be finished that way we'da done it already. We've been casing him for months and there ain't no way in hell to get a clean shot on the mothafucka. He's like that baby elephant in the wild surrounded by a herd of a hundred giant ones. Nah, this has to be done from the inside. And it has to be clean."

"I can poison him," I said, gritting my sore teeth — Goat's gun feeling like it was cutting into my ear. "I can poison him at our next meeting."

"When is that?" he asked, motioning for Goat to lower his gun, which he did. I casually sat up a bit and tried to concentrate.

"A big one is being planned sometime before the trial. We're to discuss all of the logistics regarding who will be in charge of what if he is forced to serve time. I may be asked to oversee all of the Black Star Line affairs."

"When exactly?"

"I just know it's to happen before the trial. Probably in a few weeks."

"Poison him how?"

"I always show up early to our meetings

490

and am alone in the boardroom for a few minutes. Only his top men are allowed in that room. There's heavy security everywhere. But a servant always delivers his mango juice, cheese, and crackers before anyone else arrives. I can slip something into his juice. I can kill him."

"Sounds mighty loose."

"It's solid. I can guarantee it. I just need you to get me the poison."

"What do ya'll think?"

Cleo and Goat nodded their heads with approval. Drake kept his eyes on me and tilted his head to the side. I could see his brain working. He puckered his lips.

"Who do you think our inside man is at the Bureau?" he asked. "And could there be more than one — a Bureau courier, a Bureau telephone operator?"

"I have no idea," I mumbled.

"Mr. Banks told me to ask you that. He said to ask yourself that question before you think about sending the Bureau a telegram with the hopes that they'll come rescue you. Ask it before you think about calling them or trying to get in touch with another agent. You never know who you might be talking to. And the big bosses got plenty of New York policemen on the payroll. So you see, you can't be saved."

"That seems clear."

"Find out as soon as possible when Garvey intends to have this meeting."

"I can do that."

He picked his gun up off the table and pointed it at me. "Just know that every time you step out of this house there won't be a second of the day when we won't have one of these aimed at you. We own you. When Garvey's dead, you can have your life back. Until then, your job is to keep on livin' the same life you've been livin'. But do anything stupid and you're as dead as that smart-ass Darwin mothafucka. And we'll decide what *is* and *isn't* stupid."

"How do we communicate?" I asked. "Garvey's secret service is more aggressive now than ever. None of us connected to the UNIA ever know when and if we're being watched by them."

"Perhaps they were watching you tonight. That's gonna require some creative explaining on your part."

"I was simply robbed."

"Good. Good. Nevertheless, since we have to assume they may continue watching you, your living habits must appear the same. You will stay in good standing with them that way."

"I don't see why not."

"Now . . . how do we communicate, you asked? One of our men, Bingo Jones, will be meeting you at the church every morning to report for duty. Your new assistant!" He smiled. "Wherever you go, he'll go."

"I can't enter UNIA headquarters with —"

"You'll have to. You're a trusted man around there. Make them trust your new protégé. If you have to meet privately with Garvey, Bingo can wait just outside the room. But that's the only exception. You can never be out of his sight otherwise during the day. You go to the market, he helps you pick out fruit, you go to take a piss, he holds your pecker for you."

"When I come home at night?"

"Your regular comings and goings have to appear the same to Garvey's men. So you and Bingo can part ways at the church come evenin' time and we'll follow you home from there. Figure you might wanna at least have supper alone for the next few weeks — finish packin' up all these boxes for that move to San Francisco. I'm sure your wife can't wait to see you. Anytime you need to call her, go ahead and use a telephone near the church. Just make sure to have Bingo dial the number for you. Clear?"

"Yes."

"Our inside man says you stay in touch with the Bureau by calling from your fake-ass office."

"That's right."

"Keep on checkin' in with them as usual. Bingo will be more than happy to take notes for you. He's good at it, and I'm assuming you ain't got no office secretary, right?"

"No."

"One more thing," he said, surveying the living room. "That front door. Never open it again. We'll have some men parked right out front around the clock. And never step out onto that upstairs balcony either. You're to come and go only through that Seventh Avenue gate. Is that back porch light always left on like that?"

"No. I forgot to turn it off this morning."

"Well, keep forgettin' to turn it off. Leave it on 'round the clock. Change the bulb as needed. One of us will be parked along Seventh Avenue all night. You do remember showing me how visible your back door is through the gate when that light's left on?"

"Yes."

"You won't be able to enter or exit without us seeing you. So get what you need during the day, 'cause once you're in at night, ain't no leavin'. And if you even think about walking toward that Eighth Avenue gate you'll feel a bullet in yo ass."

"My neighbors?" I asked.

"What about 'em?"

"The man next door, the doctor . . ."

"Say 'good morning' or 'good evening' if you have to, but no carryin' on. You have one job: to get through the weeks without any hiccups — to attend that meeting."

33

At UNIA headquarters the next day, I explained to Amy Jacques that my battered face was a result of my having accidentally fallen from a ladder at the church. Seemingly embarrassed by my explanation, she explained that Garvey was in Detroit. But I didn't care. I'd simply entered the building to satisfy Drake, who was parked about a half block down.

He and his sidekicks had left the house on foot at three in the morning, but as I'd pulled through the gate onto Seventh Avenue at around nine, there he was, parked in a cream-colored Oldsmobile with brown trim, just waiting to follow me. Goat and Cleo were probably resting up back at their base, waiting to relieve him when it was time to rotate shifts.

I said good-bye to Amy, and with the Oldsmobile following in the distance, drove straight to the church, now a tall, massive shell of two-by-fours with a makeshift roof attached to keep out the rain or snow. Waiting near what would soon be the front door was a young man wearing khaki pants, gloves, and a very thick brown topcoat.

I figured he must be the lucky one assigned to be my new best friend because all of the other workers shuffling about — the ones carrying slabs of wood, saws, hammers, etcetera — I'd seen before. As soon as I opened the car door and stepped out into the cold morning air, he approached.

"Let's make this real simple," he said, reaching out his hand, which I shook. "Name's Bingo Jones." He handed me a sheet of paper. "Just stand here and act like you're reading these work orders to me."

"Okay."

"I'll be at your side all day, every day, but we don't have to speak unless it involves the job. I'll do my part and act like the ambitious young engineer-in-training, and you just go about your business as usual. Understand?"

"Yes."

"When's the meeting?" he asked.

"In two to three weeks — late December, early January. The specific day is being nailed down. Garvey's traveling constantly. And because this will be the last business meeting he oversees before the trial, he wants to make sure all the key players are in attendance — lawyers, architects, accountants, investors . . . even some Liberian land developers are expected."

"Good. Let's go to work."

Nothing eventful happened the rest of that day. I spent most of it leaning over a large, schematics-covered worktable, advising laborers, collaborating with other engineers, and trying to stay warm by drinking a lot of hot coffee.

Bingo sat close by and pretended to make notes on the architectural drawings for the church ceiling. He was quite the actor. But when the two of us were alone for a brief moment, he acted like the serious agent he was and searched me from head to toe, doing his best to make sure I hadn't slipped something under my coat.

The following days went along in much the same fashion, save for the fact that Bingo spoke more and more freely to the other workers, having convinced them that he'd graduated top of his class at Tuskegee. Maybe he had. He was a well-spoken young man, no older than twenty-five, and in many ways reminded me of myself, both in looks and temperament.

How in God's name he'd found himself

smack dab in the middle of some plot to assure Garvey's assassination was hard to figure. In fact, the Timekeeper, Drake, Cleo, and Goat were also educated-sounding, refined men, save for the cursing and slang when they were angry. Whoever had recruited them was most assuredly paying each top dollar. It was all I could guess.

But then again, colored Americans as a whole were lost, still scrambling about, fighting amongst themselves for the scraps left over from Reconstruction. What else could be expected from a people stripped of their native languages with no respected language to replace them, devoid of specifics about their African roots, legally denied an education, whose souls were still being ripped out, whose collective mind was still haunted by thoughts of whips tearing at the flesh of kinfolk?

I pondered questions like this as I lay in bed each night, alone in the house, my mind exhausted from trying to figure out an escape. Drake had dumped out my briefcase on that first night but had left all of the items on the floor, even the new maps James had given me. My gun was all they'd wanted.

But during their sweep of the place, they hadn't discovered my storage spot under the slabs of wood in my closet. My second gun, the holster, etcetera was still stored there.

All this being the case, I'd begun studying the new maps religiously, each with dozens of updated routes just as James had said. In fact, the railroad system as a whole had improved dramatically in a short time and was so much more elaborate that the old maps I had under the car seat were now useless.

But even with these new ones at my disposal, they only allowed me to dream of a way out. The more I lay there and examined the dizzying lines, the more I was reminded that America's wide-open space was inaccessible to me. Still, I was hoping against hope that something unexpected would occur and provide an opening for me to slip through — a brief moment when the Timekeeper's hired eyes were not fixed on my every move.

December twenty-second was no such day. With a light snowstorm having set in, I motored up to the gate bright and early. Ivan stopped me with a big smile as he pulled the gate open.

"Mornin', Mr. Temple. Just need to let you know that the undercover police will be staked out across the street and around the corner until they catch who they're looking for."

I was listening to him but looking across the way. A police car was parked right behind the Oldsmobile. Two white officers were inside and Drake was standing by their driver's-side door. He reached inside and shook both their hands before heading to the Oldsmobile as they drove off, each officer flashing me a serious look. Cleo was behind the wheel of the Oldsmobile. Drake went to the passenger's side and got in.

"They done spoke to me real clear," continued Ivan. "So ain't no need to be suspicious of that Oldsmobile being there all the time, mainly at night. I guess a couple of our tenants along 139th have been robbed, real close to this here gate, not the other."

"By the way," I said, "what's the brotha's name who works that Eighth Avenue gate? I've never used it."

"For this block?"

"Uh-huh."

"That gate's for them west end tenants anyhow, Mr. Temple. But his name is Howard. Then, at night, a man named Leonard relieves him."

"I see."

"But back to them houses that done been

robbed. Has your front door been damaged?"

"No," I said, as Cleo opened his door, got out, and stood there, squinting at us through the snowfall, obviously trying to hear our conversation.

"Anyway," said Ivan, "they want all the residents to know they're safe. No need to worry. Just keep your front door locked. That's the only way they can get in, especially as long as them police are watching over the gate with ol' George at night."

"That's awfully reassuring," I said, eyeballing Cleo. "Thank you, Ivan."

"My pleasure," he said, turning and waving at Cleo who waved back. "You have a wonderful day, Mr. Temple."

I decided to make a left on Seventh this time, then another immediate one onto 139th. I wanted to see the vehicle parked near my front door. With the Oldsmobile tailing, I slowly passed a plum-colored Chevrolet with two men inside. The Oldsmobile briefly stopped and Drake engaged them.

Obviously, their job was to watch my front door around the clock — to make sure they could see anyone who might come knocking. There'd likely be no one, save for maybe James, perhaps Ellington, and, of course, the postman. As soon as he dropped my mail off, these men would certainly filter through it. The last thing I wanted was them intercepting a letter from Momma or Professor Gold, revealing the Vermont address.

Driving along 139th, I studied the row of houses to my left, most of them filled with Strivers' Row tenants I'd never met. I wanted to stop the car and run to bang on one of their front doors for help. Passing one similar set of stairs after another, one similar set of windows after another, reminded me that the row was simply one block-long continuous building with no spaces separating each house. In fact, each home was distinguishable only by its unique set of curtains. It was the first time I'd thought about the disadvantages of living in such confined quarters.

On a whim, I drove straight to the real estate office to see if there was any news on the house sale. Not a good idea. Just as I parked, the Oldsmobile pulled up right beside me, so close that I couldn't open my door.

"What the hell do you think you're doing?" asked an angry Cleo, his pistol pointed right at me — his voice surprisingly squeaky and high-pitched. First time he'd spoken to me.

"Hold on!" I frantically replied, holding my hands above the wheel. "I'm simply seeing if there's any news about my house."

"You go from the house to the church, nowhere in between, unless Bingo's with you. Thought this shit was crystal clear."

"I was simply . . ."

"Fuck simply! I almost *simply* put your ass to sleep for good. I'm itchin' to kill you, fool. I don't have a dog in this fight. I'm just paid to pull this trigger if the plan looks like it's going bad. Drive to the church mothafucka!"

I did just that. An hour later Bingo drove back with me to the real estate office. I could only hope that he and the others had no interest in stealing the money I'd receive from selling the house. Time would tell.

With him sitting beside me while I spoke to the sales agent, I learned that there'd been an offer made for $9,000, a thousand more than we'd originally paid for it. I accepted, signed the necessary paperwork, and was told that the deal would be final within days.

As we headed back to the church, I eyed the gun Bingo held on his lap. There was never a moment in the car when he didn't have it there, ready to use if I so much as sneezed the wrong way.

"Why are you-all willing to shoot me in broad daylight?" I asked.

"Because we can. No one gives a fuck about you, at least no one that matters. Lotta no-name niggas get shot and killed every day. It would suit me just fine to splatter your brains all over that car door window."

"There's no need to do that."

"We'll see."

"I need to pull over right here and mail a letter."

"Then do it slowly. You yank that wheel even a lick, I shoot."

As I calmly pulled in front of the post office, he tightened the grip on his gun.

"Hand me the letter," he said.

I reached inside my coat pocket. As soon as I pulled the envelope out, he snatched it away. He read the address. It was a letter to a nonexistent person in Los Angeles. I was just trying to see what I could get away with.

"You got another envelope you can use?" he asked, tearing it open.

"I can buy one inside."

"Good."

He began reading my note to a fictional college friend in which I asked how his family was doing and apologized for not staying in touch. I mentioned my intentions of moving to San Francisco and the possibility of our being able to visit each other more often.

"What's in your briefcase?" he asked.

"Nothing."

He grabbed it from the backseat and began rummaging through the contents. He'd find nothing of interest unless he was suspicious of writing paper, pens, a few novels, and a bag of peanuts. But I took note. I'd have to be careful about what I kept in there from now on.

"What you got on you?" he asked, reaching over and patting me down, checking under my suit jacket.

"Nothing. You can search me from head to toe. There's nothing."

"Let's go," he said, putting his gun in the holster under his topcoat. I hopped out and he followed. There'd be no way of mailing Professor Gold or anyone else a letter anytime soon.

Fortunately, using the mail service to correspond with James wouldn't be necessary. He was there waiting to see me when we returned to the church. In fact, he headed our way before I'd even finished parking.

"Who is this?" asked Bingo, as James neared my car door.

"My best friend."

"You better make him feel real comfortable with me. Make him feel like he can talk openly. He better not act the least bit suspicious of anything."

"How am I supposed . . ."

"Figure it out," he snapped, reaching under his coat.

There was no time left to discuss the matter, so I gave James a wave and rolled down my window.

"I ain't been here but a minute," he said, rubbing his hands together. "Them boys inside said you'd be right back."

"You're back!" I said.

"Not for long. Nonstop travel, brother. And I see you still ain't shaved a lick. I gotta razor over there in the car."

"It suits this cold weather," I said, rubbing my scraggly beard.

"Who we got here?"

"Oh . . . this is Bingo Jones. Bingo, this is Reverend James Eason."

"Good to meet you," said James, reaching across my chest and shaking his hand. "Bingo, huh? All right. All right."

Bingo didn't say a word. But his steeliness spoke to me loud and clear. It only confused James — that along with my unusually reserved demeanor. He probably expected me to hop out of the car and give him a

507

hug. Instead, I just sat there, waiting for him to speak. He began looking up and down the street, then at the church.

"Looks like ya'll been mighty busy 'round here. My goodness it's done gone up quick. Praise God."

"Won't be long now," I said.

"Well, look here, brother. I don't wanna keep ya'll. Just wanted to run this Louisiana business by you. I'm leaving tomorrow for Georgia, then I'm off to Florida, but I'd love for you to meet me in New Orleans on the thirtieth. I'm due to speak there on January first."

"You see all this work I'm . . ."

"I know. I know. I'm just puttin' the invitation out there 'cause I love you, brotha. You like family to me now. Come on! You know that."

"I love you too, brotha," I sincerely said, reaching out and grasping his hand, shaking it like it might be the last time I'd ever do so. He seemed so alone, so uneasy, much like myself. I was certain he felt the hand of Garvey squeezing him tighter and tighter the more he tried to build his new movement.

"Anyhow," he said, "if you do decide to come, here's the information." He handed me a folded piece of paper. "It's all written down there . . . where I'm speaking and the hotel where I'll be staying. You're officially invited. It's probably the most important speech I'll give, considering how big the UNIA following is down there. This thing is really startin' to take off."

"We knew it would."

"But Marcus's boys are causing us an awful lot of problems. Well . . . let me tell you about that later. I'm sure Bingo there don't wanna hear all this."

"No . . . he's real good people, James. Bingo's my right-hand man. Go on and talk. Go on."

"Don't pay me no mind," said Bingo, smiling. "Just tryin' to stay out that cold as long as I can."

"Ha-ha!" laughed James with a big grin. "Young brotha say he tryin' to stay out this cold. I hear ya. I hear ya. That hawk is out, boy!"

"You ain't lyin'," I said, watching his breath hit the air. "Go on and tell me about Marcus's boys."

"Look, it ain't nothin' surprising, Brother Sid. They just keep showing up at our meetings and threatening our followers, even puttin' their hands on folks in some cases."

"What?"

"Mm-hmm. Marcus has certainly put the

word out. He done told 'em to stop us from gaining momentum. Gettin' ugly out there! His Los Angeles, Philadelphia, and Pittsburgh divisions are real bad. Sometimes they even block off the streets so folks can't get to the church where I'm speaking. Sight to behold, brotha! But we find a way. There's too many of us. We growin' fast. We attractin' them well-meanin' American Negroes. Most of them roguish West Indians stayin' with Marcus."

"Sounds like you need some protection."

"Nah. They just tryin' to intimidate us. What I need is your support. Wanna see you standing in the audience come the first. But ain't no pressure on it, brotha!"

"Oh, you got my support. You know that."

"Right. Well, listen . . . next time you speak with Loretta, send her my love. Sure do miss that sista."

"I will."

"Ya'll take it easy now," he said.

He tapped my door twice and headed for his car. It was impossible to fathom not being able to ask my best friend for help. Even if I could, how would he react if I told him I was a spy? It was all so terrible. He needed my support, but I couldn't give it. I needed his help but couldn't get it. Hell sounded better.

As I drove up Seventh later that night, I came to a brief stop in the approximate position where the Oldsmobile had been parking. Looking to my left, I noticed two distinct things: One, my back door was indeed very visible; and two, there was obviously no way anyone could see the plum-colored Chevrolet parked around the corner from this position. How any of this mattered, I was still trying to figure out.

With the Oldsmobile fast approaching, I turned left. There was Ivan, standing in his usual position, the inside southern end of the gate. It was from that end that he always lifted the lever and the heavy, black-iron gate opened.

"Evening, Mr. Temple," he said.

"Evening, Ivan."

I reached across the passenger's seat and handed him a one-dollar bill. I wanted to see if such a simple act could slip by Goat and Cleo, who'd already parked before the exchange.

"Christmas is almost here," I said. "Hope you have a merry one."

"Why thank you very much, Mr. Temple. And merry Christmas to you, too."

I eased down the alleyway and pulled into my carport, then took a peek at the Oldsmobile. Cleo had already gotten out and was approaching the gate. I watched him have a brief conversation with Ivan, who showed him the bill.

I walked up the steps, opened the back door, then took one more look Ivan's way. I guess Cleo had made his point because he patted Ivan on the shoulder and returned to the Oldsmobile.

Later that night I ate nothing but grapes and peanuts while listening to Marion Harris's "After You've Gone" over and over before finally falling asleep on the couch.

34

The flood of folks entering Liberty Hall the next day had all us workers at the church looking across the way. Legionnaires lined both sides of the street for nearly half a block. And when the huge motorcade approached, the hammering, drilling, and sawing completely stopped.

Marcus Garvey was a living icon, whether one hated him or not, and the workers wanted at least to catch a glimpse of him. Covered by his blanket of protectors, all holding umbrellas to shield their boss from the still-falling snow, Garvey hustled his way inside.

"I want to hear this," said Bingo. "Take me inside."

"You'll have to leave that sidearm. Everybody's searched before they can enter."

"Not a problem. I should be all right without it for a few minutes, especially with Drake and them parked right across the way. I'll let you wave to 'em on our way over."

Minutes later we stood in the Liberty Hall basement listening to Garvey shout his defiant rhetoric, seemingly about everyone who'd ever crossed him. It was as if this was his last chance to publicly lambaste folks before the big trial. He took full advantage. After he finished tearing into Du Bois once again, he turned his attention to a more surprising foe.

"Those of you who remain with me I shall not forget," he said. "You are my family. Save for a few who may have me fooled. I cannot be so naïve as to think a few British or American spies are not among us. But I'm not speaking to them. I'm speaking to my family. You stand with me as I dare to set foot in the white man's inferno. It's his justice system. His laws. His evidence. His courtroom. He has everything on his side. Everything! But he's never butted heads with this fearless, African-blooded titan!"

A thunderous roar tried to blow through the ceiling and didn't relent for at least a minute. Bingo stood there taking it all in. It was his first taste of *Garvey Power.* And there was no denying the effect it had on anyone who'd ever witnessed it.

"Yes," he continued, "those of you with

me here at Liberty Hall today . . . those in our many offices across the country . . . I can trust you. We shook that big ol' bush long enough to get rid of the bad seeds. But we can't be foolish about it. There are always a few stubborn ones that manage to hang on, ones we can't see. And in this case, they may be hanging on to help the government hang me."

"BOO!" roared the crowd.

"You see, Mr. J. Edgar Hoover, that nigga-hating puppet the president put out front, has a way of making it worth their while. You'll know who I speak of when the trial begins and one backstabbing former UNIA employee after another trots up to the stand and sings like a bird."

"THAT'S RIGHT!" many shouted.

"EASON!" screamed others.

"But Mr. Hoover is no match for Britain's Secret Intelligence Service and their many rogue divisions. He doesn't have their old money, their centuries of developed resources. But even if he did, the U.S. and Britain hate me for different reasons. America simply fears me because I'm a loud-mouthed black man who doesn't know his place. They think I'm a Russian-loving communist like all the others. But! The Brits fear me because I'm going to take back what they stole: AFRICA!"

The audience erupted again. He let the noise feed him, and with every rising pitch he seemed to grow a little taller.

"You see," he bellowed, "the Brits have had their intelligence officers stop our precious *Negro World* paper from being circulated throughout many of their colonized nations. It has crippled our paper's growth. And now they want to keep me out of Liberia . . . far, far away from their beloved, *colonized* Sierra Leone. They're afraid of a revolution. I've always suspected as much, but the hunch was recently confirmed. One of SIS's little mice was caught in one of our traps."

"OOH!" cried the crowd.

"And the little mouse couldn't wiggle free without telling us a thing or two. Like who he reports to here in New York. What was his name?"

Garvey turned and looked at Marcellus Strong, who was standing stage right, arms folded. He gave Garvey a wry smile but said nothing.

"Ah, yes!" said Garvey. "Mr. Banks is his name."

Bingo and I locked eyes. Hearing that name may just as well have been a slap across my face to wake me up. *My God,* was all I could think. The Timekeeper and his men worked for Britain's Secret Intelligence Service — better known as SIS. It all made sense. But Bingo and I hearing this news did little to change my predicament. If anything, it only raised the stakes for Bingo and company. They had all the more reason to kill me if I tried to run.

"Beware of him," Garvey continued. "The little trapped mouse said Mr. Banks is a high-yellow Negro with thick, black glasses who smokes cigars all day long. I tell you all of this man's appearance so as to weaken his plots and schemes. We must all be on the lookout. So, to the British Secret Intelligence Service . . . my Liberty Hall family and I are aware of you. We've got a few more traps set for your little nibbling rodents. We're ready for your high-yellow man. Your Mr. Banks better not show his face in Harlem again."

"STAY OUT OF HARLEM!" yelled several up front.

"Oh, those British!" he mockingly went on. "Think they own my beloved Jamaica! Think they own me! The greed! Sickens one! And let us not forget the man who's beginning to do as much damage to the UNIA as that uppity Du Bois. You all know him well. That sly James Eason actually had

517

the audacity to once call himself my loyal friend. He lied! And now . . . now that he's up to his schemes . . . we must keep our eyes on him as he trots across the country bad-mouthing all that is sacred about our organization. He is our enemy! He is the grand traitor!"

This roar was now an angry one. The remaining Garvey loyalists seemed ready for a fight.

"So," he went on, "as I ready myself to step into the white man's inferno, you all must be on the lookout. Keep your eyes wide open during these trying days . . . for the mice are lurking. And whatever the judge may rule, 'AFRICA FOR THE AFRICANS' MUST REMAIN OUR GOAL, MUST REMAIN OUR RALLY-ING CRY. THE FIGHT MUST CON-TINUE."

"GARVEY! GARVEY! GARVEY!" the chant began.

We finished listening to the speech and returned to the church. There was a different feeling in the air. Bingo seemed more on edge, fidgety. He insisted I find out exactly when the meeting would take place, that we go see Miss Jacques. So at around three that afternoon, we did.

UNIA headquarters was beginning to take

on the look of a capitol building. There were more flags hanging out front, newer, fancier automobiles parked along the curb, and at least fifty Legionnaires were standing guard. Some had formed a large U-shape around the stairwell. The rest were draped along the entire front of the building. It was an awesome display of uniformity.

The blue-uniformed men looked ready to march at once if given the order, all of them standing tall, dress swords at their sides. We'd gotten no closer than ten feet when two of them stepped forward and created an opening for us to walk through. My clout hadn't waned.

"Stand there and let them search you," I said to Bingo.

"Excuse us, Mr. Temple," said the taller one, seemingly uncomfortable with having to approach me. "Sorry to bother you but we've been told . . ."

"It's fine," I said, lifting my arms.

They patted us both up and down. But they were more thorough than before, checking every inch of our clothing.

"Can you remove your shoes and hand them to us?" asked the shorter one.

We followed orders and watched them take each of our shoes, turn them upside down, and shake them.

"Sorry to bother you, Mr. Temple," said the taller one again, handing them back to us. "Please make your way inside."

Amy Jacques was busy at her desk when we approached. She and I had developed a very cordial relationship over the years. I quite liked her.

"Ah . . . Sidney," she said with that thick Jamaican accent. "Good to see ya."

"You as well," I replied. "This here is my assistant over at the church. Name's Bingo."

"Nice to meet you, Bingo."

"You as well, sista."

"Any word on the meeting, Amy?" I asked.

"I believe it's been organized finally. Let me go upstairs and speak with Marcus."

"He's here?" I asked, looking at Bingo, who stood there stone-faced. "He said during his speech earlier that he was departing for Boston straightaway."

"Not just yet. He had to meet with Henrietta Davis, but she just left. I'll be right back."

As she headed upstairs, Bingo took a seat and I surveyed the place. It was as busy as ever. Office staff typed away at their desks and ran back and forth from one room to another, upstairs and down. Many of them, I gathered, were hard at work putting together the latest edition of the *Negro*

World. And, as always, Legionnaires covered every door of every office.

One face I hadn't seen on our way in was a familiar one. Peavine was standing guard just inside the front entrance. He looked to be daydreaming, probably wishing he were off playing music in some swanky cabaret.

"January seventh," said Amy, returning to her desk a little out of breath. "We've been trying to coordinate it with the arrival of a cruise ship coming from Africa. And now we know the arrival time for sure. Mr. Green and Mr. Stark from Liberia will be arriving that morning and the meeting is to be held at eight o'clock that night. Marcus would actually like to see you upstairs right now."

"Certainly," I said, eyeing Bingo, who discreetly nodded his approval.

Some ten minutes later I was still sitting in Garvey's office as he went on and on about the need to hire a new slew of Black Star Line mechanics once the trial was over and he was free. He was confident his lawyers could get him off. "If they can't make a solid defense for me I shall represent myself," he said. "I just got through telling Lady Davis as much."

"How is she?" I asked. "I haven't spoken to her in a while."

"Very well," he said. "She's managed to organize even more divisions for us in the West Indies during her trip. She also has some new ideas for growing the Black Star Line."

"Excellent. Will she be attending the meeting on the seventh?"

"Indeed, Sidney. She has much to share. You know, I'll never grow tired of saying to anyone who will listen that I consider Henrietta Vinton Davis the most magnificent colored woman in the world today. She is a true UNIA loyalist. Whatever comes of me, our organization would be in good hands were she to take the helm."

"She's a visionary to be sure."

"Back to this business of me representing myself. I certainly could have been a lawyer had I so chosen."

"I have no doubt," I said.

"I could have also been head of an intelligence agency. I know how to catch bad guys. I've had many men followed. Many men! You included."

"Why me?" I asked, my blood rushing.

He leaned forward; grabbed one of the many thick law books stacked on his desk, and opened it. It was a big blue one entitled *The Fundamentals of United States Law.* His eyes went from me to the book and stayed.

"Don't worry, Sidney. You checked out clean. I never doubted you would. I knew when I hired you that all you cared about was being an engineer. It's just you . . . that church . . . that wife . . . and my ships. I know this."

"I'm a simple man."

"It was Reverend Eason who introduced you to that church project, correct?"

"Yes."

"That is what kept you two so close?"

"It was all business," I said. "It was all about the Abyssinian. He introduced me to Reverend Powell."

"So if I was to see you two together . . . you and Eason?" He slowly turned the page and waited for my response.

"We'd be discussing Abyssinian affairs. The community certainly is excited about it opening soon."

"Hah! Half these niggas in America don't know what the hell they want. Thinkin' some imitation of a white man's church is gonna bring them hope. Please. Is Reverend Powell paying you well?"

"Enough."

"Enough, you say. And I believe you, Mr. Vermont. You've never once asked me for anything . . . never pushed for some political position like all the others . . . never begged me for more money. You never speak unless spoken to. Again, that is why I share so much with you. That and the fact that I trust my instincts."

"They've served you well."

He turned the page again and began to study the content more intensely.

"We need more colored lawyers, Sidney. Perhaps you should have been one. You could have helped me sue the NAACP for slander. It is certainly Du Bois behind this *Garvey Must Go* campaign. He's appealing to the very group that's against our people — the U.S. government. He's joined by A. Phillip Randolph and Chandler Owen over at the *Messenger.* Those two have committed themselves to launching a vicious editorial campaign against me as well."

"The people won't buy it," I replied.

"My secret service men have come to believe that these house niggas plan on sending a letter to the U.S. attorney general claiming that our various UNIA divisions across the country have become violent, that they aim to kill our opponents if need be."

"Sounds utterly desperate. Why would they notify the attorney general?"

"They want to put pressure on him to speed up the trial. These fools supporting this campaign have the nerve to call themselves the 'Friends of Negro Freedom.' As if I'm not the same. Haven't you always seen me as such?"

"Of course," I said, surprised to see him displaying such self-doubt.

"We just disagree on what the meaning of freedom is and how to get it."

"Right."

He slammed the book shut very hard and finally looked up at me, his sternness never more pronounced. "There was the Revolutionary War — George Washington versus King George. There was the Civil War — Abraham Lincoln versus Jefferson Davis. Both wars fought on American soil. And now this may very well be the initial phase of America's Negro War — Marcus Garvey versus W. E. B. Du Bois."

35

The train ride to New Orleans had been a long one, so long that it allowed me more than enough time to think, fall asleep, then think some more. Shortly after my one-on-one meeting with Garvey, I'd lied and told Drake and them that I'd been given specific instructions.

"Garvey's demanding that I go and hear what Reverend Eason has to say," I'd said. "He says the New Orleans gathering is pivotal because the city ranks second only to New York in UNIA constituents. I'm to report back to him during our big meeting."

"If that's what it takes to ultimately get you in that meeting room, then go," said Drake. "Just know that Bingo and I are coming with you. When will we be back in New York?"

"By the fourth," I'd said. "Three days before the meeting."

Bingo had also accompanied me to my office while I'd informed Speed of Garvey's fictitious demand. He was all for my going and wanted a detailed report on Eason's new organization.

"You do exactly as Garvey wants at this point, Q," he'd said, my eyes on Bingo and his gun as I'd held the phone. "He's busy testing everybody's loyalty, Q. He'll be in prison soon but you're still our insurance policy. Continue to placate him. You're a damn good agent, Q."

As we'd chugged along through the various Southern states — North Carolina, South Carolina, Georgia, Alabama, and Mississippi — I'd found myself gazing out at the Confederate terrain, so much of it soaked with the blood of those recently beaten and lynched. New York seemed like a foreign land in comparison.

We'd arrived in New Orleans in time to hear James speak at St. John's Church on First Street. In fact, he'd just finished and was in the midst of shaking hands as he filtered through the crowd inside. I waited out front along with Drake and Bingo.

My reason for making the trip was simple: to find an opportunity, any opportunity, to break free. But the more it sunk in that I was dealing with trained SIS men, escape seemed a more daunting task. Before leaving New York, Drake had spoken to me about the SIS spy whom Garvey's men had caught. Apparently the "little mouse" had only ever dealt with the Timekeeper.

"Look," said Drake, "yes, the sloppy SIS spy who got pegged worked for Mr. Banks, just as we do, but he's never met any of us. He knows nothing about this particular mission. You're not stupid enough to think that all us SIS men know each other are you, Agent Temple?"

"Of course not."

"Just like we're not stupid enough to think you know every man working for Mr. Hoover. Besides, the important thing is this: Mr. Banks never made this sloppy fool aware of you. So, you see, it's full steam ahead."

His point made sense. So now that I'd succeeded at making it full steam ahead to New Orleans, I needed to make a move. The sun had already set, but I'd taken the time earlier in the evening to study the neighborhood surrounding the church. Harlem it was not. There were no row houses, no brownstones. Instead, there was nothing but shotgun shacks lining the narrow streets — little rectangular dwellings no more than twelve feet wide. We were in the heart of colored town. In fact, I hadn't seen a white face yet — some light-skinned Creoles, yes, but they were simply mixed-race Negroes.

James finally made his way out of the church, surrounded by several high-ranking members of his new Universal Negro Alliance — all of them smiling, beaming with pride. He had introduced each of them during his powerful speech. There were at least eight.

"Brother Sidney!" he cried out as he hustled down the steps. "There you are." The two of us gave each other a big hug. "I saw you standing in the back while I was preachin'. Boy I mean to tell ya!"

"I heard every word," I said. "Words of wisdom, James. Words of wisdom." I turned to Bingo and Drake. "You remember my assistant, Bingo?"

"Of course," said James, the two shaking. "Good to see ya, Brother Bingo."

"Once he found out I was coming to New Orleans," I said, "Bingo here was dyin' to come see it for the first time. This here's his older brother, Drake."

"Had to bring him along too," said Bingo, grinning. "He's the one paid my way. Was either that or stay home."

James smiled and shook Drake's hand. "Smart man, Brother Bingo. Gotta brotha with some cash, might as well bring him on with you."

Bingo just stayed with his grin. "That's right. That's right."

"Well look here," said James, "we're all on our way to Sista Constance Toutant's house for dinner. And you best believe you comin', even if I have to tie you up and throw you in the car. Sista can cook! She got a house full of gumbo, jambalaya, fried catfish, chitlins, collard greens, and cornbread."

"Always wanted to try me some gumbo and jambalaya," I said.

"Boy, you ain't lived 'til you tasted some gumbo. Ain't that right, brothas?"

"Mm-hmm," said his colleagues collectively.

"Let's hit it," said James.

I looked at Drake, who signaled his approval with a quick nod. And with that, we joined James's group, casually making our way down the busy sidewalk, heading west. There were folks everywhere who'd streamed out of the church, many huddled in groups near the front stairs engaging in sprightly conversation. One thing was clear: James had left them all in a festive mood, full of hope and pride.

"Did you notice anything different about the audience this evening, Reverend Eason?" asked one of his colleagues as we walked.

"Uh-huh. Sure did, Brother Turiaf. Was quite a few Jamaican brothers up in there. I heard 'em mumblin' to one another when we first arrived. Reverend Clemons said he recognized one of 'em from the area but said he ain't never set foot in the church before."

"That's right," said Mr. Turiaf. "I spoke to Reverend Clemons too. He told me the same thing."

"It don't matter none," said James, as we all continued down the sidewalk. "We already know Marcus be sendin' fools everywhere we go. Ain't no doubt he's just the latest one."

Just then a loud shot rang out from behind. I flinched, turned, and saw three colored men standing no more than twenty feet away. I couldn't make out their faces in the dark, but one was surely pointing a gun.

Immediately another shot. We all ducked, but this time I heard James groan and flail like he'd been hit in the back. Bingo and Drake, as if they'd been trained for President Harding's Secret Service, grabbed me and forced me to the ground, both of them covering me like a blanket.

As James tried to gather his balance, he

531

turned around and another shot was fired, this one hitting him in the face, the force so great his head flung violently back. He fell to the ground and the assailants fled. Most of the men in our group gave chase, save for Mr. Turiaf, Drake, Bingo, and me.

"JAMES!" I yelled.

"STAY DOWN!" screamed Drake. "IT'S TOO LATE!"

I watched my friend lie there gasping for air, Mr. Turiaf hovering over him. With every bit of force I could muster, I tried to break free from the grip of the SIS men, wanting desperately to tend to my bloodied brother, but they had me by both arms, protecting me like gold. I was just that to them. God forbid the man they'd assigned to carry out Garvey's murder were to get shot before the big meeting.

"NO!" I hollered. "HANG ON, JAMES! I'M RIGHT HERE! HANG ON!"

All I could think about during that long train ride home was how cowards had been responsible for murdering two of the most significant people in my life — my cousin, at the hands of a white man, and now James, who'd been shot by a Negro, most likely a Garveyite. In both cases, neither had stood a chance of defending himself.

Now that James was dead, I found it difficult simply to put one foot in front of the other. I'd barely been able to make it to my seat on the train. I was nothing but a limp being — heart still beating, mind and soul: gone. But it didn't matter. The SIS men were handling me like a mannequin, pulling me to and fro, propping me up here and there — making sure I remained usable.

In less than a minute after James had been shot, Bingo and Drake had dragged me to the car. They drove straight to the station and made sure I joined them in boarding the next train to New York. They weren't about to let the police show up and question me as an eyewitness. And now, with nearly two days of travel in front of us, I could hear nothing but the nightmarish sound of that popping gun over and over again.

Cleo and Goat picked the three of us up at a chaotic Penn Station around noon on the fourth and drove me back to Strivers' Row. We stopped by Tony's so I could order some dinner. I hadn't eaten since New Orleans.

On my way out I grabbed a copy of the *Messenger* from a paperboy. Word of James's murder was all over the front page. It was clearly being blamed on Garvey. But proving that would likely be impossible. Still, the *Garvey Must Go* campaign had ratcheted up its public outcry.

Later that night I lay on the couch near the fireplace downstairs, thinking about James, agonizing over the fact that he was gone. It had happened so fast.

With the fire crackling in the background, I rolled over on my side and reached for the half-empty fifth of whiskey there on the coffee table. I guzzled a bunch down without even sitting up. Then I put it back down and grabbed the paper bag from Tony's. There was still half my salami sandwich inside. As I pulled it out, the receipt fell onto the floor. I reached down and picked it up. The size and lightness of it triggered something in me.

I rubbed my eyes and sat up, examining the backside of it, which was blank. It was about a three-by-five-inch slip. I put the sandwich back on the table and focused on the receipt. I began folding it until it was no bigger than half a piece of Chiclets gum.

I stood and put it in my right pants pocket, patting the outside as if searching myself. It could not be felt in the least. My mind raced.

Taking it back out and sitting, I began unfolding it. Then I flattened it out on the coffee table. I took a pen from my briefcase and began writing very tiny words on it. I was crafting a letter to the one person who just might be in a position to help me. I'd have to hand-deliver it of course, right in front of Bingo at that — quite the risk but my only option.

I leaned over the table and squeezed the pen tighter, my face up close to the words. With the sparkle and pop of the roaring fire keeping me company — its warm glow allowing me to see my pen glide across the receipt — I began to hatch a plan.

I woke the next morning, having slept on the couch again, determined to put the plan into action. I headed upstairs and found my three rarely used fedora hats hanging inside the closet door — one black, one brown, one gray. I put the black one on and stepped in front of the cheval glass. It suited me rather well, even making my scraggly face a bit more presentable. Nevertheless, I decided to shave.

Standing in front of the washroom mirror, face lathered in white cream, I glided the blade along my right cheek before dipping it in the cloudy sink water below. I jiggled it and watched the curly black hairs float to the top, the splashing sound accentuated against the morning silence of a cold house.

I looked in the mirror at the smooth, narrow strip of skin my blade had left behind — then back at the floating hairs — nothing more than dead cells. They symbolized my deathlike existence. Again, I glided the blade along my cheek, wanting to see more fresh skin, more of the old me. It was time to try living again.

Minutes later I backed the Baby Grand out and approached the gate. I needed to buy myself a minute or two, so I turned the engine off and pretended to have trouble restarting it.

I stepped out, lifted the hood, and began tinkering around. Ivan quickly walked over and stood next to me. My intentions were for Drake and Cleo across the way to think nothing of the conversation we were about to have. I also wanted them to notice my hat.

"What you think it is?" asked Ivan.

"Just something loose probably," I said, jiggling a wire. "Listen, Ivan, my cousin Peavine is coming in from Chicago today. I want him to be able to go on inside and relax until I get home tonight, but I don't want to leave my front door unlocked. He'll park down the street, but can you let him walk through the gate so he can use the back door? I left it unlocked."

"No can do, Mr. Temple. Strivers' Row policy."

"Look, Ivan, you been knowin' me some three years. Been nothin' but good to you."

"But they pay me to —"

"I'll pay you ten dollars," I said.

"Well, now . . . I just don't —"

"Make it twenty," I said, closing the hood, rubbing my hands together and nodding across the way at Drake.

"Oh my!" he said, eyes wide open.

He followed me as I walked around, got back in, and started the engine. Again I nodded at Drake, who nodded back as I rolled down the window.

"So what you say, Ivan? Deal?"

"Deal."

When I got to the church, I told Bingo that we needed to pay another visit to UNIA headquarters. "I want to reconfirm the day, time, and place," I said. "This news about James's murder may have changed things."

In my heart I believed that Garvey had ordered the killing, that it wasn't some angry, revenge-seeking Garveyite acting on his own. Still, I wasn't certain. And I didn't have some newfound desire to go through with murdering Garvey. Besides, even if I did poison him, the SIS men would still find it in their best interest to get rid of me.

As we got in the car, I reminded Bingo that I needed to pick up a bank check that was probably waiting for me at the real estate office.

"That'll be fine," he said. "You do whatever you need to do to put your mind at ease before that meeting."

We picked the check up and then visited my bank where I had it cashed. I'm sure Bingo was happy to allow such a transaction. Once I was gone, he and his partners could split it up and consider it a salary bonus. But I had my own ideas about how to spend it. Still, until then, walking around with $9,000 in my briefcase would be uncomfortable to say the least.

The two of us arrived at UNIA headquarters and went through the usual pat-down routine with the Legionnaires before visiting with Amy. "The meeting is definitely set in stone," she said. "Try to relax, Sidney. I've never seen you so unsettled."

"Just worried about Marcus's trial, that's all," I replied, casually placing both hands in my pockets — keeping them there as if trying to show her a more relaxed side. "But I'm fine. Ain't I been actin' fine, Bingo?"

"Been as calm-actin' as ever," he said, putting his hands in his pockets as well, probably upset at me over the fact that she'd noticed my initial fidgetiness.

"How are you holding up, Amy?" I asked.

"Staying strong. We must."

"True. So true. Well, listen, we best be getting back to the church."

"All right, Sidney. You two take care."

As we headed for the front door I nodded at Peavine and stared at him like never before, begging him to do what my eyes were screaming. I had the tiny paper wedged between my right middle and index fingers.

"How you doing, Peavine?"

"Fine, Mr. Temple. Just fine."

"I saw you last time I was here but you were gone when I finished visiting with Marcus."

"Musta been my lunch break," he said.

"Well, this here is my friend Bingo."

As the two shook hands, I pressed my fingers tighter and tighter, the nervous sweat dampening the receipt more and more with each passing second. My gut told me Peavine was a street-smart brother — his plight had demanded it.

"Nice to meet you, Bingo," said Peavine.

"You as well."

"You got yourself another good post," I said, reaching out to shake his hand, clutching it the way I might if he were pulling me to safety from cliff's edge. With eyes alone I implored him to take the wadded up letter without making a scene. He obliged by discreetly fisting it as I slid my fingers from his grip.

"Worked awfully hard to get it, too, Mr. Temple," he replied. "All them boys wish they had this post."

"Won't be long 'til you're one of Marcus's drivers."

"You said it."

"All right then. You keep up the good work and I'll holler at you later."

I patted him on the shoulder, gave a subtle wink, then walked out the door with Bingo following.

36

Pulling through the gate and into the dark driveway felt different this time. Ivan was there as usual, the Oldsmobile had followed and pulled into its normal position, and the alleyway was as quiet as ever. But the setting was almost too quiet, too still, as if a theater stage had been perfectly set with just the right amount of artificial moonlight shimmering over the ground between my car and the back porch — as if when the director said "action," the world would watch me nervously walk to the back door, open it, and find no one inside.

Luckily, Peavine was sitting at the dining room table in the dark as planned. As soon as I turned the lamp on, he sat up and gave me a big grin.

"Thank the Good Lord!" I said. "What time did you come in?"

"It was just about two in the afternoon,

Mr. Temple. Did it just like you wrote down."

"Good." I took a deep breath, loosened my tie, and skittishly looked around, knowing we were alone, but conditioned at this point to assume the worst. "Real good, Peavine. I'm glad your love of music runs so deep."

"Can't get to Chicago soon enough, Mr. Temple. You done made my dream come true."

"Not yet."

I approached the front door to make sure it was locked, took my coat off and threw it on the couch, then sat with him at the table. He had the crinkly receipt lying in front of him.

"Boy," said Peavine, "I 'bout fell dead when I saw them numbers. You're not serious about giving me one thousand —"

"Yes. I am. You do exactly what you're told, and you'll have a thousand dollars cash to take with you to Chicago. You said you wanted to go learn Hot Jazz from those new cats. Here's your chance."

"Thank you. What's this all about?"

"First rule: Don't ask me anything about what this all involves. I say this to protect you. Just know I've broken no laws and don't intend to. Nor do I intend to ask you to. Just follow the directions I give you to a T . . . no exceptions. One mistake and there'll be no Chicago. Got it?"

"Got it."

"You're to stay here, inside the house, without leaving. Don't set foot outside. Don't even crack the door open. I'll come and go as normal, and the men who've been following me will continue their routine. All the while, you'll be hiding away . . . right in here. You're to stay here tonight, tomorrow night, and then drive my car to UNIA headquarters the next night, dressed in my suit and this hat."

I took off my fedora and handed it to him. The two of us were roughly the same size. I was about an inch taller and outweighed him by a few pounds, but he'd certainly be able to wear my suit.

"Fits perfectly," he said, running his fingers along the brim. "What do I do when I get to headquarters?"

"Let's start with you leaving here first. As you approach the gate, Ivan will nod, may say hello, and may even try to engage you. Oblige him. He'll be expecting you to drive my car that night. I'll inform him on my way in that evening. Take a right on Seventh and drive at a normal speed. An Oldsmobile parked across the way will follow you.

Don't make any abrupt turns. Be very steady. They'll think you're me."

"You mean because it's gonna be dark out?"

"Yes. That and the fact that following me has become second nature to them."

"You in some kinda trouble with . . ."

"What did I say about this deal, Peavine?"

"No questions."

"Just do as I say. You'll be taking my briefcase with you. In it will be your cash. Once you arrive at headquarters, park as close to the building as possible, and definitely not across the street from it. There'll be several folks arriving for the meeting, even some Liberians. The Oldsmobile will park a good distance away. They won't want any Legionnaires to see them. Once you park, immediately get out and head for the stairs. Do not turn around. Don't stop for anything until you get inside."

"Yep. I'll just go right on in. Them boys on duty will let me pass. I did just like you said in the letter and let Mr. Grant know I had to go to New Jersey for a few days and wouldn't be back in town until later on this week. Told him my grandmomma was deathly sick."

"Where did you put your uniform?"

"In the supply room closet . . . way in the

back corner behind some dusty boxes of old *Negro Worlds.* But it ain't no thing to keep it in that room anyhow. Other boys be stowing their uniforms in all kinds of places. I just hid it to make sure no one moved it."

"So the guards out front won't think anything of you changing clothes at headquarters?"

"Oh no! I'm supposedly coming straight off the train from New Jersey, right?"

"Right. So once you're inside, change into your uniform and take a post. After the meeting, you wait to be dismissed as usual. Leave the Baby Grand parked there. Don't even go near it. The boys in the Oldsmobile will have their eyes glued to it. So walk in the opposite direction and don't turn around. Your next stop is Chicago."

"But what about the car? What about you?"

"Don't worry about that. At this point, your job will be done. Leave town and try not to look back."

"Like I said . . . ain't nothin' here for me no way. Darn sure ain't got no sick grandmomma."

"There's food in the kitchen for you during the day. Don't move around a lot. There's another car parked out front that's watching me. Stay away from that front door. Don't *ever* open it, even if someone comes knocking. One bad move on your part during the next few days could cost both of us our . . . well . . . just make sure we're clear here."

"We are."

"I'll be sleeping on the couch down here and you are to sleep upstairs in my room. And stay off of the balcony."

"I will. And thank you."

"No . . . thank you, Peavine."

The next forty-something hours were the most intense of my life. Not because something unexpected happened, but rather because I was constantly worried that Peavine might mess up while I was away at the church. My life resting in his hands was anything but comforting. But I continued the routine, exiting through the gate in the morning, entering at night, all the while making sure to wear my fedora.

My latest conversation with Speed had been entirely about Eason's killing. He'd kept asking me if there was any way to tie Garvey to it. I'd told him that only in the coming weeks, as the New Orleans Police Department finished their investigation, could that be determined. Speed was sure Garvey had ordered the killing.

Finally, the hours had whittled down. At around lunchtime on the day of the meeting, Bingo had a little gift for me. We'd ordered up some sandwiches from Tony's and were parked out front eating. I was just picking at mine, nervously eyeing my watch.

"Here it is," he said, handing me a small, brown leather pouch.

I unbuttoned it and removed a thin, glass, two-inch vial with a black top. Inside was a clear liquid substance.

"What is it?" I asked, tilting the vial back and forth, watching the liquid move about.

"That's a question for someone above my pay grade."

I placed it back in the pouch and watched him take a big bite of his sandwich — fried egg and ham. The smell was strong and the sound of his smacking lips irksome. He devoured it with such pleasure, perhaps excited that Mr. Banks would soon have a hefty paycheck for him.

I buttoned up the pouch and slipped it inside my suit jacket's inner pocket.

"You know," he said, chewing, "when you're finished tonight, Mr. Banks says you can resign from the Bureau and come work with us. That's assuming all goes well."

"I'll do my part."

"The poison won't take effect immedi-

547

ately. But when it does, Garvey will react as though he's having a heart attack. When he falls to the floor, his handlers will, of course, rush him to the hospital with the hopes that he'll survive. He won't. Drive straight back to your house while he's being transported. Go inside and exit your front door. We'll meet you there and drive you to meet Mr. Banks. Once Garvey's death is one hundred percent confirmed, Banks will want to speak to you about joining us."

"Ya'll wanna keep me around, huh?" I asked, sure they intended to kill me afterward.

"Why do I detect doubt in your voice?" he asked, licking his fingers.

"Just a question, that's all."

"Well . . . have a little more faith."

"I'm curious," I said, "how does it work — all you American Negroes working for the British?"

"Simple. SIS is global. If they want a Mexican watched in Mexico . . . they're gonna hire a Mexican. They want one of them slanty-eyed mothafuckas in China followed . . . they're gonna hire a chop-suey-eatin' sucka from Shanghai. And in this case here, we was hired 'cause we're experts on Harlem. Experts! All of us . . . born and raised right here. We ain't no pretend

Harlem niggas like you."

"You gotta interesting worldview there."

"You damn right," he said.

"Isn't it the height of disloyalty for all you Americans to be working for the British?"

"You feel like an American?" he asked.

"Yes."

"Why?"

"Something in my bones," I said.

"Well . . . a Negro in America can be loyal to whoever's willing to pay him. Shit! Besides, there ain't any institutions in this country loyal to us colored folk. So why should we be loyal to them? Especially the U.S. government!"

"What about the NAACP?"

"Fuck the NAACP!" he said.

"And, of course, the UNIA, right?"

"Fuck them too. Garvey . . . Du Bois . . . President Harding — each one of these deceitful devils is interested in nothing but lining their own damn pockets. So some of us niggas done figured out a way to line our own. In this day and time it's every brotha for himself. Eat or be eaten. Kill or be killed. When you gonna catch up, fool?"

I nodded and watched him take another bite before talking with his mouth full.

"The bosses in London are paying us to do something they can't do: be black in

Harlem. And also to follow exact orders."

"Like making sure I don't run."

"Exactly. You run . . . we kill you . . . we've proven we can follow protocol."

"I'm amazed by your utter disregard for human life."

"Like I said . . . protocol. By the way, Mr. Banks is a very important man for SIS here in America. The fact that you can now identify him is no small matter. The London bosses could have ordered your death the minute Garvey blurted out Banks's name at Liberty Hall and you looked at me like you'd seen a ghost."

"So, it sounds like I'm a very lucky man?"

"No," he said, "just a very needed one."

I let that sink in before attempting to end this little chat.

"Well . . . this offer to join your team is flattering," I said, putting my uneaten sandwich back in the bag, "but, when the job is done, I'm resigning from the Bureau and going to San Francisco like I previously mentioned. I'll tell Banks to his face. No more shadow work for me."

"All I know is this: Once you impress Mr. Banks by pulling this off tonight, he'll be awfully sad to see you go."

"Well, I aim to impress."

37

I drove through the gate at around five that evening, Drake and Cleo tailing me closer than ever. Though the meeting was to commence at eight, my job was to arrive at headquarters between seven and seven thirty. I'd told Drake that it would be nothing for me to fiddle around the offices before entering the empty conference room at just the right time.

"Evening, Mr. Temple!" said Ivan.

"Evening, Ivan. I meant to give you your money this morning. It's in the house. I'll bring it out to you before you head home for the night."

"Boy, I sure do thank you, Mr. Temple."

"Look, my cousin will be heading out in a couple of hours. He's taking my car to Club Deluxe. Wants to hear some live music and maybe find him a lovely young lady to dance with. Been cooped up in there for too long, if you know what I mean? Please let him through the gate the same as you would me."

"Will do! You have a good night, Mr. Temple."

I parked, opened the car door, stepped out, and glanced across the way at the Oldsmobile. I took my time, adjusted my hat, and gave them a nod. Drake nodded back. The sun had just set, but it wasn't completely dark out yet, not nearly as dark as it would be in two hours. I stood there looking at them for just a few more seconds, hoping this fedora-wearing image of me would be stained in their minds for good.

I wondered if Drake might approach Ivan about what we'd just discussed. Perhaps he hadn't pulled up in time to notice such a brief conversation. Either way, it was too late to turn around and do a thing about it.

I opened the back door, entered the dining room, turned the lamp on, and there sat Peavine, dressed in my finest black suit, his posture as upright as could be, his eyes looking straight ahead at the wall.

"How long have you been sitting there?"

"Oh, I reckon 'bout two or three hours, Mr. Temple."

"Well, you look ready."

I walked over and sat my briefcase down directly in front of him. He didn't budge. I approached the front door and jiggled the knob, acutely aware, as always, that it was locked but still fearful that the men parked out front might come bursting through.

"Where is your bag?" I asked, loosening my tie.

"Right under here. And it's empty, just like you asked."

"Good."

He reached under the table and grabbed his old, beat-up leather bag. I took it and set it beside my similar-sized briefcase and began transferring the stacks of cash from my briefcase to his bag, save for the one thousand I left for him.

"This briefcase has your future in it, Peavine. Use it wisely."

I checked my watch and loosened my tie a little more. I began pacing, then removed my black fedora and placed it on his head. Walking to the opposite side of the table, I began examining his appearance.

"Pull the hat down a bit," I said, taking my overcoat off and resting it on one of the chairs.

"How's that?" he asked, pulling on the brim.

"Good. Stand up."

As he did, I walked around the table again and looked him up and down. He was wearing my newest black shoes, and the suit seemed to fit him even better than it had two days ago when he'd first tried it on. I patted his shoulders, trying to smooth out any bunched-up areas, then adjusted his lapels. Our faces were nearly touching so I stepped back.

"Turn around," I said, wiping my brow. "Slowly. And hold your arms out."

I took my suit jacket off, nervously folded it into a ball, and placed it on the table. The intense once-over had me in a trance. I eased back around to retrieve my overcoat, my head still turned toward him. It's a wonder I didn't trip. Grabbing the coat, I returned to his side.

"Put it on."

As he slid his arms inside the sleeves, I walked in the kitchen, poured myself a glass of water, and drank it down in one shot. I approached the back door, wiggled the knob a bit, wanting desperately to peek outside and make sure the Oldsmobile was there. I didn't. Instead I began pacing from one end of the kitchen to the other. After about a minute I returned to find him standing there like a statue with the overcoat on. I walked over and grabbed his old bag.

"I'll be right back," I said. "You can relax."

I headed down the hall to Loretta's studio

where I had several of my new railroad maps laid out on her desk. I grabbed a pencil and began running it along several routes — one from New York City to Kansas City, another from New York to Seattle. Easing over to another map, I ran my finger along a route I'd highlighted as another option — New York to Santa Fe.

So many possibilities I'd figured out, but I'd have to choose one. Still, the thing each had in common? All departed Grand Central Terminal before nine p.m. I'd grabbed several departing train schedules for different railroads while purchasing my ticket to New Orleans. The SIS men had been busy purchasing their own in the line next to mine and hadn't seen a thing.

I began studying the routes again. By the time I'd finished losing myself in the various American destinations, the time had drawn near. I headed upstairs and into my closet. Removing the slabs of wood on the floor, I gathered my pistol, holster, magazine, and boxes of bullets. I placed all of it in the bag, headed back downstairs, and sat with Peavine.

"Do you need anything?" I asked. "Some water?"

"No, sir."

"Remember, no deviations. You open that

back door, head straight to the car, and calm yourself. Back it out smoothly, slowly enough for Ivan to already have the gate nearly all the way open by the time you pull forward. As you turn right on Seventh, tilt your head down just a bit and give the Oldsmobile a subtle wave. Subtle."

"Got it," he said. "Subtle."

"From there, everything should unfold just as we've planned." I looked at my watch and stood. "It's time. Are you ready?"

"Yes, sir."

"Let's go."

38

As my train pulled into Grand Trunk Station in Portland, Maine, I exhaled, it seemed, for the first time in a long time. I felt free. With my sleepy head leaning back against the soft seat, I looked out at the light snow beyond my window and thought of Loretta.

She'd gone on and on about the beauty of this place — the docked fishing boats, the distant view of Mount Washington, the Victorian architecture. And now, just seeing the town for myself made me feel a little closer to her. I couldn't wait to check into the little hotel she'd gushed about — The Inn at St. John.

Exiting the waterfront station, I stepped out into the white weather and fell in with the thick-coated crowd standing along India Street — most of them New Englanders I was guessing. We were all waiting for the streetcars to pick us up and take us somewhere — Congress Street, in my case.

During the shuttle ride over, I marveled at the bustling little city — so many muddy-shoed, wet-hatted folks acting cordial to one another while hustling in and out of coffeehouses, restaurants, filling stations, food markets, bookstores, and novelty shops. We passed a little white church that looked like it'd been plucked from a fairy tale, constructed so perfectly square, its steeple overpowering the rest. I half expected to see little white angels appear just above, smiling with their hands held out as they tried to catch some of the fluffy, floating snowflakes.

The image got me thinking of the Abyssinian I'd left behind. Construction on it would be finished any day now. It also got me thinking of Peavine. I'd walked out the back door with my pistol in its holster no more than ten minutes after he'd left, but not before I'd paused to realize how many boxes and furnishings I was leaving behind.

I'd tried to take solace in the fact that our most precious family items — letters, pictures, books, personal files, etcetera — were in a secure storage facility. But even though I'd placed them there with a watchful eye, I was keenly aware that the Timekeeper might have been observing me, even back then. He'd probably watched me shake hands with the facility manager and on-duty security officer. And now, he might forever be waiting to track the items to wherever I'd eventually have them sent. Whatever the case, it was a problem to deal with in the future, so I had opened the kitchen door and headed out.

With only Peavine's old bag in hand — stuffed with cash, boxes of extra bullets, my brand-new railroad maps, and some personal items — I had approached Ivan and handed him his money.

"Boy I sure do appreciate this," he'd said, pocketing the money.

"Well, I just appreciate your help, Ivan."

"Way I see it . . . you've always been good to me, sir, and I was just returning the favor. Besides, Strivers' Row policy is still very well intact. By the way, if you don't mind me asking, Mr. Temple, where might you be off to dressed so nicely?"

"Club Deluxe. Figure Cousin Peavine could use some company."

Ivan was right. I was dressed nicely, wearing my favorite brown suit, brown patent leather shoes, and brown fedora. My other suits would go to the lucky man who found them hanging in the closet.

"You walkin'?" he'd asked.

"Come on now, Ivan," I'd said, just beginning to walk south on Seventh before stopping. "Us Strivers' Row folks ain't so well-to-do that we can't walk one block over to Lenox and up a few streets to 142nd."

"But why you headin' toward 138th?"

"Need to stop by the Abyssinian Church first. I got it all planned out."

Of course, I was simply avoiding 139th and the plum Chevrolet. I also wanted to steer clear of the 135th Street Station, as it was far too close to UNIA headquarters. Figured I'd instead take 138th over to Lenox and up to the 145th Street Station. From there I'd hop on the Lenox Avenue Line en route to Grand Central Terminal.

"Say you got it all planned out?" he'd asked. "I hear you."

While en route I planned to write a resignation letter to Mr. Hoover and drop it in a mailbox somewhere near Grand Central. In it I'd explain the Timekeeper, his men, my abduction, their claim of having a mole inside the Bureau, my escape, etcetera. If Hoover or Speed were *not* in cahoots with SIS, at least I'd be giving them the courtesy of a resignation letter. But, of course, they'd never know where I was going.

"Is Club Deluxe still owned by Jack Johnson?" Ivan had continued.

"I'm not sure."

"Well, word on the street is he done sold it to some white hoodlum who's in prison. Heard somethin' 'bout he fidna turn it into a place he gonna call the Cotton Club."

"Wouldn't that be something," I'd pretended to care, beginning to walk south again.

"Ya'll don't get in too much trouble now, Mr. Temple."

"We won't. But tell old George not to be expecting us home anytime soon."

"Will do. He'll be relievin' me here shortly."

Two hours later I'd already dropped off the letter and was on a train heading to Portland, and presumably, Garvey was in the middle of conducting his big meeting while Drake and the others were still parked out front. But I could only imagine.

As my Portland streetcar came to a stop near 939 Congress Street, I looked out and made note of how many colored men were working different jobs, everything from deliveryman and paperboy to streetcar driver and food vendor. In fact, I'd noticed more colored folks in general than I'd anticipated.

I walked through the brown snow sludge with such great anticipation and relief. I could see the sign I'd been looking for straight ahead. Loretta had probably taken these same steps. And she'd been right — Portland *was* wonderful. Perhaps it was the smiles on people's faces as they embraced the snowy weather, their kind nods, or just the overall sense of community on display that put a pep in my step.

"Welcome to The Inn at St. John!" said the salt-and-pepper-haired colored man working the door.

Nodding at him, I approached the check-in counter with nothing on my mind except taking a warm bath and sleeping for a long, long time.

"Checking in, sir?" asked the young woman at the front desk.

"Yes. Two nights if you have it."

"Oh . . . we've got lots of space. Let me see here . . ."

"Pardon me, ma'am, but you wouldn't mind checking your logbook there for the name of an artist friend of mine, would you? She stayed here about a year and a half ago, sometime in June I believe. It'd be nice to stay in the room she raved about."

"Certainly, I will happily do that for you, sir. What is her name?"

"Ginger Bouvier."

She ran her finger along the shelved logbooks to her left until she found the one she needed. She opened it and flipped some pages for a while.

"Looks like your friend . . . Miss Ginger Bouvier . . . stayed in room . . . 1-C. That's one of our larger rooms on the fourth floor."

"You wouldn't happen to have that room available, would you?"

"We sure do."

"Wonderful. I'll take it."

The following day I rose in the late afternoon and headed out, bag in hand, to go buy myself a new overcoat before visiting the Portland Museum of Art. Afterward, with my mind fed plenty, I decided to feed my stomach and have dinner at a place called Chester's.

The hostess sat me next to the window facing Cumberland Avenue, a kind gesture to be sure. Looking out at the dim European-style streetlamps and casual night strollers made for a pleasant setting. I tried to stay in the moment, to think of nothing heavy. But with every bite of my juicy porterhouse, I thought of James. He would have liked this restaurant, none of its patrons so much as raising an eyebrow at the colored man enjoying a fabulous table with a view.

I still couldn't believe my friend was gone. It pained me to no end. And if he had ever learned of my being an agent, could I have explained it enough for him to forgive me? After all, he'd slowly grown to detest Garvey himself. It's a question I'd have to ponder 'til my dying day.

As I walked down Congress Street and neared my hotel, I anticipated the warm night of sleep ahead of me. Meanwhile, I kept switching my bag from one hand to the other, blowing on the free one, unable to ignore the freezing night air.

As I got close enough to see the friendly doorman through the very light fog, my focus shifted to the man standing just beyond him next to a black automobile parked along the curb facing the other direction. I slowed down and squinted to make sure my eyes weren't deceiving me. Just then, another man on the driver's side got out. Again, I squinted, but this time stopped walking completely. My eyes were not deceiving me.

Standing in the distance were two men I thought I'd never see again — Drake and Bingo. I felt a deafening ring in my ear. I reached under my coat to feel for my gun. At the same time, Bingo spotted me. The two of us stood there locked in a stare briefly before Drake eyed me as well, flashing a wry smile as if to say, *You're not as slick as you thought, mothafucka.* The visual worsened when the back doors of the automobile opened and Goat and Cleo stepped out.

There was no more time to think about my predicament, so I turned and ran, initially bumping into a man, knocking him over. I turned and saw them get back in the car, prompting me to run even faster. With the cold air stinging my face, watering my eyes, all I could see were blurry streetlights, blurry passing car lights, and a few oncoming pedestrians dodging out of my way.

I slowed down enough to turn and see them racing after me, dodging in and out of light traffic. Again I sped up, but it was clear there'd be no outrunning them, so I stepped in front of an idling car that was readying itself to turn left onto Congress.

"GET OUT!" I yelled, pointing my pistol at the driver.

The white man of about fifty did just that, stepping out with his arms raised high. I ran around and got behind the wheel of his cream-colored vehicle, slamming the door as he backed up onto the sidewalk. He never lowered his arms.

Stomping all the way down on the gas, I accelerated left onto Congress. The fog appeared to be thickening as I weaved in and out of light traffic, trying not to kill anyone in the process. I made a violent right turn onto State Street, careening so much that my back end nearly slammed into a car heading in the other direction.

Looking in my side mirror, I could see their headlights in the distance. But their car was weighted down with four men, giving me an advantage. I looked straight ahead and poured on the gas. It wasn't long before I came upon a sign that read: YOU ARE NOW CROSSING THE MILLION DOLLAR BRIDGE.

I crossed it and pushed ahead, both hands on the wheel, jaw clenched, head bobbing like a prizefighter's — trying to avoid the road's edge and anyone driving toward me. But only a few cars had motored by, and with each passing mile, it was clear that there'd be even fewer.

Portland's lights were disappearing, the remote darkness approaching. I felt the road veering left a bit and wondered if I was heading too far east now, unknowingly heading right into the Casco Bay. And the fog wasn't helping matters. Fortunately, the stolen vehicle *was,* for I had sped well beyond them, so much so that their headlights had vanished.

Again the road curved the opposite direction, and I passed several smaller intersecting roads, but I chose to stay on the main one for the time being. Able to go only about fifteen miles per hour now, I wiped at the inside of my damp, frosty windshield with one hand while trying to control the steering wheel with the other. Luckily, not enough fresh snow had fallen to affect the roads.

I'd been traveling for roughly an hour now, aimlessly motoring deeper and deeper into a land of mystery and darkness — perhaps only circling. The fog, the cold, the stolen car, the chase — it was all too perfectly terrible.

Rolling my window down to help defrost the windshield, I glanced in the mirror and saw their headlights reappear from way back. Part of me was glad they'd kept up — relieved to know the inevitable face-off was drawing close. I just needed somehow to tip the scales in my favor.

It was only a matter of time before I'd run out of petrol and it was now pitch black out, save for the road immediately in front of me. I decelerated to ten m.p.h. to make sure I didn't smash right into God knows what. Just as I did, a slow-flashing light appeared in the distance, likely one of the many lighthouses in the area. This would have to be the place where I made my last stand.

39

I slowed down and pulled over, sharply turning the wheel until the car was facing the lighthouse. Then I drove several yards into the open field and parked, leaving the headlights on to help me see the beginning of my walk path. I also wanted Drake and company to spot the empty car — to follow me.

Stepping out into the snowy vegetation, bag in hand, I headed straight for the tower. It wasn't long before my headlights faded away and I felt my feet getting wet and numbingly cold. But I pushed forward, the ever-so-slight glow of the powerful slow-flicking light allowing me brief moments to barely make out the contours of things.

I'd been walking for maybe half an hour when I felt the vegetation turn to uneven rock, forcing me to move even slower. With every careful step I took the fog grew thicker, the sound of crashing waves a bit louder.

The rock was gone now and the frosty shrub-like surface began to ramp downward. I squatted and grabbed at the long marram grass for balance and eased down into what was most likely a sand-filled gully — currently covered in snow.

I stood at the base and blew on my hands. I'd probably descended about ten feet, but the dark had made it feel like twenty. I began the climb up, using the marram grass as if it were rope. My patent leather shoes weren't helping matters, as with each long upward lunge, I slipped, even taking in a mouthful of snow a few times.

At the top of the gully was a wire fence. Without hesitation I thumb-hooked the handle on my bag and began to climb, clawing at the wire, digging my shoes into the diamond-shaped openings for leverage. At the top I clutched the frozen, horizontal bar, flipped one leg over, and straddled the high fence for a moment, trying to keep my balance. I had one hand in front of me, the other behind, and could feel the sharp edges of wire just above the bar, cutting at the crotch of my pants. As I looked out at the darkness from where I'd come, a tiny moving light appeared. One of them had a flash-light.

I climbed down the other side and continued on. I could now make out two distinctly different beams of light ahead — one flashing, the other fixed — obviously signifying two towers. Pushing my way through a patch of high, thick bushes, I tried to protect my face from the bare, stubborn branches. Wasn't long before I exited the other side and began moving through an open field.

The crashing waves grew louder, and though the tower beams were pointing in the other direction, their powerful glow seeped through the thick fog the way a full moon might. I hoped to reach shelter before one of them stepped out from the bushes behind me.

The closer I got, the more defined the setting became. The towers were about three hundred yards apart and each had a large house attached to it. Situated about halfway between the lighthouses were two smaller sheds.

I was running at full speed now and wondered if the keepers' families might be asleep in their respective living quarters. Even if they were, whatever noise might ensue would go unnoticed, as the violent sound of crashing waves would drown it out. A big storm was surely approaching.

I skidded to a stop near the larger shed on the right and turned around. No sight of them. Trying to catch my breath, heart pounding, throat and lungs burning so much I could taste blood, I circled around until I was out of sight.

Approaching the shed door, I saw a lantern hanging to the left, along with a matchbox. The wind was too heavy to light it outside, so I tried to enter the shed first, but the door was locked. Still, with the absence of a padlock, I kicked the area above the knob twice, easily breaking the lever away from the frame and flinging the door open.

With only darkness inside, I grabbed the hanging lantern and matchbox and entered. Kneeling down, I struck a stick, lit the wick, and stood again. The lantern leading me now, I stepped forward and saw the illuminated front end of a green tractor. I glided the lantern to the left where a big, silver snowplow was parked. Both vehicles were plausible hiding places, but not ideal.

Shutting the door, I stepped to the right where several small rowboats were stacked to the ceiling. The shed was at least fifteen feet high. I walked around the boats toward the back where piles of rope could be seen along the entire wall. As I got closer, I realized they were actually breeches buoys.

I eased my way along the back wall toward the opposite corner behind the snowplow. Pushing away some dusty spider webs, I squatted down, placed the lantern in front of me, and took out my pistol.

I opened my bag, removed a box of bullets, and emptied it into my coat pocket. Out of pure impulse, I also removed the magazine — even though I knew it was full — took its bullets out, and held them in my hand. For some reason, this simple act was reassuring. As I reinserted the first one, I felt its tip and imagined whose chest it might enter.

Beads of sweat began dripping on my fingers and my hand was shaking. In fact, the nerves throughout my body were beginning to dance, so I finished, popped the magazine back in, blew out the lantern, and listened for the door to open.

My gut told me that the four of them would split up — perhaps Drake to one tower, Bingo to the other, while Goat and Cleo each picked a shed. But if they decided to stay together, my chances would be slim.

I waited several minutes and — nothing. Each time I thought I heard a creaky hinge I flinched and pointed my gun at the darkness. But it was my racing mind fooling me.

Then, the faint sound of crashing waves slowly grew louder, as if the volume knob on a record player were being turned up. The loudness then faded back down. I could hear walking on the opposite side.

Leaving my bag, I stood and crept alongside the snowplow until I reached the front wall. I got on all fours and crawled to the door, then opened and slammed it, prompting whoever it was to fire two shots at nothing while I backed up again.

Pistol aimed straight ahead at blackness, I listened to him retrace his footsteps. He stopped and opened the door, the soft light from outside bringing his image to life. It was Goat.

He stood there for a moment looking out. Then, as if he could somehow see my dark image out of the corner of his eye, he spun right and attempted to shoot. But his motion wasn't quick enough, because before he could pull the trigger, I fired twice at his head, dropping him instantly.

Rushing to his body, I took the contents from his coat pockets and placed them in mine. Standing, I peeked my head through the doorframe and scanned the outside, making sure the attached house to my left still had its lights off. So far, I was in luck.

Surveying the entire landscape, I tried to calculate distances. One lighthouse was about 150 yards to the right, the other, the same distance to the left. Assuming an SIS man was in each tower, it would take them quite a bit of time to finish climbing the respective inner stairwells. Each tower appeared to be about seventy feet high.

I began a slow trot toward the other shed about thirty yards to the left. I'd taken about ten strides when I saw a flashlight appear from the doorway. I stopped as he turned and shined it directly at me. Before he could make me out I aimed and fired one shot. The flashlight fell to the ground, and he cried out. I waited for any movement. None. I cautiously continued forward.

Approaching the injured body, I picked up the flashlight and shined it at his face. It was Cleo. My bullet had entered his stomach and he was coughing up blood, trying to lift his head. As he struggled to breathe, steam rose from the blood oozing out of his gut.

I looked at his right hand and saw that he hadn't released his pistol. As if summoning up one last bit of strength, he clutched and lifted it, attempting to fire a final shot. Watching him struggle, I unloaded two more slugs into his chest, finishing him.

With the flashlight aiding me, I took the items from his pockets before reloading my magazine. My head was on a swivel, and with no one approaching in either direction, I began dragging his body inside the dark, kerosene-smelling shed.

Moments later when I arrived at the left tower, the thick, heavy, cast-iron door was shut. Rather than pulling it open, I contemplated whether Bingo or Drake might be standing just inside. There was a fifty-fifty chance, but I needed to move fast before one of the two arrived from the opposite tower.

I turned the flashlight off, grabbed the coarse vertical handle, pulled the door open, and stepped inside. Pulling it shut, I stood there in the dark. It was silent. Then, from high above, the faint echoing sound of hard-soled shoes began lightly tapping the iron steps.

Stepping forward, I felt my way onto the winding stairwell, then stopped again and listened, unsure whether he was ascending or descending. It dawned on me that Cleo had likely been the only one carrying a flashlight. *Why not pretend to be him?*

The footsteps were indeed descending, so I turned the flashlight on and started climbing, stopping after about five steps.

"You get him, nigga?" I asked in my best high-pitched Cleo voice, all the while shining the flashlight upward.

"Is that you, Cleo?" he asked. It was Bingo.

"Don't be a damn fool," I replied. "Who the one been carryin' the light? That keeper up there see you?"

"Nah!" he said.

"I asked you if you got him."

"He ain't in here," he said.

"Then Drake musta shot that fool in the other tower . . . 'cause he wadn't in nary one of them shacks."

"Where's Goat?" he asked, still circling down the narrow stairwell.

"He went on to the other tower. We best join 'em."

"Get that light out my face," he said, covering his eyes with one hand and reaching to grab the flashlight with the other.

I fired a shot, spinning him around, forcing him to fall on top of me. He dropped his gun and I dropped the flashlight. Both went clanking down the stairs. With him clutching my coat at the shoulders, the two of us tumbled down the bottom few steps until we came to a stop at the base, but not before I banged my head against the rail. The flashlight lay right next to us, reflecting off the wall enough for him to see my face.

"Son of a bitch!" he groaned, the two of us tangled together.

I rolled away and tried to shoot, but he grabbed my wrist and kept my arm extended. I was disoriented from hitting the rail, and he was able to slam my hand against the bottom step several times until I released the gun. He then kicked it away, sending it flying against the door until it came to rest next to his.

I violently shook my head, trying to fight off the dizziness and get up, but he jumped me and delivered several heavy punches to my face, damn near putting me away. Instead, I kneed him between the legs and he fell away.

Crawling on all fours, I tried to go for my gun, but he took a knife from his coat and stuck it in the back of my right calf — the force so great it stopped my forward motion as he leaped on my back. I lay there face down, stiff as a board, his left arm wrapped around my neck, his right hand reaching for the embedded knife. But I was able to reach back and beat him to it.

As I yanked it from my calf, he clutched my fist and kept it pressed against the ground along my side. I couldn't move my legs, the weight of his body too much, both of his knees digging into my hips. He began pulling me back by the neck, bowing my spine until it felt as though it might snap.

When he'd bent me as far as I could bend, he tried repositioning himself in order to gain more leverage. Inching his knees farther down my legs, he unknowingly loosened his grip around my neck just enough for me to fling my head back into his nose. As he let go, I rolled over and cracked him in the jaw with my left elbow, thrusting him back against the bottom step. Quickly getting to my feet, I stepped back and he stood.

With the flashlight lying on the floor about halfway between us, we sucked air and waited for the other to make a move. Behind me some ten feet back by the door were our guns. He couldn't risk trying to get by me, and I certainly didn't want to turn my back on him. The knife would have to settle things.

As he turned and raced up the stairs, I scooped up the flashlight and followed. Despite the leg gash, I continued climbing, certain that I was simply stronger and physically superior to him.

After winding up about twenty steps, he realized I was gaining and turned to confront me. He swung his right fist, which I ducked, then a left, which I sidestepped —

all of my motion causing the flashlight to flicker in every direction. Then, as he revved back to swing another right, I stepped up and drove the knife into his chest, holding it there as he cried out. I could feel the blade cutting through the bone as he desperately gasped and grabbed at the knife with both hands.

"Just call this protocol," I said, looking him dead in the eye.

While I focused on keeping my footing some three steps below him, his arms fell limp. Slowly he leaned downward and began to softly hug me, struggling to take his last sips of breath, his weight forcing the blade to cut deeper and deeper in until I began easing him down to a seated position on one of the steps in between us. I pulled the knife out and tilted him onto his side so he wouldn't go tumbling down.

Pointing the flashlight at each of his pockets, I found nothing except a stick of gum, some cigarettes, and a box of matches. The pain in my calf growing more intense, I put the knife down, sat beside him, lifted the bottom of my pants, and shined the light on what was a two-inch long gash. It looked deep and was bleeding considerably.

I set the flashlight down, undid Bingo's necktie, and wrapped it around my wound several times, pulling it as tightly as possible before tying it off. Taking the knife and flashlight again, I stood and began limping downstairs. But after only a few steps, I heard the door open. Drake had likely arrived.

I climbed back up, put the knife in my coat pocket, and sat beside Bingo's body. Propping him up, I put my left shoulder under his right armpit and extended my arm around his back, holding the flashlight just above his left shoulder, maneuvering it so it shined only on his face. I then wrapped his right arm around my neck and held his right hand with mine. I was now in a position to lift him to his feet. Meanwhile, it was time to become Cleo again.

"Who that there?" I said, surprising myself with how high I could make my voice.

"That you, Cleo?" he asked.

"Yeah!" I replied. "I got him! He laid out up there at the top!"

"Good!"

"But he cut Bingo up bad. We got to get him to his feet and get him up outta here fast. Need ya to help me here."

"Comin'!" he said, beginning to move quickly — the *ping, ping, ping* sound of hard soles to metal reverberating.

I tightened my stomach, widened my

stance, and lifted Bingo to his feet, keeping the flashlight pointed at his face, wanting that to be all Drake could see as he approached.

"Hurry!" I begged. "He barely breathin'!"

"Shit, I am! Lotta damn steps!"

Huffing and puffing, he was now close enough to see Bingo's face, only four or five steps below.

"I think he gonna make it," I said, just as he got close. "Step on up here and grab his other arm."

He reached up and in one motion I released the dead body and kicked him flush in the chest with enough force to lift him off his feet. He was suspended in midair for a while before crashing down on the stairwell below, surely breaking his back or neck. I turned the flashlight on him and watched as he went flopping downward, his bones banging on each and every step.

I reached into my pocket for the knife and headed after him. But there'd be no use for it. He'd come to rest some twenty steps down — his body twisted up like a pretzel. I kneeled down and began searching him. All of his pockets were empty, save for the one inside his topcoat.

Setting the flashlight next to me, I pulled out a folded-up paper. Holding it close to the light, I recognized it as one of my old railroad maps. I opened it and saw it was the one I'd given to Loretta way back before her trip with Ginger to pick up Momma and Aunt Coretta. Drake had obviously found it under the seat inside the Baby Grand. *How foolish of me!* In my haste to cover all of my bases, I'd forgotten about the old maps I'd stored there. The memories of that time period came rushing back — how she'd gushed about their trip, and particularly the state of Maine.

I flattened the map out on the step and pointed the flashlight along the route she and Ginger had traveled. She'd circled the town of Portland and had written something quite revealing next to it, words I'm sure Drake was pleased to stumble upon. They read, "The Inn at St. John. The perfect escape for me and my one and only love, Sidney. A magical town where we could reside forever."

I dropped my head for a moment and closed my eyes, knowing she'd written those words while pregnant with my son. I also realized that this current state of affairs had all come about because she'd simply done exactly what I'd asked her to do upon returning from her trip — placed the map back under the seat. I rubbed my fingers over the words, trying to feel some of her. Her writing was so lovely, so pleasing to the eye. Why I'd ever longed for anything other than to have her by my side seemed greedy now. God had blessed me with the most elusive thing in the universe: love.

I folded the map up, placed it in my pocket, and headed down the remaining stairs. It was time to retrieve my bag from the first shed and retrace my footsteps back to the stolen car. I'd bypass Portland and head straight for Brunswick. Once there, I'd find a doctor to stitch me up before catching a train north as planned. I was finally certain that I'd made it impossible for anyone to trace me. Well . . . at least I forced myself to believe that. My only other option was to go completely mad.

40

Paris felt like home the minute I stepped off of the train from Le Havre. Having left Halifax as planned, after purchasing a new suit, of course, the long ship ride across the Atlantic had given me time to reflect and heal. I knew not what was to come but tried to remain optimistic. Just knowing I was in the same city as Loretta warmed my heart and put my mind at ease.

"Où est-ce que tu veux aller?" asked the short, mustached young driver standing beside his taxi on the busy street outside the Gare Saint-Lazare Station.

"Can you take me to the University of Paris?" I asked.

"Oui! La Sorbonne! Oui!"

He hustled to open the door and I hopped in the backseat. It was around noon and traffic was heavy, but he seemed oblivious to it, gripping the wheel with his dry-looking, olive-skinned hands and steering us right into the thick of it.

"Dépêche-toi!" he yelled at the surrounding vehicles, honking his horn. *"Dépêche-toi!"*

We quickly came upon a stunning grayish neoclassical stone building with a sign out front that read LYCÉE CONDORCET, a name I recognized. I counted ten arched windows on the bottom floor and wondered which one the great Marcel Proust used to peer out of. The Lycée Condorcet was famous for being the boyhood school of the great French novelist.

Moving on, we made our way down the Rue Tronchet and approached the Place de la Concorde, where I could see the eastern end of the Champs-Élysées, a visual that prompted me to think of people from the past who'd spoken to me about Paris. They'd been right — its beauty was breathtaking.

"I take to see some sights," the driver said, turning his attention back and forth from the road to me. *"De visite touristique!* I take to Arc de Triomphe . . . to la Musée du Louvre!"

"No, no," I replied pointing straight ahead at the fast, oncoming traffic. "Please . . . watch the road."

"Oui, mon ami Américain! Je suis désolé.
Sorry."

He yanked the wheel to the left, avoiding a head-on collision, and I braced myself, putting both hands on the back of the front seat. God forbid I'd made it this far just to die at the hands of some overzealous taxi driver.

"How much farther?" I asked.

"Excusez-moi?"

"Distance! *La distance!* What is the distance . . . *à l'université?*

"Nous sommes à proximité. Uh . . . uh . . . we close. Close."

"Good," I said, leaning back and taking a deep breath. "Real good."

The front desk attendant at the university's directory office was helping a young lady when I walked through the front door. The two spoke to each other in French with such speed and volume. It was as if they were arguing, only they weren't, as the two exchanged several smiles throughout. I was quickly learning that the French simply engaged one another with more passion than do we Americans. They finally wrapped up their conversation, and I stepped forward, hoping the attendant would have the answer I was looking for. I was also hoping

587

she spoke English.

"Puis-je vous venir en aide?" she said.

"I only speak English."

"Ah!" she said, smiling. "Can I help you?"

"Yes. I am hoping you can help me locate one of your professors in the art department. Her name is Ginger Bouvier."

"Let me take a look."

About an hour later I stood outside the classroom door listening to Ginger lecture her students about Renoir's *Bal du moulin de la Galette.* The excitement with which she spoke about the painter's life was enough to make the world want to paint. I envied her students.

"Attention!" she said. *"Si vous avez quelque peu énigmatique, de terribles cauchemars ou mystérieux, beaux rêves, ne pas avoir peur de s'asseoir et d'expliquer les détails en utilisant la peinture."*

A collective "ahh" came over the class. I was dying to know what she'd said. Fortunately for me, she began speaking English.

"For you two American painters, in case you are having difficulty translating, I said, 'Remember . . . whatever enigmatic, horrifying nightmares you may have . . . whatever inscrutable, pleasant dreams . . . don't be afraid to paint them.' Never forget this.

Now. *Je vous donne rendez-vous toute la se-maine prochaine!*"

She clapped her hands twice, and I could hear the students stand and begin to move about, their footsteps coming my way. The door opened and I stepped aside as they filed out. I waited for the last one to exit before peeking my head in. Ginger was still standing at the lectern, placing papers inside her briefcase.

"Hello," I said, knocking on the door-frame.

As she turned and saw me, she froze for a moment and stared, obviously surprised to see my face. Then, without a smile, nor a frown, she looked back down and continued gathering her materials. I watched her and thought about the best way to continue, wanting to respect her emotions.

"We live in Montmartre," she finally said, in a monotone voice. "Loretta is there now. The address is Nineteen Rue Ravignan."

"Thank you."

She nodded without looking, but that was enough. She'd given me all the information I needed.

The fidgety taxi driver was happy I'd asked him to drive me around for the afternoon. He'd calmed down considerably, perhaps because he'd been able to smoke cigarettes and read a bit of Victor Hugo's *Les Misérables* while parked in front of the various university buildings he'd driven me to. From the looks of the battered old book that was resting on the dashboard, he'd likely been trying to finish it for quite a while.

"Nous sommes ici!" he blurted out, as we finished winding up a narrow, treelined hill and pulled in front of a two-story house made entirely of brown cobblestone — a unique design style completely new to my eye. "Nineteen Rue Ravignan!" he continued. "I wait here. Yes?"

"Yes," I said, grabbing my bag, opening the door, and slowly stepping out, all the while keeping my eyes on the house, trying to imagine my wife coming and going, carrying on without me.

I nervously adjusted my tie and looked down at my pants and shoes. Everything appeared to be in order except for my nerves. Still, I walked up to the door, readied myself to knock, and then held my fist in the air for a moment while I prepared my words. But there were no correct ones. True feelings would have to decide matters.

I knocked softly three times, and my heart sped up. I could feel her on the other side.

And then I could hear her footsteps approaching. With the sound of the thick wooden door being unlocked, I took a deep breath and shrugged my shoulders. She pulled the door open and, upon seeing me, flinched as if she'd seen a ghost. But it was I who should have flinched. The visual before me could not have been more shocking. Neither of us said a word as my eyes were fixed on her large, pregnant belly. A minute must have passed before I broke the silence.

"When did . . ."

"That night you awoke from a nightmare soaking wet," she said.

I thought back and remembered. The very last time we'd made love had been that past summer.

"I'm sorry," I said, "for not being there for you during this time."

"It's all right," she said, giving me an ever-so-slight smile. "Please . . . come in out of the cold."

I stepped just inside and closed the door behind me as she backed up. The fireplace in the dark book-filled den behind her was ablaze and she looked so lovely — her tall, thin body the same, save for the perfectly round ball beneath her pinkish plaid gown.

"I hope this isn't too much," I said.

"I'm just so glad you're safe."

I stood there filled with pain and joy —
doubt and hope. Never before had all of
these conflicting emotions been so present
at once. She softly rubbed her tummy with
one hand then calmly raised her other for
me to take. Just the simple touch of her
warm fingers sent me trembling. And, as
the tears flowed down my face, she pulled
me closer, wrapping her arms around me,
gently resting her cheek against my chest.
We must have stood there for half an hour
just holding each other. Life had begun
again.

As the weeks and months went by, we didn't
talk about the past. We just did our best to
move on, to plant new seeds in Paris. I
landed a part-time teaching job in the
engineering department at the University of
Paris and we moved into a house close to
Ginger's at 12 Rue Gabrielle.

I'd been able to track down Bobby Ellington through his parents in Ohio. He was
now working at the State Department. He'd
arranged, very diligently I might add, to
organize some new passports for us. We
were now the Sweet family. Loretta was still
Loretta but my first name was Prescott. She
felt that Sweet was a last name befitting an

artist and I agreed.

I also sent for Momma and Aunt Coretta. If the SIS had decided to have the Timekeeper continue pursuing me, I figured he'd have very little luck tracing my whereabouts. Still, I worried that his pursuit might eventually lead him to Professor Gold's. Too risky. Besides, I had no intentions of returning to America, and the only way I could see Momma and Aunt Coretta was to have them in Paris with us.

Sadly, we didn't get to enjoy Aunt Coretta for very long. In April of 1924, she passed away. But what little time she did get to spend in Paris pleased her very much. Momma was as sad as I'd ever seen her, but was so glad to have been with us when the end finally came. And she didn't mope around, I guess because her sister had been struggling for so long. Instead, Momma poured herself into helping Loretta with the twins — little James and little Ginger — during the day while I was at work.

On the weekends, Loretta and I walked a lot, pushing the baby carriage for blocks and blocks, both of us fascinated by everything Paris had to offer. On the weekends, while Loretta and Momma were still asleep, I tended to wake up early with the twins. I'd often put them in the stroller and push them down to the corner market where I'd buy whatever food I intended to cook us all for breakfast. The delicious cuisine of Paris had prompted me to start collecting cookbooks, to try my hand in the kitchen.

The preparation for one particular breakfast on a cold Saturday in late February of 1925 came with some added dramatics. Needing to buy some sausage and a few more potatoes for that morning's meal, I bundled the twins up and strolled them down the block. As we approached the storefront, I glanced at the fresh stack of newspapers and saw something on the front page that grabbed my attention. It was a picture of Marcus Garvey being hauled away in handcuffs. It was, of course, a French paper, and though I was quite close to doing so, I hadn't yet completely mastered the language, so I picked up a copy and entered the empty store.

"*Bonjour,* Jean," I said to my tall, thin young friend behind the counter as I set the paper in front of him.

"*Bonjour,* Prescott!" he replied, smiling and waving down at the twins. "*Bonjour, mes petits bébés!*"

James and Ginger, not yet two years old, just grinned. I'd wrapped them in their blankets like tiny mummies, so tightly that neither could do as they normally did and lift their little arms to wave back. As Jean continued making smiley faces with them, I pointed to the column next to Garvey's photo.

"Jean . . . if you wouldn't mind . . . can you read some of this for me? *En Anglais,* please. I'm sure I could read it myself, but I don't want to misinterpret even a tiny piece of it."

"Oui," he said, picking up the paper and taking the last bite of his powdery white pastry. "I would be happy to do for you." He licked his fingers, stood tall, and cleared his throat several times, as if preparing to speak in front of a large audience.

"Merci, Jean."

"Stop-uh me . . . if you want-uh me to repeat-uh something," he said in his stereotypical, thick, rich accent.

"I will."

"It-uh . . . says-uh . . . uh . . . 'UNIA leader Marcus Garvey's initial one month mail fraud trial began in New York City-uh . . . almost two years ago-uh . . . on May eighteen of 1923 with Judge Julian Mack presiding. The trial ended on June twenty-one of that year, with Garvey being sentenced-uh . . . to five years in prison for mail fraud. Mr. Garvey's appeal for bail was initially rejected and he spent three months incarcerated in the Tombs Prison in New York before finally being released on bail . . . pending the appeal of his-uh . . . case to a higher court.' "

Jean stopped reading and looked up at me. "Continue," I said. "Please."

"*Oui.* It says-uh, 'Now . . . after spending-uh . . . close to a year and a half out of jail continuing to build his organization, his appeal to the U.S. Circuit Court of Appeals, Second Circuit has finally been denied. Garvey . . . uh . . . who had been visiting Michigan in an attempt to increase his following and raise funds was arrested at New York's 125th Street train station-uh . . . as he returned to the city on February five, 1925. He was-uh . . . taken directly into custody and arraigned the following day. He was transferred from the Tombs Prison in New York to the Atlanta Federal Penitentiary on February seven and began-uh . . . serving his term.' "

"Is that all?" I asked, looking down at James and Ginger.

"*Oui,*" he said, handing me back the paper.

"Thank you, Jean."

"*Merci.* You do the shopping now?"

"Yes."

I began pushing the carriage, my mind

596

now in a different place. I'd been in Paris for two years and had done my best to shield myself from all that had occurred back in America. The only news I'd read had been a snippet about how Du Bois was successfully continuing the growth of the NAACP. It had left me feeling good, enough to continue moving on without stopping to analyze the past.

But now, hearing this about Garvey brought back all of the details. I couldn't help but ask myself a question: *Had the work I'd done been worth all that it had cost me?* I waited for an answer to come to me as I pushed my babies toward a bin full of potatoes. I thought about their futures. Then I thought about their own children's futures. If and when any of them decided to return to America, what kind of life would be awaiting them? It was then that I knew the answer to my question. It had indeed been worth it because any one man's life had to be worth risking for the good of an entire people. I needed to believe that.

And now that Garvey's separatist movement had been delivered a blow, Du Bois could make some serious gains. The NAACP's dream was alive and well. I'd helped it survive. Integration had a fighting chance.

"Daddy!" said baby James, looking up at me with a big smile. I shook the carriage back and forth a bit to soothe them both.

"That's right," I whispered. "Daddy's right here. Daddy loves you. Daddy loves you. Daddy loves you."

■ ■ ■ ■

A Reading Group Guide: The Strivers' Row Spy

JASON OVERSTREET

■ ■ ■ ■

ABOUT THIS GUIDE

The suggested questions are included to enhance your group's reading of Jason Overstreet's *The Strivers' Row Spy*.

DISCUSSION QUESTIONS

1. If the Bureau had not taken the action that they took in 1919, how might the current state of black America be different?

2. If Du Bois and Garvey had had a different relationship, how might their outcomes have been different?

3. If Loretta had been politically curious and aware, how could she have changed the course of the story?

4. Was the risk worth the reward for Sidney?

5. Is there hypocrisy in considering Sidney a sell-out while white agents are not thought of as traitors to their race?

6. Why is being a black agent in the story about race but being a white agent is not?

7. Considering what happened in the story, would James have forgiven Sidney if he'd learned the truth?

8. Why was it necessary, at least in Hoover's mind, to hire black agents?

9. What historical facts fed the Bureau's paranoia regarding communism?

10. Give two possible reasons that Hoover would think Garvey and Du Bois were like-minded on communism.

11. Which of the following do you think are factual, fictionalized, or both?

- The Harlem setting
- Young J. Edgar Hoover's role in the fledgling Bureau
- The Bureau agents in the story
- Du Bois's and Garvey's roles in U.S. and world history
- The Dyer Anti-Lynching Bill
- James Eason's trip to New Orleans
- President Warren G. Harding's stance on racial issues

12. Name some historical black Americans who emigrated to Paris.

13. Why might Garvey have been enthralled by pomp and ceremony?

14. Discuss Du Bois's philosophy of the Talented Tenth.